TUZU

"STUPID SITTING DUCK"

Allen Kuziwakwashe Matsika

To Anita and Doreen
"You're right; God didn't die and leave you in charge."

From the Author

"Tuzu" is a Shona word that is challenging to translate from the Shona language, which this author grew up speaking. At best, it comes to "sitting like a stupid sitting duck" or "chilling like a clueless ignoramus" or "standing and blinking like…" - you get the idea. In this book, I hope that we all come face to face with ourselves, and what amounts to our endless "onion peeling' revelation of our own limited capacity to reason well through the unknown future. What remains is whether we judge ourselves honestly and kindly or we run from the reflection in the mirror either through dishonesty or harshness.

Foreword

Yes, Uzumbamarampfungwe (Uzu) exists in Zimbabwe, my home country. It's a region of many towns and wonderful people with great business and political acumen as well as superb agricultural senses. I will be living full-time in Uzumbamarapfungwe, come July 2022. But let me assure you that this is a work of fiction. Space and time have been rearranged to suit the convenience of the book, and with the exception of public figures, any resemblance to persons living or dead is coincidental. The opinions expressed are those of the characters and should not be confused with the author's. You will find that in this work of fiction, Zawe exists between two rivers, the Limping river to the south with its Great Lakes and crocodiles and the Zii river to the north with its deafening majestic waterfall. (Map insert at the end of this foreword)

And in this book, Uzu is a Village State or Country within a country like the Vatican. (Map insert at the end of this foreword)

This book is, in part, my amateur attempt at comedy. I was born and raised in a country and a nation whose culture allows for irreverent laughter. We not only laugh at ourselves, but we make jokes about everything and everyone. One can think of us as a nation of comedians. I joke that we have laughed ourselves into social and economic decay. Our politics remain strong though, and we are a proud and sovereign democratic situation. And so, of course, some of these words of fiction will sound a tad bit irreverent, but to my people and me, that is normal. I hope you will take it as an invitation to laugh at yourself. Someone said once, "You should laugh at yourself sometimes; you never know you might be missing out on the best joke in the world."

In this book, one of my hopes is to reclaim the word "stupid" so it can be an asset for our growth. To rescue it from its "political" use and bring it back to its informative use under the mandate of precision of language. When stupid is used "politically," it loses its rigor. Words used politically are intentionally coined not to be rigorous. They are designed to denigrate, discriminate, and label others as equivalent to being terrorists. It's by design so that those coining the term can create an "us" and "them" dynamic, while the lack of rigor makes it so that arguing is endless since the term is wishy-washy. Words with rigor and precision have their precise meaning. For example, "Dioxide" means two oxygen molecules; we cannot argue about that. What then is the "dioxide" definition of Stupid? If one were to Google Stupid, they would find that it means:

"having or showing a great lack of intelligence or common sense"

And the example used is hilarious and spot on.

"I was stupid enough to think she was perfect."

How many of us have been stupid enough to think someone was perfect? I am willing to bet a good number of us. The informal meaning is what we are calling the political meaning. In this google result, the use example for the political meaning of stupid is full of silliness:

"you're not a coward, stupid!"

And again, how many of us have been stupid enough to think we were cowards. So there is no reason for the stigma associated with this word. Unless one misunderstands its meaning. In truth, no one is pervaded entirely by common sense. No one has a perfect grasp and use of reason. So if someone suggests that I act in a way that lacks common sense, I feel compelled to agree. I don't always know whether my action is common sense or a significant lack of it until the results. And in this book, you will read how sometimes we only recognize insanity in ourselves after we have regained our senses—all the more reason to be humble.

This reasoning has led me to reclaim the word stupid in my life. Someone called my line of thinking on a particular topic "idiotic" recently. I was far from offended, as I considered it very well may be. I stuck to my guns with no offense taken as I stood in the humility of knowing I very well may be wrong, I am lacking in common sense in many areas, and this could be one of them. It's time for us to be smart enough to know that we might be wrong, smart enough to know we might be stupid. We need to stop believing and creating facades of ourselves that are infallible, or if they are fallible: veneers that are strategically so. We need to reclaim stupid because it could be the way to find our lost tempers and be the salvation of our dysfunctional relationships. By removing the sting of the un-rigorous politically used insult, we may be able to battle shame and the propensity to be offended by others.

I am convinced that many of our actions lacking in common sense or intelligence have one fundamental lesson in their consequences. That is to say; they are first and foremost a reminder that we are not entirely pervaded by common sense or reason. I have found it to be true in every person I have encountered that humans are not wholly pervaded with reason and common sense. I have not met everyone in the world, so there may be a considerable chunk of the world that is perfect in their actions, filled entirely with common sense and reason, and act with great intelligence at every single turn.

This book was born from recognizing my own stupidity, but again, I would like to reassure the readers that this is a work of fiction. And yet a part of me wants to laugh and ask: If life hands you such hilarious stupidity, why make anything up? But make up things I did, so maybe I have an answer but can't articulate it yet. If you manage to cross the chasm called the first chapter of this book, you will encounter an upside-down world yet so upright.

One friend of mine expressed an expectation of more complex language in this work. I have a philosophy degree, so I was expected to write a little more sophisticatedly. I will not challenge that. This work of fiction is written in a way that hopefully allows for accessibility. The ideas explored are profound, yet the desire is to invite all readers to encounter the questions posed without needing a dictionary or a philosophy degree.

I am grateful to so many people for their help in making this piece of art a reality. To the legend, Gary Barbee; you and Charlene have been in my corner, helping me dream this dream of writing and publishing. Ranelle, my dear mom, thank you for being on the ball and helping with the process. Adrienne, you rock. Thanks for making sure this work was philosophically bearable. I am deeply grateful to Millicent, who edited this work and helped breathe life into the various chapters. And to my ghostwriter, no one might ever know, but I owe it all to you.

To Anita and Doreen, thank you for teaching me that God did not die and leave me in charge. Who is in charge? Definitely not me.

One last thing: This is a book about a woman, her

husband, and her family. I know many will argue with me that it is about a man, but I wrote it. And maybe I am wrong, but I want to know: since when did we make it the opposite of virtue to do something and not claim credit for it?

I am an amateur author and will only grow from your feedback. Please leave an honest review on Amazon or drop me a line with your thoughts and ideas. The best way to reach me is by joining my Patreon. Please send me a message, and let me know your thoughts, ideas, and reactions to the world I feel joyfully called to share with you in this book.

Glossary

Many of the names in this book mean something because Shona generally has proper nouns with meaning. I have translated some of them in parenthesis right along with the text. However, some of them are not translated and so here is a Glossary to help.

Uzumbamarambapfungwe - a fictitious village state like the Vatican
Simbai - be strong (plural/respectful)
Tambudzai - feel free to trouble me / make me suffer
Ruramai - walk the straight and narrow path / become orthodox /
Rasai - throw away
Tongerai - Rule on behalf of others / rule on their behalf
Riva - a wonderful name of an Ace Hardware check out attendant
Nobuhle - mother of Beauty
Nqobizitha - conquer our enemies
Leilani - Apparently Hawaiian meaning Heavenly child

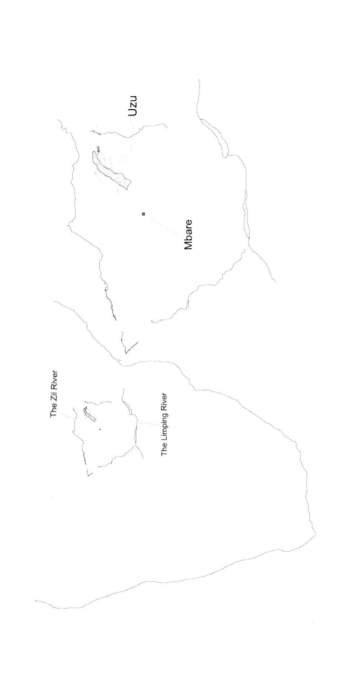

CHAPTER ONE

Uzu

VILLAGE STATE

Yes, everyone knows the village of Uzu. The three letters are short for Uzumbamarambapfungwe. Which is a conglomeration of 4 words: "Anozama kuramba kufunga," Maybe that's three words. Be that as it may, they say these three words literally mean "the one who strives not to think." Some say it's "the one who makes a tremendous effort not to think." The people of Uzu had cracked the code to the age-old problem of problems, how to live life well. There was only one reason people divorced, the people of Uzu believed. And it was thinking; thinking too much. The greed in the world? Too much thinking about oneself. Every war that has ever happened resulted from too much thinking about an offense from an enemy. Nationalism? That was thinking too much about one's own people.

'When it comes down to it,' the people of Uzu said, 'too much thought caused all the ills in the world.' Too much thought caused people to criticize and judge each other. Too much thought caused quarrels that impoverished the spirit. Too much thought caused many relational dysfunctions, dried the bones, and caused ill-health. Contemplation hurt the head, made crops grow wilted, and made the cows dry such that they produced powdered milk. When your sole mission is to think as little as possible, you find peace.

This philosophy enamored Simbai. It didn't help that Uzu came up again as he watched the cyclone's news coverage. The storm ripped across the eastern borderlands of Zawe (Zah-weh). Zawe was a small country between the Zii (Shhh) river and the Limping river. It was being battered and torn apart by the cyclone like it was a chew toy being tossed around by a ruthless canine. The banks of the Limping river and its lakes burst. Terror was spreading among nearby villages of the crocodiles let loose by the flood. The limping river had gotten its name because many who had tried to cross it had been left limping after being maimed by these reptiles. In addition to the terror, there was destruction. The torrential downpour tore apart roads like a giant centipede burrowing through the ground, ravaged villages, flooded schools, and wrecked buildings.

Yet the news coverage had zero numbers on the possible casualties and images of the survivors. The state media relied heavily on the scant footage of rescue efforts shot anonymously. The government maintained a tight grip on the information leaving its borders concerning this catastrophe. The severity of the cyclone that had ripped through eastern Zawe was still just speculation even by the next day's evening news.

Simbai was sitting on the cold floor, watching the little news coverage allowed. Children who question their mothers do not get to sit on comfortable couches. They were her couches.

The storm had skipped over the village state of Uzu. Satellite images confirmed it. The village of Uzu, bordered on every side by Zawe, had created a tunnel of dryness for itself in the passing storm. The reporter said it was like a 'chosen people" crossing a river on dry land. Except this 'river' was crossing them!

Through their ambassador, the leaders of the village state even confirmed this event. Simbai had always dreamt of escaping to Uzu and perhaps finding a 'real' home there. Not this cold floor!

And now he imagined himself becoming magical if he moved there. He saw himself moving clouds and making them rain gently. Then he made the clouds rain fire and shook his head at his thoughts. Meanwhile, the screen switched back to the rest of the cyclone coverage. Simbai smiled and resolved to start practicing the 'Uzu way' as the rumors spoke of it.

"What are you smiling about?" his mother scolded, "Are you finding pleasure in this storm and other people's suffering?"

"No, no..." Simbai stammered, caught off guard. It was too late; she had let a slipper fly in his direction, smacking him square in his face. He was disoriented for a minute and puzzled. The slipper stung a little, but the pain inside was worse. Sometimes the storms inside are more violent than any on the outside. She walked over and switched off the T.V.

"This is my T.V.," she announced, "You won't be watching any more tonight." And that was the end of the conversation.

Simbai had resolved to succeed so he could earn enough to get as far away as possible.

Even after years of emotional pain, the road to his dream looked cleanly swept; he had been an exceptional straight-A student who had landed a great job at a successful local tech company. In addition, he had an awesome marriage to his high school sweetheart.

They had met when he was a young boy visiting his uncle in the countryside near the Zii River. And then she had been sent to the same boarding school as he was attending. His Uncle had written him, encouraging him to take her under his wing. Many students born and raised in rural Zawe were susceptible to hazing shenanigans. These students would often be humiliated in ridiculous ways by their city-dwelling peers. Especially for someone as quiet as she was. The people who lived by the Zii river tended to speak very little—preferring instead; silence. It was a habit because of the constant and violent roar of the waterfall. Making "virtue out of necessity, these people had told each other over generations that 'Mankind needs to be silent when nature is speaking.' It was easy to understand when you took a walk closer to the waterfall. It was futile to speak in that proximity unless you had the headphones from a helicopter.

Simbai watched out for her while educating her "ignorant" self on some of the "city values." Values which she called 'stupid' because they seemed to go 'against the flourishing of the human soul.' But an unexpected romance had blossomed between them. Then a cute rivalry took shape as she found her voice and mastered the way of the city people. She started challenging Simbai in his domains. He had been the captain of the debate team, and she, his successor. She was voted in by the whole team to take his place. Their rivalry had kept their lives interesting and fun, and now they were married. He was very progressive, and she understood her husband. Yet, she would sometimes lean back on her default virtues of silence and submission. The values instilled in her by her upbringing in rural Zawe. The two were a gregarious team. Even though there were past events Simbai preferred not to talk about; they found a vast array of topics to discuss with the utmost honesty and joy. Simbai and his wife had talked and laughed all the way through a 7-hour flight once. Their flight attendants and fellow passengers thought new love was blossoming around them. Only to hear that the two had been married for several years and were high school sweethearts.

It was the arrival of their daughter - or rather the conception of their daughter - that set in motion the irreversible chain of events you are about to hear.

Simbai walked into their house carrying a bottle of dilutable orange juice. His wife had been craving oranges, and he thought orange juice would be a good supplemental flavor supplier. And that's when she told him about the pregnancy. Simbai was nothing but excited. And they danced around the living room. That night he didn't even touch his dinner of rice and chicken. But she was starving and eating for two. "Haha, that's why you prepared rice and chicken today. You had good news," Simbai remarked as she ate her food. Rice and chicken were the Zawe special for holidays, guests, and feasts.

They cuddled on the couch and talked about the baby and the future. Simbai was swept away by the joys of the moment. They were tickling and arguing about names and monkeying around. Of course, he wanted the baby's name to be "Cup" or "Spoon," and she had none of it. He suggested they say it in Spanish, "Taza" or something. He challenged her to a wrestling duel for the name, and she chose him as her champion, so he had to wrestle himself. They had a fun night and fell asleep on the couch. He held her, the future mother of his baby, close to his heart.

They woke up in the middle of the night when Simbai's stomach demanded food. She proceeded to bed, and he went to the kitchen to warm up the leftover rice and chicken. As the food was bubbling in the microwave, he cracked open a door to the dreaded vault in his mind. And there he was, still in his early days of elementary school. Up early as the maid helped prepare breakfast and pack lunch. Then the flood of memories ambushed him: He could see the half cockroach in the middle of the lump of sadza (Pap/fufu). The maid had said mirthfully that seeing half a cockroach meant he had swallowed the other half. She chuckled while he felt disgusted then and felt nauseated in the present. He remembered how the house could have used some more cleaning and how... And without intending to, the floodgates of memory were opened.

Nausea turned to anger, to sadness, and then transformed to despair. Simbai could feel his carefully leashed beast begin to claw at his walls. He tried to stem the bleeding by shutting off the microwave and its hum. He would watch some T.V. and distract himself. This was his T.V. now, and he could watch as late as he wanted.

He walked out of the kitchen to the empty living room. By the time he was there, he had forgotten why he had headed there in the first place. He was not going to think about this, he thought. Thinking about it would destroy him. He slumped into the couch. He would sit slouched if he wanted to, he said to himself; to her, the absent one who needed to hear it! He had not realized he was closing his eyes and was holding the sofa's edge like he was clenching tightly to his sanity. He opened his eyes, got up, and stumbled, hitting the corner of the coffee table and cursing in a subdued whisper. His vision blurred by unshed tears, he reached for the light switch as he left the sitting room and limped to bed. He made sure not to look at or touch his wife as he got into his still-cold side of the bed. He shuddered and forced his eyes shut.

That night the nightmares returned. The ones he had banished the day of the cyclone. She was crying. He held his baby boy like he held his little sister after the incident. His wife continued to cry as she looked at him with eyes that screamed, "It's your fault, Simbai!" He was not sure why it was his fault, but he felt the guilt in every part of his body. The blood coursed through his veins, delivering oxygen, nutrients, and guilt everywhere. He raised the lifeless body to his face to see if there was breath. With each movement, he felt his heart sinking lower and lower. His body twitched in revolt. He started and awoke before he could find proof of life. But he knew the ending if it was anything like the accident. His wife had been woken up by his jolt. It was light out, but he felt like he had slept but a few seconds, if any at all.

He hung around in bed and then remembered the gross "half of a cockroach." A moment later, he bolted to the bathroom and threw up. His wife teased him that he was being sympathetically pregnant. Simbai laughed it off, placing the blame on the late-night meal. Then, he got ready for work, forgetting several steps in his routine. And when he left, she found his plate of food still untouched in the microwave.

Simbai experienced unusual mood swings. At first, it was cute and funny to his wife, who kept the sympathetic pregnancy joke going. He would overreact when the stores ran out of orange juice, which she craved. Then he began to have episodes of being a vegetative being. He would sit in front of the T.V., pick up the remote and then forget to switch on the set. Only to sit for hours staring at the blank screen. Some evenings in bed, he would shudder at every one of his wife's micro touches. She was his wife and future accuser, and rightfully so because *he would cheat on her.* She was his high school sweetheart and now probably his *future ex-wife* if the beast had its way with them.

He had lapses in memory as well as in judgment. Day by day, he was taken over by anxiety. Simbai was afraid to fail his wife. He loved her dearly, and he was fond of babies. He was scared to create the possibility of raising their daughter outside a family unit. Because as long as he was the dad, *they would.* They had found out that the baby would be a girl. This news was a relief for Simbai, whose nightmares had a baby boy. But the war inside did not relent. One day he almost got fired for making a rookie mistake at work. When he arrived home, he skipped dinner because he wasn't hungry. Sleep did not visit him either that night. And each time he closed his eyes, another nightmare lurked in the shadows. He was walking away from his family into the arms of another as the family fell apart. By 3 am, he was sure he would not be sleeping that night. Around the same time, he became aware that he was no longer in control of his own thoughts. Instead, his thoughts were now controlling him. But he could not let the beast come out of the cave he had so neatly packed it into all those years ago.

If it did, he would lose everything. He knew very well he couldn't stand it for even a day more. The idea that he might eventually abandon his family hit him with full force. A force he should have expected and prepared for but hadn't. But they could get ahead of the ripples. He shook her awake.

"Hey, hey," he whispered, "Are you awake? Wake up, wake up," he whispered in a panic. His wife was comfortable rising early; she was startled only because he sounded distressed. "Let's move to Uzu," he said as soon as he perceived her present in the conversation. His lips spoke because their owner was too busy wrestling with the beast to talk.

His wife looked at him but did not answer.

"Let's go to Uzu," he repeated as if he thought he hadn't been heard the first time. She looked at his bloodshot eyes and finally admitted what she had been afraid to admit. The pregnancy had triggered her husband. "Come here," she said instead of opening her arms and gesturing for him to come into her embrace. Instead, he looked at her sideways.

"No, no, no, no, that, that won't solve anything. We need to move, darling. We need to get out of here to a place where, by design, we won't be able to have these thoughts interfering with our lives. A place where I won't think too much, and therefore won't abandon you and the baby; or hurt you and then you hurt our baby, but, but, but, it won't be your fault, it will be my fault because..." Simbai was sobbing, and she pulled him into her arms. She tried on the city values and rocked her husband to sleep. It paid off to be of many worlds.

Simbai was gone when she finally woke up. He had left early for work, most likely embarrassed by the incident from the night before.

They did not mention the incident or Uzu for a couple of weeks.

Moving there was the only solution this man could see to staying sane and keeping his beloved family together. During these weeks, he had researched the village state, and so had his wife. Uzu had applied minimalism to contemplation. If a thought did not bring one joy, they enjoyed ignoring it. They had applied moderation in excess when it came to reflective thought. It was a case of; a microscope combined with a magnifying glass and added to the Hubble space telescope. And then directing the contraption towards the process of introspection. To find the minimum viable amount of pondering necessary to exist.

On the other hand, the village state had a wonderful community. It sported excellent social structures that supported the flourishing of the living soul. With each sleepless night, Simbai anchored on the village state being the solution. Finally, one day he came home and announced that they should emigrate to Uzu. His wife had been waiting for it.

"But I won't be able to work there." She objected.

"Yes, and we won't have to worry about money either. The village has a collective treasury, and we will be paid from that."

She groaned, "Simbai, do you want *your* daughter to grow up in a society where women aren't allowed that much autonomy."

"No, honey, he replied. I want *our* daughter to grow up with a mother and a father who love each other and are still together. Not to grow up with a deranged father who doesn't live with her anymore."

The tremor in her husband's voice and the tears in his eyes crashed her already weak resistance. A Zii woman, she remembered the night she had rocked him to bed. She was cradling him like a little child. It was clear Simbai was crumbling under the pressure of the thought of fatherhood. Uzu could be the answer. It might help to not think too much about parenthood; to not dwell on the past. It might help not to worry about where the money would come from.

"What about the stories of the dragon?" she asked.

"Sweetheart, those are old wives' tales. But if there is a dragon in Uzu, that means it is a magical place, and we definitely need to go." He said with a mischievous glint in his eye. His unshed tears were reflecting the lights. He pounced, play tackling her onto the couch and pretending to be a roaring dragon. Its claws, raised, came down to her side to tickle her. They giggled before he collapsed onto her, and she held him, wiping a tear from his right eye.

Simbai's wife called a friend to share the news of the plan and departure. But, of course, her friend thought it was ridiculous. Uzu was not a place for smart people.

"Why can't you talk him out of it?" her friend asked, and the reply was:

"I know who I married, Shamwari. (friend). When my husband makes up his mind like this, he does not budge. I hope our daughter takes on my flexibility. Otherwise, it's going to be an interesting household."

Then she recounted the story of how she had met Simbai. The boy who had carried a rock up the rocky river bank and down into the village. His family had been taking a walk, and nine-year-old Simbai had fallen in love with a rock. The problem was it was too heavy for him, so he had asked his older brother to help carry it for him. But his brother had refused. His Uncle had encouraged him to let it go. Sensing their disapproval, he had stayed back a little. And then he had carried the rock all by himself. He lagged behind them. He even held in his huffs and puffs to not give away that he was carrying the rock. He even stopped and pretended he was just looking around when his brother and Uncle would look back. They had tried to coax him and turn good cops, but he continued at his slow pace. She had seen the three from a distance as she played in her yard. He was way back, and the other two were close by. And by the time he passed by her house, his Uncle and brother had long passed by. She had approached the boy as he was resting, remarking on how beautiful the rock was. And that opened them up to a strained friendship. He considered her rural, but she had approved of the rock, so she wasn't too bad. Whenever he visited the village, they would check in with one another. The man was stubborn, and his rock sat at the entrance of his Uncle's house to that day. And it was a gorgeous monument to his obstinacy.

The immigration process was arduous as Uzu tried to weed out spies.

In addition, the economic transfer of wealth needed some intricate calculations. They had to buy into the village at a certain financial level. They also had to surrender their wealth to the village treasury. By law, no one in the village owned any property. In Uzu, "property" was anything that conferred individual economic benefit. For example, a house was not considered property, so people could own one.

"But no one is allowed to sell their house to buy a cheaper one." the aide said as he handed them a catalog of homes to buy. "That's because that would create an individual economic benefit." The aide continued as Simbai's wife mocked the man by mouthing the words he spoke.

With a playful gentleness, Simbai elbowed her, and they smiled at each other.

"Focus," he whispered, nodding from the corner of his head in the direction of the catalog.

"What about this one?" His wife asked for the umpteenth time. And the answer was again, "Oh, sorry, you cannot buy that one."

"Why?" she asked in exhausted defiance.

To which came a patient repetition of, "Its classified. We encourage you not to visit the house or go near it when you join Uzu on the ground." It was a weird warning, repeated each time a "No" came. Finally, several houses later, they had a home.

Simbai kept reminding himself why they were making the move to Uzu. He learned that if he had been a religious leader, he could use the religious exemption to expedite the process. He laughed because he wished he was a famous Zawe prophet for a moment. But he reminded himself that this was about family and a better life together. He could achieve this united unit in Uzu without too much thinking. There, they could stay as 'an unit' forever. These thoughts helped him through the challenging immigration process.

Uzu was a progressive village. One that was accepting of all beliefs. Uzu accepted spiritualism, witchcraft, and the beliefs of Simbai and his family. Even though Simbai and his family's beliefs were mutually exclusive from the other two, his family was welcome. Even when the family's beliefs considered witchcraft an enemy, all were welcome in Uzu.

Contrary to the opinions of outsiders, Uzu was not a place of uniform thinking. Trying not to think did not mean thinking the same thoughts. In fact, working to keep everyone thinking the same thoughts took too much policing, which meant deputizing more people to think than the necessary two. Diversity of perspective and not thinking too much pair excellently. Like pancakes and waffles or potatoes and rice. Contemplating very little allowed Uzu to exist in harmony. At the same time, allowing people to relate diversely to life, each other, and all the village's amenities. All one had to do was not dwell too much on an incident, a word, or an idea.

It turns out that his wife's fears were partly true. Wives were not allowed to work in Uzu unless they were the only parent left in a family unit. Both daughters and sons could work when they came of age until the daughters married.

DANIEL'S BOYS

Leilani walked over to her father with a little round bottle of baby lotion. "Daddy, daddy," she said, "Would you look over at the other side and tell me if the label is there." He did not think too much about it and looked. She asked, "Is it there" and he replied, "Yes, why?"

"I was making sure that it wasn't a magic label," she replied, and Simbai chuckled. He remembered doing the same when he was a little boy.

"You were making sure it wasn't switching sides when you turned the bottle around, huh?" She beamed at him, glad her father understood. She took her bottle and ran away gleefully. She and her dad became tight friends. He also spotted her bullheadedness from miles away. Knowing himself helped them navigate their conversations without getting entrenched in a certain perspective. Something helpful as she became a teenager. Simbai's wife was ever grateful for his skill in raising their daughter. Without him, she would have struggled with the beautiful, stubborn girl.

Simbai flourished as his family flowered in Uzu. He worked in the fields and enjoyed his manual labor. He called it getting paid to get fit.

His wife, too, blossomed even though she could not work. She learned she could still contribute to the welfare of the village. That is through the Wives' Association of Crafts and Kids. They would work on crafts and create artistic monuments for the village square. Sometimes, the creations were slated for export. The Wives' Association also had free reign of the education curriculum. Instead of teaching people what to think, the schools in Uzu taught people how to think. They did this through the vehicle of liberal arts. It was easier to tell people not to think too much after they experienced the disorientation brought on by studying philosophy. Furthermore, children weren't allowed to discuss school subjects away from school. So there was no homework which meant more time for families to spend together.

Simbai's wife honed her cooking skills and became a world-class chef. Her platform was her house. She mastered the Uzu recipes, and these were intricate creations. They winked at how thinking in the kitchen was a private guilty pleasure indeed for most women. She had tried working with Leilani, her daughter, but the girl did not like to follow instructions. She preferred winging it and experimenting with food. She called it relaxed cooking and claimed - with her father's support - that it was a good way of practicing little contemplation. Simbai and his daughter were peas in a pod. It was such a gift that they were on the same side of many issues they encountered as a family.

In Uzu, they had family friends and ample time to hang out with them. They developed relationships far and wide—a great support system for Simbai, who had so many examples around him of good parenting. Tawanda (we have become many) and Shadreck and their wives were around their age when they arrived. Their children were also around Leilani's age. So they and their families became best friends.

After a good evening or weekend hangout, Tawanda would always say, as his last parting words,

* * *

"Remember not to think too much."

Shadreck would counter with, "Stay clear of them weird houses." This made Tawanda uncomfortable, which made Simbai laugh. They weren't supposed to talk about these houses—the homes with the weird shrieks and roars where the "scalers" lived.

THE DRAGON'S EGG

Simbai arrived home to find his wife and now sixteen-year-old daughter in the kitchen one day. They were talking like friends sharing a fun secret. It was a rare sight, and Simbai smiled in approval. He soon learned that they were talking excitedly about a dragon's egg. He was surprised about the two talking about a vessel of evil in his home. Many don't realize that the creatures were enthralling manifestations of galling deceit. In truth, all that the dragons wanted was food. They ate human beings and got them in the form of -- justice. Yes, the dragon, for whom all supreme thinking tasks were reserved in Uzu, was in charge of the courts of ancient Uzu. They could understand human speech and communicate back somehow.

The dragon would allow two other individuals to think, the Dragonhead and the Chief of Crops. These three made the three flames of government. The Dragonhead was in charge of the entire political landscape. The Chief of Crops managed everything related to the health of the harvest, while the dragon was in charge of justice. First firing up the criminal, then gobbling them up as the dragon did to Tongerai. He was the first native Uzu to dare think in Uzu without a title. His name means "rule for others" or "rule or judge on behalf of others." This is the story Simbai's wife and daughter were talking about. But Simbai had heard this story before and had let it be, not even bringing it home to share. So he wondered why today these two were chattering. His wife looked so happy talking with her daughter.

The story goes that a few decades back, there had been a bloody battle between various Uzu factions. Tongerai had dared to think and wanted the dragon's egg for himself. Or at least to control its powers so people could access its magical properties. The egg was said to bring all the luck in the world and ward off evil. And it was at that time held by the Dragonhead and stored in his basement. Tongerai was accused of having too much thought about himself. Thinking in Uzu was not allowed at depths such as these. As expected, the thinking of oneself too much resulted in the breakdown of Uzu society. It was contagious and infected more people creating factions. Tongerai's faction tried to steal the egg. After thwarting the theft, the Dragonhead presented Tongerai to the dragon. The man was charred and eaten.

Later the dragon would die. The astute Dragonhead decided to secure his power without the dragon. He gave a speech at the gospel forum, the famous Dirtybags Address.

"People of Uzu, countrymen, and lovers! Believe me for my cause and respect me for my honor. Four score years ago, the dragon helped create this wonderful village state. Where we get to contemplate as little as possible and are provided for in abundance. If there is here, any dear friend of Tongerai, I want you to know you were not wrong. The dragon's shell indeed has powers. This is not the reason why Tongerai was fired up. No! He claimed he wanted to help you all access the power of the eggshell, but he only was thinking of himself. And then he infected you with the disease of thinking too much of oneself. They say that the love of money is the root of evil. But the love of money is nothing but the love of self-gain. The love of self-gain is the root of all evil. As Tongerai was from Uzu, I mourn for him. But as he fell in love with self-gain, the dragon ate him. There are tears for his being one of us and death for thinking too much of himself. Today, I think less of myself and more of you all. And I break the eggshell, so many may own the gift. So, the government of the three flames may never perish from the earth."

The broken eggshell was brought out in dirty brown cloth bags. They used to be white, but someone had muddied them so they would look rustic. The people cheered with great commotion. Little thought allowed superstition free reign in Uzu. The people, one and all, were delighted to have access to the shell. Such selflessness could not be argued against, especially by those from Tongerai's faction. And those on the Dragonhead's faction felt their leader was magnanimous.

* * *

Furthermore, it was said, a part of the eggshell gave the same powers as the whole egg. So breaking the egg would please all the people. Whereas Tongerai supposedly wanted it all for himself and his faction. His manifesto had not mentioned sharing the dragon shell.

"It is undeniable that this gift is priceless." The Dragonhead continued, and people quieted down to hear. "Yet we know how much we take for granted what is given for free. Therefore, in order for this gift to be valued, it must be sold. Yet, it will be sold without any discrimination or limitation to any and every Uzu resident."

More cheers and clamor were heard. People were cheering for the breaking of the egg. They were excited to share the pieces among the people for a price, so it was treasured.

The biology of the dragons was not clear to anyone. Many thought that because the creatures had eggs, they came from their eggs. The Dragonhead was of this school of thought. Without the dragon, the Dragonhead moonlighted as chief justice at times. He calculated that he had destroyed the line of dragons forever by destroying the egg. Now he could be chief justice whenever. And by sharing the eggshell, he had also secured the favor of the people. And by selling it, he had captured value from his efforts, and the triple bottom line was fulfilled.

THE SHELL

This was the story they were chattering about. Simbai's wife was glowing, happy that her daughter was confiding in her and not her father for once. He, of course, was let in on the conversation later. He disapproved as Leilani had expected. As he was delivering his descending opinion, his daughter - who knew her father well - presented the picture of the egg to him. The beautiful gold embossed silver accented and gigantic dragon's egg. He was astounded by the image of refined adornment. He looked at the image together with them and, for a moment, was mesmerized and fell silent. He forgot that this was evil as he quietly appreciated the beauty before him. He came to as the silence became noticeable. Leilani and her mother laughed as they watched his face transform from anger to enchantment. He dismissed their laughter and behavior, murmuring "the vanity of women" as he tried to recover from how the shell had captivated him. Simbai shrugged it all off, but he didn't realize that there was more. There was so much more than mere vanity. Simbai's daughter had smuggled the picture from her history class. Only his wife knew of this infraction, and she didn't say anything to Simbai. She didn't tell him that Leilani had fallen in love with the beauty of the shell. That their daughter desired to own a piece of the dragon shell with inexplicable desperation. Of course, Leilani claimed it was to ward off evil, but the covetous gleam in her eye said otherwise.

The son of the Dragon Head sold the eggshell pieces, and they were paid for in gold. The Dragonhead was too busy with government matters, but this was an important task. That's why he had delegated it to his trusted son. People would trade their stipends for a few pieces of gold in circulation. They would save the gold until they had earned enough to buy a shell to ward off evil. A few years before Simbai and his family had emigrated, it was all the rage. But fewer and fewer people were purchasing the eggshells. Some had made it a religious experience. They used the eggshells in acts of worship. This section of the population had all but secured their eggshell pieces. Simbai trusted in his own spiritual beliefs. They were enough to bring about goodness in his family's lives and favor to their work. To be sure, he trusted Uzu's constitution, which guarded against thinking.

Nevertheless, Simbai believed it was evil incarnate, this dragon. And even though he was happy with Uzu, he found that he was suspicious of the Dragonhead and the Chief of Crops. Since they derived their authority from the dead beast. Simbai forbade Leila from ever speaking about the dragon eggshell. He forbade his wife from even thinking about it. Then he suggested that discussing the matter any further would be thinking too much, and that was the end of the conversation.

As a man, he was allowed by Uzu law to control the level of thinking of his household. In the same way, the Dragonhead controlled the level of thinking of the village of Uzu.

THE BLIGHT

Misfortune comes and goes everywhere, like day and night, or the six seasons one after the other. The same year Leilani had come home with that image, misfortune befell Uzu. It was a blight that affected food. A weird kind of rot, which, when not spotted and ingested, the blight would infect the one who ate it. At first, they thought it was only passed through food. But they found out that once a person had it, they could pass it on to another person somehow.

A few households had suffered the rot already. It was strange because it seemed selective in who was affected and how. It was rumored that it affected the descendants of Tongerai and his faction. Other rumors said it affected only tall people and that all Uzu people would eventually be of short stature. One rumor even suggested it affected only men, so the laws needed to change if all the men were eliminated. Speculation of this kind was already illegal. The Dragonhead intervened to ensure no one was allowed to discuss these topics.

The rot and the fear of it gave the Dragonhead an idea. An opportunity to get back into the public view and strengthen his power. Since he was one of the few allowed to think, he branded the rot as a prophesied curse and a village-wide challenge. He cracked down on those discussing rumors and those who thought it wasn't a curse. The gospel, which was periodical, became a daily gospel. In his daily gospel, he reminded people of an obscure prophecy by a shaman. "A score years and a decadent three, if not careful, no more will thee, Uzu, be." A prophecy he interpreted to mean 33 years. The time after the shell breaking when there would be a great threat to Uzu's existence. Coincidentally, it was 33 years since the breaking of the eggshell.

Simbai talked with a co-worker and friend as soon as he left the gospel announcement. It might be a good time to explain the gospels here. The gospels were the Dragonhead's edicts, read aloud by an aide. And they were sometimes delivered in person. They came as needed, usually every two weeks. Everyone gathered at the square every so often to hear them. They would sometimes announce new laws or new thoughts allowed. Or the thoughts which were no longer allowed. When people came to the gospel point, it was the only time listening to think was allowed. The rest of the time, people were told to listen in order to reply and to skip the thinking. Thinking too much was possible as soon as thinking began. To eliminate thinking too much, people were advised not to think at all whenever possible. Simbai didn't bother attending the gospels. But this morning, he was allowed to be late for work if he attended this important and long gospel.

"Did he say a decade and three or a decadent 3?" Simbai asked.

"I don't know, does it matter" his co-worker, Tawanda, answered.

"Yes, it does, to make sure the interpretation is correct and..."

"Aaaaaand you are thinking too much. Remember, you came here not to think too much. Besides, are you sure you want to challenge the Dragonhead man?"

"What are we challenging the Dragonhead about?" Shadreck chimed in, joining the walk to work

"Nothing," Tawanda answered, giving Simbai a look. One, he ignored with a smile.

"How long ago was that prophecy given?"

"Oh, that was 20 years ago." Shadreck replied. "My grandmother has been talking about the prophecy and the rot recently. She even brought out her record of the shaman. He disappeared, of course, like all who try to preach any deep thought about our dear village state." he finished.

"Sssssshhhhh, guys," Tawanda said furtively, casting his eyes about, hoping no one had overheard them.

THE SOLUTION

A few months later and the blight was continuing its hop-scotch around Uzu. It afflicted one person in the family and skipped over the rest. The rot affected some neighbors but skipped a household in the middle. It was a tragic and mysterious time for Uzu, and none could solve the riddle the blight posed. Then the scourge began to affect some food plants. Since the rot began in food, it started attacking the food not yet harvested. The Chief of Crops projected that enough food plants would be destroyed to cause a famine. This news brought more people to the Gospel forums and more attention to the Dragonhead. He enjoyed his almost daily speeches and updates because he was not only amassing wealth but also gaining influence.

That year, the rot affected the harvest as it destroyed some plants in the fields. But the numbers were not as terrifying as had been projected. The Chief of Crops announced this news. It was received with relief and joy by the people. The rot remained, but soon, death and the blight became normal. Buzz dies down pretty quickly for people who strive not to think too much. The news from the Chief of Crops helped calm down the village state even more. Fewer and fewer people came to the Gospel announcements. So the Dragonhead had to think of another scheme to come back into the public eye.

He announced that his son had been deputized to think. First, it would help break the tie between himself and the Chief of Crops whenever they voted on measures. Then, the three would come up with a solution to the blight and easily vote on implementation. It was important to stop the curse in its tracks, especially now that it had been seen to affect plants. The harvest was now in jeopardy.

And find the solution they did. There was hope.

The solution was right there all along—the dragon's eggshell. The eggshell would allow people to ward off evil and be safe from the curse. So the second year of the rot was greeted with hope. The dragon shell was declared the village-wide solution to the curse. It would now be given for free to the people in good faith. The village treasury would take care of the costs. All they had to do was wear it, and they would be able to ward off evil from themselves and the village, which would save the harvest.

DIVISION

Many began to wear the shell to protect themselves and the harvest. After all, it was free. The dragon shell began to be talked about in the public markets and arenas. Some people had been staunch supporters of the Dragon egg story for a long time. People who had made the dragon story into religion turned the three governors into gods. Some sad stories began to re-surface about some of these people. That they had turned into "scalers." Many of them had been wearing the shell for years. And some of those people had developed strange scales. The scales began on their body parts, where the dragon shell rubbed onto their skin the longest. For some, the scales spread, and they became shut-ins. No one was allowed to approach or buy or trade these houses. Houses where strange shrieking and roaring had been heard.

Some had worn the shell around their necks such that it rubbed onto their chests. They suffered from the same scales. Then later, they suffered chest constriction, and usually, they died not long after. Many were happy to give their lives for the dragon eggshell. Those who had kept it in their pockets lost limbs to amputation. They chose to remove the scaled limb so the scales would not spread. This information had been unpopular and exchanged among people in Uzu for years. But now it became hot stuff as the rot spread and the solution spread with it. The Dragonhead announced that these stories were officially declared too much thought. As such, they became unallowed thoughts. As the prohibition took hold, people could not even look or point at the houses where the "scalers" lived. People had to put their heads down and focus on work. While they also lined up daily to claim a free piece of the beautiful golden shell.

CHIEF OF CROPS

Before long, the curse befell many people who wore the shell. It started looking like the shell was not a solution to the blight. The Chief of Crops returned to the people, as was his job. He had evidence that showed that the dragon shell did not ward off the evil. And news that it did not prevent the rot's jumping from person to person either. He was adamant, though, that the shell was worth holding onto. Until another solution came along, it would be good for everyone to wear one to protect the harvest. Famine was not an option ever, in Uzu. It would only prove right all the people in the world who wanted the village to fail for "not thinking." So the Chief of Crops encouraged people to try two or three eggshell pieces. Or to get a huge shell of breastplate-like proportions. There was always a chance that more or bigger shells would likely have amplified powers. They could offer the possibility of a partial modicum of protection to those who might believe enough. The hope was that this amplified power could perhaps prevent the curse from possibly doing its worst to them all.

Those Dragon religious gladly wore the shell and claimed more free shells. Some of them even began to trade in smaller shells for bigger ones. They were wearing these bigger pieces as breastplates and as helmets. Some people didn't think it was a religion. But they wore the shell at the recommendation of the Chief of Crops to protect the harvest. They also traded in smaller shells for bigger ones and sometimes wore multiple ones at once.

Simbai claimed it was witchcraft to trust in the dragon shell. He even dismissed the newly minted rumor that the rot was targeting all-female organisms. However, others in his faith claimed that sometimes it's practical to wear shells. Their beliefs demanded that they care for the welfare of the village and the harvest. And that they also care for their loved ones, especially the vulnerable ones like women. "Would it be ok to let the whole village down and let the harvest be attacked by evil? Or to not care for the lowly and vulnerable in society? Wear the shell, brother," they said to him.

His wife was supportive, standing by her man, even though she had doubts and concerns about the recent rumors. Leila, on the other hand, was adamant. She was getting the shell no matter what. After all, it was recommended by the chief of crops; it was beautiful and free. And she added the recent rumor to her list of reasons to procure a shell with haste. Her father was not getting in her way of the possibility of the probability of being likely protected from the worst case when the rot caught up with her. And he was not getting in the way of her finally possessing something so beautiful.

She lay in her bed on many a morning, contemplating how she would get the shell. She smiled and visualized how she would get a chain to wear around her neck. The necklace, she imagined, would be silver and a little jagged like the cracks she noticed in the ceiling. First, the cracks made a loop that came together at the edge of the ceiling. Then, they joined and continued as one down the wall.

Uzu had its own cracks developing. Some of the shelled were uncomfortable being around them unshelled. The Dragonhead even suggested that the shell might work only if everyone wore one, which added to the people's concern for one another wearing a shell. The bar server said, "It's like having a fortified city next to a village without walls. The strong walls can repel a threat and protect the people inside the walls and those outside the walls. If more people wore the shell, it would be like expanding the wall and protecting everybody. But the walls may not work to ward-off attackers if the village next to it is itself not protected." he said. Simbai had carried this thought home, mauling it over as he struggled to grasp the idea well. He wanted a reason to change his mind, grounds to compromise his beliefs, and be on the same side with Leila. He wanted to keep his family together. He was willing to break the law and examine the bartender's thoughts to save his family unit. Finally, he gave up and resolved to stop drinking altogether. He only drank once a year or so, but now he felt even that made him think too much. And by stopping drinking altogether, he might also avoid the bartender. That man sounded like he was suffering from thinking too much as well.

WEIRDNESS

Few people wore the shell in a way visible to the general public. Which meant one couldn't always know who had it and who didn't. This made it difficult to determine who was ok with your presence and who wasn't. In addition, there was a rumor going around that the Dragonhead would soon order everyone to wear a shell. If people didn't wear one, they would have to give up work. Simbai dismissed this entirely as he was talking with Shadreck.

"Uzu not only depends on a good harvest for its reputation but for its entire welfare as well. If enough people were disallowed to work, the harvest would suffer. And so would the welfare of the village." "You may be right," Shadreck replied. "But, don't you see the way the tide is going right now. It is better - politically speaking - for the Dragonhead to support the shells. Better to make a statement of concern for the welfare of the village than to actually be concerned." Tawanda was enraged that they were even discussing this subject. The three had decided not to ask each other about the shell wearing or not. They had done so out of respect for each other's privacy and autonomy. They also did it to avoid thinking too much. But Shadreck, who was native to Uzu, had the freedom of speech that he got from his grandmother.

It was Shadreck's grandmother who discovered the secret. The news was that the dragon shells were being paid for by the Dragonhead out of Uzu village gold storage. The payments went directly to the Dragon Head's son. His son was the only one who seemed to own an economically viable property. One which was not connected to the village coffers. He claimed that he didn't own anything and was operating on behalf of the village. But also that he did not need to connect his funds to the village treasury. The shell he "bartered" was a gift to the collective society since it warded off evil from the village. He could not give the gold earned from the shells to the treasury. He would then contribute double to the village's welfare. Once in warding off evil and twice in gold. It wasn't only like duplicating efforts, but it was like taking twice from the treasury but in reverse. Anyone could agree that taking from the village treasury twice, even in reverse, was not fair. So him pocketing the gold was fair and good for the collective. The village paying him the gold for the shells was good for the collective who may not afford the shells. He called it a triple bottom line. It was wellness for the village, shells for everyone, even the poor and marginalized, and gold for him. That all sounded like too much thinking, but he had been deputized to think.

Simbai tried to ignore all these thoughts, but he was getting troubled. Things were not making sense as easily as they usually did in Uzu. He wondered if he was thinking too much and tried to keep it all in and not show his wife he was puzzled. He watched all around him as families and friendships fell apart. Friends were afraid to ask each other if they had the shell, and some stopped visiting each other. Simbai believed he was powerless to influence the village discourse. But he could deal with his daughter with a caveat: as long as his wife stood by him. She was his anchor, which he had moved to Uzu to keep. She and his daughter were his world. It was on his wife now to keep them together, as it had always been. He needed her support to get Leilani to back down.

And then, the unthinkable happened.

NO SHELL, NO WORK

The gospel that day had been short but super important. It was the "No shell, no work" decree, and Simbai had not attended.

He was greeted along the way to work by downcast heads going in the opposite direction to his. No one ever got off work early, and this was a considerable number of people walking from the farm. People were walking with their heads tucked in their chests. The way dogs tuck their tails in terror, supplication, or defeat. The people would not talk to him. They were afraid he had a shell, but he didn't know. They were scared he would do what the crowd had done to them. The mob surprised Simbai as he approached the entrance to the gate. They were looking at him menacingly. Simbai refused to think at all about this surprise grouping of people. Groups of people were not allowed except at the gospel reading and as task clusters at the farm. This was illegal, but he ignored the crowd's eyes as he waded through them. He would not think too much, he repeated to himself. He finally made it through the sea of faces and responded to the usual question.

"I.D.?" with

"Simbai, badge number 047," He showed the citizenship card to the attendant. He brought his wallet down, zipping it up with a smile on his face -- hooray for routine. Then, glancing briefly toward the crowd, he folded his wallet and tucked it into his pocket. He patted his pocket twice as usual, like Santa checking his list. He waited to be buzzed in when he heard another question. Another word was spoken as though it were routine. Another question, in addition to "I.D.?"

"Shell?"

* * *

A murmur rippled through the crowd behind him. It was echoed by the horde beyond the entrance to the collective farm. The one he had not noticed. He was distracted for a moment by the two crowds.

"Simbai, badge number 047, would you please show me your shell?"

The crowd on his side of the gate seemed to close in on him like a tide coming in. They leaned in to hear his response. That's when he realized what was going on. Once you passed the entrance, no one was allowed to leave and pass back outside. Once buzzed in, you were in until all the work assigned for the day was done. It looked like the shelled had split into two groups. Those who had the shell and had passed through the work entrance. And those who had the shell and had not passed through the farm gates. These were the welcoming party and the shaming party, respectively. At that moment, Simbai was caught between them; between welcome and shame. He was standing at the crossroads of acceptance and rejection and the consequences thereof.

"Simbai, badge number 047, would you please show me..."

"No, I don't believe in the shell."

"It doesn't matter if you believe in the shell. Do you have the shell or not?"

"No, I don't have the shell."

"No shell, no work," the attendant said, as though this too was routine.

Simbai was flabbergasted. A murmur arose in the crowd, moving across it like the bristled hairs on a monster's hands standing on end.

"But I have worked here forever," he replied

"That doesn't matter. No work, no shell. It's the law. The Dragon head announced it this morning."

"But, but," he swallowed and looked at the sea of man around him. Their movements like a wave about to engulf him. He had to surf it with skill. "But, I do this work for the welfare of the village," he said, finding his tongue.

"Again, that doesn't matter. No work, no shell. It's the law."

He did not want to look like a man who skipped the Dragon Head gospel announcements. He, however, could not find a suitable honest reply, and though he could play defiant instead. But nothing could come out of lips. He was so accustomed to filtering his thoughts. People generally filter their thoughts before they speak. Simbai added a second sieve of thought, well before the regular filter of speech. Uzu helped him justify this double filter and this structure held back the raging tsunami of thoughts as he stood there. He was trying very hard to tow the line of the law and balance his beliefs and thinking as little as possible. He could feel his head start to burn like a car burning rubber, the air filling up with smoke and reducing visibility for perception.

"But I can't wear the shell, it's, it's, I don't believe in it..and...and...and...and." The wave of men descended on him as they surrounded the stammering-Simbai.

"If you want, we can give you a shell right here for free. The village is paying for it." The attendant said, raising a shell for Simbai to see.

"Is that your shell?" Simbai asked.

"No, I am exempt from wearing a shell. Being a direct employee of the Chief of Crops and all."

"What, won't the evil curse affect you too, and then the crops and the harvest? Are you exempt from the curse as well"

Silence.

"You value my life and the welfare of the village to enforce the law to wear shells. And yet you won't value your life enough and how you could affect the harvest by not wearing the shell?"

"Yes, it's called putting other people's needs first? I am here to serve and protect you and the harvest. Do you want to work?"

"Yes, I do," Simbai responded, encouraged by the question.

"Then here is a shell," the response came.

"No, I don't want the shell. I don't believe in the shell," said Simbai.

The crowd had been unsure of how to respond thus far. But with Simbai's new refusal of the shell, they hissed and hummed. The noise crescendoed as they gained confidence and unity in response. Simbai, quelling the fear in his chest, held out. He would not be bullied, and he would not be forced. He did not own any property which conferred economic benefit besides his body. It was the only thing that was his and which could work. And it conferred an economic benefit to his family in the roundabout way of adding to the village's wealth. It was his only property, and now they were trying to take it away from him. Oh, yes, he could keep it, but he was no longer in charge of driving it or taking care of it. The village was now in charge of it!

But hadn't he already allowed the village to think for him? This was simply the next step in the evolution of their community. He stood there, petrified by self-pity and anger. He had escaped from the mouth of the lion into the paws of a bear. The attendant broke his reverie, "Remember, it's a crime to think too much. I can see your gears turning, and I would like to give you a verbal warning. You can be arrested if we think you are thinking too much" The crowd closed in on him. They wanted to hurt him for not wanting to "not-hurt" himself by wearing the shell. One could say perhaps they wanted to hurt him for not caring about the welfare of the village. But assaulting him showed little care for his welfare. It reminded him of the joke Ruramai, one of his good friends, made when he left for Uzu. "If you die there, I will kill you." Simbai was lost in thought when a funny one popped up. Maybe the shell did ward off evil after all. If he took it and wore it, he could save himself from the crowd closing in.

But it was no laughing matter. Simbai was frozen like he used to be when his mom rained fire and brimstone down on him. The crowd might get physical, he thought. So he began dissociating in preparation for the pain he would feel later when his body was no longer in shock.

Only it wasn't his body that was in shock, it was Uzu's body now, or at least they were trying to make it so.

IN CIRCLES

"What's going on?" intervened a familiar voice. Simbai looked over to see Rasai, the farm's manager, or "Owner." He didn't own anything, but that was his title; Rasai joked that he was the only one who had his own Kingdom in Uzu. That earned him the nickname Rasdom, short for Rasai of the Kingdom. He preferred to be called "Rainstorm" or just "Storm." but no one cared to call him that.

"Oh, it's you, Simbai. What's the matter, attendant? This is my favorite and best worker?"

"He doesn't have a shell," came the reply.

"Oh, the business of shells," Rasai said. He tucked in his already tucked-in shirt and raised his belt with a proud sigh. "It's the only way you will work, chump," he said, finishing with the wagging finger.

"But if I don't work, the harvest will suffer."

"Yes, but if you work on farmlands without the shell, the evil might befall the harvest. And the harvest will also suffer."

"Yeah, yet the attendant is working on farmlands without the shell."

"Oh, he has them in the drawers. But, for all intents and purposes, he is wearing all the shells--they're just not on him right now."

"And when he goes home without a shell, aren't we worried about him being attacked by evil?"

"I don't govern home issues, Simbai. So what he does out of that booth and away from the farmlands is not my jurisdiction."

"Oh, so I can get a shell for the sake of work and then leave it here when I go home?"

"Where did you get that idea? That's ridiculous. You need the shell on you at all times to ward off evil. The evil can catch you anywhere, and we wouldn't want you to bring it to the farm."

The crowd jeered and began chanting, "Rainstorm! Rainstorm! Rainstorm!" And Rasai raised his hands to quiet them down. He was loathe to do it because, for the first time, they were getting it right. But in Uzu, people had a right to be heard as long as they were not thinking too much.

"Let's let the man speak."

Simbai wondered how else to proceed in the face of what seemed to be a breakdown of logic. He would lose his job, but the attendant who'd taken his job from him wouldn't lose his?

"But, but...but..."

"But what? Look at my shell. I am protected from the evil, and I am putting the community first." Rasai said, pulling out a golden shell from where it hung on a gold chain.

"But we all know that the Chief of Crops said that the shells do not ward off evil. And can't prevent people from giving it to one another."

"What do you mean? Everyone was invited to wear many shells for a reason," Rasai exclaimed, exasperated,

"What's the reason?"

"To ward off evil."

"But they don't. We are being forced to wear a 'solution' to a problem which does not solve the problem."

"It's in the name, Simbai; it's the solution to the problem. How -- by definition -- would it not solve the problem."

* * *

"Ras, if I call your wife my wife, does she become my wife?"

"Whoa, hands off my wife, buddy. This is about the shell." Rasai replied. His eyes flashed for a moment with protective anger. Then he remembered to remain professional.

The crowd laughed and eased the tension.

"Look, you are being unreasonable and un-neighborly. It's all about the welfare of the village." Rasai responded

"Yes, that's why I am here to work, for the welfare of the village. If there is a shortage of workers, there is a terrible harvest. And the village suffers."

"Yeah, but if there is evil, and the crops suffer from the evil, the village will suffer too."

"Yes, but there is nothing you can do about the evil affecting the crops."

"Oh, there is; you can wear the shell."

"But we have already established that the shell does not ward off evil."

The crowd was getting worked up as the conversation went in circles. They started chanting.

Then someone yelled, "Let's go, Rastorm."

And the new chant caught on.

"Let's go Ras-storm, let's go Ras-storm."

Simbai turned away from the booth into the crowd, defeated, dejected. He tucked his head in his chest, like all the other people he had passed on his way to work. He tried to remind himself of the reasons he had emigrated to Uzu. The reasons he could never forget with each day that passed. To keep his family together.

* * *

People not working in Uzu was unprecedented. Simbai suspected his wife would not be allowed at WACK. Maybe they could let their daughter wear the shell and work for both of them. He came home to his wife, who had been booted from the Wives Association of Crafts and Kids. She, too, didn't have a shell. She was sobbing when he arrived. He thought it was the job situation, and then he heard the rustling and cluttering. He walked down the hallway to find their daughter packing. Her brand new shell dangled from her chest. As soon as she heard him approach, she turned around to explain:

"The Dragonhead said that the shelled could catch evil from the unshelled," she began, preempting Simbai's questions.

Simbai closed his eyes gently.

"No," he murmured under his breath and closed his eyes, exclaiming, "No!"

Leilani started, and he noticed he had scared her.

"Where are you going?" he asked her, pointing to the bag she was packing.

"To Mr. Tawanda's place. His family said they would take me in until you and mom come to your senses. People with shells cannot live together with people without shells," she finished. She zipped up her bag and slung it over her shoulder. "It's only logical."

THE "U" IN YOU

The conclusion was that the shell could only work when everyone wore it. The three flames had to take drastic measures to safeguard the harvest and save Uzu. The gold from the shells had made all three decadently wealthy. They tried to hide it by parading themselves as suffering due to the collective suffering. Suffering mostly blamed on those who didn't wear the shell. They introduced new measures. If one wasn't shelled, they had to wear a red "U" to warn others to stay clear of their unshelled selves. This was a measure to prevent the blight from spreading around.

This made everyone less tense since now they could tell who was shelled and who wasn't. It, however, created visible divisions. There was a physical chasm between the shelled and unshelled. The two groups stayed away from each other everywhere with ease now. Simbai could no longer visit some of his long-time friends and acquaintances. After close to two decades in Uzu, relationships crumbled in the face of the 'red U.' Some of the unshelled people tried to be positive about it. They made beautiful embroidered 'scarlet U's' and pridefully wore them. It was almost a fashion statement, and they made so many beautiful new styles. Some wore them on their chests like superheroes—heroes to themselves for being persecuted for their beliefs.

All this while, the rot had not stopped ravaging Uzu. The reputation of the village was in jeopardy. A magical place that once passed through a storm unscathed. Now it was at the mercy of a mysterious rot. Only the three at the top knew the world was watching them. So they took even more drastic measures to save face and hopefully save the village. They were not going to let the village state die on their watch. It was their source of wealth, and they did care for some people in it.

There was a new decree from the three. All those who had emigrated to Uzu but refused to wear the shell to protect Uzu were guilty of treason. Since there was no dragon to fire them up, they would be banished. The natives of Uzu who wore the 'red U' would remain. But they would be moved to their own special area reserved for their comfort.

OLD WIVES TALES

"Mom, mom, mom, listen. Listen, mom, I have a shell for you, mom, mom." Leilani was saying. Her voice was undecided between anger and sadness as tears streamed down her cheeks. "Please stay!" the girl said and half-whispered the scream to her mother. Her mother was the only parent she could appeal to because she knew her dad was stiff-necked. Her mother was a Zii woman at heart. She was nothing like her independent and intractable daughter. She sat there, next to Simbai, sobbing and silently proud she had raised Leilani. A young woman so outspoken and sure-willed.

Simbai sat on his couch like a derelict ship at a port. Rusting, water sipping into the hull in places where holes had developed over time, and no plans of sailing. He was about to lose everything he had come to Uzu to protect. But he was not crying; he was not falling apart. Leilani was eighteen now, and the rot had started when she was sixteen. Simbai was tired from all the thinking he had forced himself not to do in the last few years. Simbai was exhausted from all the work to control his feelings and thoughts. Especially in the last few weeks. He had tried to explain himself to Rasai, the others, and even himself. He had tried to do this all without thinking too much. Leila was not budging, and they were about to lose the unit. He was on his last legs as he fought the beast inside the cave as it gloated at his family falling apart. He could never outrun that monster though he tried. He remembered his and his wife's last visit to the village by the Zii river. His wife was saying goodbye to her family, and he was visiting his Uncle. He remembered his Uncle's response when he shared the news about telling his parents that he was leaving for Uzu. He had asked what their reaction was,

"Well, dad was silent as usual, but mom was prophesying doom for my family and me. You will suffer, never be happy, all that usual stuff." Simbai had replied calmly, pretending to himself that he was over it.

"Hmmm, the usual," his Uncle replied knowingly. She was his sister, after all.

"All the more reason to go. I have needed to leave for a long time." He had replied. His Uncle had looked off into his yard at the beautiful rock. Simbai had followed his gaze and chuckled, remembering the journey with the rock.

"Do you remember the day you and I ran from Kurauone and Garakunzwana from the neighbors across the wash?" he asked instead, grinning. These were the two vicious dogs belonging to the hunting neighbors across the wash. The family had done well to settle further from everyone else. On this day, his Uncle was on his black horse bicycle, and Simbai was trailing on foot, limping. They had been coming from the store. As usual, rather than take the straight road home, the two had taken one of the many long winding scenic routes. Unfortunately, Simbai had sprained his ankle on an exposed tree root. So when it came to his turn to ride, he had opted to keep walking instead. Unfortunately, they had forgotten that this scenic route passed by the neighbors and had startled the two dogs. They had both ended up on foot. His Uncle had lost the butt off of his pants to one of the dogs, but they had escaped. They were laughing as they recounted the story in turns.

"There is no looking handsome when you are running away, you know. I fell from my bicycle into the dust. You kicked a rock, opened your big toe, and got leaves in your hair. We didn't stop to clean up or attend to our wounds. Your body ignored all the pain. It even forgot you had a sprained ankle, consumed by one objective, to flee. Even as your big toe bled and my head was ringing from hitting my head. Now imagine that, but not in your physical body. I'm talking about fleeing your country, your circumstances, your own family, anything. You take it in stride when you get banged up in your heart and mind as you flee. Commendable, you think, but not until you sit down and take stock."

Simbai came back to the present, wondering if this was time to take stock. But his mind was dog tired from thinking and feeling. It was spent as he tried to balance logical inconsistencies. The memory from his Uncle's conversation effortlessly took over his reality, pulling him back in time.

"What are you suggesting, Kule (uncle)?" he had asked.

"Fleeing is freedom from, but it is not freedom to do. 'Freedom from' is a sigh of relief, but it does not give you purpose in the long run. But 'freedom to be and do,' now that is empowerment, vision, and purpose. So you either escape or take your banner and become a leader to lead others into the light. We could have stood our ground with those dogs. If you had stayed, I would have stayed. If I had stood my ground, I imagine you would have too. I stand my ground these days, and those two dogs know I'm alpha. But they are also old and worn out." he added, chuckling. "Stand your ground, Simbai, and lead; don't run from Zawe. In this case, it's your wife we're talking about leading. Having a child without a father in these parts of Zawe is tantamount to eternal damnation. So you lead your family."

"Are these the only options?" Simbai asked.

"I don't know; let me think." His Uncle pursed his lips into his customary thinking pout. A few moments went by as Simbai hoped for a third viable option.

"You could always become a hedonist!" The man said, and they both laughed. Then, after their shared mirth, Simbai asked.

"So, run, lead, or become a lover of pleasure, any more options?" His heart hoped desperately that this man's wisdom would produce more options.

"No, I don't think so. It's two options; escape or face it. Pleasure or running are both 'escape.' Leading others means you have led yourself first, so that's facing it.' Look around you, Zawe is full of pleasure seekers, and most of our escape artists are abroad. Someone needs to face the beasts."

"For good reason, though, Uncle. They fled for good reasons."

"There is always a good reason to flee. An intoxicating reason too. I know; I fled my family to come live with my wife's family in her home village by the Zii river."

Simbai remembered when they had fled the dogs. He had experienced an intoxicating clarity of adrenaline and the single-minded purpose. Not only does the one escaping always know precisely why they are where they are and doing what they are doing. But everything they are doing serves the fleeing purpose and its auxiliaries. It's an intoxicating, unified purpose, and it's deceptive. Eighteen years in Uzu, and he had never forgotten why they were there even for a day. It felt like 'clarity of purpose,' but apparently, it's adrenaline in charge for years.

He looked at his Uncle, "But Uncle, at least fleeing is taking action.

Working together with another means a lot of waiting and less action. Waiting makes you a victim of circumstances, a sitting duck."

"Oh, my son." the man said, adopting the cultural motherly tone all Uncles are allowed in Zawe. "Fleeing from oxygen is not a sign of agency, but a sign of ignorance, stupidity even. And suffocation will show you that in acting this way, *you* are being stupid. So as you escape to the diaspora or into pleasure and money, you will get whacked by the consequences of your own choices and actions like a sitting duck. In the end, you can't escape pain and discomfort in life, that's…"

Leilani interrupted his thoughts as she continued her supplications. "Mom pleeeeaazzuh! Just take it, take it, take it, mom, pleeeease…" Leilani said with a little jump and tremble. The way teenagers do as they try to implore someone with their whole body. Leilani's arm was outstretched as she held the shell out, stabbing the air with each "take it." Her tears continued to flow as she waited for her mother to make a move.

Her mother shook her head slowly and began articulating quietly to them both as tears streamed down her face. It was as though she was reading his mind and hearing his desire for her to speak up. "What are values for if we abandon them when we are in peril. We chose to believe in the way of life that won't let us wear the shell. It is who we are. And when these beliefs produce good, we enjoy it, and when they produce suffering and pain, we endure it. I will stand by my values, our values," she corrected, looking at her husband, "I will stand by you." She finished, tears continuing their cascade from her eyes. "I am proud of you, my daughter. You have become strong and independent as we hoped." She continued getting up, arms open for an embrace.

"I am proud as well," Simbai said, getting up and reaching out too, grateful that she had spoken up. So now Leilani will know her mother had a mind of her own, too though it differed from hers.

"What about the rot affecting women," Leilani asked in frustration, "Aren't you afraid?"

"If death is my lot, what am I afraid of, that I will go to paradise? Don't threaten me with a good time," she replied with gentle levity.

"That's almost like suicide; you know that, right?" Leilani asked, raising her hands in exasperation.

"Leila, I can see how that sounds to you. But to me, to us, maybe I'll speak just for myself. If I become afraid of death, my daughter, what becomes of my faith?" she replied, arms still open. She was flicking her fingers, urging Leilani to come into the hug.

Leilani hesitated but ultimately refused to come into the group hug. She wanted to blame her father, but now her mother had spoken up. They were two people hiding behind each other at the same time. She hoped she would find something like them someday. Deep sorrow and panicked anger overtook her being. What if this were the last time she would see them? At least she could say goodbye and hug them, right? The three flames had told them to stay clear of the unshelled unless they wanted to catch the rot. Leilani did not wish to catch the rot. But she was already in the house, and she had come to convince them to stay. She believed in wearing the shell. It was who she was as well. She couldn't stomach going any nearer to them until they changed their minds and joined her in the shell-wearing. Even though every pound of flesh on her body told her to hug them, she stayed rooted in her spot. Her heart told her to hold on to them and never let go, but instead, more tears gushed out of her eyes. She spun around and ran to what used to be her room and shut the door, sobbing.

It hurt them to stand there, their arms open, and be rejected. Simbai's wife whirled around and buried herself into her husband's chest, crying. He held her tightly. He was working on overdrive to contain his thoughts, to be strong.

Leilani wasn't the only person Simbai and his wife could not hug goodbye. Some of their long-time friends would not even look at them, let alone speak to them because they did not wear the shell. The "U" was their curse of separation. Simbai was banished, unemployed, running out of food, and about to lose his daughter. He looked down at his wife, kissed her on the top of her head, and smiled weakly. At least they still had each other.

* * *

Simbai nuzzled her and gestured at their luggage with the top of his head. They picked up their two bags and walked out. Uzu had helped them downsize to only the essentials in life. He put one bag on his back and carried one in his left hand. With his right, he held on to his wife. To comfort her, make her feel safe, and lean on her for strength. Slowly, they walked away from their reason for coming to Uzu; their daughter and family. Some unshelled neighbors were waiting on the roads to bid the banished farewell. At the same time, other neighbors were jeering at the treasonous bunch. Simbai and his wife walked past them, heads down. They had the scarlet letter emblazoned on their chests.

They made it to the only airport in the village. They boarded the only plane allowed between them and the outside world. It took off in the sombreness of all low flights: everyone on board, a banished citizen. Simbai's wife looked out of her window, bidding Uzu farewell. Only to see something break out of the roof of a house. She was petrified. Another one of these things broke out of another rooftop. This one screeched loud enough for Simbai to hear. He came to the window in time to see two dragons flying and breathing fire down onto the village. His thoughts bolted in every direction. They were like a relay connecting messengers to knights in medieval times. Calling them to gather at the mouth of the dragon's cave. At the same time, his heart sank for his daughter's life as he thought - 'dragons exist.' There was too much to worry about, too much lost, and much that did not make sense. Simbai made an exhausted last-ditch effort to apply his thought control skills from years in Uzu. He banished the complexities from his wearied mind. "Hmmm," he remarked, placing his butt firmly back in his seat, "it's not an old wives tale."

CHAPTER TWO

Rusty Velvet

BLUE BLOODS

"In short then," the narrator of the book said, "We all bleed blue." Simbai chuckled at this part, excited to discover how this narrator would make her case. All practical knowledge disagreed with this assertion. Curious, Simbai continued reading. "You see, blood is blue. It gets red when hemoglobin combines with oxygen. Hemoglobin is the iron-containing oxygen-transport[ing] metalloprotein in the red blood cells. This iron metalloprotein is one of the two keys responsible for the red color of the life-giving blue liquid. A question: What happens when iron combines with oxygen? The answer: Rust. If a blue car was rusty, would you say it's a brown car, or would you say it's a rusty blue car? Oxygenated blood is red because oxygenated blood has rusted hemoglobin. So, in truth, blood is a rusty velvet blue liquid. Some may recognize this as an ontological oxymoron. One which at its simple core says, we bleed blue."

Simbai smiled and looked away from the book.

As a student of logic, he could not argue against this syllogism. It was somewhat well constructed and airtight. It was even sprinkled with some science in there. For example, hemoglobin contains iron which facilitates the transportation of oxygen—all true. The only way to destroy the fallacy was to pull out its foundation, and then the rest would crumble. The foundational assumption or axiom was wrong.

Blood is not blue, ever. Unless, of course, one is an octopus. For most vertebrates - and all people - blood is light red at most. It becomes darker with a bright redness when it has absorbed oxygen. And people thought Uzu was the one full of dubiousness. Simbai snorted with ridicule as he thought all this through.

He awoke from his reverie as the noise of crunching wheels reached his ears. A brand-new truck was rolling down the driveway. It took him a minute to recognize Ruramai, who was at the wheel of the truck approaching their farmhouse. They had received the plot of land from the local government of Zawe. Ground paid for by The Three Flames through the government of Zawe.

The car door slammed, and Simbai chuckled, calling to his friend.

"Ruuuu, Ruuu, my friend who bleeds blue. How are you?"

Ruramai (Which means "get right with" or "get with the program") was puzzled by the greeting, but he expected his friend to have a few screws loose now. After all, he had chosen to go live his life in Uzu. And Simbai had sounded strange on his return from the place. Ruramai brushed the greeting off and said,

"Only when the blood is not oxygenated is it blue."

"Would that blood be in its purest form or its dead form?" Simbai asked as he embraced his friend, who rolled his eyes.

"I don't know, but I know you need an upgrade in life, my friend. Country living won't do for my best pal!"

"Ha-ha, come in, come in! See how well we live, me and my beloved," he said, noticing how the sentence lacked the third member of their family.

He ushered his friend into the house. His wife was beaming at Ruramai. A welcome visitor and great help since their return. She embraced Ruramai, who smelled the smoke off her. She was using the fire pit oven. He didn't say anything but scrunched up his nose involuntarily.

* * *

"It's good to see you, Tambudzai (which means "trouble me)," he said instead.

"Aaah, aah, aah, you can't call her by her first name like we insisted when we first arrived from Uzu. This is Zawe now. We do what all of you do and use titles and last names."

"It's good to see you too, Ruu." Simbai's wife said. She shook her head with a playful smirk on her lips. "Would you like some water?" she said, brushing off her husband's half-kidding comment.

"Yes, please," the man replied, "and whatever you are making on that fire of yours."

She chuckled again, "You must have smelled the smoke on me." she replied.

"Ah, yes, country living," he said, looking around the beautiful house. He was trying to reconcile his disdain with his approval. They seemed to be living well, but Ruu could not shake his bias toward city life.

Tambu smiled at him, "You won't be using that tone when I bring out the scones and tea." She said, walking out of the living room.

"I'm sorry for your state of affairs, my friend," Ruramai said, sitting on a fluffy, comfortable couch.

"Why would you say that?"

"I mean living in the here, as opposed to..." he replied with a motion of his hands like he was pedaling a bicycle with his elbows.

Simbai knew what he meant: "living in the rural areas instead of the bustling city life." But he just stared at Ruramai and waited for him to finish his sentence. Ruramai squirmed under Simbai's gaze until finally, Simbai relented.

"Oh please, this is perfect for my gentle wife and me." He smiled, his mind drawn to how his wife had been a pillar of their relationship. He

41

was lost in thought as Ruramai continued to inspect the well-kept farmhouse. He was searching for the crack, for something out of place to confirm his thoughts on the place.

"What's ideal about this? How are you making money?" Ruramai blurted.

"We have a small settlement from Uzu. They banished us but to our surprise; they did not abandon us." Simbai replied, looking pensive.

"Most likely for the PR. We don't know much about what's going on in that place there. But the dragons showing up changed things the world over. What are you going to do when that money runs out?"

"That might take a long time since we don't spend much. We run on solar, water comes from the river, and the food comes from the land."

"How about vacations. Or vehicles. Or, or, or..."

"Ruuu, don't you rent a place in the city?"

"Yes, it's a beautiful place. It's luxurious. You should see the new artwork I have added since you passed through on your return from Uzu. Some large prints of the missus on vacation at the falls and me."

"I see, so what happens to you when your money runs out? You don't own your house or land. I'm assuming you are making payments on your truck, so you don't own that either. I mean, that does not sound ideal."

"Yes, but I am earning money,"

"And we own our land. We are living the retirement and vacation life many people wish for. We don't have any of your touch screens, but our goats and chickens are great!" he ended with a laugh. Ruramai did not join in the laughter.

Tambudzai was in the kitchen arranging some tea and scones onto a tray. She brought it before she had finished, hoping to break the tension she felt on Ruramai's side. The aroma from the scones brought an unexpected smile to Ruramai's face. He picked one before the tray was set down. He was at home with these two.

And as he took a bite, he closed his eyes, inundated by the flavorful crumbly scone.

"Hmmm, nhapitapi (sweet music to my tastebuds)," he said

"Those are banana orange scones. I learned the original recipe from Simbai's dad. Then I modified and perfected it in Uzu." she said

HOME

At the mention of his dad, Simbai called to mind the memory of the last time they visited his family. That was on their return from Uzu. Other people had been housed in a hotel in preparation for other travel plans. The Uzu ambassadorial vehicles had also driven other people to their hometowns, while Simbai and his wife had been taken to his parent's hometown. His father had been there, to their surprise.

As they walked into the gate, they were greeted by his mother, saying, "I told you it was a bad idea to go to that dragon place." She embraced him. "Let me look at you. Did the dragon burn you in any way?"

"Welcome home, my son?" His father said, trying to get ahead of the conversation

"Yes, welcome, welcome. You see, it was a bad idea to go to Uzu, right?" His mother said, briefly realizing she had forgotten the welcome part. She embraced Tambu and turned to face her son to continue her victory lap. His siblings were nowhere to be seen just yet.

He hung his head a little. He raised his eyes to look at the house where he had grown up.

It never once felt like home in all his short life. But, it felt a little like boot camp and a lot like, "When will I leave?" if that could be called a feeling.

* * *

To be sure, he had learned a lot about life from both his parents. Hard work had been impressed upon him and his spiritual beliefs. He was sighing at his fate, having to return here, when his mother chimed in: "Now you don't have anything but two bags. I told you it was a bad idea, didn't I? I told you so." Simbai's mother had said.

Simbai looked at his wife, who shook her head to urge him not to speak. She knew this look. It only came over her husband when he visited home. Simbai shrugged with apathy though he was about to act. He looked at his mother, "You know, 'I told you so' is actually witchcraft?" he said, his mouth drying up with each word. Then, he cleared his throat, moistened his lips, and amplified his voice a little. "It's people who..."

"Are you calling me a witch?" his mother asked, her anger roused.

"Some people want to be so right; they are willing to wish evil on others." Simbai continued his somewhat subdued tirade. The rant of one who felt defeated.

"Why, no, I would never wish evil on you," she replied, trying to calm down.

"Oh yes. So would you be happy for me if I had called you and said, "You were wrong; Uzu is great?" No, you would feel defeated. But now, you are deriving joy and satisfaction from being right. This means you wish to be right about this somewhere in your heart and mind. To be right meant we had to fail and suffer. You wished for our downfall. That is witchcraft!"

"Baba waSimbai (Father of Simbai), do you hear your son?" she said, looking to the sad man caught in the crossfire.

"Stop, just stop, everyone," Simbai's wife whispered with vehemence, spittle accompanying her delivery. Then she sighed, straightened her blouse, picked up her bag, and walked out the gate, back to the Uzu government car that brought them to the house. She informed the driver they would be sleeping at a motel.

* * *

"But you don't have any money," Simbai's mother called over the gate. Tambudzai informed the driver that the government would be footing the bill. She said it loud enough for Simbai's mom to hear. Simbai followed her to the car. He didn't bother to apologize to anyone. Sitting beside her, they both clasped hands in silence. They hoped fervently that the government would pay for their motel that night.

HARBINGER

Ruramai snapped his fingers in front of his friend's face. "You are missing out. I am almost done with these scones."

"Are you thinking too much, honey?" his wife teased, walking in with more scones. He responded by trying to trip her as she walked by. She gave him a look, shook her head, and laughed.

"You should come to the city?" Ruramai said as he took another scone from the tray on its journey to its demise.

"We prefer the rural folk," Tambu replied, sitting by her husband.

"Yes, here they preach less about money and more about life in the spirit." Simbai chimed in mischievously, eyeing Ruramai's new truck. His friend smiled knowingly.

"But they are all up in your business a lot," Simbai's wife said more to her husband than Ruramai. He nodded, "Yes, you are right. It's almost like they are always thinking about your business and not their own."

"Aaah, that's a cultural thing, remember?" Ruramai replied. "You might be better off going abroad if you don't like that sort of thing. And even then, we will call you to nose around your business."

"Interesting suggestion," Simbai said, looking at his wife and genuinely considering the option.

There was some silence.

* * *

Then he looked at his friend and started shaking his head with another knowing smile. Simbai could trust Ruramai with his life because they went way back. But Ruramai was a complex maShona type, and he spoke in circumlocution and innuendos. To get at Ruu's meaning was like going hunting. And Simbai was not always in the mood, so he would sometimes choke it out of Ruu. There was no bad blood, but no prisoners were taken either, just two friends playing an old game.

"So, going abroad, huh?" Simbai asked, reaching for a scone and eyeing Ruramai. His gaze forced Ruramai deeper into the couch. Their guest squirmed, and Simbai.

"You got me, you devious scheming man."

"What, what?" Tambudzai asked, lost.

Ruramai laughed uneasily, glad this would not be a wrestling match. He meant well and wanted to get his boy out of the rural setting. "What gave me away?" he asked.

"Your silence. You are never quiet unless…you haven't changed much, Ruu." Simbai said, shaking his head and smiling. When Ruu was not nervous and not carrying news, he would generally talk a storm. But he struggled to say the more profound things on his mind. Like when he was against them going to Uzu and had joked about it.

"Ok, so abroad, is it?" Simbai asked again in different words. He broke his scone and urged Ruramai to keep eating the sumptuous baked creations.

"Yes, yes, abroad," Ruramai said, clearing his throat. Then, he took a sip of tea and cleared his throat again. "That's why I am here. I found you a job at a big tech company in Orange Valley (Oh-rah-nkeh Valley).

"What, I didn't know you were looking for a job," Tambudzai said, looking at her husband doubly lost.

"No, no, it's a joke. Simbai wasn't looking, and I didn't find it. The company was trying to get in touch with you. But you don't have a phone, and you don't check your email. So, someone put them onto me as a contact for you guys. And I drove all the way here to tell you the news. It's an all-expenses-paid multi-year trip," Ruramai glanced around the farmhouse as he finished responding to Tambudzai. Still no cracks, the house was simple, well kept, and yet comfortable and welcoming.

Later, Ruramai took a land tour and saw the goats and chickens. That's when he told Simbai about the Uzu asylum program. Some tech companies had partnered with the US government to help "rehabilitate" people from Uzu. He urged Simbai to consider it a cultural exchange exercise.

"You know, I will have to tell my wife the truth, right?"

"Yeah, I know. I was nervous in there to face the both of you. Your wife though quiet, has formidable resolve. And you, we already know."

The friends laughed.

"So, facing two unmovable objects was challenging, so I had to divide and conquer."

"With a lie," Simbai asked as they began the loopback.

"It's not a lie. The asylum program asked for names from Uzu, and I believed you were great candidates for the program. Tambudzai will love it, too, because they will have her partner on UN women stuff. This is a pretty big deal, and I wanted it for you."

Simbai smiled.

When they were getting back, Ruramai smelled the great cooking. So, he stayed for dinner. Food cooked over a fire tasted wholesomely different. And this food smelled delicious, but unlike any food aroma he had sensed in Zawe because it was an Uzu recipe. They bade him farewell after dinner, and Simbai closed his truck door for him. He and his wife waved as Ruramai drove off. When he had left, Simbai sat down on the porch. Tambudzai sat by him, leaning her head on his shoulder.

"Did you guys talk more about the job abroad?" she asked, sighing with contentment.

Simbai sighed with joy in response, adding a little snort.

"What's so funny?" Tambudzai asked, raising her head. And he smiled.

"Put your head back. I like it there." Simbai replied instead. She pushed his legs in protest and laid her head back on his shoulder. She knew he had news but had to wait a few seconds. Then he took a deep breath and told her about the asylum program and the rehabilitation. He made sure to mention the UN and how this was an opportunity for both of them.

"So, thoughts?" he asked, pulling her closer.

"Well," She said, moving away from him as he groaned in fake pain. "What, I'll be back. Let me grab us a cup of tea." When she came back, she had two cups of tea. And she looked at him and poured the one into the other, then smiled and handed the cup to him. He took a sip as she resumed her position, and she laid her head on him and raised a hand to signal for the cup. He passed it to her, and she took a sip and sighed. They sat like that for another moment, and he nudged her to remind her to answer. She sighed again and replied, "We have tried to keep to ourselves. But I am starved of human contact. And the more alone we are, the more I think of Leila. I feel like my bones are drying up. And the goats are drying up too, so I can't get good milk to bake. The garden isn't looking so good either." she finished.

"What, you mean our stress may be affecting our animals and possibly our plants." He asked, half-serious and half-joking.

She looked at him, "Stop it; I don't know" she shrugged. "I just don't feel ok here."

"Me neither. Going somewhere far from family and nosy neighbors might be great." He replied, gathering her up in his arms as they snuggled.

"Yeah, I don't like thinking of it as running away. More like going towards more community with more freedom to be and do." Tambu said, thinking back on what she wanted to run from.

People said they were in denial. Strangers shed tears for Leilani but not her parents. A daughter who was lost in a village overrun by dragons. Theirs was the only banished family that had left a child. Simbai wasn't bothered by the people's criticism. He was annoyed by people who were not themselves happy until they forced him and Tambudzai to be troubled by what happened in Uzu. They also wanted them to be troubled by what other people said. Simbai remained unperturbed. He regularly stated that many thought it was normal to be bothered by the past or what other people said. He told that if this was the case, he desired to remain abnormal. His wife rallied with him. She had faith that she would see her daughter again someday. "If my daughter were gone, I would feel it." she would say, smiling at whoever asked after Leilani. People were unnerved by the two's capacity to not care about what other people think. So, the two began to spend more time shut-in, like the scalers. The memory of these events came to mind as they snuggled and considered going abroad. They had shed tears in Uzu for Leilani. They could not go on crying forever.

Simbai had cried for years when his sister died. Especially when people sang her favorite song, he would feel the tears coming. Back then, he had promised he would never cry at a funeral. But when they carried her little coffin out of the hearse, tears gushed out of his eyes. The little girl who was so outspoken and independent was no more. He remembered the day she was told she could not come with him to the mall. Mom had thought she would fold. But, instead, she had filled up the kettle. He had been afraid to help her because he would get in trouble with their mother. But he had encouraged her to put less water so she could carry the pot. Then he had helped her put it on the stove because her little arms could not though she tried. Then he had made sure she didn't get burned when the water boiled—next, helping her pour it into the bucket in the bathroom. And then she had bathed herself, picked out her clothes, and joined them on the excursion to the mall. He chuckled to himself, and he thought how much she would have loved her niece Leilani. She would be proud of him, too, that he could speak for himself now and stand his ground. She had been his mouthpiece often, and they were inseparable. So inseparable that when she came for his birthday at the kindergarten, she refused to leave. She cried and made such a fuss the teachers finally decided to keep her. And the next day, she dressed up for school, and he went with her again, and that's how she started kindergarten. He sighed and came back to Tambudzai.

She had been speaking for a while and now was saying,

"Plus, living here is making me feel Old. Yet, we still have tons more to offer the world."

He grunted in agreement, hoping she wouldn't notice he had been lost in thought. She continued,

"Though I should say, Orange Valley is an individualistic place, which isn't ideal." They both preferred more community like in Uzu. Yet, the valley was in a country that carried the same, 'leave the thinking to the professionals' philosophies of Uzu. Which meant it would be comfortable even though it was less communal. Over there, they could live with others, but they would also not need to interact with anyone. They could hide in plain sight. It was a sad alternative to Uzu, but it mimicked Uzu in many comfortable ways. It was better than this place full of community and discomfort. In Zawe, everyone was all up in everyone's business. And no one could stop thinking of what others were thinking about concerning them. The image was everything, and looking wealthy was preferred over being wealthy.

So, it was decided on that porch. Simbai and Tambudzai were going to move abroad!

And it was because of that, that they found themselves going to stay with Ruramai and his family every other week or so. They had paperwork to complete, virtual interviews to take, and offives to visit in the city. Simbai was enrolled in a primer for IT. At the same time, Tambudzai received her training and briefing on current affairs and global politics. They didn't realize it, but they were high-profile asylees. Uzu was an international sensation, mainly because of the new dragons. And they were some of the few who had seen the beasts.

* * *

Half a year flew by, and they were on the plane to Orange Valley. It felt like redemption to be packing for happy reasons. It was a welcome relief to be on a comfortable and happy flight again, and they were flying first class. They talked, reminisced, and philosophized. Simbai found Tambduzai way more talkative on their travels, and he loved it. They touched on having more children but did not explore the topic much as they felt strange. When they arrived in Orange Valley, they were housed in a luxurious apartment on the tech company's campus. It even had an indoor fire oven. The oven didn't smoke the house at all when they used it. Tambudzai remembered she had noted in a questionnaire that one of the things she enjoyed in her home was an authentic fire oven. Uzu had gotten Tambudzai addicted to the well-cooked food that such an oven offered and stove. Simbai and Tambu had other excellent customized amenities they had not realized they were 'requesting' when filling out paperwork.

DEFLATED TIRE

Simbai was on his way back from a meeting in LA. When the cop lights lit up like a fireworks display, he witnessed the whole thing. He was a couple of hours from Orange Valley, which was home.

"Let him go," someone said, looking at the car. The driver filmed all that was happening, afraid of saving the dying man. "Let him go," the driver pleaded, hoping his words would do what his body could not. Simbai looked away but was jolted back to the main scene when the man pinned down began to convulse. He thought they would let him up now. He had not seen anyone die before. But these seemed like the last kicks of a dying horse, as they said, death throes. The involuntary struggle continued for a few moments. Simbai was stunned at his inability to look away. The bicycle, the police, the man, the lights.

Then the man on the ground went limp. And Simbai thought out loud, "He is not moving."

And someone added, "You killed him right there..." and Simbai had to jump out of his car. The police looked his way, many of their hands placed on their guns. Simbai was, however, running away from the scene. He tried and succeeded in going a few feet from his car. Then he began retching violently. He felt nauseated, but nothing came up when he tried to throw up. Nothing but memories; thoughts: He had failed his family...his solution had failed his family. Going to Uzu had been a mistake. He thought, tears welling up in his eyes.

A policeman caught up with him, tackling him to the ground. They arrested him, saying it was only a precaution if he was connected to the limp man on the road.

A supervisor was on the scene, and he recognized their mistake immediately. Simbai was a high-profile civilian. Some higher-ups would take issue if they detained him any longer. They apologized profusely, quietly, and quickly let him go. Heavy at heart and bruised from the tackle, he collected himself. He did not realize he could make trouble for the offivers if her wished. He drove back home to his wife, distracted all the way. A few hours were like an instant in that mindset. He felt agitated like in the pre-Uzu days and was concerned as he walked up the stairs to their apartment. They lived in an on-campus apartment graciously provided by the software company that brought them hither.

Simbai threw himself onto the designer couch, defeated. He winced as the pain of the tackle came through. He had grown a little stiff from the drive. As he relaxed a little more, pain coursed through his body. But at least he was alive. Then he sighed as tears streamed down his chicks. Tambu ran over from the kitchen when she heard the stifled sobs. He looked bruised and dirty. But his eyes said it all. She didn't know the specifics, but the tears were about Uzu and not what happened that day. She came over, arms stretched, and knelt to hug him. They embraced as she joined him in weeping. He pulled her on top of him, wincing as he did so. They held each other on the couch.

When they came to, it was dinner time. The two got up, and Tambu made a quick Uzu dish. They ate in silence, occasionally exchanging weak smiles over the delicious food. At one point, Simbai stood up, came over to his wife's side, and hugged her from behind, above the chair. She held his forearms.

* * *

Simbai and his wife sat on the couch after dinner. Soon they were lying down, and that's how they spent the night. The next day was Sunday. They had another whole day without work to distract them. They had no escape from each other or the issues at hand.

Tambudzai had finished making her coffee and made his cup of tea. She had sipped her cup and looked up to heaven like someone who had just had a refreshing swig of a cold Coca-cola on a hot day. He chuckled, "Your drug tasting good?" she smiled and shook her head. "Please, as if your tea doesn't have caffeine in it?" He was going to argue, but today he couldn't find the wherewithal. So he smiled, and they stood across from each other in the immaculate kitchen. A white marble-top kitchen island stood between them like a chasm of beautiful white sands waiting to be crossed. The day before hung over them and the day ahead, a blank canvas.

"I think," they both said and smiled,

"You can go," her husband said

"Oh no, you are the man, you go..."

"Aah, that is not how this country works. So you go; first," Simbai said.

She laughed, eyeing him resolutely. He could not read her expression, so he decided he would speak. She was delighted at going first.

So, they both spoke again:

"I think the whole police thing yesterday was racially motivated?" he said

"I think you might want to try therapy?" she said

"Of course it was," she responded.

"Ewww, no," was his response.

They looked at each other, amused. These were serious issues, but they

53

smiled.

"Therapy is not for people like us. "He replied, pinching and pulling his forearm skin.

"I'm serious, Simbai. I know you shun working out, hiking, and this sort of thing. But it's all offered for free at your job."

"I don't get it. Why would people shun manual labor? There you get paid to work out. But people choose instead to pay for a gym. For what? So they can all spend time lifting things and putting them down in place. And they don't produce anything but bodies that look like people who do physical work. So do manual work already, like I did at the farm in Uzu!"

"Oh, so you did that for the body?" she asked, distracting her stubborn, caring husband.

"You know it," he said, winking at her. "And hiking, why would anyone climb a mountain when they aren't gathering firewood or hunting? Imagine then what therapy must be like. Most likely another pointless exercise like the gym or hiking. One which probably can be achieved through other rewarding and productive social means. I bet it's like that show you were telling me about."

"Which one?" Tambudzai asked.

"Oh right, you tell me about a lot of shows. I mean the one where the main actress talks about her problems only to blame her parents for everything. And then I bet after I do that, I will then you receive a prescription and pop pills for the rest of your life. Is that what you want for me to be drugged-up forever?"

Tambudzai was losing her patience. She walked up to her man and pulled him by the ear.

"Ow, ow, ouch," he said, stunned.

Then she kissed him while twisting the poor man's ear. She walked away.

CORPORATE SOCIAL RESPONSIBILITY

Simbai was pacing the next day at work. He was standing in the hallway leading to the sports arena, the meditation room, the yoga theatre, and the therapy rooms. The nap pods were on the other side of the cafeteria. He did not want to go to therapy, but she had done the thing with the ear and the kiss. She meant business, and he had to make something happen.

Finally, he decided that no stranger had a right to advise him about his life. Especially if that stranger did not understand his spiritual beliefs. Simbai chose yoga as the better evil. Not meditation or therapy, but yoga. It was halfway to meditation, and all the yoga people he knew were quite zen. Until, of course, someone messed up their energy, but at least they were calm for the most part.

Simbai tiptoed awkwardly into the yoga theatre. He was the only man there. Even though he had taken off his shoes, he did not look dressed for the occasion. He resolved to change his dress next time and bring his own mat. Finally, he decided on yoga, and that was it.

He came home chipper, but they did not discuss the day much. Tambu had chosen to give him room to come around. Two weeks went by, and he sounded a tad bit better. She suspected he was going to therapy but wouldn't tell her until she asked. So, she asked.

"Hun, you look effortlessly relaxed lately. What's your secret?"

"My secret, my dear Tambu." he said dramatically, making her laugh, as he nuzzled her face and whispered, "Is yoga!"

Her face moved so fast away from his that he thought he had messed up. "You are lying. No. No way you are doing yoga. No way!" she said, chuckling and punching him playfully.

"Yes, ways. Here are my yoga clothes and my yoga mat. I have been hiding them from you just because." He said, pulling them out of a drawer underneath the cabinet at the door.

"Wow, alright!" Yoga was one step from therapy, she thought, smiling. So she took her win.

THE COLORS

It started like a purple hallucination from the corner of his eye—a purple reverberation of the reflection of his body in a mirror or a body of water. And, sometimes, when he moved his hands fast enough, he would notice a purple blur. Then, he started seeing colors as people interacted. Yellows, pinks, reds, and Tambu's green - a whole kaleidoscope. Especially in the yoga theatre. It was strange but also did not disrupt a lot of his work.

What was interesting was that sometimes people would change colors. It would be an overnight change, but they would not change colors again for a while. It was all strange business, but he didn't want to worry his beloved wife, so he did not tell her.

Simbai had researched enough a few months later to know that the colors he saw were called auras. The ability to see these auras had been helpful in his negotiations and interpersonal conflict. These colors also inspired out-of-the-box ideas tailored to people. This extended skill became invaluable to his collaborations at work. He landed some fantastic projects and was recommended for a raise a couple of times. The higher-ups were glad they had chosen an Uzu refugee to join them. Simbai certainly had unique perspectives.

One day, Simbai was doing his breathing practice at the beginning of yoga. He saw a flash of color with no corresponding body. It darted hither and thither. And he tried to remain calm, hoping the colors were not about to become a problem. The color did not have a body but was aura-like.

He closed his eyes to center himself and sang in his head. "Don't be suspicious, don't be suspicious," He opened his eyes to a formless face right in front of him. Everybody else in the room seemed to be moving like a slow-motion instant replay.

"He is awake," the face said to no one before it darted away, not to be seen in the room again.

This was super strange, so he confided in the yoga instructor after the session. The instructor looked thoughtful as he narrated his vision. But unfortunately, he did not tell her about the auras.

"It isn't uncommon that people with trauma could have a mental breakdown during mindfulness practices without a guru. And you have some trauma from Zawi. Did I say it right, Zawi?"

She asked, eyeing him innocently.

"Yes, yes, Zawe," he replied, correcting her.

"Aaah, yes, Zawi. The country must be carrying trauma indeed as a nation. Bloody elections, droughts and famines, and general hopelessness. It can be a lot to carry in the body. Have you considered the generational trauma in your country as well? Imagine the heritage of trauma of the wars, the colonial trauma of the people in your country. Your country needs not only a cleanse but wholesale therapy. Normalized trauma of a whole group of people can look or sound like culture. I know a guy who could run a national workshop...."

It was at this point that Simbai realized she was fading away. He thought he was fading away, but she was the one changing into a ghostly figure outlined in blue, which replaced her usual black aura. Then she erupted into a fire, head first. He started and took a step back and gulped. The figure was overtaken by a consuming and overwhelming blue light or flame. It still had a little black in it, but the color which made up most of the flame was blue in hue. And then she slowly came back to her bodily self.

"What?" she asked as she tried to decipher the look in his eyes, "Did I say something wrong?"

No words came from Simbai, only a look.

57

* * *

"I'm sorry if I projected on your country," she began her apology, but he cut her short.

"I have to go. I am starving." Simbai said, surprising himself with the tactful truthful lie. "National Trauma," he thought to himself, then the word emerged by itself, "Trauma." He instantly thought about Leila, the dragon, and how Tambudzai must be feeling. His wife, with whom he had not discussed the aftermath of their lives in Uzu. His loyal and trusted sidekick was, in fact, the leading superhero all along.

He walked dazed to the cafeteria. He was distracted by people melting into magnifivent blue-lighted flames—the figures shown brilliantly like the sun breaking through clouds. They leaped about like flames burning energy in a gentle breeze. The fires looked like they had a source of fuel for their subsistence and an unending supply of oxygen or whatever sustained the combustion. Each flame flashed a different color now and then, which he realized was the person's aura. Some fires had their edges lined up with these colors, almost like a silver lining on a cloud.

He went straight to his car. The tech campus was big enough that their apartment was a short drive away. On his drive home, Simbai encountered blue flames driving other vehicles. Blue flames in sports cars, blue flames in Lincolns, Teslas, and old beat-up cars. There were blue conflagrations everywhere. He was greeted by the aroma of good food cooking in the slow cooker. Tambudzai's constancy and care floored him. She was patient, dedicated, and fed them both so well. He walked over to her offive, weighed down by how neglectful he had been. 'Did she too have trauma to work through?' he had never asked himself or her that question.

Tambudzai worked online mostly, so she could work from home. She was a UN ambassador, among several honors. Tambudzai was seated at her desk when he unexpectedly opened the door to her offive. She was torn between removing her headphones and continuing the call. Simbai decided for her. He walked over to her table. Tambu was on a video call with a Prime minister. Simbai overheard them talking about The Three Flames and negotiations with the UN. He didn't care, and he walked right up to the call dressed in his yoga clothes and greeted the VIP on the other end. Then he excused his wife from the video call. The Prime minister, though surprised, was gracious about it.

Tambu was astonished by her husband's interruption.

"What now?" she asked exasperated.

And then the sweaty man from yoga pulled her up from her chair and held her close. He kissed her on the forehead and held her tightly. "I'm sorry," he said, close to tears. "For what?" she replied, puzzled. "For not talking about us, about Uzu. For not talking about how you are doing?" Tambu smiled briefly before breaking down into tears. Finally, he was getting there, she thought. She had been waiting a long while, but he was getting there.

They cried together.

When he opened his eyes, he saw they were engulfed in flames. He could see his body, but Tambudzai was now a beautiful blue conflagration in his arms. And the flame was consuming them both. As he smiled with tears still on his face, he started turning into his fiery self. And they became one flame, one fire; they became one - an unit.

He felt her body shake as she sobbed, and he saw her tongues of fire leaping with apparent excitement. Her emotions increased the brilliance of her hue. She was blue, a little green, and a lot bluer. He was blue too, and he thought he noticed an occasional purple flare. Together they made a brilliant turquoise ultramarine blue flame that was unique.

Later, as they sat down for dinner, she said, "I didn't know yoga could open you up to think of others like that?"

"Aah, and the beauty of it all is that no stranger knows our dirty laundry?"

She paused mid-bite.

"What did you do?" he asked like a parent who knows the face of a red-handed child.

"Watch your tone, my love."

"Wow, deflecting, are we?"

She swallowed and put down her fork and knife.

"I have been seeing a therapist," they said in unison.

"Wait, what?" she asked, surprised.

"Oh, not me. No. No. No way. I was anticipating your words, and it looks like I was spot on." he replied, smiling and shaking his head.

She threw her napkin in his face from across the table.

"You are not mad?" she asked.

"Oh no, a little sad that you had to do it in secret."

"I wasn't doing it in secret. I followed your lead, my love. Held onto the news for a few weeks before telling you."

"I suppose I started it," he replied.

"That's not what I mean. Are you sure you aren't mad?"

"No, not at all. I was trying to take responsibility for my actions in starting the secret-keeping game."

"It's not secret-keeping, and it's not a game!" she retorted more passionately than she intended. Simbai looked at her, placing his eating utensils and placing his palms flat on the table. The way he usually did when he was giving way in their conversations.

She repeated herself more calmly. "It's not secret-keeping, and it's not a game. I was hoping you would notice me doing better and ask me as I asked you."

* * *

He stood up and walked over to her side of the table. "All this time, I thought your strange behavior was because you were hiding that you were pregnant. I only suspected it was a therapist thing today as we were eating." She laughed nervously for a second.

"We haven't talked about kids in a while, Simbai."

"I know," he replied. "I thought you wouldn't want to have any more with me."

"And I thought you didn't want anymore? The weight of one child almost crushed us."

"It did crash us," he whispered.

"But we are rising again," she said," raising her voice poetically. "We are rising again. We may fall eight times, but we will rise ten times!"

"Huh, the other extra two times are we flying?"

"I don't know. I know we have a future ahead. There is hope."

He kissed her hands and walked back to his seat. He wiped a tear from his right eye and sat down to finish dinner.

THE NIGHT LIGHTS

As he lay in bed asleep, one mosquito was bugging him plenty. It somehow left Tambu alone but was in and around his ears often. It was like a phantom haunting him rather than a mosquito looking to bite him. For a minute, his heart skipped as he wondered if this was a message that Leilani was in trouble or, worse, moved on to the other side. Then the buzzing slowed down to a drawl. It was as though the mosquito had grown bigger and sluggish. The drawl was persistent and wouldn't go away. Then suddenly, he felt a surprising warmth on his face which came with a light. Like a warm, soft glowing hand was resting on his face. He started and woke up to the formless face he had seen before. He could not scream even though he was terrified. Tambu had been through enough without exposing her to this new delusion. He would have to deal with this one alone. Finally, he realized that the drawl was a mosquito moving in slow motion. The formless light darted around the room, and suddenly there was a host of them illuminating the bedroom.

Simbai marveled at the beauty surrounding him. "This is what it must have been like when the shepherds saw the hosts of angels on that night in Bethlehem.' he thought. "It was even better." a beautiful voice sang from everywhere in the room. Then the faces rearranged themselves and illuminated a staircase. Resigned to his hallucination, Simbai got up, walked over to the window, opened the panes, and began climbing the stairs. The faces of light were darting around him, up and down to and fro so fast. But everything else around him was going at half the speed of a sloth on a bad day. He was in a slow-motion dream - the thought - and the faces of light were moving at breakneck speed. He wondered what they looked if this was real life and everything was going at regular speed. He chuckled to himself, wondering how his mind was working this dream.

Simbai walked for a considerable time. Enough for the hallucination to wear off, he thought. Then he was ushered into a room that wasn't dark, but it wasn't light either. He looked up and noticed that a shadow cast over the place caused the dimness in the room. The room without a roof beside the stary sky. He could not see what was casting the shadow.

"It's 'who'?" the formless face replied, reading his thoughts.

"What?" Simbai asked

"It's not what. It's who."

"Who 'what'?"

"Who is casting the shadow."

"Who is casting the shadow?" Simbai asked.

"The one shining the light," the face responded.

* * *

And Simbai gave up. More doors to the room opened as large flames of light entered from different angles. Simbai counted six huge flames, and none of them was blue.

The face darted around the room, whispering at this flame and that one. Then, each being's flames sizzled out, transforming them into physical entities. The shadow prevented Simbai from clearly seeing each one of them. But their forms were unmistakable.

One burly being with dreadlocks was like a giant to every being in the room. Two of these entities looked almost identical, like twins, but one was slightly shorter and skinnier than the other. One being was constantly shifting sizes as he 'breathed.' This one looked Simbai squarely in the eye, yet its eyes kept moving places on its body. Simbai shivered. There was another being who was spikey and spindly. And then one being who looked almost human. About the height of a short basketball player so taller than Simbai. He had some golden scales, which reminded Simbai of the dragon shell from Uzu.

After they transformed from the enormous flames, they all found their seats and sat down. Simbai awkwardly took the chair, which remained empty, and the meeting was called to order. The formless face darted to Simbai and asked him to stand up and bow.

"This is Simbai, the new and recently awakened representative of the Living Souls from the earth below. Since the last representative is now gone to the union (died), we, the faces of light, picked this one because he can see."

All the beings laughed.

"Another one of them, huh." - The shifting being said.

One of the beings grunted and huffed a little. Simbai could not tell which one made the guttural noises. As he tried to figure it out, the skinnier of the twins said,

"Might as well call it our vote, huh?"

* * *

"Or just dispense with the fake representation," burly dreadlocks said. "I know its cosmic law to have a living soul present at our deliberations. However, they never really suggest plagues, and they always agree with our recommendations."

"All cosmic law is life, and to dispense with the representation would be death." The face of light replied. There was reverend almost terrified silence over the mentioning of Death. These being's revered their superior and tried not to cross Death lest they perish.

"Hey, isn't that the guy from Uzu?" the spindly one said, trying to relieve the tension.

They all howled and hollered loudly.

"These are the principalities in charge of Earth," the formless face said, ignoring the laughter. "They have the authority over this level of the heavens. And they tend to be up to some shenanigans targeting people's auras."

"Hahaha, 'shenanigans' is right!" The basketball player said.

They all went silent. "Order in the meeting!" burly dreadlocks said, hitting a gavel that Simbai had not noticed until this moment. Every being cast a disapproving glance at the basketball player who had laughed and spoken last.

"What did I do? You guys were laughing too." He said, shrugging disappointedly.

"Silence, Drogo," said Dreadlocks.

They all looked at Simbai for some reason. Simbai didn't know that he wasn't supposed to know their real names. Because if he was armed with their real names, he could rule over them. The beings didn't realize Simbai was trying very hard to keep track of them. So he held on to Drogo's name for the convenience of following the conversation.

"Alright, it's time for the annual wack-a-color." Dreadlocks said, trying to move on quickly.

* * *

One of the walls immediately flashed images of people walking about on earth. Simbai could see faces and places and was surprised.

They all laughed uneasily at this and howled, hoping Simbai would not remember Drogo.

"As usual, we will choose a color to wack into oblivion." They all proceeded to laugh again

"Unless, unless, the Living Soul vetoes us," Drogo said. Another stretch of silence fell on the group and an air of contempt. This being was certainly the outcast.

The formless face whispered to Simbai and said, "That one is in love with the truth though dispossessed of him. So all he has left is the lust for him."

Simbai pretended to understand. "The rest are bent on malice and destruction against all living souls." The face said.

"That is not true," Dreadlocks said.

"Yeah, defamation. I say we take this to libel and file a complaint," the spindly one said. And there was an uproar of indignation. Then the face suddenly had the other faces surrounding it in solidarity. They glowed brightly, revealing more of the figures around Simbai. There were six of them, with Simbai to make seven, and they looked hideous. Only Drogo was of the same stature as Simbai; the rest were somewhat colossal figures. Simbai was used to nightmares, so he wasn't waking up anytime soon. But he was impressed at how his imagination was producing such realistic images. "I need a 48-hour psychiatric hold." he thought to himself.

"This is not a dream." The formless face of light said to Simbai, and everyone in the room burst out laughing. One of the beings grunted loudly, and the skinnier twin said, "He thinks it's a dream." They laughed some more.

Soon, dreadlocks called the meeting to order. Only colors were to be negotiated and advocated for in this whack-a-color meeting. No names and no individuals unless they add up to white. No wholesale groups and words such as 'all,' 'everyone,' and 'everybody' was allowed. No sweeping statements and no generalizations. In addition, any plague could be announced from frogs to locusts and boils. The decision had to be unanimous for all the measures to whack a color. Speaking was only allowed for anyone standing. And lastly, they would refer to each other by numbers. This was so they could include Simbai in their communications without Simbai knowing their names. The Living Soul -Simbai - would be number seven and counting back, going anti-clockwise.

Drogo, the basketball player, would be six.

Spindly would be number five.

Shifty would be number four.

The twins were three and two.

And Dreadlocks was number one.

It was quite a challenging rule set to keep in mind. The numbers were easy because all Simbai had to do count clockwise. The formless face was about to answer Simbai's questions as he thought them. However, the principalities said it was not allowed to explain the rules. Which was a new rule, and sadly, the formless face had to comply. These principalities were in charge of the Light Room and its surrounding heavens up to the sixth ring. They could not disobey cosmic law but could make other sub-laws like this one.

The beings stood up, and each, in turn, took out their eyes and placed them on the table. 'This way,' they said, 'they would only see colors when they looked at the living souls on earth and not bodies or individuals. Simbai was told to remove his eyes as well. He was shocked that he could do it without pain. And when he looked again at the wall, all the people had turned into a sea of flames. Only colors! The primary color was blue, but Simbai could also see the auras.

Number four stood up from the triangle, shape-shifting into a larger stature, and loomed threateningly.

"I'll kick us off," he boomed, "green must go."

The wall flashed with images of Blue flames with green lining. They were everywhere in the world.

Number four continued thundering, "I say a mentally debilitating affliction causing mental instability and memory loss."

"Green must go indeed," number one said, casting his gaze at number five. The being had green-brown skin like a tree whose leaves had fused with the bark in the fall. "Don't look at my skin. I am not part of the measures, you blind gluttonous oaf." spindly replied, and they all laughed. That's when Simbai realized somehow though they had no eyes, they could see inside the Light Room as though they had eyes. Removing the eyes only made the Living Souls body-less and turn into flames.

Then 4, the shifty angry thunderous one stood up again and spoke. "My reason for choosing green is that the greens are peaceful and harmonious. But, unfortunately, these traits are in violent opposition to our goals." They all agreed with nods and grunts.

Then one said, "Two votes for green means it is now on the table for final unanimous ratification."

Six stood up in all his basketball glory, "Eh, eeeh, I don't know, maybe we leave some of the green."

The rest of them hollered and complained at this opposition to their will.

"You are supposed to be on our side," two moaned.

Number one asked, "Is this an objection of conscience? You are like us, an old god. Why do you side with the living souls every time."

"I do not, my Lord, I do not. I believe it is easier to deceive these earthly beings if we can show them that a few of them can attain goodness. But of course, we make sure it's all on the outside. Only greens can fake it that well unless we possess the other beings ourselves and through proxy."

"Hmm, six speaks a good scheme," Spindly five said, standing up briefly to speak and then sitting down.

"Ok, ok. In that case, we will leave some." Dreadlocks said, acquiescing and writing something down.

And then four stood up from the square.

"I believe that Pink is also a threat to the order we want to bring. We need more upheaval in family functions and in the hearts and minds of children. This would bring about isolation from family, which gives rise to the correct order of independent and individualistic thought on the earth. This will breed all manner of unbridled immorality fueled by loneliness and the thirst to quench it. It will also produce self-pity and consumerism as people try to assuage their 'Woe is me' feelings.

"Woe is me," Spindly five echoed, and all the beings roared and laughed.

And then Simbai got it. These six spoke in opposites. Good was terrible, and evil was good. For them, 'order' was 'chaos,' and 'chaos' was 'order.' They were plotting the demise of all these colors. The colors were the people who had those auras.

He did not get how they thought they could get him to be part of the unanimity of these votes. They were plotting the suffering of hundreds of thousands—all for the fun of it.

The other beings proceeded to pick a color or add an affliction to a color already selected. Wars were planned, outbreaks organized, and even some storms. They could not control water, but the wind was a good way of moving water around without touching it. Then finally, they were supposed to ratify these measures for the year.

"I veto these measures," Simbai said, speaking for the first time.

* * *

No one paid attention to him at all. Then, finally, one of the faces darted to him and whispered for him to stand.

"Silence, you face of light. We said 'no explaining the rules.'"

The other invisible faces joined the face of light. "I did not explain a rule. I only ordered number seven to stand," it said

"And do you, seven, take orders from these faces?" The other principalities held their breath.

Simbai had a sense that the correct answer was 'no .' So he stood up and said, "No," and the other principalities moaned. "We almost got him." If Simbai had said yes, he would have subordinated his vote to the faces who had no voice in the meeting. That would have made him a non-entity in the discussion, which would have allowed the vote to pass quickly.

He looked at the face of light. It egged him on with facial color gradients that looked like expressions of thought. "And, and, and, and, I would like to repeat my veto for the measures."

All the principalities waited for him, expectantly. Simbai did not know that it wasn't enough to express an intention. Intention and action are not the same. "I would like to repeat" was not in and of itself a repetition of the thought even though it sounded like it. It did not point to the existence of the thing to be repeated. It instead merely pointed to the presence of the intention to repeat something. So, when Simbai thought he had finished the repetition, he had simply stated the intention. A little patience and open-mindedness were required to settle into the meeting. And Simbai had tones of practice with controlling his thoughts and emotions. The proceedings were literal because the precision of meaning rules creation. Sloppiness in expression would miss the mark. The creatures spoke the language of being, the pure language of genesis. Slipshod sentences had led many representatives to be stuck on the outside. They were stuck watching other living souls suffering. When with carefully thought-out words, they could have stopped the measures.

The beings ignored Simbai again and continued with the ratification process. "Didn't you hear me? I would like to veto these measures."

Six thought out loud, standing for a second, "Number seven, would you like to, or are you vetoing the measures?"

All the other beings roared in anger.

"Come on, six; we were going to pass this once again this year if you didn't help the guy."

It sank in for Simbai; Shoot straight and only straight - the orthodox speech!

"I veto these measures," Simbai said, exasperated by the rules but getting it. He slumped back in his chair.

Number one responded gleefully at the exhaustion of the representative. "You are required to pick a color to veto, number seven. In addition, keep in mind the fact that you can't save "everybody" or "all" of them because such words are prohibited." Dreadlocks was enjoying enumerating the limitations to the scope of the veto. Simbai had to craft an argument that could encompass the salvation of every color in the measures. Otherwise, he had to pick one color to save.

He thought that he could save his wife by choosing to save green. But he also knew that people leveled up to different aura colors, and she might not be in the green by morning. He also knew he could not mention her by name, which was a dead end. He also did not know Leila's color, and he had to be careful of leaving her out.

He then noticed the whispering in his ear. All these weren't his thoughts proper. They were tainted somehow, and he noticed. Then he jumped up, and the other beings burst out laughing. The green being had gone invisible and was whispering in his ear. Once recognized and acknowledged by Simbai, spindly five materialized, defeated.

Number two grunted and shifted lazily in the chair.

"Nice try five," three said, standing up briefly, and for a moment, he flashed his flame and glowed enviously. Then, the beings all laughed some more.

Frustrated, Simbai remembered at that moment that if you mixed every color, it turned into white. So, he said, "I veto the destruction of white." they all looked at him and away. Then he realized he wasn't standing.

Simbai had to watch his thoughts and words as he followed the rules to speak.

He stood up, "I veto the destruction of white."

Number one smiled. He looked at the colors on the wall. They had designed the choices so that not all the colors were present. They added the ones there, and they barely made it to white.

"Well, if your veto can't hold its own, it will have to become our vote."

Simbai looked at the formless face, which said without speaking, 'these are the rules.'

"But all these lives matter," he said, standing and trying to appeal to pathos.

"Aah, you can't say "all" in your statement of advocation." number four said vehemently.

Simbai threw his hands up, sitting down.

The principalities bristled with excitement. "Alright, I am passing the resolution for wack-a-color." Dreadlocks said. The numbers were called to vote, counting from one to seven. There was a hold-up with six, but eventually, six keeled over. Then one said, "by not having an argument to base your veto, we count your vote, number seven, as one of ours, and so the res...

"Blue," Simbai murmured, standing up, "Blue lives matter. I pick blue." Simbai said, gaining confidence.

* * *

They were all stopped in their tracks. There was no blue aura on the list.

"Each of the Living Souls on your list is blue?" Simbai said.

"Yeeeeees," Number one said hesitantly, looking around the room for help in arguing.

Three stood up and said, "But the primary color we are looking at is the other color."

"No," Simbai said, "The primary color you are focussing on is the superficial color. Blue is the primary color of all these living souls. The auras are like a silver lining on the edge and sometimes not even that. Like skin color on a body with the same flesh as all the other bodies."

"I motion to have that statement struck from the record," four said, standing up and looming more significant than ever. The table shook at the thundering voice, and all but number two seemed to tremble. Number one of the twins was too lazy to be moved. Shifty four continued, "Number seven said "all" several times.

"Statement struck," One said gleefully.

Simbai swallowed hard, "I would like to repeat, nay, I repeat." He realized that by repeating the statement, he would repeat it. It was needless to say, 'I repeat' - Simbai sighed and murmured to himself, "Not now, brain!"

"The primary color you are looking at is not the primary color. Blue is the primary color of whichever living soul on your list of measures." Simbai said, removing all from his sentence.

"That is so," one assented. They were beaten, but all was not lost.

"Why do you pick this color?" burly dreadlocks asked as procedure.

"Because it is the color of each flame on earth. Any living soul is at the core blue in color."

* * *

72

Six chuckled, standing up, "But that is a mere fact. It's like saying I pick yellow because it's a color we can pick." Everyone else smiled. six's lust for truth worked for them occasionally.

And indeed, Simbai had picked blue because it was a color he could choose. And for a moment, he had myopically focused on that victory. He needed a reason to save the blues, to keep everybody from the suffering. He made up reasons on the spot. First, he said, "Since the primary color of these superficial colors is blue. My mentioning of a particular color other than blue is immaterial. It only targets each measure as it is particularly targeted to the specific superficial color. And we have already agreed that auras are superficial and subordinate to the primary blue." Simbai said, enjoying the lawyer-speak and loving the "dream" if it was a dream. Number one allowed Simbai's statement to stand.

Simbai proceeded with the argument. "Now, you will realize that each living soul in its current state is the raw material for your shenanigans. So it is to be valued for what it is and not to be altered. In fact, I argue that as things stand, entropy will help you achieve the order you seek. And I, therefore, veto the measures in favor of leaving things as they are. I favor the status quo without the interference of this illustrious council."

Four of the six beings nodded all around the table. Shifty number four was heaving in frustration. At the same time, burly dreadlocks was shaking his head and sighing heavily.

And so, each color was saved from the shenanigans of the malevolent beings.

Though Simbai's arguments were allowed to stand, they only allowed for the resetting of the meeting. Once the forum was reset, everyone had to pick new colors and reasons to whack them to oblivion. Old colors and old defenses could not be used in the 'new' and last meeting of the year. The second meeting had never happened before. It was good that the only rule changes were; 'no picking colors' and 'no using old justifications.' The beings, however, proceeded as though it was normal so as not to alert Simbai to the unprecedented moment.

* * *

New colors were picked, more plagues announced, and Simbai was horrified. It seemed they had chosen the tame afflictions the first time around. But this second round was unfathomably horrific. They got to the resolution stage again. But this time, they each looked at Simbai in turn.

Spindly, Number five began the address "Number seven," if you vote with us, we will give you and your wife all the wealth you want. We oversee this realm, the gold, the jewels, the cars, and houses. Anything. Just ask for anything, even money, and we will give it to you. You can even check back in when you go back to earth and call on us for more."

Twin Number two began to grunt and shift.

And number three spoke up,

"We can even make it, so you don't lift a finger and can sit back and relax as we fill your bank account. And no one will know; they call it miracle money. We will even protect your family, clan, and descendants. And none of these plagues shall come near you or anyone you love. And in fact, we will target all your enemies and make sure they suffer but not you."

This usually worked on other delegates in centuries past: wealth and fame and a promise of protection for their circles—all the things everyone desired and sought after regardless of race, creed, gender, or nationality. The Galilean had tried to shift this focus, but people still worried about what they ate and wore.

Six stood up with a sad face, "The order of the century cannot be disrupted. We are a part of nature, and our work here is merely nature. Ecosystems balance because of us. You wouldn't want the collapse of the ecosystem, would you?

The others smiled at Drogo's reasoned speech.

Then four added in the ominous, threatening tone as usual. "And we can tell you where Leilani is if you allow us to pass this resolution. Otherwise, we will hide her from you until the end."

* * *

"They are only for a year." They all said in unison, standing up to intimidate and persuade Simbai simultaneously. Number two's words dragged on comically after everyone else had finished their sentence. But the words hung in the air for Simbai to consider. Access to Leilani in exchange for a year of evil was the offer or trade. There was also a lifetime of wealth but Leilani.

That got Simbai's attention. Humanity or Leilani. He would lose his daughter. He would also lose out on the safety of his beloved family and loved ones if he didn't ratify these plagues for the year. And also lose out on wealth and fame and the guaranteed safety of his property.

Simbai looked again to his left, where the whisper in his ear was coming from. He noticed that only five of the beings were standing and present. He realized number five was invisible and suspected he was whispering in his ear again. Exasperated, Simbai ordered number five out into the shadow. Number five materialized, but no one laughed at his being discovered this time.

Simbai continued thinking. Each of the principalities was standing, waiting. Simbai stood up too. Then he paced a little, deep in thought. He breathed deeply to center himself as he thought of all the suffering on the earth. Could he stop it all tonight? Was this even real?

They had presented riddles to support their color picks and the plagues. They had airtight syllogism. Simbai chuckled as he remembered the logic from the book about how everyone bled blue. It was false, but the syllogism was airtight. Then an idea struck. With these beings, the truth was wrong, and false was true.

"I pick blue," he said,

Number two slumped back into the chair, and the others remained standing.

"But you can't pick the same color as before." number one replied, trembling with the excitement of a probable win.

"I am not picking the same color, Simbai retorted. "I picked blue flames before. Now I am picking blue, which is the color of the blood of all living souls."

The other five looked at number one, who asked, "Is it really a different color because it's in a different form."

"Yes, exactly!" Simbai exclaimed, overjoyed.

"Yes, a pdf file by the same name is considered a different file from a word doc by the same name," six said. This made everyone exasperated. "Shut up, number six!" Number one barked.

"But from experience, blood is red, is that not right?" Number one asked everyone at the table. This was an unanticipated argument, so no one had a ready answer, but they all were shrugging yes except for number six.

"Let me school you guys on this matter. You see, red blood is actually rusted blue blood. I suspect that you have used rust to destroy a structure and cause an accident. You know how rust forms, so you will understand the analogy. When iron combines with oxygen, it produces rust. Hemoglobin is the iron in the blue blood which combines with oxygen and becomes rusted, and gives blood its red hue."

"Whoa," blurted Number six in disbelief. "That's not tr…"

"Shut up, number six!" the other five beings screamed, their voices fraying in their fit of passion.

Simbai felt he was winning, so he turned on his pleasant tone. "Come on, guys, if a blue car has rusted and turned brown, one is still within the confines of reality to say, "That's a rusted blue car." The metal has rusted and corrupted the blue color, but ontologically the car is blue." he finished.

Number one looked at the living soul in front of him, surprised. Number two finally spoke slowly like a sloth and asked the question all six of them had in mind.

"Ok, maybe money and fame are not what you find important. Are you going to throw away your daughter, though? Throw away a life of peace, comfort, wealth, and family in favor of people you don't know. Some of whom have worked against your good. You would choose your enemies over your family?"

Number two spoke so slowly that the words hit home. Simbai was silent. He was not even thinking it through because he had already decided according to his principles. Some things are bigger than any amount of self-interest, even concerning his own beloved family. The other representatives would ask for powers and favors to let the measures pass in the past. But this guy seemed detached from all of this, including his daughter. These values opposed the will of the six evil beings. So, number one resigned and asked, "What's the reason for picking blue?"

Simbai now had to pick a reason to save all their lives. Yes, his daughter mattered, not just his daughter, and not just his loved ones; but all lives mattered.

"I pick blue because all lives matter," he said,

"I would like to motion to strike that statement because he said "all." four said gleefully, shifting to the size of a dwarfed human.

Number one responded gladly, "Statement struck."

"I pick blue because blue lives matter," Simbai repeated with a modification. He was adamant.

Number two grunted, and number three asked, "What was that?"

Number two sighed and shifted. Then grunted and croaked. Number three looked in Simbai's direction,

"Why do blue lives matter?" Three replied. Simbai was blank. "That, eeeh, that is, umm," he was flailing. "That is a question asking for a secondary reason. The fact that blue-blooded lives matter is primary and enough." Simbai answered, hoping he had won.

Five jumped in, hoping to save everyone, "But it could also be a clarification question. We can't simply state things that others don't understand and then expect them to agree."

All the beings were still standing except for number two, who had sat down long back. Drogo cleared his throat, "Each of us here knows the intrinsic value of each of the living souls on earth. It's inherent in their very existence and so..."

Drogo stopped in his tracks as number four shifted from a happy dwarf to a furious colossal serpent. The being grew so large he had to coil up to fit the room. "Shut up, D...number six!" he snarled, shaking everything and everyone. Drogo whimpered and gulped in terror.

Number one was angry, and number four roared at their inability to sway this living soul and defeat him. They had had their way for eons, even with each representative from the earth. They had developed wealthy and influential families. They had cultivated relationships to awaken various family members so they could be chosen as advocates for the LightRoom. Thus furthering family wealth and power.

The beings were stumped with Simbai. Who was this one who promises of personal enrichment could not buy? They would make him suffer, ensuring he never saw his daughter until the end.

"Meeting adjourned, eyes on," dreadlocks said quietly. Then he looked at number seven and back at the other beings.

Exchanging glances with dreadlocks, number five asked, "Would you please repeat your reason for picking blue again."

BRIGHT

"Blue lives matter," Simbai replied victoriously with a smug face.

He looked around and was greeted by a sea of angry faces. It reminded him of Uzu and the shelled and unshelled workers at the farm.

"What did you say?" someone else asked, turning around. Simbai squinted, confused. It was too bright out compared to the shadowy LightRoom. He wasn't sure what was going on, but he knew what he had said and was happy to repeat it. "I said, blue lives matter," he repeated with vehement emphasis like one speaking truth to power in victory.

"Did you hear that guy," someone in the crowd said? The dream-like experienced of the lightroom was fading. Simbai looked around like one sobering up slowly. He was dressed in his pajamas, wearing no shoes. Had he sleep-walked to a crowd of people? He never sleep-walked; that was an Isaac thing. Was this a new stress side effect? It was dazzlingly bright out, and he was squinting and struggling to see all around him. To the protestors, he looked worried, like he was aware he had kicked a hornet's nest.

"What do we do?" someone called out close to him.

"Stand up and fight back," the mob responded.

"What do we do?"

"Stand up and fight back."

And they roared and rained blows on the unsuspecting Simbai. He went down. "Maihwee kani, maihweee"(Oh mother, oh mother) he yelped. "I just saved all of you," he screamed. "Maihwee, maihwee" (Oh mother, oh mother)

As he fell to the ground, he saw the face of the beings smiling and ascending effortlessly away into the sky. Number 6 was looking down sorrowfully. Then they burst into flames, and each shot off into the ether in different directions.

Simbai sighed at his fate.

They had set him up. The entities had brought him back from the meeting but dropped him off in the middle of the protest. The crowd didn't spend too much time on him as they had to keep marching. But it was enough for him to look horrible to the news camera following them. He was on TV and for the wrong reason. The real reason for being on TV was that he had just saved all their lives! He was angry with himself for being in these circumstances, which could stress his wife. He did not know how he had come to be at the march. If that meeting was a dream, it was a nightmare, he thought, his tears hanging on tightly to the corner of his eyes. What if Tambudzai was watching the news coverage of this march. Was he putting her through too much?

He got up, ignored the reporter's questions, and limped into the first door he found. It was a dive bar. The bartender was making a cocktail and using a flame thrower. The whooshing sound of the flame was vivid for Simbai. The brilliant and hot blue flame was, for an instant nauseating. Simbai threw his hands up and sighed. He planted his resigned butt at the bar and said, "I'll have what he's having," pointing at the flaming drink.

The bartender looked at him in the dim light. "You look bad, man, even in this light." Then, he said in a valley accent, "Here. Have this one. I'll make another one for you, sir," he said, looking at the other patron and sliding the flaming drink down the bar.

"Thanks," he said, catching the stem of the flaming sliding cocktail glass. What is it called?"

A voice with a familiar Zawe accent replied,

"Shamwari, you are about to drink the Rusty Velvet!"

CHAPTER THREE

Pro Gay

IN THE BAR

"Shamwari, you are about to drink the Rusty Velvet?" The voice with a Zawe accent said.

Simbai looked over slowly, shaking his head. It seemed to him that someone from Zawe would be there no matter where you went. Be it the south-pole, Antarctica - anywhere really. Even in this random bar, early in the morning, on a workday too. Someone from Zawe was drinking a Rusty Velvet. And now there were two of them.

"Wangu, uri kuitei drinking early on a Thursday morning?" Simbai asked (My friend, what are you doing drinking on a Thursday morning?)

"I would ask you the same thing," Learnmore replied; he looked down at his phone and chuckled. His friend Lani had texted, "I'll be going home with Biz. Also, watch out; a crazy right-winger is coming your way." He put his phone away and slid down the bar to sit next to his fellow countryman.

Simbai took a sip. His companion watched and waited for the verdict.

"Ndinonzi, Simbai," Simbai's hoarse voice said after swallowing the burning cocktail. By the time he had taken a swig, the flames were long extinguished. But his throat was suggesting he had swallowed the fire instead.

"And my name izi Learnmore," Learnmore said, exaggerating his Zawe accent. They shook hands, beaming at one another.

"Thoughts?" Learnmore asked, pointing to the cocktail.

Simbai cleared his throat and replied. "It burns, but it's helping."

"Hmmm, yes, you look like you could use a lot of help," Leanmore replied thoughtfully as he eyed Simbai up and down before continuing with his reply. "Were you the cause of the commotion outside? The crowd was already loud, but it got quite intense for some time. It quieted down right before you stumbled in."

Simbai chuckled, holding back his tears before replying matter of fact,

"Yeah, I was the cause."

"Mans, is that blood on your forehead?" Learnmore asked, scrutinizing Simbai in the dim bar lighting.

"Aaaah, forget that. I'm only glad to be alive. It's such a pity that this is my reward for helping save everyone."

Learnmore was puzzled by the words. He cocked his head to the side like a dog after hearing a strange sound. "I sense a riveting story. What do you mean you saved everyone?" he asked.

That's when Simbai realized he might have said too much. So he tried to play it down, and Learnmore was even more interested and would not let it go.

" Look, the long and short story is that I moved to Uzu a long time ago."

Learnmore burst out laughing. Uzu was well known in Zawe. The dragon village had also made its way to the news some years back when the dragons returned.

* * *

Simbai paused; he had expected a reaction but not such hearty laughter that had no trace of malice. Before long, Simbai was laughing too. Learnmore gasped and tried to speak. "Tuzu kunge munhu wekuUzu." The man struggled to birth these words in the middle of guffaws. When he finished, he renewed his mirthful roar. "A dumb sitting duck like someone from Uzu" was a well-known saying. They laughed together for a while. Simbai laughed at his circumstances for the first time.

Another gentleman in the bar joined in their laughter. It weirded out the Zawe men causing them to calm down prematurely.

"So yeah, you can imagine the freedom of thought I came with from the place?" Simbai continued when they were both finally composed.

"Really? Freedom of thought? I thought they didn't allow people to think much at all down there?" Learnmore asked. He wondered in secret whether he was speaking to a man who had lost his marbles. Lani had told him all about Uzu. How the place had deceived her into believing they were free. And how her parents had abandoned her there, but she felt she couldn't call it that since she had decided to stay. "They should have forced me to come with," Lani had often said but had also added, "it goes to show you how dumb we all were because of that..."

Simbai replied to Learnmore's question. His words cut through his reminiscences of hanging out with Lani. "You are right about that, Learnmore. Thinking is not an activity that was or is promoted in Uzu. However, the effect of it all is that people think in-depth and freely. While also allowing others to do the same."

Learnmore's eyes grew in disbelief. "So you are saying there was no tyranny in Uzu; people were not forced to think certain things but were free to think about whatever?"

"Hmmm, well, listen, listen," Simbai said, his thoughts racing. Something about this inquiry made him feel unsettled, almost nauseous. His shame about participating in Uzu-life was like a lump in his throat. It was stuck and required a gentle Heimlich maneuver to dislodge. But it felt like Learnmore was slapping his back hard with the butt of an AK47. All so that Simbai would not die by choking on the embarrassment but once saved, the gun would be used on him. As he sometimes did when he was thinking on the spot, he raised his two fingers and began his reply. "Two things: Thinking is harder when an authority tells you what to think and what not to think. This is what modern society is doing with grassroots censorship. Many people don't think; they simply regurgitate the words of thought leaders. These people then work to stay updated on new and evolving thoughts. That's why everyone is on their devices all the time. They need to stay up to date with the new Gospel of approved thoughts. People are now like cellphones or computers needing software updates with the new approved thoughts. No one asks sensitive questions, and no one dares ask seemingly stupid questions. No one dares to ask any questions at all besides the ones already asked by thought leaders. I suffered instant justice moments ago from the new powers that be "the mob." That was because they wanted to tell me what to think. They punished me for not thinking about it their way.

On the other hand, in Uzu, we could all think about the topics within our jurisdiction, in whatever way we chose." Simbai was making some of it up, but it made sense. At least it sounded within the script he had created for himself. He wondered if his thoughts contradicted those of the protestors.

Learnmore grunted long and hard at this remark. Then he asked, "Topics within your jurisdiction, is it?"

The man who had echoed their laughter also echoed the grunt as if to say to Simbai, "You are delusional." At least that's how Simbai took it. The man was grunting and fidgeting in his chair like he wanted to stand up and come over. Simbai and Learnmore looked in his direction, and the man froze. He looked like a homeless drug user.

"Yes, freedom within our jurisdiction," Simbai said, collecting his thoughts and turning his gaze back to the bar and Learnmore. "And the second thing is that thinking is also hard when one is afraid to hurt others or be hurt. And in Uzu, people shrug things off and do not hold on to grudges and the like, making it a place of utter freedom to think as much as one wants within the allowed parameters. Thinking about politics, the health of the crops or wearing shells was reserved for the professionals. No one at all could opine on those matters except the experts. Oh, and one could also let go of one's past before Uzu, which gives way to peace in the present." he finished. And with unwavering determination, he shut the door of pain, which opened whenever he reminisced about Uzu. He also closed the door of integrity that always popped up when he was churning the truth into solid butter to drink.

"Hmmm, I guess it does make sense that we would not understand Uzu as well as someone from there. Okay, so you are a free thinker, huh?" Learnmore replied in a reflective tone. He wanted to tell Simbai that his words were suspicious. He wanted to tell Simbai that his words did not describe the Uzu that he had come to know from his conversations with Lani. But he did not want to antagonize a man from Zawe who was willing to share a drink with him when many would not touch him with a six-foot pole.

"Yeah, I am a free thinker - free to be and speak - and the crowd outside did not like my free-thinking and free speaking. So, the crowd tried to silence me." He did not say what he had said to the crowd. He did not tell Learnmore that it was a carryover from a conversation with beings of light that had set him up. But, on the other hand, Learnmore had come alive by degrees during this conversation. Now, his eyes gleamed with a brilliant fire.

"I wish I were free to be as well," Learnmore said in a hoarse whisper. "Free to be and to do," he mumbled, then cleared his throat, "I mean, I am suffering for the same reasons as you. But unfortunately, the kangaroo courts of social media have seen it fit to sentence me to exile from all online presence. And to exile me from earning a livelihood through creativity."

Learnmore waited for Simbai to recognize him after dropping these hints.

Silence

"I am *THE* Lenny of the Phil and Lenny Show," he said finally. He pointed to himself the way a famous painting points to itself if ever one could. The bartender stopped shining the spot of the bar he was wiping down. His co-bartender stopped drying the glass she was working on with the white cloth. And the two exchanged glances. At the same time, the man who had been eavesdropping made his way to the bar but stood a little ways from them. The bartenders were deciding whether to throw Learnmore out or not. Simbai had a blank face, and Learnmore realized that the man did not know he was speaking to a celebrity. The bartenders looked at Simbai, surprised that he did not know the man to whom he was talking. Learnmore was now more infamous than famous but a celebrity, nonetheless.

Simbai took another sip of the cocktail in silence. All the while, Lenny struggled to accept that someone from Zawe did not know who he was. "Does the movie Tanganyika ring a bell?" Learnmore asked, and Simbai shook his head and sounded. "Hmm, hmm"

"So, you don't know who I am?" Learnmore asked again, pointing to himself in disbelief.

Simbai took yet another gulp of the burning cocktail in silence. This time he grimaced and spoke. "I don't, unfortunately." His voice emanated from clenched teeth. His eyes were teary and fixed on the burning cocktail as though he was getting purified with each swig.

Learnmore laughed. "Mans, let me tell you my story then. And before we go any further, remember, I am innocent."

The bartenders rolled their eyes. "But you lied," one of them muttered pretty loud. Learnmore neither heard nor saw these two at this time. He was too busy reveling in the delight of having someone he could share his side of the story with. Sharing and not as a 'defense' but as a 'telling of his life story.' So he decided to start with college.

"All I am saying is, I want a redo. If only I had known that coming to the United States would determine a massive change in my future. I would have thought twice about making the journey. I came over thinking it would be four years. Only four years and then maybe one more for practical training. Then back to Zawe to help build the motherland. I was dead set on returning. I mean, I had promised to return to help develop the country. So, it broke my heart when Zawe's politics and the economy took a plunge and made it difficult to return.

And so I had to create a new plan for my life.

In the meantime, the culture of this foreign country sipped into my bones: the consumerism, the hoarding, and the storage facilities. The freedom to do whatever you want with whomever you want was alluring. All of it rubs onto you, especially as young as I was. Then you start following your passions as rich people do. You begin chasing your dreams even if it means being hungry as you pursue them. I was on my way to the American dream, and I could feel it. That's when I met Phil in college. We became roommates. He is the one who got me into acting. We were inseparable for years. Our history online made it plausible when we finally decided...

Lenny was about to reveal the big secret. He wondered if he had earned enough goodwill points. Points enough to elicit the empathy Lenny believed his story should engender in a good listener. He could not read Simbai's expression, so Lenny slowed down with the words, "I am getting ahead of myself. Let me do this in the proper order."

When Phil got a gig on a commercial, we moved to LA so we could pursue acting full time. I don't know what I regret most. Whether it is meeting Phil, moving to LA, or coming to this dreaded country, to begin with. This country with all its loneliness and the struggle to fill that gaping lonesome hole with achievements and...and...and...things, and...

Anyway, let me stop ranting and paint this picture for you. So, Phil and I were in this apartment in LA. There was Big Betty who was always in our apartment and...

ORIGINAL SIN

Phil and Lenny sat down in front of their TV. LA had been unkind to many who had come searching for fame and glory. They were part of that many. One film executive had walked Lenny out of his offive for the umpteenth time. With his hand on Lenny's shoulder, the man told him some peculiar word. "The pile of bodies of industry failures could stake up to rival the pyramids of Giza." Lenny had envisioned himself piled up there as well. Phil was the one who had landed a few gigs, and for Lenny, none.

They had trained and practiced as actors and joined an improv troupe. The two had also managed the wardrobe in their troupe's theatre appearances. They were pseudo fashion designers at this point. They didn't have access to share their sometimes-brilliant ideas with the fashion world. They also did not have access to female models. The models had expressed their discomfort with their heterosexual designers. It helped to dress your models yourself to ensure quality presentation. And sometimes that happened backstage in siloed cubicles. In fashion, the article fits better when the client is confident and comfortable. Sadly, too many models were insecure and uncomfortable working with Lenny and Phil.

Lenny switched on the black and white TV they had swapped for their big-screen color TV. They had barely made rent because of that pawn shop trade. And now, here they were, making do with their entertainment.

"It's like being back to Charlie Chaplin days," Big Betty said, laughing at their black and white television.

Their neighbor, Big Betty, came over to talk to them. She got along with Lenny, who was an immigrant from Zawe. Many found Learnmore's full name bizarre. That's why he had shortened it to Lenny. Big Betty liked Lenny because she could vibe with him, and she did not get along much with Phil.

Phil was the son of Jewish immigrants. His mother had fallen in love with Phil Collins literally. So, Phil Collins was supposedly married to another woman, and he met Phil's mom and got involved with her. And Phil's mom, in turn, was having a love affair of her own. They say Phil's mom was responsible for the song "In the air tonight ." She had two-timed the famous two-timing musician, and a great hit was born. They also say that Phil Collins' actual wife was also having an affair, so it was a double-triple betrayal of one another.

"Come on, son," Big Betty retorted. "Stop claiming that song. That song was about his wife's affair, not Phil's affair with your mamma."

* * *

"Well, that's just it. Phil had an affair with my mom, and his wife decided to..."

"Clap back." Lenny jumped in, finishing the sentence. He and his roommate had been good friends for a while. They were so stupid together, and that's how they ended up in LA, almost going hungry.

"Yeah, so she 'clapped back,'" Phil said, and Big Betty made a face at Phil. She disliked it when Phil used the Negro Vernacular / Harlem Register. She was very adamant that it sounded strange when it came out of his mouth. And Phil knew it was weird too. And that's precisely why he did it. To make her uncomfortable so she could leave.

Big Betty was the fly on their wall. However, Lenny tolerated her, and Phil liked her cooking more than her company.

"And when Phil Collins' wife clapped back, boy, it produced a hit."

"But roomie," Lenny jumped in, "Is that why you are named Phil. You think you might be his...?" And all three of them made such a raucous as they launched into bouts and fits of laughter.

They continued with their fun-filled evening while multitasking with watching the news. That's when Big Betty asked her usual question.

"So, what are you boys going to do about rent?"

You see, Big Betty was the superintendent of the apartment complex. And she collected and enforced rent. She lived at the complex for free to do that job. Her unpleasant demeanor made her ideal for the job. She was partial to Lenny, though but liked to give them a hard time when she collected rent.

"Well, Betty, you know we don't have to worry about it until next month," Lenny replied with a smug look.

"Oh baby, I will be waiting to come down on you like Thor's hammer then." She fluttered her eyes, feigning innocence.

* * *

Lenny liked to believe it was harmless flirting, and Phil enjoyed harping on it to make Big Betty uncomfortable.

"Hmmm, do I sense some tension in this one room?" Phil asked, teasing. This, too, made Big Betty unhappy.

She pressed on, "What's the deal with your jobs anyway. Can't you do something to make ends meet?"

"Well, we don't have the spark, we have been told. Lenny here looks good, yet he hasn't landed a role except in the troupe. And me, I am hopeless at the action. But with fashion design, our clothes get picked up all the time. Sadly, they stall somewhere between design and dress rehearsal. Somehow, gender plays a huge role there even in the freest of places."

"Yeah, fashion and design are the freest of places." Lenny jumped in. "I remember when I did my first photoshoot in college. We had to strip and stand at a street crossing. The clothes we had were art pieces hiding only the essentials. And then the cops showed up to our unlicensed shoot. Phil here ran like a baby with his tooshie in the air for all to see and a bunny covering his essentials. It was ridiculous and funny. But all day long, our genders did not matter, dress change did not matter who was male or female."

"Yeah, you would think that would go all the way to the top. But here, some of the top models aren't comfortable." Phil said, "And that's because, at times, it's either Lenny or me with them alone in a dressing cubicle. And we are heterosexual males, which makes us 'creepy.' Especially when you think of this 6-foot hunk from Zawe here. He is menacing already."

"Well, if the problem is being heterosexual. Why not become gay?" Big Betty asked.

"Well, Big Betty, it doesn't work like that? You need to be, to be, to be..." Lenny stalled. "How does one become gay again?" he asked, looking more at Phil than Big Betty even though he meant to ask her.

"That's an inappropriate question," Phil replied instead.

* * *

"Well, what's an appropriate question about the subject then?" Lenny asked

"I don't know, but don't get caught by the gays asking that question!" Phil replied

"'The gays,'" Lenny said, laughing, and Big Betty joined in. They laughed hard, repeating the word over and over again.

Phil shrugged and tried to escape being the brunt of the joke. "Anyway, aren't people born gay like, like, like, 'some people are born great'" he stammered.

"And others have greatness thrust upon them," Big Betty chimed in. Lenny joined her in her reverberating laughter. Phil only shook his head, disappointed and embarrassed.

"Don't make fun of me," Phil said, as he tried to be heard over their laughter, and then he continued, "Stop it, stop laughing, stop it, guys, this is serious." Phil's mind had a hard time thinking in politically incorrect terms. He was always sure to be respectful of others, and his discipline went beyond action and words. Phil policed his thoughts with great care to not offend even in silence. He looked at the laughing pair and said with enthusiastic resolve,

"Plus, aren't gay people gay, only during sex, but they are simply people the rest of the time? How then can we act gay? Doesn't everyone have different personalities no matter their sexual orientation?" Phil finished his questions feeling triumphant.

Lenny found the sentiments thought-provoking, then he smiled mischievously and said, "So if one is gay, but they aren't doing the deed at that moment, do they stop being gay?

Big Betty grinned and chimed in, "Yeah, is it something you pause and resume, or is it a thing that is always there like my being a woman."

Phil gathered his face in determination and replied, "Well, I don't know what it's called, but people can identify as a woman one week and as a man another and fluidly switch many times over. It's not always there."

Lenny said, "I don't know what that is called either, but we are talking about being gay here, Phil." Phil made a face of frustration, raising his hand and pointing at Big Betty. Lenny knew his friend so well, so he continued without skipping a beat and addressed the injustice Phil felt, "I know. I know. I know you didn't start the man-woman thing but let's get back, anyway. So, seriously, Phil, you can't claim there is no behavioral aspect to being gay. I mean, I know it might be uncool to generalize, but..." and Big Betty jumped in, interrupting Lenny.

"Child, it's his political correctness that's getting in the way. Look, Phil, dear, if we are being politically incorrect, there is definitely a way to act that we can call gay. And one can get by with the act, and people can assume that person is gay without that individual even saying so."

"But sometimes people assume wrong," Phil replied with a self-righteous air.

"And sometimes they assume right even without the person ever saying anything," Lenny said with an impatient emphasis.

"I don't know; I don't know!" Phil replied. He felt like he had to make a concession but on his terms. So he said, "Sometimes people say they are gay, and everyone has to take their word for it. So you can do that, and no one can question you on-pain-of being called a homophobe. Well, maybe the gays can question you. But yeah, someone might get away with claiming to be gay or thinking they are acting gay, as long as they claim to be, first."

Lenny stifled a laugh while Big Betty grinned at the phrase, "the gays." Then, finally, Lenny cleared his throat, trying to get serious.

"I know, I know, rent, serious...serious, serious stuff. Rent is serious. Umm, Big Bee's idea is crazy, but it's worth a thought, right?" Lenny said as he tried to get serious.

"It's a dangerous thought, especially because we can't answer the fundamental question of what it means to be gay?" Phil answered.

"Maybe, then, we just act like we are gay," Lenny replied, and Phil took a deep breath to say something back when Big Betty jumped into the fray and faced Lenny.

"Child, child, let me help you and your friend here."

"Why, what do you know about being gay?" Phil asked even though Big Betty was addressing Lenny.

"I am a woman; I know everything about being gay. Who do you think had a gay best friend?" There was silence. "Well, none of you two, that's for sure." she ended with flair.

She was right. They hadn't had a gay best friend or a gay friend to speak of. Instead, they simply looked at one another. "Why haven't we had gay friends?" their eyes interrogated each other.

"I've had a couple of gay best friends, and I can coach you both on what you should do, dress, or even speak like." Big Betty continued after they remained silent.

"Ewww, that sounds like appropriation," Phil said, disgusted.

"How else are we going to do it?" Lenny asked, raising his hands with his palms facing the heavens.

"I don't know, but this way sounds wrong. Isn't there another way? Also, why are we doing it again?" Phil replied, confused.

"It sounds like the right way would be to become gay, Phil. And we don't know how that works." Lenny answered, ignoring the question. "Plus, as you said, people simply come out and say they are gay, and everyone has to believe. No one can question it at all. That could be one way of being gay; to identify as gay," Lenny replied

"The only proper way is to actually become gay. And again, we don't know how to do that." Phil said, entrenched and getting frustrated. This was the only way of pretending to be gay, which silenced his conscience.

"Hmmm, I don't know, it's not about becoming gay or identifying as gay. It's about saying we are gay like a black person passing as white. They don't truly become white or identify as white, but they look, act, live, and eat like it. They pass. Am I right, Big Betty? It's not about becoming..." Lenny answered

"Yeah, it's nothing personal like becoming. It's simply good business and making sure you pass as gay," Big Betty replied and asked her voice an octave higher. "And Lenny, how does anyone eat like they are white again?"

Lenny smiled and was about to burst out laughing when Phil spoke, annoyed,

"Don't you have a color TV to watch Big Bee? You are out here corrupting my Lenny." She gave him a sour look and sauntered away, heading towards the kitchen.

"What's for dinner anyway?" she asked instead. In a studio apartment, heading to the kitchen was crossing the room. Finally, Phil realized what was happening.

"Your feet must be killing you, Big Betty..." he said and paused when she turned and eyed him curiously.

"I mean from walking up and down the stairs to speak with tenants. I should give you a foot massage later after dinner if that works for you?" Big Betty shook her head and rolled her eyes. They had settled well in their love-hate dynamic.

"Do you guys need some privacy?" Lenny asked, paying Phill back for a similar comment.

"See, you wouldn't ask that if Phil was gay." Big Betty replied.

"He can be Bi," Lenny retorted.

* * *

"Yes, but that doesn't sell well these days. Phil needs to be an outright underdog." Betty replied

"Everyone loves an underdog," Lenny murmured thoughtfully.

"Everyone loves an underdog," Big Betty said, and Lenny smiled.

"And besides, it's the new cool these days. Cool underdog!" Big Betty added as she began to hum, forgetting the conversation. Instead, she had turned to focus on the food she was making.

RENT

Lenny was sitting staring at the black TV. The small black and white TV was off, but he was staring at it, lost in thought. It was a week and a half before rent was due. Lenny did not know how to find a gig and get paid in the short time frame. His next prized possession to sell was his gift bicycle. He had been reluctant to let it go all along because it was a gift. Did he have to now? He took out his phone to read text messages for movie set locations. He would gate crash the movie sets to scope out opportunities.

Midmorning, he walked confidently onto the third set of the day. It was a retro shoot. He noticed one of the actresses trying on colored scarves. She was testing for compatibility with the rest of her outfit. She tried the green one, then the red one, and skipped over the orange one onto the gray one. Lenny was cringing at each try. An assistant was standing by her. The assistant seemed to echo the actress's actions, not lead or guide them. She would reach for the shawl the actress just picked. The assistant corrected a wrinkle that the actress had just fixed. It was like a silent game of, "Simon says ." Lenny grimaced at the scarf choices like one who cringes at a wrong musical note in the middle of a symphony.

"Oh, stop it, get out," the actress said sharply to the assistant by her side. The lady walked away, head hanging. Lenny dropped his fake papers absentmindedly and hopped onto the actress's side. The master had arrived, and a masterpiece was afoot.

* * *

"Sweety, you want to try the orange one," Lenny said. The actress looked at him for a second. Her face said to the taller than her man, 'you are beneath me; how dare you.' She looked away without a word. She tried on the orange shawl, and it popped. It clicked right in like a trigger ready to fire good tidings. "Why, thank you, eh Lenny." the actress said, looking back to read his nametag.

"There you are," someone with a clipboard said, looking at Lenny.

"Who, me?" He asked.

"Yes, you, you, you, you umm."

"Lenny," Lenny replied

"Yes, you, Lenny." The clipboard character winked at Lenny. She had watched him drop his papers to help the actress with her wardrobe.

"Lenny, here is your new stylist," the lady with the clipboard announced to the actress.

"Wow, and he is doing a great job already." The actress replied, smiling at Lenny.

"Why don't you help this superstar into her frock, Lenny." The lady with the clipboard asked Lenny politely.

"I don't want any creeps, though," the actress said, looking Lenny up and down.

"Don't worry, I'm gay," Lenny said as he took off his reflective jacket. He had a new profession now.

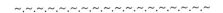

Wangu (my friend), the words rolled off my tongue effortlessly. It was as if I was born to lie. At that moment, I felt like someone born to act and star in big productions. I was lying effortlessly to an audience that had suspended disbelief. Deep down, I knew my ancestors would howl at this day. Even though I wasn't gay, it was enough that I was only pretending for the moment. My baptizing pastor would roll in his grave. This kind of joke is not tolerated in Zawe, as you know. Let alone the behavior itself.

The funny part of all this is that, when I was young, I was terrified of being gay. It's why I didn't want to be a fashion designer, to begin with. Yes, I was fascinated with the female form. Sometimes I would fall in love with a dress worn by this or that girl. So, I would fall in love with her too. Only to see her in another outfit and quickly fall out of love because she was wearing the wrong dress. It didn't help that all the TV shows I watched in Zawe had only male gay fashion designers. I thought I was gay because of my interest in fashion design. I wasn't terrified of the state of being itself. At the time, I was more terrified of how the world would treat me. So, I abandoned all my fashion and design dreams and the adjacent sexual orientation. But here I was, embracing that fear in order to pay rent.

The man who had made his way to the bar chuckled at this remark. Lenny ignored him and continued with the story.

~.~.~.~.~.~.~.~.~.~.~.~.~.~.~.~.~.~

Lenny helped the actress into the clothes. All the while making banter. He tried to imitate Big Betty as much as possible. From the topics to her tone. The actress enjoyed his gossip, and they had a blast. Lenny surprised himself by how much he remembered Big Betty babbling about celebrities. He helped with wardrobe through the entire day's shoot. At the end of which his new boss handed him a wad of cash

"$5,000 for your trouble, playing ball, and being cool," she said and turned around to go. Then changed her mind and whirled back. "My name is Letty, by the way?"

He looked at her closely for the first time. "Is that short for Letwin by any chance.?" She furrowed her brow. No one had used her full name in ages. "Yes, that's too wild a guess. Are you a creep like she was worried about?" she said, gesturing with her head in the direction of the actress.

"Learnmore Huku," Lenny replied instead, extending his hand as he introduced himself. His accent deepened, and his cisgender self appeared.

"Letwin Mukoto," she replied with an accompanying massive grin on her face. "Zviri sei" (How are things), she added, and they both laughed.

"Good, good sister, I'm glad we could help each other."

"And I take it you are not gay." She remarked offhandedly.

"Only professionally," he replied, acting like a spy dropping a secret.

She chuckled. "Well, you did great today. I run a small firm here, doing wardrobe and such. It's been tough to find good and reliable help. Today was my last probationary day after some failures on set. You saved my skin. Any chance you can be gay again tomorrow?"

He eyed her, mischief emblazoned on his face, "I can be two gay people tomorrow."

She was puzzled, and she looked the part.

"I have a friend who could use a job." Lenny clarified

"Well, to be sure, I don't pay $5,000 a day. I just thought I would show my gratitude today. But if your friend is gay and hardworking like you, I wouldn't mind trying you both on for the duration of this movie. So meet me at Vermont and Los Feliz tomorrow. And be dressed for your roles," she said, walking away and throwing her words behind her, like a girl boss from Zawe.

ALL TOGETHER NOW

"I can't believe you are going with Big Betty's ridiculous idea," Phil whispered vehemently. This was his fighting voice, the nice man he was. He continued, "No offense Big Betty but you both see how ridiculous..."

"...this construct is?" Lenny finished the sentence.

"Exactly," Phil said, pausing and feeling heard. "I hate how you seem to know what's in my head?" He said, sighing.

"And you know what's in my head. We've been friends a while, Phil." Lenny replied, and Phil grunted. He knew Lenny had fallen for Big Betty's idea weeks ago.

They had the $5,000 to cover their rent on the small side table in front of them. Big Betty was standing in the doorway.

"You can even buy back the TV. Maybe even get a car to get you places easier." Betty said, and Phil looked at the crisp bills peeping out of an envelope. They needed the gig; they needed the money.

"Well, where do I sign over my soul?" He asked, making a writing gesture.

"I'll take a handshake," Lenny said as they shook hands and embraced in camaraderie.

"I guess we are ordering take-out today." Big Betty said, riffling through the take-out menus by the door. She was going for the menus from the one fancy restaurant which delivered. They all laughed. When Big Betty left to pick up the food delivered downstairs, Phil looked at Lenny and asked:

"So, we are doing this?"

"You tell me," Lenny replied, anticipating the response.

"We are going pro, baby, pro-gay," Phil replied. He was trying to galvanize himself into the courageous act of deception.

"I've always wanted to go pro," Lenny replied, making the motion of shooting a basketball. They both laughed. Big Betty opened the door, and they both yelled "Yeaaaaah" in exaggerated excitement.

PROFESSIONALLY GAY

Big Betty seemed to know more about how they should behave than any magazine or TV show. And so, they stayed in the apartment where they received easier and ready coaching from Big Betty. By degrees, they gained confidence in presenting themselves as two gay men. Instead of moving to a more excellent apartment, they had used their extra income to buy into Letty's business. They were also gaining equity in Letty's company by degrees. Not to mention they had a keen eye for fashion! Letwin was only grateful to have them on board.

As their company grew, Phil and Lenny had to identify as gay to a broader audience. Which meant they had had to turn down requests for dates and such. So, they added to their fabricated life a romantic relationship with each other. Which was easy considering they had been to college together. The social media profiles had plenty of photos of them together. With this relationship in place, no one asked too many questions. Fewer people asked them out.

Following the promulgation of this relationship, Letty began to behave strangely. She put to task, the two of them like rookie employees. Always on their cases. Phil received the worst of it. The two men did not understand why but they choked it up to Letty being stressed with work. Her behavior did not let up for years.

One day, during one of these years, Phil called Lenny into a closet at work, "Dude, I am worried. Letty and I fought with each other today. She was and still is pretty miffed."

"Yeah, but she can't fire you. We are all partners here. So, what are you worried about?"

* * *

"It's not the job, Lenny; I am afraid I may have gone too far today. My therapist says I should embrace my masculinity and fight. And today, I brought my lion out and may have insulted Letty."

"Mmmm, that's not cool. I can smooth things over with her, though,"

"Yeah, you may be able to. But what if you can't, and Letty outs us as not being gay." Phil replied

"Hahaha, dude, you are funny. Of course, she won't do such a thing. If it's any consolation, we have been pretending to be gay long enough that we might as well be gay. That's how many people become anything. They pretend long enough, and everyone around them joins in playing pretend. Letty is in it with us."

"Dude, what are you saying. Have you actually become gay?"

"No, not really," Learnmore replied, "I was just kidding."

"You are scaring me, mans. What do you mean "not really," and what are you kidding about?"

"Okay, no, I am not gay. Are you happy now?"

"No, I am not happy. Are you, or are you not gay?" Phil asked. His stance was firmer than he usually took when asking anything.

"I am not!" Learnmore replied, creating a painful schism in his brain. He winced at the words a little. That's because pronouncing them aloud forced him to shift something in his brain. Something which allowed him to live in the duality. To live both in the lie and in this truth of who they were, namely, not gay.

"Okay, if you are not. Aren't you afraid Letty will rat us out?" Phil asked.

"Didn't I say I am not?"

"Yes, yes, I suppose you did. But I was leaving room for your whole pretending long enough spiel."

* * *

Lenny rolled his eyes and sighed, "You are so worried about the truth coming out that you are attacking me?"

"Yes, yes, but no, I am not attacking you, am I?"

"Look," Learnmore said, adopting a patient and upset tone. "Letty is from Zawe. We are born hustlers. Hustle secrets are a norm in Zawe. Everyone has them. It's how she and I vibed the day we met. Remember? She was hustling, and I was hustling; she pretended I worked for her, and I pretended I did work for her. I also happened to pretend I was gay. Remember?"

"I hope you are right, mans. I don't want to lose all this. The money is good, mans, it's good. And Letty is miffed today. Go talk to her, please."

THE FALL

Lenny made his way to Letwin's offive.

"How about some sadza for dinner tonight," he said as he entered her offive. She smiled weakly. Sadza usually worked to cheer her up.

"What's the matter?" Lenny asked, knowing full well what had happened.

"Playing dumb today, are we?" she asked mirthfully, which was encouraging. Lenny chuckled, shaking his head. He had a playful air and could get her out of any funk. They had discovered this early on in their working relationship. And now, it had been years of the same. It was almost like her mind and body anticipated alleviation whenever he showed up. Showbiz was stressful, and it was always good to have him, her anti kryptonite, around.

"Phil called me an 'old and cranky bachelor' today," Letty said

Lenny furrowed his brow.

She got up from her chair and responded to his facial expression, "Right? That's not cool, right?" she said

"No, not at all. But think about it. Phil had to pull that one from his formal archaic dictionary?" he said, grinning, and she stifled a laugh and shook her head. They found Phil to be formal and overly friendly. He was a proper gentleman.

"But he isn't lying, though. I am 32 and have no prospects and no time to find prospects."

"And I am 35, and I don't know how I will extricate myself from this lie. A lie which is paying the bills and keeping the lights on. When I am out of the game, maybe then I can settle down?"

"You can always try to be bi and get married and move on," she said.

"Naaah, that doesn't work. I need to look like I am not attracted to the female models I work with."

Letwin sighed and walked over to the front of her desk. She leaned back on it, eyeing her golden goose, Lenny. He had led the company to its expansion and was clearly the most talented on their team. And he was also the man she wished she could be with for the rest of her life.

He came over to her side, and together they looked out towards the door onto the factory floor.

"You know you are not gay, right?" She asked him

"Yeees," he answered hesitantly.

"So why haven't you asked me out?"

Silence

"I know you haven't asked out anyone since we started working together five years ago..."

* * *

"Yeah, and that's because..." he didn't finish the sentence.

"because of what?" Letty asked, goading him.

"Because I am gay," Learnmore replied sheepishly.

"But you know you are not gay," she replied emphatically.

Lenny was quiet, and she was grasping for words as emotions were rising.

"And I know you and I..." she stopped talking, choking up a little. Lenny sighed and looked at her. They looked at each other awkwardly in that proximity. He had hinted at wanting to be with her over the years. While she, in turn, had hinted at her openness to the idea. But their lingering glances and long hugs had come to naught.

"You wanna count shoulders?" he asked, interrupting her thoughts.

"What?"

"Do you want to count shoulders?" he asked again.

"I don't know, maybe?" she said, sniffling.

"Ha-ha, you don't know what it means."

"Well, teach me," She replied, punching him in the shoulder.

"Ouch, well, that's not how it works," he replied as he started counting his shoulders. His right-hand reaches for his left shoulder, "One," then back at itself, "Two," then over to Letty's shoulders. "Three, Four," he said, reaching over. And then he had his arm over her shoulders, and he drew her to him.

"Smooth," she chuckled, shaking her head. He laughed.

They were quiet for a while as she sobbed softly. Her body shaking was the only sign of her emotions. Then, moments later, she was composed, but they were still by her desk.

* * *

"You know, I have thought about it almost daily? Seeing you close deals, meet deadlines, and be kind to the employees, is alluring," he whispered.

"Then why haven't you pulled the trigger she asked?"

"You know why?" he retorted.

"Really! Hello, my name is Lenny, and I can't do this because gay people don't do this." she said, mocking him, "And now you can't let us be together because of the lie. Is it more important to you to be gay than being with me?"

"Whoa, whoa, hold on. How do you know we would even make it as a couple?"

She quickly extricated herself from his arms.

"So, I am just not worth the risk?" she asked.

"Come on; you are from Zawe too. You understand these things. This is our shot at the American dream. We are all close to being multi-millionaires."

She looked at him in disbelief. "I didn't know you loved money that much."

"I don't. I am only saying I am good at what I do. I am good at pretending to be gay and designing kick-ass fashion. That's solid ground for me. On the other hand, you and I might not work. It's risky and could blow up our lives, not just our hearts. I can do a broken heart, but a broken life or both together would be devastating. And we can't go back to Zawe; you know how the economy is."

She scoffed at him.

"Really. It's all about comfort for you, huh?"

"It's all about...I don't know what it's all about. Have you ever been poor? The "can't pay your bills" poor. Where you hawk every one of your possessions from graduation gifts to essentials?"

He looked at her knowing look,

"Okay, yes, maybe you have been just as poor. But people respond differently, alright. And I need to make sure…."

"you get more money until you are secure?" she asked, jabbing at him.

"No, it's not that…"

"Then what is it, Lenny. What do you want?"

He looked at her, his eyes screaming, "You," but his lips remained immobile. She was exasperated, but the silence and the look in his eye gave her an idea.

She decided she would try to help him say the words,

"You can't come out as "bi"?" she asked as she had asked before and many times in years past. Now he understood why she asked.

"No, no, no, no. Then I won't be the underdog," he replied, "Plus, we'll be back to creeping people out again."

"What's this about an underdog? what are you talking about."

"I don't really know, but I felt its power when Big Betty sai…."

"This Big Betty, again?"

"No, no, it's not like that with her. She was just…"

"…your mother away from home. Because you can be a big baby when you try," she retorted.

"You are not good at finishing my sentences, so stop!" he exclaimed, his voice deepening - his cis-gender self emerging.

* * *

"There he is," Letty said mockingly, "There is the man inside all the pretend..." she stopped short of finishing the sentence.

"I guess we are done here," Lenny said, realizing they were close to hurting each other irreparably. But unfortunately, he didn't even know she had been repeatedly cut deep over the years by the lie.

As he was walking out, she called out his name. He stopped, hesitating, and paused without turning around.

"I'm not a rat," she murmured like a gentle breeze.

He closed the door after himself, and she slumped on her desk, deflated. Head in her hands and tears dried up with no more coming. He walked away, confused. He wondered who he was becoming in all the success and the money.

THE BIG SHOT

Life became even more awkward between Letty and Lenny. They miscommunicated on crucial projects. They dropped things when handing them to each other. They even bumped into each other as they tried to navigate their shared spaces. As though they were using a GPS which made each other the destination. There was a general clumsiness between them. He would look at her when she wasn't looking, and she would stare at him when he wasn't aware. Finally, the workers were beginning to notice. Phil, too, noticed.

First, he released a statement to the company. He suggested that Lenny and Letty were preoccupied with the Dragons in Zawe. The Dragons in Zawe were all the buzz in the world and on the news. The world did not exactly recognize Uzu as a state like the Vatican. That was because Uzu's statehood derived from magical creatures, and that wasn't science. Officially, Uzu, the village state, was lumped together with the ocean of land surrounding it - Zawe. The headlines read, "Dragons in Zawe?" and not "Dragons in Uzu." Many employees did not know the distinction between Uzu and Zawe. They wondered if their bosses had family around the dragon areas.

* * *

No one had filmed or photographed the dragons. So artists had tried to get descriptions from some of the banished. The news was awash with artistic renditions of the Dragons in Zawe. The hairy, scaly creatures looked strange to a world accustomed to other dragons. That too distracted people. This worked for a short while. But Phil needed a permanent strategy, so he started sending Lenny to TV sets farther and farther from LA.

When Lenny was in New York, he met the future director of the movie, Tanganyika. The one Lenny starred in later. They met at a gay bar, and they connected over showbiz. Later, the man would introduce Lenny to a TV executive, and the Lenny and Phil show was born.

Big TV gave them a platform to earn more and influence culture. Of course, Zawe sought to boycott the show as much as possible. But the unofficial word was that Zawe was touting Learnmore's success. It was supposedly a sign that the country could affect the international discourse. "Pop culture is simply the best way to influence the world anyway, and politics is second best." This was the unofficial quote from the president of Zawe.

With increased publicity and money, Lenny began to feel the need to protect his private life. So he made some changes that made it possible for him to spend more time with Letty. She was willing to take whatever she could get even though she desired more. Theirs was an on and off weirdness which made them both uncomfortable. Yet still, they held on.

Meanwhile, Lenny was falling deeply for Letty. He was beginning to sense the futility of a life unshared by another. Lenny debated disrupting the Lenny and Phil show. After a couple of movies, he wondered how much more of the same he could take. As a role model to many, the lack of authenticity in his life was killing him.

THE THREAD

Lenny was picking at his sweater before they taped the show. It aired every Friday and re-ran over the weekend. They taped it on Wednesday.

He had been bringing more and more of his personal clothes on set for a more authentic look. Plus, their company supplied the show's wardrobe, so he had some leeway. He was wearing his favorite sweater, and he had discovered a loose string. He was pulling at it like a child playing with a scab. He stopped mid-action, wondering whether he honestly was bothered by it. The OCD was part of the act of being gay. He did that in public, yet he was alone in his dressing room right then. He wasn't sure what was him and what was an act anymore. But he was sure of one thing, or one person rather: Letty. It was time, he thought, time to let go of all this. He could confess, or he could come out as bi. The second option was a better option for the show. It was also better for Phil, who was not slowing down.

As he came to this conclusion, he realized he had been pulling at the string. It had lengthened considerably and unraveled his sweater more. He decided to cut it and go on the show with the tiny hole anyway. As they started taping, he swiveled, and the small hole got caught on the desk. The movement tore the sweater considerably. Lenny was so happy with his resolution to care to change. After the producers checked in with their OCD host, they were surprised he was good to go, and the show went on.

That day, the show discussed the footballer kneeling at the football games. Lenny was, as usual, being the devil's advocate. Phil was presenting the "Pinterest" perspective, as they called it. Their on-camera dynamic worked so well and with ease. That was because it fit perfectly with their heterosexual personalities. It was also congruent with the dynamic of their long-time friendship. Lenny came out in favor of kneeling. However, Phil was suggesting they should not mix up football and politics.

"Really, I think at this point anything that anyone with brown skin does is political."

"Well, I don't know about that?" Phil replied sheepishly. He was trying to maintain his resistance but acknowledging the danger. This debate could quickly backfire on him on social media if he pushed back too hard.

"I mean anything. And so, I say kneel, sit at a Starbucks, drive; anything you do in brown skin is political nowadays." Lenny continued

"All I am saying is I came to watch football, not a political statement."

"As though anything we do is separate from the politics of the world. Or race or the gender, or even the sexual orientation we find ourselves in." Lenny replied.

"Come on, really, from kneeling to gender and sexual orientation." Phil said, swiveling in his usual, "I am wounded signal," the signal to slow down and move on. Lenny had to wrap up.

"Well, I am sticking to my guns," Lenny said, and then he looked directly into the camera. He was addressing Phil in this dramatic move, but it looked to many like he was now addressing the audience. He delivered these words, eyes locked with the camera. "We need to kneel with this player, and if you disagree, come at me, bro. Come at me." He beat his chest like a gorilla and made the mic drop gesture. He didn't realize he had challenged some resourceful vindictive viewers.

After the taping of the show, he sat down to change. The tear in his sweater reminded him of his resolution to give up the life of a lie. He called Letty,

"You sound very light," she said as they spoke over the phone.

"And that's because I have finally decided," he said

"Wow, okay, you decided to give up the con?" she asked playfully. He was quiet. She thought she had offended him.

"Oh, come on, Learnmore. It's a joke. You know how sometimes I call you a con man. It's just a..." she was explaining.

Lenny interrupted her, "It's confidence, man," he said, cutting through her words.

* * *

"What?" she asked,

"Confidence, man, I am a confidence man,"

"What does that even mean?" she asked. "That you are cocky?"

"No, no, that's the original term. Confidence man was shortened to con-man. His role or her role was to gain the confidence of those around him and then reap them off. So come over this weekend, Letty wangu" (My Letty)," he said, mixing the two issues.

Letwin sighed deeply and replied in a subdued voice, "I am not yours, Learnmore."

"Maybe so. And maybe we could change that this weekend?" He asked her

"Maybe you could drop the con?" She asked in reply

"This weekend," he said, "come over." She sighed in resignation. It was set.

The weekend never came, or at least the weekend they envisioned never came. The show aired on Friday. By Saturday morning, someone had leaked photos of him and Letty from a few years back. Images that showed them in a more romantic light than friendship. Someone had searched for pictures of Lenny and Phil behaving like a romantic couple. People wanted pictures where they held hands or something. There were none. Though they claimed to be a couple, no images online suggested romantic attachment. But there were plenty of pictures of him and Letty. Over the years, the rumors had said he was her gay best friend. But now, it looked suspicious.

By dinner on Saturday, Lenny was putting out multiple fires. All thoughts of Letty and his resolution to stop playing pretend had to be set aside. She, in her turn, was helping him cope with the situation. She tried to comfort him. He had bought a ring to propose to her. He had planned to leave it all behind. He had schemed to get ahead of it. But now it was unraveling like his sweater, and he was playing catch up.

* * *

There was enough social media evidence to suggest that Phil and Lenny were not gay by Monday. The world was on fire. Lenny had already given up, so he came out as heterosexual. He released a very brief press statement. He had drafted this before the unraveling, so it was more optimistic and joyful than he felt that Monday.

"I have lived a lie for so long. I have lived under the shadow of inauthenticity. I have lived like a king sitting under a throne with a huge sword hanging over it by a horse's hair. I have lived with the risk of being found out and the fallout of being discovered. The threat of persecution and losing my career. The fear of hurting loved ones loomed over me as I hid my true self from the world. And now I am glad to say that; I am not bi, I am not gay, I am a proud, heterosexual male. This is my coming out day!"

~.~.~.~.~.~.~.~.~.~.~.~.~.~.~.~

"To me, it was a statement of victory," Lenny said, breaking the cadence of narration. "I had to abandon fashion design because I thought it would be my downfall. But after years of designing and pretending to be gay, I still am here, an unflagging heterosexual man. I was no longer afraid of being gay."

The bartenders groaned at this, and so did the mysterious eavesdropping man. Lenny was happy for an audience to hear him out.

Needless to say, "He continued, there was an uproar in the world in response to this. But the worst were the lawsuits. Some models were filing sexual assault lawsuits. Maybe a touch had lingered, here or there. Nothing a gay best friend would be sued for, but a heterosexual man could not do that."

~.~.~.~.~.~.~.~.~.~.~.~.~.~.~.~

112

In all the chaos, Learnmore invited Letty to Hawaii. She was eager to go. She wanted to get her beloved friend away from the scandal and its fallout. He had other plans. On their arrival, he whisked her away to what was supposedly an isolated spot. He had surprised her with the ring. She had taken long to reply, and the musicians and such who had been invited came out prematurely. She was not surprised but was instead shocked. Shocked and overwhelmed by the unanticipated cameras, musicians, and witnesses. Letty ran away in tears without responding. Someone leaked the images of all this, and the scandal became even more prominent.

60 MINUTES

Hearing about the lawsuits and how Lenny had been suffering, Phil stuck to his guns.

He released his statement,

"I am shocked and saddened by the fraud my long-time partner has maintained. I always knew there was something more between him and Letty, but I didn't think to investigate. He was such a great pretender and good at gaslighting me." With this statement, he ascended and sat on the throne of the ultimate underdog.

The world had nothing better to do for a month or so besides following the story of the two-man.

In an interview of *60 minutes*:

"Look, Phil was in on it. We had failed to find success in the fashion and entertainment industry. So we thought, 'why not become professionally gay?'" Lenny was saying.

"Yes, and you keep saying there was a witness, but you won't name that witness. If we find this witness, we can verify and share with the world."

* * *

"Hmmm, I see. But the witness is dear to me, and I won't have her embroiled in all this. Become an accessory to fraud and such."

"Is it Letwin you are talking about," the interviewer asked.

"Of course not. I wouldn't have said 'she' if it was that easy to guess who."

"Aaaah, the smart brain of a con artist," the host responded, and Lenny was quiet for a second, then smiled and replied.

"I prefer the more elegant term, a confidence man." he retorted

The host of the show laughed.

"Phil and I confidently embraced the gay identity. Then we invited many people into that confidence, and soon we were gay."

"That is sad. Using such a minority identity to make it in entertainment. Don't you feel sad for those who are actually gay and the discrimination they suffer?"

"Of course, I do. But I suffered the same even as I walked the world as gay for the last decade or so."

"But you weren't in effect, gay. And besides, you are successful."

"I am successful because I lived life as though I was gay."

"Exactly, you pretended."

"Maybe, in the beginning, I pretended to be gay. But in the end, I identified as gay. I have experienced the discrimination gay people have to endure. However, I have also been availed opportunities which my gay identification afforded me."

"But you could shake it off, right? I mean, because you aren't really gay, you could let the insults roll off you. Unlike those who are truly gay?" he pressed.

* * *

"I don't know, do the insults of those who identify as women roll off them because they aren't actually women?" Lenny shot back

"Well, that's different?"

"What's the difference?" Lenny asked

"Well, they truly believe in what they identify as."

"And you are saying I didn't believe?"

"Well, your actions don't suggest you believed you were gay?"

"What do you mean? What actions are you talking about? I didn't have a girlfriend, even a secret one." Lenny shot back

"You didn't behave like a gay person" is what I am talking about

"And how should a gay person behave?" Lenny asked

The host was stumped, so Lenny thought, "victory." But Lenny was not winning in the court of public opinion. And this interview exacerbated things. Had the world been firing at him from one corner of a square world? If so, now it was firing at him from all four corners. Lenny had just won himself more enemies.

His only friend Phil had distanced himself from him and the scandal. In fact, in a few months, Phil had found himself a celebrity gay partner. The story was he had met this other man in his grief over Lenny's lies. And in being comforted, they had fallen in love.

Lenny could not believe it. But what was most difficult to stomach was how everyone clamored for him to be canceled. He was removed from the show, but the show went on. It grew in popularity due to the scandal. He was blacklisted for jobs in Hollywood. Letwin had to make a statement about distancing the company and herself from him. Secretly, they stayed in touch and stayed close. It was a good business move, though.

~.~.~.~.~.~.~.~.~.~.~.~.~.~.~.~

"It surprises me," Lenny said, breaking cadence again. "If the government was doing this to me, it would be censorship, and there would be an uproar. But we do it to each other, and it's alright, which defeats the idea of democracy where we are the government. In that case, we should not be censoring one another. Because that's what it is, we have become our own censorship where we cancel one another. Somehow, we are hoping those we cancel never get jobs and lose any means of livelihood. It's almost like a prayer to render destitute the people we don't like or people we disagree with. And society answers the prayer by distancing itself from you and boycotting your business. I don't think people know that the guillotine eventually killed the man who invented it. Those who cancel others will themselves be canceled eventually."

Simbai laughed, "It's tragic indeed. People don't realize they, too, run the risk of being canceled. And with that fear in mind, more conformity is created. We regurgitate the safe opinions already expressed and allowed. So new thoughts and new opinions become risky."

"Hehe, it's like we live in Uzu, but without the dragons," Lenny said, winking at Simbai. They laughed the way people from Zawe do. Laughing at themselves no matter how bad things go.

Anyway, let me tell you what I did next, Lenny said, "or rather what happened next."

~.~.~.~.~.~.~.~.~.~.~.~.~.~.~.~

So, Lenny sold his houses, settled several lawsuits, and moved back in with Big Betty. Or instead moved back to her apartment. Of course, he lived more comfortably there than before. He had quite a lot of money left after the dust settled. He was not planning on spending much since jobs were scarce for him.

* * *

Pictures of the apartment building he had moved back to were everywhere in the news and tabloids. "How the mighty have fallen," read a headline, "Back to square one," read another. Even though a book deal was thrown at him, he refused. It would be too intrusive to their lives, to Letty's, to Big Betty's secret.

So now he was single, back in his old apartment, and he was turning 37.

~.~.~.~.~.~.~.~.~.~.~.~.~.~.~.~

"And that Shamwari is why I am here in theeeee uh...." he said, looking at his watch to make sure it was still morning. He had taken his time to bare his soul, and he told everything.

The bartenders were listening attentively. But, unfortunately, so was the man who was eavesdropping.

"Eish, man, you sound like you lost everything," Simbai remarked.

"Yeah, but methinks I lost it all a long time before acquiring it. I lost it when I lost myself. I was lured by the luster and allure of the American dream."

"Hehe, all that glitters is not gold, am I right?" Simbai asked

"Rightly said," Learnmore replied pensively.

"I don't know if I was inspired by the colonial dream - company house, company car, or American dream when I was growing up. But after Uzu, I found everyone in Zawe preaching about getting rich. Sounds like the American dream being adopted across the world."

"Yes," Lenny replied, "It's being adopted worldwide. It's why many of us come here. To chase the American dream. Isn't that why you and your wife are here? You are here to get that money, give back to society, and go on splendid social media-worthy vacations. Am I right?

Lenny asked

"No, no, no, no, no, no, no, mukoma (brother). If anything, my account of my Uzu story should have shown you that I can't be bought by money or the promise of belonging. Also, I can't be deterred by the threat of persecution either. Besides, the American dream pales compared to my faith's vision for humanity."

"How so," Lenny asked, "What can be greater than having money, giving back to society, and making the world better? While also enjoying your money in the Maldives or Dubai? And please don't say, God. I would not understand that."

"I hear you; I think. I know now the American dream includes giving back to society once you get rich. Yet, in the end, the dream is founded on the clamor of "Me! Me! Me! Me! Me!" Being selfless is giving up your right to do whatever you want, whenever you want, with whomever you want. It means doing no harm even to those who harm you or others. It's giving up your desire to have it now, whether it's money or change in the world. In that regard, the American dream and the Divine dream are not synonymous. And those who think so have inevitably and ignorantly made America their god."

CHAPTER FOUR

Imogene Pass

THE HOBO

"Hehehe, hic, you sound very wise," The homeless man finally said.

Simbai and Learnmore were silent, unsure how to respond. Should they entertain this man or let him be.

"Jus, hic, jus, hic, why did you go to this place anyway?" the man asked. One could feel many in the bar approve of the question. Some eavesdroppers wanted to know.

Again Simbai was tempted to raise his two fingers. But this time, he did not know where to start. He took a swig of the Rusty Velvet, but it did not burn enough this time.

"Eh, ahem," he cleared his throat for no reason. "Eh, em, that's too private for this setting?" he replied in a hoarse whisper.

"Private for this setting? Too private for a bar? This is the modern-day therapist's house. How, hic,...look, this repentant lying man over here just gave you the tea on his life story, and you, you, you, hic say your reason is too private?"

Learnmore shrank back at what sounded like a diluted accusation. Simbai fidgeted on his bar stool.

* * *

"Yes," Simbai replied uncomfortably. He felt he was a lying man, though unrepentant just yet.

"Go kick rocks and pound sand, man! Hic, I bet you went to Uzu to remain the man of the house. Instead of waiting like an ignorant sitting duck, you saw the wave of equality sweep across the world. Then in a bold act of cunning, you ran."

"I did not run!" Simbai replied, slightly agitated. The man evidently wanted him to lose his cool, but this day had seen much worse already. By now, all he could give him was a slight show of emotion.

This man had inserted himself into their conversation. Now he was showing all intent and capacity to steer it. He was at best a five foot eight who could pass for six-foot when he was talking. He had eavesdropped and giggled and grunted along with Simbai and Lenny for a while now.

He had a terrible case of the hiccups, as anyone could tell after about two minutes of listening to him talk. His clothes looked rustic in the dim light. Like they had spent several nights with the wearer rolling in the deep somewhere.

Simbai continued a little more subdued, "I did not run. I left for my mental health, afraid I would lose my mind and let my daughter down. The world is a crazy stressful place, and my childhood trauma..."

"Gobble gobble gobble," The man interrupted, mimicking a turkey. "You were afraid that you would let your daughter down, but her mom would remain solid. She would end up being in charge of the family. And your ego could not...hic...could not...hic...take it?

Simbai was surprised at such a drunk-looking cogent man. He remained silent. He was unsure how to extricate himself from the conversation this man was forcing upon him. It brought back memories and inspired the very thoughts that could throw him into a loop. He wished he had taken his wife's advice. Had he done so and agreed to see a therapist, he would have a pack of pills waiting for any moment that looked like this—moments when he did not want to deal with himself or the truth.

"You see, I contemplated being the first white family in Uzu. When I saw that I was about to lose my family and could no longer rule over them, I considered the move. The gender roles in Uzu made it clear that if I flew over, I could keep my family together. I could tell them what to think. I could even control their level of thought on those topics I allowed. I could control my household and as such be at peace."

Simbai froze. Was that it? Did he feel better in Uzu because he could control his wife and daughter's level of thinking? Simbai could control their perceptions of him. Did that make him feel better as he slowly marched towards derangement? Marching and normalizing his steps towards insanity. Had he gone crazy like the proverbial frog in the warm water? The water is gradually turned up until the water boils, and the frog dies. Wasn't it madness to go to Uzu in the first place? Especially to go there to keep one's family together, only to blow it up. Wasn't it insanity to purport to tell others what to think and how far to think it? Wasn't it craziness to see blue flames and auras? Who would not call it stupid if he said he had attended the galactic spiritual meeting of colors in the Light Room? And after the meeting, he had woken up half a day's drive away from home?

Lenny saw Simbai's mangled face in the dim light and decided to help with the conversation:

"Alright," Lenny said, "That's enough of attacking my fellow countryman."

The drunk man chuckled. He turned his attention to Lenny, who felt the shift before words were sent his way. The homeless man made you feel like you were on stage, and the limelight was focused on you alone.

"Aaaah...hic...the almost gay one. Your name reminds me of her name. Lane, the lesbian who destroyed my life. Her friends would not have taken her up that mountain if she had not come out. She and her friends made my life miserable. Look, look, look, look, loo...hic. I am

121

not describing your friend here or attacking him, but I am talking about me. I did my research on Uzu when my family was falling apart." The man paused. He looked pensive, how a man looks as he remembers something severe but beautiful.

Then dreamily, he said, "I wish my wife had taught me about submission?" He paused again. Lenny and Simbai exchanged 'what now' looks before the man slowly continued. It looked like he was tying threads together in his mind on the spot.

"She was so skilled at submission, and I was the militant one. Maaaaaaan..." his voice trailed. Simbai was quiet, his mind on Tambudzai, his beautiful and loyal wife. The woman could teach him oodles about submission. "Had he learned anything from her?" he wondered. Lenny felt obliged to carry on the conversation in the face of Simbai's silence.

"What are you talking about?" Lenny asked.

The drunk man felt encouraged to continue with his monologue. After all, it needed an audience like all monologues.

"They say once the pope took some men on a tour of his treasury. And he said to them, "No longer shall the church say, "silver and gold have I none." One of the visitors responded, "No longer shall the church say rise up and walk." Now I say, no longer shall a woman tell us or teach us what it is like to be under authority. Soon submission as a virtue will be lost in the world. In the same way, the church lost the invisible power to heal and fight invisible enemies. By focusing on fixing visible problems in the world with visible means such as money. There is a place for soup kitchens; the problem is when it becomes all you do."

The story was a jumbled mess for Lenny and Simbai.

"If submitting is that big a deal, why is only one gender forced to submit and the other isn't?" Lenny asked, smiling to himself. He was self-satisfied with what he thought was a confounding question.

The man laughed. "Imagine saying to your father, 'Dad, why do I have to do mathematics, right? Everyone else in my class is doing it wrong. I will avenge myself and do it wrong also.' Now. I am not saying it's fair to demand one submits and the other not. But it does make you wonder if one should stop listening because the other isn't? Submission is the way of a child. Remember, the ones who were supposed to come to Him because the Kingdom belongs to such as them. A husband submits as a leader does and must - to lead well - and he must learn it from Christ. Though Jesus was the leader of the twelve, he washed their feet. A wife must submit as one under authority should, and she must learn it from Christ. Because though equally God, Jesus finds a way to submit perfectly to the will of the Father to the point of death."

"So women are equally men," Lenny retorted, hoping he had defeated the homeless man.

"Wait, wait, did I say that?" He swayed a little hiccuping some more. "Oh yeah, I guess that's what it means, huh?" he said more to himself than anyone else. Then he looked at Simbai and Lenny, "You know, some, hic, say, hic, that gender is a human construct. Fine, let's give them that, but biology is a concrete place to stand for my next point. We are biologically made to safeguard and represent different elements of God's image. So that we wouldn't be self-sufficient but need each other for different things. We are pieces of a whole, one only recognizable when we come together. That is why, why, why, um...can I just use gender for simplicity here?" he asked no one in particular. People were captivated, and some grunts were heard, so he continued. "Think biology here, but I am trying to say, each separate eh, eh, hic, biological gender has increased capability or responsibility in recognizably different things. And equal capability in a great many numbers of the same things. So yes, men are equally women as Christ is equally God." he paused, and Lenny was about to jump in when the man raised his finger swaying a little with the movement.

"Aaaah, but submission is not the absence of authority. In fact, submission is the...hic, the epi...hic...submission is clear evidence of the existence of authority. Information or knowledge gives us authority. Experts are called experts only because they hold specialized knowledge of a subject. In the past, men were experts at war and sacrificing their lives. This made it so they could sermonize on that. Women could preach about nurturing and submission. Or rather, they were used as good examples of both in the sermons by men. Now both genders are jacks of all trades and masters of none. And destroying the marriage and family structure in the process."

"Yeah, because marriage is outdated." Lenny retorted

"Says the almost gay man who wanted to marry his business partner." Bishop Hooper shot back, silencing Lenny.

"I am saying that those naturally fitted to nurture are no longer keen on nurturing. Those naturally fitted for war are trying to do the nurturing. And so nurturing is falling through the cracks. Heartbreak and heartache ensue, and shootings are on the rise."

The bartender jumped in at this one, "Sir, women too can go and fight a war. Men aren't the only gender naturally fitted for war." The whole bar was tense as many more were eavesdropping.

"You know, in Uzu, we had a saying, "Breasts are for fighting wars," Simbai said, trying a come back into the conversation.

"What does that mean?" Lenny asked in a hoarse whisper.

"I don't know. We weren't supposed to think too much there, remember?" Simbai replied in similar hushed tones.

"I don't know what that is supposed to mean, but I hope I never have to fight a war. If there was a draft, I would be happy to be cut from it to make room for women who want to fight. I just heard that a draft announcement was made in Bahrain. You know the European country that was recently invaded. First, women and children would be evacuated. Then men, nineteen years of age and above, were to stay and fight. Then, of course, some women stayed. But what I haven't heard is any gender watchdog protesting these draft measures. No one has come out angry and demanding equal treatment of all genders, equal evacuation, or equal drafting. I bet you tons of men would rather be evacuated.

"and probably tons of women would rather be drafted." The bartender said, jumping in. Bishop Hooper gave her the stink eye.

* * *

"If, if, if, if, hic, if only the draft announcement made that a possibility, many men would leave without shame. And, and, and, many more women would be required to stay." he finished looking at the bartender.

There was a resounding echo of silence in the bar.

"Look, look," said the drunk man, who quickly realized he was not making any friends at the bar at this point. Lenny, Simbai, and the bartenders all were disengaging from him and his ranting self. But he desperately needed an audience. He, like Lenny, needed to tell his side of the story. The side the newspapers had ignored. He needed someone to know his own pain and suffering.

"Look, look," he said, quieting down as much as any tipsy person could. "I believe that the end goal of this dress rehearsal of life is to make male into female, and female into a male. I am not talking about becoming transgender but transcending gender. That is to render us all one race, one people, one love. But, but, but, hic not through fighting one another. Nooooo! Not through silencing or destroying the 'other.'" He said with air quotes, making him sway dangerously with both hands in the air. "I don't want any violence, even verbal. I am a natural man, and nature knows no violence. We find that metamorphosis is not brought about by violence, anger, or malice as we walk in nature. If there is any force in nature, we can easily see that it's a necessary force or ignorant vehemence. Nature works over a duration, eroding slowly, gently, and patiently. Yes, storms come through, but we are the ones who ascribe morality to nature's actions. The sun gently coaxes a flower to bloom; any more heat and the poor flower burns. And I got burned y'all. I got burned badly when gender and marriage equality entered my church; I got burned." he repeated, muttering and shaking his head. He looked like a man in need of a 24-hour psychiatric hold now.

Now the man's story was slowly taking shape. Finally, the room eased up a little. A crazy person with a reasonable account of why they are crazy seems less threatening to some people.

"You all do know gender equality opened the door to marriage equality which opened the gates for designating as a sexual orientation things like pae...

"Stop, stop! Lenny interjected. He had been silenced before by Bishop Hooper's comments. Now he raised his voice to signal his unwillingness to back down. "Do you have any idea how these people you mention have suffered? I know first-hand what it is like!"

"And do you know how much people like myself have suffered because of these very people? I lost my church, my own family, and my life..." his voice trailed, "Does the name Bishop Hooper ring a bell."

"Oooooooh," everyone in the bar who was listening moaned! Only Simbai did not recognize his name.

Bishop Hooper looked at Simbai, beaming. This man in his dirty pajamas did not know about Imogene Pass. The place where the decked-out four-wheel-drive 4Runner rolled backward on the ice. Even L4 could not gain traction as the vehicle dovetailed into the abyss. The fear as the back wheel tipped into the air. The lurch of his stomach as the car flipped over, half flying. Before it made contact with the side of the mountain. The jerk of the impact of that contact, the sound of metal crunching and glass shattering. His mind worried for Timothy's safety, and his heart going out to Riva (River) who would be alone; widowed and without a son.

Bishop Hooper shook his head quickly to dismiss the memory of his thoughts on that day as the car rolled down the side of the pass. Then he turned his whole body toward Simbai. He gave the rest of the bar his back to pelt with invisible tomatoes.

"So, I am Bishop Hooper from Arizona or was, was, was Bishop Hooper. I was the Bishop of the Interfaith Liturgical Life Society. The ILLEST," he said, pausing and making a "cool" gesture with his hands. "Anyway, the ILLEST..." Again he broke the narration and did the hand thing and started chuckling to himself. Tears glistened in his eyes. Then after finally composing himself, he tried again. "The ILLEST," and again, he did the hand gesture. This time he burst into laughter which threatened to turn into tears. "Ok, ok, ok, I'm going to tell the story. "The ILLEST," - he paused, his hand twitched, and he grinned - "adheres to scripture as its unifying factor. It was unlike other interfaith denominations. The ones which integrate worldly practices to fill their benches. My story truly started as I was preaching. No, wait, it was the camp booking by the Flagstaff group. Maybe it would be better to go way back to the dinner when she first brought up all the equality stuff. Or when Timothy brought up the ILLEST?"

We were having some grub with my family. But, of course, my son, Timothy, was up to his usual troublemaking and challenging his Father."

...and the man's words came like a slow-motion flood—one with waves just as powerful but whose impact reverberated much deeper. The words were accompanied by vivid emotion. It was no wonder they were all effortlessly transported into Bishop Hooper's world. It was as though another person was telling the story for him.

REPAST

Timothy was criticizing Bishop Hooper's work. To top it off, he was making absurd suggestions about the changes they could make. His mom was playing along with him as usual. Bishop Hooper felt like he had to be the only reasonable one at the table.

"Dad, have you noticed the Interfaith Liturgical Life Society's abbreviation reads, "ILLS." It's like we are advertising that we are the "ILLS" of the world."

He chuckled, and his mom laughed with him. But unfortunately, the father did not laugh.

Riva (River), the Bishop's wife, had tried to steer her son a little. She suggested to Timothy an alternative meaning. "Maybe we can say it's from the phrase, "Behold, the lamb that takes away the ILLS of the world."

"Mom, if we do that, then that would be like saying He has come to take all the Liturgical Societies of the world. Which might not be such a bad idea." He added chuckling

"Timotheeeeeee," The mother said, punching him playfully in the shoulder.

"Owwww, see what I mean," the boy said, laughing and his mother joined in.

The Bishop was willing to admit the acronym was not the best. Yet, he felt his family had gone from critical to sacrilegious at that moment. To make matters worse, they were laughing about it. He was getting angrier with each decibel of laughter and each pixel of joy he spied at the dinner table. The son knew his father and noticed the El Niño winds kicking up a storm. So he shifted gears,

"But as dad reminds me often. 'When you find a problem, be sure only to criticize when you have a solution. So I propose that we call the church the "ILLEST."

The Bishop slammed his fist on the table, rattling the plates and the kitchen wear. Only his wife flinched. Timothy had been accustomed to these outbursts now. Riva would be too if the Bishop lost his temper around her as much as he did around Timothy.

"What, so we can become the sickest?" the father asked, irritated.

Timothy chuckled.

"What, what's so funny?" Bishop Hooper Asked genuinely puzzled.

"Dad, it's slang. It means great or awesome. If we changed the acronym, we could be even more hip and inviting to the younger demographic. And I know it's a goal the church has been aiming for in recent years."

The Bishop felt foolish. He paused, and his wife smiled. "I think that's a great suggestion, Timothy," she said. She punched him on the shoulder again, this time with more gentleness than the last. Timothy responded by falling out of his chair and exclaiming, "Owww!" The two laughed, but Bishop Hooper again did not join in.

"And where will the E and the T come from?" The Bishop asked victoriously. He was winning the battle against what could be favorable for the church and the greater Kingdom mission.

"Dad, it's like a rap lyric. The T is implied in SocieTy." If you want, you can skip the E and add that air comma, like - ILL'ST. But then, in the end, you see the E is implied in there as well, so it would be fine!"

The boy was correct, but the Bishop wanted to be right.

"You have been listening to rap?" the father asked, throwing his napkin on the table. "What have I said about rap music?"

Timothy had looked at his father with disgust. "The things you choose to focus on, Dad, are surprising." He threw his napkin on the table, stood up, and walked away from the table.

"Come back here, come sit down?" The father vociferated.

Timothy did not come back, Bishop Hooper exchanged glances with his wife, and Riva shrugged her shoulders.

Three weeks later, Timothy had done the welcome greeting at mass. He introduced himself well. Then he said, "I would like to welcome you all to the Interfaith Liturgical Life Society. Or as I like to call it, 'the ILLEST.'" He had accompanied the words with the dab gesture, and the entire church had laughed.

People around town could be heard saying, "Oh, I attend the "ILLEST," and they would make the hand gesture. Even older people were in on it, and it soon became a calling card.

"Come join us next week at the "ILLEST', and the hand gesture would follow. The Liturgical Society had managed to appropriate a pop-culture gesture. And a few more high school students were added to the flock and young adults as well. Timothy's victory further soured his relationship with his father somehow.

DIVORCE

When the couple came over to their house unannounced, Bishop Hooper had little time to dismiss his family. He had taken the couple to the study, but the raised voices could be heard around the house.

The couple was bickering because one of their children had come out recently. The mother and father were not in agreement on how to respond. Bishop Hooper tried to keep his response neutral. He could not come out in favor of one of them, or the conversation would break down.

The couple started throwing around the "D" word as the conversation heated up. Bishop Hooper cringed. Just the word itself appalled him. He believed it was a sin to get divorced but did not say so for fear of alienating the couple he was trying to help. But he sounded sterner with them, and they noticed his change in demeanor.

Interestingly enough, his tone unified them against him. And one question resounded from the couple. What did the ILLEST have to say about the rainbow nation?

They left in a huff, walking past Riva with a nod and a wave. She had wanted to join in the counseling session to help amplify the woman's voice but had struggled to find a good time to knock and butt in. Timothy had been in his room enjoying the drama. Unscheduled visitors were not too rare an occurrence for the Hooper family. Timothy used to sympathize with the people who budged in for emergency counseling. But lately, he had taken to enjoying his father's foibles when interacting with these home visitors.

Riva came in after the couple left. She saw her husband sitting on the counseling couch with his head in his hands. He was frustrated. Bishop Hooper spied his wife in the room and, raising his head, said out loud,

"Amen."

* * *

Riva smiled. "You weren't even praying, honey."

He gave her a weak smile back. He looked drained and exhausted. She walked to the couch, sat by him, and rubbed his back. "It's their job to be in disarray and yours to facilitate their conversation with the real teacher."

He smiled, grateful for her perspective on the matter. "It's exhausting, though, and this rainbow question needs to be addressed head-on soon," he said to her.

"What's your opinion on the matter?" Riva asked continuing to rub his back.

He raised his head out of his hands where he had replaced it and looked at her in disbelief.

"My thoughts? My thoughts? I have no thoughts; I only follow the Bible." he replied to her.

"I am not the enemy here. I am only trying to help you articulate your thoughts. But if you prefer discussing it with yourself, I will gladly drop it." Riva replied as she placed her hand back on her lap.

Bishop Hooper sighed and looked at her. Then he picked her hand and dropped it on his back. "I could also use a massage," he said sheepishly.

"So, your thoughts?" she asked as she resumed rubbing his back.

"I don't know; I have too many. But I may not be able to remember all of them right now. If that's alright with you." He replied, scooting back and making room for her legs. He brought her feet to his thighs and took her shoes off.

"Let me massage your feet," he said

"She chuckled. I am not looking for a tit for tat, you know?" She replied, smiling.

* * *

"I know, dear. It helps me to have something to do with my hands as I talk. So I thought I would return the favor," The Bishop replied as he removed her socks.

"Suit yourself," Riva replied, leaning back and closing her eyes.

"I think the church is headed towards a watershed moment. This conversation is going to destroy many congregations. And it's sad because the virtues of tolerance and love will go out the window as people aim for right and wrong. But it may not be helped, you know." he replied. Riva was sighing in contentment. She asked her question quietly.

"So, what do you think about flying the flag?"

Bishop Hooper chuckled. "Well, I am concerned on every side. First endorsing sin, and then...you know what, endorsing sin is a big deal enough. Sin is death, and death is a big deal." He replied, pausing the massage.

She opened one eye, "Don't forget, as you minister to my spirit right now, you also have feet to minister to, mister." She replied, and he laughed, shaking his head. He enjoyed talking with Riva, though they didn't always see eye to eye.

She looked upwards, throwing her head back, and sighed with pleasure, without forgetting her mind. She murmured her question slowly and with sass, "But think about it. There are people out there, confused young people. They are making tough decisions about their sexual preferences and core identities. I want them to know that this is a safe palace to have this conversation. If, as a church, we are judgemental, they won't come to us. So who are they going to? Who is giving them counsel and advice? You leave them no choice for good advice. And in so doing, you keep the kingdom from them. No one who keeps the kingdom from others can enter. It's impossible. What do you think about that?" She asked him as she moved her foot so he could reach a spot, murmuring. "Right there," when he got it. Bishop Hooper chuckled.

"Are you trying to tell me something about Timothy?" He asked in a playful tone.

Riva raised her head and jerked her foot, trying to kick him, but he held on to it. "This is seriously silly, I'm trying to help here," she replied, and they laughed.

"I get what you are saying. And yes, maybe being a place for conversation is good. It's just that the flag alienates some people as well. And those who remain usually feel they are better than those who left, which is not true and is a path towards destruction. It used to be sinners in the hands of an angry God. Now it's 'virtuous people and doing all kinds of good in the world, in the hands of a loving and forgiving God.' And I think that's wrong. So the true balance is 'sinners in the hands of a loving and forgiving God.' Sinners who are no better than any other whether they leave because of the flag or stay."

Riva liked what she heard from her husband. But she also disagreed, so now she knew she had to find another way of getting this idea to the board.

SERVICE

It wasn't long before another dinner brought an excited Timothy full of new ideas to the table.

"Mom, how would you like to pass communion around or lead worship?" Timothy asked, reaching for the sault and winking at his mother, who had to pass it because it was too far for Timothy. She shook her head and handed him the salt.

"What are you talking about?" Bishop Hooper had quipped without delay, laying his fork and knife down.

"I am saying that the world needs a church that does not ignore 50% of its attendees when serving. Actually, women make up a larger percentage of most church demographics. So it might be more like 70% of its attendees." Timothy said, then returned to salting his food.

* * *

"Where did you get those numbers," The Bishop asked, raising his hands and enfolding his fingers.

"I think he is onto something, love." Riva had said. She had a way of washing away the dross and mud to leave the gold.

The Bishop could not resist his wife's gentleness much. He disliked it whenever she came to Timothy's defense because it meant the boy would win. Nevertheless, he stopped pushing and listened.

"The world is moving forward whether we like it or not. Either we embrace gender equality, or we wither and die," said Riva.

"I don't know," the Bishop replied, assuming the didactic airs. "We don't need to be gimmicky and appeal to the world on its terms. And, if they aren't buying the Kingdom wares we are selling, we need to shake the dust off our shoes."

"That sounds harsh," Riva had said, and Timothy had echoed the sentiments. But, she continued, "If people are not buying what we are selling, maybe we need to improve our packaging. That doesn't change what's inside, does it?"

"No, but nowhere do we see an example from the master. On the contrary, he made an effort to be obtuse so that only those who were willing to work for it would get it."

Riva shook her head, "Even after we embellish the packaging, people will need to open the container. It's the only way to get to what's on the inside. That's work. First, we throw the burning bush out there. People still need to turn towards it and take off their shoes. That's work! We are not gatekeepers. Our job is to invite, and to invite well at that."

Bishop Hooper could not argue against this. So they continued dinner. The father was sulking, but the mother and the son enjoyed their meal in good spirits.

QUORUM

"I think that's a great suggestion, mother Bishop," one of the elders said, using their endearing title for Riva.

"What suggestion?" the Bishop asked as he walked into the church board meeting. He was 25 or so minutes late to the monthly undertaking. Next to his wife was the hollow space meant for him. She sat at the end of the table in his usual spot. The long brown table looked lopsided like that. The Bishop proceeded to sit down, jostling his wife out of her end table spot.

"Aaaah, Bishop, welcome, welcome. Your wonderful wife just pointed out how we all bring our wives to the board meetings as leaders. And how they participate minimally in the conversations here. But the fact that we bring them means we are willing to acknowledge they make a huge part of the leadership here. And that we let them speak also means we already consider their input as valuable. She suggested we might be missing out on more by not acknowledging the same on a more public scale."

"What happened to wives being silent in the church, and only consulting and speaking with their husbands when they are at home?" The Bishop asked

"Well, with all due respect, Bishop." The chair replied, "Our wives speak and have spoken for years in this board. Even though they don't speak as much as the men."

"Well, we allow that, and that's alright." The Bishop said

One of the ladies in the meeting spoke up. "I think mother Bishop is saying if you allow it on a smaller scale, you might do better to allow it on a larger scale."

"Why, what for?" The Bishop shot back.

"To empower more people, Bishop. And to acknowledge our being equal in the eyes of the Lord." one of the elders said, smiling at how they would be doing the Lord's work by making this possible at the church.

"If we add the rest of what Mother Bishop was saying, we would most certainly be the real ILLEST." one of the other elders chimed in.

"What other suggestions are you talking about?" The Bishop asked.

"She thought we need to discuss flying the rainbow flag to show we are a welcoming and safe place." Someone replied. The Bishop did not even recognize the voice which responded. Whoever it was, noticed the look on the Bishop's face and quickly backtracked. "I thought you had discussed this at home." he had said.

"Why do you look shocked?" one of the elders asked. The Bishop did not want to admit they had not discussed the matter. He did not want to reveal that his wife had sprung this on him and the board.

"Well, if you are for it, Bishop, we can continue the discussion another day. We have a lot to think about already from these few remarks. But we have the budget to work through. Also, it's always best to think about things before discussing them. So let's take some time to think and pray, and we will pick up this conversation next month."

The Bishop was still in shock, "I'm sad to have missed the beginning of today's meeting. If you don't mind my asking, we usually don't start the meeting until I'm here since I'm the Bishop. What happened today?" The Bishop asked.

"Oh, Mother Bishop reminded us that I was the chair and that we had a quorum. She said she would brief you just as you brief her at times when she isn't in the meeting."

THE DERRINGER

When the meeting was over, the ladies gathered around Riva animatedly. The Bishop was pow-wowing with the board chair. The other men had formed their group discussing this, that, and the third. Riva had quickly answered her questions from the ladies. Then, finally, she encouraged them to stand their ground on the matter they had started and left to make some food for her husband.

When he arrived home, Bishop Hooper was fuming. The Bishop opened the door and was smacked by the aroma of delicious food. He had to work hard to stay angry, but he was less angry now than when he opened the door. "Sit down, honey; the food is almost ready. Timothy is out gaming with his friends." Riva said from the kitchen.

There was a lot for the Bishop to take in. First, there was a friendly and warm welcome from his wife. She looked like whatever had happened earlier had been washed away. Water under a bridge flowing gloriously and joyously towards the ocean. A place where all the puny ills would dissipate in the large volume of water. Then there was the aroma that made his knees weak with anticipation. He had rushed with no breakfast to answer a family emergency. He had only left that house call after 2 pm, only to be late for the board meeting. And then there was Timothy. He was out with his gamer friends, which made him anxious about how they were influencing his son. And then his anger at being blindsided.

The Bishop sat down; then, he stood up. He cleared his throat, and Riva paused whatever she was doing. "Would you like me to stop and listen?" she asked. "No," Bishop Hooper had replied, hungry, angry, sitting down again. Moments later;

"Alright, come make your plate," Riva said, standing aside and holding a plate.

Bishop Hooper got up, unsure of what to do. He wanted to compliment her on the smell of the food and tell her she looked beautiful as she stood there waiting for him to go first. He only managed to give her a long and appreciative kiss on the cheek. Tears threatened to come to his eyes with the kiss, and he felt like Judas Iscariot. His smile was weak and mournful, sad at what was coming later. He made a plate, and he sat down. She fixed her plate and joined him at the table. They sat down, and joining hands; he said grace. And they dug into the sumptuous dinner. Later after dinner and after helping her clean up and put away some dishes, he cleared his throat. It was the "gong" to announce the talk they both anticipated.

* * *

"Quorum, really? That's what you used to blindside me and get your marriage and gender equality agenda onto the floor?" he said, sitting down at the kitchen table. He picked up the pepper shaker to fidget with.

"A technicality for the greater good," she replied, sitting down. She picked up the salt shaker and held on to it.

"What about the Kingdom good, Riva. What about the Kingdom Good?"

"Do you think I am not thinking about the great commission for a second? I want women to take part actively in this. I dream of everyone having an opportunity to hear the offer of true life. Regardless of sexual orientation."

"Aaaaaah, you can want what you want, Riva. It's hard when I am associated with it as though I endorse it. When you speak at the board meeting, you carry my authority. And I refuse to have my power abused like that." he said, shaking the pepper. It sprinkled on the table, and he froze for a second.

"Then separate us like I was asking. Stop making men the gatekeepers to the women's opinions. I bet you those women have many ideas and suggestions that even you would love to hear. But their husbands hold those ideas back from you and everyone else. But if we say it in the open, that women can speak, they can start speaking in their own authority." she said, getting up, tearing a paper towel, and coming back to sit down.

"But that's not how the Apostle Paul prescribed it to work," he said, receiving the paper towel and wiping the pepper off the table.

"You figure out the theology. I am saying I refuse to be a derringer in your pocket. I am a bazooka. Albeit a peaceful or peacekeeping bazooka, but a bazooka nonetheless." she slammed the salt shaker on the table.

He crumpled the paper towel in his hand.

* * *

The air hung between them, still. It was as if every atom in the room dared the other atoms to move. The derringer was her gift from his father. The small gun fit in her bag, and he sometimes carried it for her when she didn't have a bag or pockets. It was kept unloaded, but it was between them, a sign of remembering their glorious wedding day —a daily reminder of their commitment to one another and their roles in the relationship. The Bishop's father, the great Hooper man, had gifted her the family heirloom with the white bone. He had whispered to her the words, "Carry this for your husband, and give it to him to keep you safe." She had loved the gift, and Bishop Hooper had been a little jealous since he had eyes for the gun since he was young. And now she was using the gun as an analogy for something sad. It jolted them both a little, and Bishop Hooper calmed down. He rose, walked over to the trash drawer, and pulled it out. He sighed and gently placed the crumpled paper towel in the almost full bin. He turned around:

"Riva, my sweet, gentle bazooka. When the church looks like the world we live in, don't you see that's when the problems begin? Replicating the world's mores and customs in the church to attract people, really? It sounds counter to the mission of reforming the world."

She stood up, "We are not here to reform the world. We are here to make disciples. And if, in doing so, the world is reformed, then great. But if it isn't that's, alright. As long as disciples are made."

"Yes, I agree with you," he said, coming over, placing his hands on her upper arms, and holding her to reassure her. "Let me find the right words. I can see and relate to the derringer analogy. You are not in my pocket, love. And I am willing to think about it some more. But to endorse sin, Riva, to fly the flag. You don't see the problem with that?"

"Maybe it's endorsing, or maybe it's simply becoming a welcoming, friendly presence. How else will we convert people if they never come through the door?" She said, sighing.

"I think it's better to call a spade a spade. It's best to call a sin a sin. That's what love does, don't you think?" He asked, pulling her into his embrace.

"That does not sound like love. Loving others is not persecuting and condemning others in the name of helping them. It's not tormenting others by pruning them or weeding their garden. It's not this constant stoic and logical pursuit of right and hammering people about it," Riva spoke with a muffled voice. Bishop Hooper heard it all. He pushed her just far enough to look her in the face.

"Maybe so," the man replied, putting on his didactic airs. "But people are always good at saying what things are not. So instead of telling me what it is not, tell me what love is. And don't say God is love."

She noted his tone, took a step back, and disentangled herself. "Let's sit down for this one." They both sat down. He reached for the pepper, and she snatched it before he did. Then she grabbed the salt as well and looked him in the eye. "Love is uprooting in you the things which would hurt and harm others. That is what it looks like to take care of others! It's growing to become incorruptible like God. You don't grow like that by weeding someone else's garden. It's only possible when you keep your eyes on the log in your eye. When you keep your lips away from slander, persecution, and condemnation. But keep them deep in prayer and meditation upon the word."

The Bishop was astounded by the wisdom his wife had just delivered. He always led their home bible studies. He led the church ones as well. He had not heard her teach much, and he felt a tinge of shame at that moment. She was supposed to be his best friend, but he treated her like a personal assistant. But shame rarely produces goodness as in this situation. He felt angry at himself and did not let her words continue melting his heart. He replied instead;

"If you are so enlightened, why do you side with Timothy against the Bible?" He was referring to a plethora of arguments with his son." Without the pepper, his hands struggled to find a place in the air, on the table, on his face.

"I don't side with Timothy or anyone. I side with letting people be. God leaves us to be without forcing, tricking, or manipulating us. He invites people to trust Him and allows us to respond in whatever way.

Instead of trying to guilt-trip people, scare them, or shame them so they can believe. I am all for leaving them alone to grow in their own time. You can't force freedom and life on anyone. It's just another kind of tyranny at that point." Riva replied, slamming both the pepper and the salt on the table.

These accusations saddened Bishop Hooper. That was because he believed he never shamed or guilt-tripped people and was far from being a tyrant.

"I'm sad you think I shame and guilt-trip people."

"No, love, that's not what I am saying," she said, reaching to hold his hands to reassure him. But, instead, he pulled his hands away from hers, and she paused, sad. She thought her zeal to share her opinion had pushed him away.

"I am only saying that we need to invite people in if we want to convert them. And then, like the sun, we need to love them and gently coax them, so they bloom and transform or re-form if you like. We can't expect them to be repented when they come in; otherwise, why do we exist. And we can't expect them to change on day one. People need time; even nature takes nine months to bring human life to term. So why not give everyone as much time, if not even more. From the day they come into the church to the day they repent; from whatever sin you believe, they need to repent." she added, smiling playfully.

"What if it takes forever. Should we live with sin in the church?" The Bishop asked, leaning back in his chair and folding his arms.

"What, we don't already live with sin currently?" Riva shot back, raising her eyebrows.

"I meant openly. You know what I mean, living with sin out in the open."

"Aaah, you want it hidden. Does it work better for you when it is hidden?"

"It's impossible to reason with you when you get this way." the Bishop replied, getting up and throwing his arms up in surrender.

"I am not the one who is making logically inconsistent statements. Also, I am not the one who feels like ad hominem attacks will help him." Riva replied, then quickly switched to a new subject. "Coffee? I bought some of that cinnamon pound cake you love."

The Bishop was angry, but he loved cinnamon pound cake. And it went well with coffee after a delicious dinner. He mumbled something, and Riva got up smiling and put together the desert.

THE SERMON

Timothy kept growing in his involvement at the ILLEST. The conversation around marriage and gender equality was growing in the church simultaneously. As expected, it caused stark divisions, and neither side wanted to talk to the other. Accusations flew across the aisle, and they gossiped about one another, making up stories of what "they" must be thinking and believing the stories they made up. They were like a novelist who wrote fiction, thought it to be true, and started attacking windmills and baobab trees because they were dragons. The incestuous conversation in the siloed camps led to the incredible, outlandish characterization of one another. Even the Bishop did not know how to reconcile the two sides and bring them to dialogue with each other. The thought of the two camps emerging in his house was terrifying. The stories he was hearing about one camp's concept of the other were untenable. It would not be easy to bring both camps to the table of communion with the divine and have a productive time together. Heaven was going to be awkward if this continued.

The Bishop began to contemplate moving to the village-state of Uzu. A weird traveler passing through the town had told him about it. The man had cool dreadlocks, the name of a Lion, and claimed to be from Zawe. The Bishop trusted that the man knew what he was talking about when talking about Uzu. The rest of the world only knew of Uzu from rumors and maps of Zawe, the land between the two rivers. He might be able to stop the inevitable by going to Uzu. He was concerned that Riva would soon ask for a divorce from him. Especially since he was so conservative in his views and she was progressive, and the prevailing logic meant he was an irredeemable monster on the wrong side of history.

Timothy had connected the church with groups of youth groups from all over Arizona. The Flagstaff team was leading the conversation. They were organizing a camp that would bring young people together from all over the state. And the Bishop had volunteered to be the grown-up point person for the conversation. Unfortunately, he had missed out on the acronym - the ILLEST. So now Bishop Hooper wanted to share some of the credit for this camp coming together. With all this on his mind that week, he preached about forgetting our worries.

> "Do not be anxious about anything. Fear not, little flock, for it is your father's good pleasure to give you the Kingdom. So, sell off your possessions...stay dressed for action and keep your lamps burning."
>
> The carpenter's words sounded more radical as he journeyed closer to his death. The words he spoke demanded more of the listeners. Even Peter had to ask, "Lord, are you telling this parable for us or for all?" Peter began to wonder how the riff-raff of that time could obey such stringent words. He must have wondered why his master's tone sounded like he was speaking to everyone. This was a word for the chosen 12 at most, Peter thought. But Jesus did not respond. He kept going...."

The Bishop's phone rang, disturbing the sermon. The Flagstaff team called for the umpteenth time about the camp arrangements. The Bishop was exasperated. He had placed the phone in front of him to use as a timer and had forgotten to silence it. And now it was disturbing the moment of his punchline and diluting his impact. The horror! Flustered and annoyed, he silenced the handheld machine and composed himself. Then he continued attempting to re-capture the tone and atmosphere before the phone rang,

> "Jesus kept going as I will," he said, and people laughed. "Jesus kept going because the question was

irrelevant. The word is for those who see it fit in their lives. It is for all but not for all. It is sown in all the land, but it takes root and grows well only in the ready soil. The net is let down in the entire river. It sweeps to the very depths of the river, but it catches only the fish that swim into it. Are you the one for whom these words are meant? Some think because they are in this auditorium, they are automatically chosen. But if you ask, 'Are these for us or for all, ' you might be missing the whole point. If you have decided these words are only for you or for us and not the rest of the world, you are also missing the point. Peter was missing the whole point even though he was one of those on the "inside." The invitation into this life is for every living soul."

Displeased by the call, the Bishop needed a sacrificial lamb when the sermon was over. He stepped down and signaled to his son about who was calling. They signed that they would discuss it later.

The service went on, and then it came to an end. The Bishop made his way down the aisle as usual. His eyes avoided people but still tried to make eye contact simultaneously. Had his words hit home? Did the phone call mess up his choreography of language? He stopped at the door as usual. He stood there to shake everyone's hand as they left. And then he walked to his son with murder in his heart and a sarcastic smile on his face. "Your people are quite exhausting. Trying to make sure all their plans are in place for the winter retreat." He said, fiddling with candles and other paraphernalia.

"Father, they have so many different youth groups coming together. They are only making sure they get these kids again next year. So, everything has to go through without a hitch."

"Well, their problem is not my problem!" the Bishop said

"Hmmm, it depends if these problems are for them only or for all people," the son replied

His father stopped everything he was doing. He looked at the son with

144

fierceness in his eyes. He felt like a hypocrite caught in his own words. "I guess we will have to make sure everything is in great shape for them then. Of course, you will be coming with me to every one of the drives up Imogene Pass. You can watch over my preparations for them in person."

Timothy, the boy of 16, was not happy about this. The camp was not too far away, but it was a long drive because the road up was a winding mountain pass road. Moreover, they did not have cell service on most of the drives up. Without cell service, they could not stream music, and Timothy could not play his video games on his phone. But of course, he put up a soldier's face. He had landed himself this gig with his mouth.

"I'll be happy to serve. You know how hard it is to get young people together. Each congregation has like 3-5 young kids or even young adults these days. Having them all in one place helps with friendships, dating, and more. At this point, I wonder why churches bother with denominations. It's isolating for the few young people." He said, referring to their church. Though interfaith or interdenominational, ILLEST was still exclusive in various tenets.

The father looked again at his son, seething. He had criticized his son's choice of friends often. But there was a small selection of young people in their church. The small pool made friend-making a challenge, so his son had to find friends and dates at school. Or worse, online, and he ended up with some interesting characters.

PUNISHMENT

The father only gave the son a stink eye and walked away. They walked home one after the other like an army marching in a single file.

After lunch, father and son drove up the Imogene hill, one of the many hills which made up the Gray Mountain range. They were on an errand to send pictures to the morning callers. A pictorial map of the camp could help them better prepare for activities.

* * *

Because of their tension, the father had resorted to playing music. A third of the way up the hill, the young man's streaming service stopped working as there was no coverage. They were streaming gospel songs and had none downloaded. He had only downloaded the secular rap songs, which he enjoyed. Without cell service, they switched to regular radio.

They had to switch from FM to AM halfway up the mountain pass. And soon, even that was useless. So, they were driving in silence when the road turned to gravel. After that, the ascent got bumpy and even slower. Imogene pass was ill-maintained, but it worked for this 4-wheel drive 4runner.

They finally got to camp with tense silence surrounding them. The father wondered how to get through to the son. The son wondered how his father ever became an ILLEST Bishop. The man seemed more suited to being a corrections offiver of a juvenile detention center. Pictures were taken as the father tried to be funny, but the boy was sulky. This trip was a punishment for his smart-aleck comment. It was a punishment for connecting Bishop Hooper with the Flagstaff team. Timothy was being punished for bringing together the church with people who could use their empty camp and pay the church.

To send pictures over, they had two choices. One was to walk to the cliff on the east side and get cell service. This option was a beautiful nature walk. Or they could head down, which was a long ride to cell coverage. Walking with his father in the beautiful forest to the cliff was unpalatable for the boy. Even his father could not impose on him to make the short trek though he tried. So, they headed down, back, towards the church where home was.

The two had been up and down the mountain several times before camp. Pride held fast, and the father could not find a way to release his son from the punishment while saving face. Timothy had not forgotten why they were driving up together. A week before camp, they went with a crew from the church to clean up and prepare the place even further. The weather had been excellent, and Bishop Hooper saw his son enjoy the camp with some of the other fathers present. He watched as his son smiled and laughed and roughhoused with these men. It brought tears to his eyes. He did not know whether to be jealous or happy for his son.

The snow that came the next day was a surprise to everyone, including the weather woman. She had given the Sunday update for that week, and 'all sunny skies' was her winter forecast for this area of Arizona. So, when the snow came hard and fast on Monday, everyone was surprised. The Flagstaff people called again to check if the mountain road was still viable with the snow. And the Bishop responded, "I don't control the weather. But I am confident that this snowstorm will be over tomorrow."

And it was. The Bishop felt like he did control the weather. The rest of the week was beautiful and sunny. Flagstaff made no more calls, and the Bishop was delighted for both. Then Saturday came to a head up the mountain to welcome the Flagstaff people. The father was in a good mood, happy for a week of not being bothered. And, of course, the son had to come with him. Timothy wasn't pleased about the situation as usual. He lost sight of how he had helped bring these young people together. He forgot to celebrate the prospect of having more peers around.

The two went through their usual stages. Streaming music, FM radio, AM, and then silence. As they got higher, they started seeing pockets of unmelted snow. Finally, they hit the gravel and started seeing some ice patches. The altitude and shadows of the mountain had not allowed the snow to melt entirely. The week of warm, pleasant weather did not do much to help with this. The driving got slower and rougher than usual as they continued their ascent. In the silence of the slow and arduous trek, the father finally spoke, "Why do we have to stream the music you play? You know you can download music to your phone, right? I am paying for the premium streaming service. You can download the music; you know that, right?"

Timothy felt insulted, "I know I can download music, Dad. I have tons of music downloaded here." He instantly regretted his response. The tone of his voice had been enough to continue the fight the father had started—the war they had been waging with each other for years now. At that moment, the boy wished he had done the whole 'Gentle answer calms anger thing.'

* * *

"Is that so? Let's play what you have downloaded then, shall we."

"Ummm, maybe let's focus on driving, Dad," the boy said, not striking the right tone again.

"I can drive and listen to music. What are you saying?"

"Nothing, dad, just that maybe silence is okay." he was trying to backtrack. And this made Bishop Hooper suspicious.

"What music do you have downloaded, son? Show me what you have."

The boy did not move. Instead, he remained slumped in his chair, terrified.

"Let me see!" the father demanded.

"No," the boy replied defiantly.

"I paid for that phone, and I pay for that music service. Show me what you have on my phone, boy?" the father vociferated.

"The church paid for the phone and for everything we have," Timothy replied. Again, another unfortunate statement. Especially for someone trying to get away with having the "wrong" music on his phone.

And so, the father snatched the phone from the boy, who immediately tried to reach back for it. Timothy unfastened his seat belt to reach further. He was fighting for the right to hide his secret from his father.

Even with Timothy reaching and his father shielding, the treacherous gravel road might have been navigable. However, the vehicle hit an unexpected large ice patch. The car skidded, then lost traction and dove-tailed backward. The father tried to engage four-wheel drive, but it was too late. The car tipped over the side of the road, and it rolled over the short drop on the side of the mountain pass. It would have rolled further down had it not been slowed down and stopped by a heap of slow-melting snow. The impact was loud as metal crunched. The impact rendered Bishop Hooper and Timothy unconscious.

TO CAMP OR NOT TO CAMP

The camp organizers were rushing to camp to prepare to receive the campers. The campers were meeting in the parking lot of a chain store to board one bus together. One bus meant they would arrive like an avalanche, and the organizers needed to be ready.

These organizers were in their van filled with supplies. They also had registration packets and materials to kick off camp that very day.

"Do those look recent to anyone?" the driver asked as they rolled to the ice patch. They had noticed some tire marks heading over the edge.

"Yeah," someone chimed in, concerned.

The person on the front passenger's seat looked over the edge of the road and exclaimed,

"There is a car; there is a car!!"

The van stopped, and they all disembarked. One of them with a hatchet. She went to work on the ice, breaking it apart.

"What are you doing?" the driver asked.

"Division of labor," this young youth minister replied. "You all check out the car while I prevent us and everyone behind us from sliding as they did."

"Smart," someone called out from the edge of the road.

"What would be smart is to call 911," someone else called out. The same voice was heard yelling down the ravine a second later, "Is there anyone in the car? Tap on something metal if you can't speak."

They all paused in silence. They were straining to catch any sounds from the car.

* * *

"Maybe they walked out of the car."

"I doubt that," the hatchet lady said, looking down at the upside-down car. She had made quick work of the ice and was now standing by the road's edge. "The windows are smashed but not enough to let anyone out, and the doors are still closed," she remarked.

"I don't have any bars on my phone," someone said, "But I see a path down. It's windy and looks roundabout, though, which may take some time to make it down."

"We are already behind time, and camp desperately needs to kick off well this year. Since we have done the ice and we don't have cell service. Let's head up and call 911 from camp. We can kill two birds with one stone. We can be at camp on time to welcome everyone and also call 911." someone suggested. They had been working on this camp for months, and they were afraid to start with this hitch. They all piled back into the van and drove on.

THE CONVOY

Later a small convoy of parents and volunteers were driving up Imogene Pass. They all came up to the ice, and it looked actively axed. The first two cars made nothing of the ground disturbance in the area. Then, finally, the third car down noticed the skid marks, and the driver, Neil, a science teacher, stopped his vehicle. He honked for everyone to stop as well.

The leading driver was the minister at the church that Niel attended. He wasn't happy that Neil was taking charge again.

"What now?" he asked, walking towards Neil's car.

"I am stopping to check out the disturbance on the road's edge. It looks like someone may have gone over the edge there."

"Well, Neil, I'll be..." The pastor stopped as Neil looked at him with a sideways glance. He was daring the pastor to finish the sacrilegious statement.

Annette, the minister from another church, came up from the 4th car in the caravan.

"What's the matter?" she asked. The minister looked at her and interrupted Niel who had started replying.

"Nothing to concern yourself with. Neil had another one of his scientific hunches. It's a man's job, though, so don't worry." he ended, dismissing Annette as he usually did. He was uncomfortable with the idea of female ministers.

And then finally, the driver of the 7th and last car in convoy caught up with everybody panting.

"Did you...did you..." he panted, "see the" he swallowed. "car," he ended, pointing in the direction of the crash.

For a minute, everyone froze, then they scurried into positions of concern. Two people were dialing 911 in an exercise in futility. The lead minister was yelling at the car.

Though not too long, the drop and the impeding brush around made it a daunting task to get down to the car. It was possible, but who would try?

Neil assessed the situation and said, "We need a cutlass to cut through those bushes. Plus, neither of us is a professional at wilderness rescue. And the car hasn't burst into flames and looks intact."

"Finally, some useful information," the lead minister retorted, agreeing disagreeably. "It sounds like you are saying there isn't much we can do for them besides call 911. Let's go find some cell service." he finished loudly, heading back to his car and angry that they had stopped for futile reasons.

Everyone else proceeded back into their cars. Annette was the only one left standing at the road's edge. She spotted the winding path and signaled Neil to come back out. He walked over to her as the other cars squeezed around theirs. She pointed out the path to him, and he shrugged, afraid of further incurring the pastor's wrath. Eventually, all the cars went around them, and they had to shrug and follow those in charge.

THE BUS

The bus finally came through. All the campers were singing together and having a good time. They varied in age from first-year students in college to Seniors in high school. There were some outliers, of course, younger and older. But they were all grooving as one and having worshipful fun as they were coming around the mountain.

It was Roberto who noticed the wheels in the air. He thought of how cool it would be to have cars drive on top of upside-down cars. Imagine a road where the cars rolled on other car tires. He smiled to himself as he began to add more tires so the road would be contiguous —a seamless road flowing like a railway line. Fine-tuning the imaginary road, Roberto smiled and thought of rollerblades for some reason.

"What are you thinking about, Berto," Nancy asked her crush. She knew that he was always dreaming about something or another. She liked his weird thoughts and she liked him very much.

"Oh, nothing," he replied, not wanting to sound ridiculous.

"Come on?" she said, nudging him and making him blush. He liked her braids and smiled shyly.

"Did it take all night again to do your hair?" he asked her.

"Yeah, my aunt Monique came over to help too so I could be ready for camp."

"Cool, they look great," the boy said.

* * *

"And I bet whatever you were thinking was great. So tell me, you know I like your dorky thoughts," Nancy said, sidling up to him.

He didn't like that. So, he decided to sound as less weird as he could muster.

"Well, I was looking at that upside-down car and thinking..."

"What upside-down car?" Nancy asked, gasping loudly and silencing the whole bus unexpectedly.

Everyone on the bus looked at her and then in the direction she was looking. And they spotted it.

"What is it?"

The driver echoed the question every counselor on the bus was asking. And the bus came to a sudden halt.

The driver was first off the bus. "Whoa," his lips and mouth said before his voice caught on. The counselors followed. The last counselor off the bus looked back towards the kids standing at the threshold of the bus door. "Stay on the bus," she instructed them.

Nancy pushed her way to the front and disembarked.

"Nancy, I said stay on the bus," the counselor repeated emphatically. But the counselor's attention was divided between the bus and the car crash. She could not pause to make sure her instruction was followed. Instead, the other kids followed Nancy.

And then the gasps and the chatter began. The driver was yelling down at the car, hoping to get a response. One of the counselors was clambering around the rocks to get some bars on her cellphone. And the kids were trying to help the driver call to the car. It was chaotic.

One of the parents had tagged along on the bus. She finally took charge of the situation.

"Alright, do you have any cellphone bars up there?" she asked, looking

153

behind her. One of the counselors, an avid climber, had squirreled up a few rocks to call 911. She answered the mother, "No, no cell service here."

"Well, come down, and let's get those bruises cleaned and bandaged. You tried, and now we need to get to camp. There is cell coverage there, I am assuming. If not, we can regroup with the people who have gone ahead of us and see how we can organize help. I bet there is no one in that car anymore. So, everybody, come on, back on the bus."

"Everyone, back on the bus!" the counselors echoed, and the bus driver hopped back on. He turned the ignition, and the bus bellowed to life. As the bus idled, the embarkation onto the bus became a little more frantic for everyone. It was as though people were afraid of being left behind with the wreck below.

LESBOS THE ISLAND

"Time to hide from the big bad wolf," Kara said, giving Lane a reassuring shoulder squeeze.

"If only the old Island of Lesbos was close by. We would escape to it." Lane replied, grinning and patting Kara's hand.

"Time to time travel," Diana said, stepping on the gas and screaming, "Back to the future!" They all joined in the screaming and laughing. They were driving towards the Gray Mountains. Lane was in the shotgun seat beside Diana. Their hatchback was packed with everything they needed to enjoy a weekend up Imogene Hill. And to enjoy an extended stay if Lane needed it. They didn't use the truck because the pass would be clear of snow by this time of year.

"You know, I take back my use of the word escape," Lane said, "Let's call it a tactical withdrawal. We are not retreating, but we are advancing towards tomorrow's battle." Lane said, hoping Diana would approve.

"It's okay," Diana said, "It's okay to call it hiding. Hiding from the world, from the church and its persecution."

Lane had recently come out of the closet as non-binary. As a result, she faced some backlash from her church and her family.

"Mmmm, Amen, sister," Kara echoed as she was used to, having grown up in church. She was serious about her remark, but Lane and Diana exchanged looks as they tried to hold back laughter. They failed. Soon all three were giggling hysterically.

"Amen, the church is persecuting us. Amen!" Diana said, mocking Kara, who did not mind and added to the laughter.

The three lesbians were jamming. They enjoyed some of Kara's mixtapes on CD as they went up the mountain. Diana's grandparents had a cabin up Imogene Pass and not too far from the church camp. The family had parceled out its land years back and given some of it to the church. So, they knew the church people well since they still had some dealings with them over the land.

Diana recognized the body of the 4runner lying upside down in the cold ravine on the side of the road.

"Girls, girls, girls." she said, coming to a halt, "That's that pastor's car. What's his name? Hmmm," she snapped her fingers a couple of times and gave up. "What is it doing upside down?" she asked instead.

The girls gaped at the sight. Then, they all scrambled out of the car.

"Anyone down there?" Lane called out. "In hell?" Kara added in a whisper, and they all looked at each other and stifled some giggles.

"Come on, girls," Diana said, working on getting composed. "There may be people down there needing our help. It doesn't help that the snow is not all melted in that space. Let's get some warm stuff and get down there."

"What if there is no one there, and we carry and dirty our blankets for no reason?" Kara asked

* * *

"What if we get there and there are people. And we don't have the blankets." Diana replied

"I guess we need the first aid kit too," Lane added.

"Yeah, but we are forgetting. We are going on a retreat because of these pastors. And all their persecution."

Lane and Diana looked at Kara.

"And we are taking Lane on the retreat so she can regroup and choose her way of walking in the world given her coming out. We all need to pick a path. On the one hand, we can live out of anger and bitterness and stand militantly and ready for combat. But, on the other hand, we can choose to let go of the pain of rejection and stand with open arms to love those who scorn us?" Diana finished and turned around to dig for the first aid kit.

Lane looked at Kara, who made a facial expression questioning the speech. Lane shrugged. "It sounds like why I'm here." she mouthed and whispered simultaneously.

"That's right; it's why we are all here." Diana added, "Tactical regrouping remember. To martial, our invisible forces and get our armies standing at the ready. Then, maneuvering them into whatever stance suits us best – peace or war. I believe love works way better at changing the world. It works way better than any rules of conduct and better than fighting someone for my rights or freedoms."

"Come oooooooonnn," Kara moaned and then caught herself. This wasn't about her; it was about Lane. And for Lane's sanity, she would believe some hogwash for a weekend.

"So how are we getting down there. I don't see a good path from here?" Kara asked

"Oh no, we are not going that way," Diana replied, "My family has owned this land for generations. I practically grew up here. Going down that way is impossible. We will take the back path over there. It winds down, and you can see it pop up over there. Do you see it?

* * *

"Oh, yeah," Kara replied, following her gaze and index finder.

"Where do you see it?" Lane asked, leaning on Kara and Diana as they pointed to the different spots on the mountainside where the path popped into view. They followed her through the roundabout path and finally made it to the car.

"Whew, it's chilly down here," Diana remarked.

"That's right, girl," Kara echoed. " And there are people in the car, y'all"

"Must be the pastor and some of the church people. Bishop Hooper!" Diana exclaimed excitedly. "That his name, Bishop Hooper."

"Poor Bishop Hooper," said Lane

"Them church people," Kara said quietly, shaking her head.

And they walked around the car in the crunchy snow mixed with ice.

"It's a boy," Kara said to everyone waiting for her to report who was trapped with the pastor.

"Aaaaaand, it looks like there are only two people.

The doors weren't jammed but required some effort to open. More force than the three ladies could muster. After trying for 10 minutes, they all were bent over, panting, and wondering what to do. Finally, Kara came up with the idea to go in through the windows instead. It meant some cuts, but it was doable. They smashed the windows clean and crawled into the upside-down car. They cut the seat belt holding the pastor up and helped him down. He came to when his head hit the roof of the vehicle. He moaned, then gasped for air and tried to yell, "Timothy, Timothy," but only managed to croak.

Timothy was more banged up. He seemed reanimated as they pulled him out of the car, his head bleeding but quieted down quickly. Both survivors were unconscious and cold to the touch. It seemed they hadn't broken any limbs. The ladies wrapped them up in warm fleece blankets and then dragged them up the roundabout way. It was slow going, and the sun had long crossed over the noon mark heading towards the mountains to rest. The three ladies were scraped and scratched all over by the bushes.

It took them a while, but they made it to the mountain road where the weak winter sun shone. As they were panting and resting, Lane remarked, "We look so red, you would think we were in the accident too."

"Well, not Kara," Diana responded, winking. Kara was the only one who wasn't red from the lightly bleeding scratches.

"Leave me and my melanin alone," Kara responded, grinning.

"I wish I had beautiful skin as you do!" Diana replied, smiling back.

"Me too," Lane jumped in, "Alright, what's next fearless leader?" Lane asked Diana.

"Well, I think we should take them down to the hospital ourselves, no? They look like they need immediate attention. If we try to get medics up here, it will be a while before we can even get to a spot with cell service to call them. And long before they get here."

The three ladies looked at their full hatchback. Lane and Kara sighed, "What we do for them church people!" Lane said, reading Kara's mind.

The three ladies proceeded to empty their hatchback to make room for the two men. Diana would drive, and one of the two ladies would ride on the passenger side. The boy in the back seat and the pastor squeezed in the trunk.

Kara volunteered to stay with their belongings while the other two drove to the hospital.

It was a warm day outside, weak sun or not. But on their way down, they cranked up the AC. The two ladies were sweating profusely. They endured it as they tried to warm up their unconscious passengers with the hot air.

* * *

As soon as they reached cell coverage, they called the hospital to get ready to receive them. They spotted a cop on the road and stopped. They then shared with her the news, and she lit up her lights, switched on the siren, and led the way.

The doctors say the two would have likely died of hypothermia had the ladies not been there. They both had head injuries, with Timothy having more severe injuries than his father. But it was the cold that would have gotten them.

A LIFE FOR A LIFE

A LIFE FOR A LIFE

A LIFE FOR A LIFE

This was the title of the special sermon for the day the Bishop would return to work. The day the three women who saved him and his son would visit. The day the whole congregation waited for with trepidation. What would be the conclusion of the debate which they had been having? People were waiting for the verdict on the questions surrounding marriage equality and allowing women to serve in the church.

Bishop Hooper had spent three weeks in the hospital and three weeks at home taking a break. But who takes a break from the work of the Lord? He heard the conversations the church and its board were having. How inclusive they wanted to become. Some hoped the accident would soften Bishop Hooper's stance and change his mind.

When they heard the sermon's title, they expected some words which reflected this softening.

Lane, Kara, and Diana had driven from the city. On the way up, Kara kept saying, "I want a medal, y'all"

* * *

And while Lane would laugh, Diana would not tire of asking back, "What for?"

Kara would reply with variations of, "Look girl, we done saved that man's life. He is like their president, am I right? We saved their president. We deserve medals!"

That Sunday, they walked into the church, heroines. They not only felt like it, but the people welcomed them warmly. They received a standing ovation when they stepped into the building. Most people stood up, and many people wanted to talk to them. Bishop Hooper's wife, Riva, had met them at the hospital, so they knew each other. The three ladies gravitated towards her. She was grateful for their choice to sit with her. She welcomed all three women with hugs and kisses like in France.

"Mmmm, bougie?" Kara murmured

"No, it's a Holy Kiss," the Bishop's wife shot back with a playful glint in her eye.

They talked a little more and finally sat down as the mass began.

The songs they sang were of joy and celebration. They were hymns of being saved and receiving a second chance at life. The music recalled the salvation of the Bishop and his son by the three lesbians.

Then soon, it was time for the sermon.

"A life for a life"
"Many have tried to reinterpret the letter to the Romans. " The Bishop began, "For example, trying to make it sound like the practice of homosexuality is wrong. But being a celibate homosexual is not. Well, I say, Jesus is concerned with our hearts. You may not steal, but if you are a thief at heart, it still counts against you. But to make matters challenging, the book of Numbers is unequivocal...

The tension in the building seemed to threaten to push the building apart. Some church members claim they heard the building crack in many places; as it strained to hold in the tense atmosphere. Some were seething, and others nodded self-righteously.

"It's the word; it's not me."

The Bishop was saying.

"Do not be angry at me. I am only the messenger."

And Kara stood up. She paused as she looked at the Bishop, resisting the gesture everyone on her side had in mind. She shuffled to the aisle and started walking towards the exit. The Bishop paused his delivery, and a hollow silence ensued. Kara's steps echoed in the packed auditorium. Diana got up and ran after her friend.

Lane was left sitting next to the Bishop's wife. She was on the other side of the pew without an exit and felt stuck. Her only way out was to say, "Excuse me," to the woman who had shown her genuine kindness for saving her husband and son. To walk away from a woman who welcomed all three of them with genuine expressions of friendship. That morning, the Bishop's wife did not look like she knew how the sermon would be that day. So, Lane remained sitting and even reached out to hold the Bishop's Wife's hand. Riva appreciated the gesture.

"And so, a life for a life," The Bishop continued, grateful that at least Lane had stayed. His message would have been wasted if all three women had left. "a life...my life, was saved by the most amazing kindness. It reminds you of the story of the good Samaritan. The purpose of the story of the Samaritan was to make people realize how neighbors act and then copy. That people come before our work even work for the Lord. People come before our comfort, and people come before our plans. If serving God gets in the way of being considerate of people, you may need to re-examine. If you have a gift prepared for God but realize you had an unresolved issue with another person. Go first and resolve that issue and then come back to offer your gift. This is how the equation works. People first! Though the Samaritan matters, what matters more is being a neighbor. And today, I am being a neighbor by sharing this word of life. So, I may save those who saved my life..."

AFTERMATH

Meanwhile, Diana had caught up with Kara.

"Hey, hey, stop. We drove up here together, and we are leaving together?"

"Well, I am leaving. Are you coming?" Kara asked, stopping but tapping her foot with impatience.

"I am not leaving, so neither are you."

"You really can't tell me we have to sit there and take what he is dishing out like that."

"I agree. We don't have to take it. We have to leave people to carry their garbage without us helping them."

"What are you saying, Ms. Wisdom?"

"Diana's eye flashed briefly, and Kara slowed her roll a little.

"A wise man once said to someone who insulted him. Suppose someone buys you a gift and brings it to you, but you refuse to take it. To whom does the gift belong?"

"Of course, it belongs back with whoever bought me the gift," Kara replied angrily. Her thoughts had gone back to an ex-boyfriend. The one whose proposal she had turned down when she was about to come out of the closet. The gorgeous diamond ring had stayed with him.

"Exactly, you don't need to carry what he offers you. Even the people in every church can leave without the sermon touching them. They can leave without carrying the words home. I think it is a weekly occurrence."

* * *

This made Kara pause and smile reluctantly. She liked poking fun at church people.

"If them church people can do it every week..." Diana said, catching the wave of cheer and surfing it. She used Kara's vocabulary and maximized her punchline. "We can do it too for this one week." Diana finished and giggled subduedly. They were still close to the church building, so she didn't want to laugh aloud.

"But it's hard to do all that, Diana," Kara said with a tone of one placated.

"It is very hard, I agree. So, we do the hard things hard, and the easy stuff we do easy."

"If it's hard, do it hard, and if it's easy, do it easy," Kara repeated, sighing. She closed her eyes to breathe and center herself and said, "I have lived this all my life. First, it was my gender, then the color of my skin, and then my sexual orientation. It gets hard to ignore the noise. To shut it all out and keep walking."

"And they are all just opinions, though, Kara. Wrong ones too!"

"You have the luxury of calling them opinions. But, to me, they are facts of life."

"Okay, yes, the way you have been - we have been treated - is a fact of life. But these people are acting out of wrong opinions and not facts. We should be able to act like people who believe the facts. People who believe that we are able, equal, and powerful."

"Easy for you to say?" Kara replied, referring to Diana's skin. She passed for white despite being light-skinned Asian Hispanic. Her family on the Hispanic side owned the land up Imogene Pass.

"And it will be easy for you to say too when you finally stop thinking you need anybody's permission. You don't need anyone's permission to be able, equal, and powerful. Sure, people will give you strange looks. But will you stand there and say you haven't given other people looks for being different? So, stop asking the world to change for you.

You don't need its permission."

"I don't know about that because society tends to control our actions." Kara replied.

"In my opinion, society only controls people who have become its slaves. It controls people who are slaves to its opinions. Society controls people subjugated by its trends and those trapped by the need for its approval. As able, equal, and powerful people, we set the trends and create our own opinions about ourselves. And we live by them...."

"With the help of God," the Bishop added calling from the door.

Mass was over, and as custom, he was the first out the door to get ready to shake the hand of each person leaving. He had caught the last part of the conversation and was eager to join in. Bishop Hooper was anxious to save the lives of these women who had saved his.

Diana looked back, startled, and Kara scowled and walked away.

TEACHING THE TEACHER

Riva remained seated with Lane holding her hand. The church emptied quickly as people tried to avoid each other. No one knew which side anyone was on, and so to avoid confrontation, they left quickly. No one commented on the sermon even though it was on everyone's mind. Timothy did not know how to feel. But he wasn't surprised by his father. He walked out of the church feeling sorry for the ladies who had saved them.

The Bishop walked back into the echoing empty building towards Lane and his wife. He was pleased with himself.

"So, what do you think?" he asked Lane.

Lane was stammering, trying to find words to tell the Bishop to take a hike politely. They were in a church building, so she chose her words carefully. She could not leave because Riva would not let go of her hand.

"You see, I am grateful for you saving my life and my son's life. And as a token of my appreciation, I prepared that sermon. It would be sad that such kind and wonderful people would be cast out of eternal rest."

It made some sense, Lane thought. She disagreed, but she could see where the man was coming from. Diana had taught her well. She could sit and listen to this man who was oblivious to how hurtful he had been. Clueless of how he had done the opposite of appreciating them for saving his life.

"Listen," he said, "Listen. I understand that it may take time for you to see the truth. And I am willing to walk with you to the light. My wife reminded me a couple of weeks ago to take it slow. It seems we've lost the appreciation for slow brewing mastery in today's world of hacks. We live in a "5 ways to" and "3 steps to" world. We have lost sight of the slow brewing relationships and slow brewing discipleship. Some convictions like tea need to be steeped to lead to spiritual growth. So, you will see soon that I was right about sharing this sermon today."

Riva scowled, which startled the Bishop.

He decided to add some words of gentle affirmation. "I know you will find the right path, Lane. I am grateful for you and want you always to know I preach out of love to help others grow. It's not personal, per se, but I am on a mission, doing my job."

"Your job today was to appreciate these women," Riva interjected. They saved your life, love. They rescued you and my dear Timothy. And you slapped them in the face with the Bible."

"It's my job to kick people in the butt, Riva!" He replied impatiently and raised his voice.

She stood up, "And who kicks you in the butt. Am I kicking you right now? Are you enjoying it? Is it helping?"

Lane, too, stood up. She wanted to walk away but didn't know how, even though her hand was free now.

"What then is my job as a preacher if it's not challenging people but letting them be in their sin?"

"Are you not a sinner yourself, or has the Bishop title gotten to your head? Your job, our job as disciple-makers, is to tell people the good news. Let them know that they are so loved that their father sent his son to die for them. And once they fully grasp that fact, they will want to know more. And when they truly know God, they will want to be in a relationship with him. They will stop wanting to fix everyone else. And they will seek transformation for themselves. They will stop wanting to fix the world and its broken systems and realize that broken people will always ruin even a good system. It's not the system; it's the people thats the problem. And then, they will start focusing on healing their relationship with God and one another. No one ever got to heaven by being the devil who helped everyone else be like Christ. And if they don't receive your good news, shake the dust off your feet." she took a breath. "Don't persecute them!"

"So now you are on board with shaking the dust?"

"I am never against the words of the master teacher. There is a time for everything, and there is a person for everything. You may be the person who gives up and shakes their dust. But there is someone out there, someone who will take ten years to help someone get to know eternity. So why don't we give that person an easier time with Lane? Rather than wound her today with our lack of gratitude for saving your life. For saving our son's life!"

"Come on, Riva, the truth is the truth!"

"You are so dedicated to doing the right things and policing everyone you don't even see your own log. Your son cannot even understand why and how you became a pastor."

"A Bishop!" he corrected her sharply.

"You see. You can't even remember you were once a lowly pastor. Your pride has blinded you, and you are hurting our son. I feel hurt at times by your oppressive take on religion. You sometimes fight against the very good you claim to represent. At this point, I am not sure who I married."

The Bishop froze. His fears of divorce rose, going real quick from zero to 100% it's happening.'

"I am not throwing stones here, but I thought I married a man who wanted to be like Christ. Willing to die even for the Pharisee. The teacher who keeps his mouth shut against the accusers who spit at him —holding back the angels from coming down to destroy his torturers. And withholding calling fire from the heavens to devour those who would have deserved it in our eyes. Instead, he said, forgive them for they know not what they…

"Enough, enough! I am not that man, and no one can ever be..."

"I guess that means you aren't even going to try?" Riva continued.

"Why try to become what is futile?" Bishop Hooper replied, throwing his hands up.

"In our own strength, it is impossible, but in His stre…."

"Come on; we can't all be Jesus, Paul, or the 12 disciples."

"My love," Riva said, "You forget that there are countless people who have given up their lives besides the big names. Unknown martyrs who believed that Paul meant it when he said, "He too was only a human being."

"Are we getting a divorce?" the Bishop asked, looking at Riva and Lane.

"No, of course not," Riva replied, puzzled.

"It's just that you sound so unhappy. And I sound like a tyrannical monster, and I can't stomach putting you through that." He said, his shame getting the better of him. He felt like he had failed at loving her.

* * *

167

"Exactly, that means you love me. And I am kicking you in the butt because I love you. Right?" Riva asked, hoping *he* believed his ideas.

"Okay, so kicking me in the butt is love, but kicking others isn't love. You are confusing me here." He said, sighing in exasperation.

"Don't be confused, dummy," Riva said, walking over to her husband, who took a few steps back.

"What's going on?" she asked,

He was close to tears. "I just need some time to think. I don't think I'm ever going to change my opinions and some of my actions. I believe these things to be indisputable, and I am not sure how I can stop hurting you." .

"Come on, if you hurt me - and you will - I will forgive you. And you will hurt me. It's how relationships work. And I am always going to forgive you. That's my rule passed down from Abba, of course, and it's got nothing to do with you." she replied

"But why does it have to be you? Why do you, the one hurting, have to be the one making peace." Bishop Hooper felt more ashamed and ignorant. He was the Bishop. He was the one who should be in her place, always forgiving and teaching these things.

"Are you unhappy, Riva?" he asked.

"Only a little. Maybe a lot, but nothing we can't work through," she said playfully.

The Bishop's pride could not digest his failure at making his wife happy. The shame was overwhelming.

TOGETHER APART

There was an uproar when the church heard that the Bishop was getting separated from his wife. He broke the news at the next church service, and more than half the church left right there. The Bishop had great qualities, but to many in the church, the Bishop's best quality as a human being was his wife.

"We are not getting divorced," he had tried to announce, "Only separating for a little while. And before you blame Riva, I need you to know it was my idea."

People were distressed by the news.

A month and a half after this showdown, the Bishop was alone, lonely, and absent-minded. Bishop Hooper had pushed his wife and son away. Riva had been adamant and refused to divorce. Finally, they had settled on separation. The church was significantly smaller, and he knew they would have to cut costs soon. He was now living in a huge house alone, paying the mortgage. Riva took Timothy, and they left to serve the underprivileged in Zawe.

The icing on the cake of the story is when the youth minister gives the Bishop some paperwork to sign. She was on his right side of the desk and had bent over the paperwork. He needed to sign some of the papers, and he was sitting down. As he raised his hand up to grab the pen, his thumb caught the hem of her dress. They had an embarrassing misunderstanding. He knew he had lost it all when she, red in the face, asked, "Did you just try to...." and she stormed out of the offive. The secretary was right there by the door and looked in to see a distraught Bishop pacing.

"It's not what it looks like," he had tried to say.

He was fired from the church after the youth minister registered her complaint. The secretary had corroborated some of the details of the story. And the destruction was complete. No church and no family. Sure, they were still married, but he would have to fly to Zawe to patch things up with them.

~.~.~.~.~.~.~.~.~.~.~.~.~.~.~.~

The whole bar was silent. So many had read the articles, and it had sounded like it always does—the fall of a homophobic debaucherous man who deserved to suffer. But now, to all in the bar, it was simply another human being suffering. Another clueless living soul trying to do his best at living. He wanted to save those lesbians. He did not violate the youth minister at all.

~.~.~.~.~.~.~.~.~.~.~.~.~.~.~.~

And you know the sad part about all this? The Bishop asked Simbai, "No one from the church has ever reached out. No one has ever said, "Brother, we all mess up, let me help you stand back up."

"Whose fault is that?" Lenny asked

"What do you mean?"

"Well, you are the one who had been teaching these people stuff for years. Did you teach them to be neighbors to those misunderstood or labeled as sinners? Or did you teach them to tell the truth and kick the sinners in the butt?"

"I don't think you realize how similar our situations might be. It's quite surprising that you would cast the first stone because…." The two continued arguing as Simbai retreated into his mind.

Simbai wondered what he had learned himself. All he had to show from all those years of church and trying to do well was a broken family who had passed through Uzu. He got up and started leaving. His thoughts led his steps through the dimly lit bar towards the door, towards his wife. He opened the door, and the bright afternoon sun threatened to blind him. He had to wait for his eyes to get used to the radiance. He felt like one coming out of a dark cave where he was chained to the wall—forced to watch as people projected their lives like shadows on a wall. It still felt more comfortable watching the shadows than living the ideas out. If Tambudzai had not been on his mind, he would have returned to the seemingly risk-free darkness of the bar. To ask if anyone else had a story they needed him to hear. As he stood there, his eyes getting used to the light, Learnmore came bursting out. He was also stopped abruptly by the sun's brilliance, and squinting, he said, "Oh, you are still here. Do you need a ride somewhere?" and Bishop Hooper stumbled out at that precise time. "Ouch," he said, covering his eyes, "May I come with you guys?"

CHAPTER FIVE
Petrichor

RAIN

The car smelled of newness and wealth until Bishop Hooper entered. Both Lenny and Simbai looked to the back seat when the stinky man sat down. The Bishop froze, and the other two men shook their heads.

"Hey, Lenny - can I call you Lenny?" Simbai paused for an answer as he looked at Learnmore in the driver's seat. Learnmore ignored him, put the key into the ignition, and started the car. The car made such a racket that Simbai and Bishop Hooper jumped, and Lenny laughed. "Yes, you can call me Lenny," he replied as he began backing out of the parking spot.

"Lenny, I think we should roll down the windows," Simbai said, amused.

"On it, boss!" Lenny replied, shifting gears and then lowering the windows.

The drive back to Orange Valley was a journey of smells. The natural ones helped cover up Bishop Hoopers'. The cattle ranches were way worse than Bishop Hooper. If only they were driving through the rain or after it. The smell of wet sand would be a glorious reprieve. The thought transported Simbai to a memory.

* * *

It had rained while he was riding the bus. The precipitation had let up about half an hour before his stop. He remembered getting off the bus after the rains. The fulfilling, rich smell greeted him and approved of his trip to his Uncle's side. He had heard that his Uncle had up and left to the village by the Zii river. It was a few months after the accident. But the incident wasn't his Uncle's fault; it wasn't anyone's fault. They had all gone swimming at his Uncle's first motel. He had slaved years to get enough of a down payment to swing the deal. The man was enterprising, and he had given them an open invitation to come swim whenever. So they had. He had promised his mother he would watch them. And Simbai had promised his mother and then his Uncle that he would care for his sister and protect her in the pool.

His older brother was now talking to one of the gorgeous girls at the pool. Simbai was shy, and he stayed far away from that side. Their little sister had also swam to that side, and Simbai sighed. He was not designed to go over there. He was not going anywhere near the scary, beautiful girls. What would he say to them? He had decided to spin around in the water to impress some of them and get their attention. After several spins and bobbing, he paused for a breath. He could see his older brother laughing and talking. His little sister was...

He stopped; she was nowhere to be seen. Then the pointing. The girls were pointing. The lifeguard ran and dove, but Simbai was already on his way through the water. He got to her first, pulling her body from the bottom of the pool. He had climbed those steps out of the pool with her body. He shuddered at the memory. She was not breathing, and he raised her face to his to see if she was alive. Nothing. The lifeguard had snatched her from him and tried some first aid stuff, but it was in vain. His mother had arrived before the ambulance. Simbai hadn't even decided how to feel or think about what had just happened. His body felt like it was on the verge of shutting down or crumbling into the earth. Like it was being crushed under a heavy load but one he had to carry for someone else. With his mother scolding him in the middle of her desperate crying, he felt his body get heavier by the minute.

"What were you doing?" she asked him. "I told you to watch her. It's all your fault." she was almost screaming, but grief kept her voice low.

"Don't mind her, someone was saying. She is hurt. Have you ever lost a child? It's devastating." This person was saying trying to comfort Simbai as his mother was raging.

No one asked him what it was like to lose a sibling. No one thought about his loss, their loss as siblings. His sister was his world, his advocate. Without her, he had no one to laugh with or go on adventures. No one to scheme all the philosophical weirdness in the world and discuss church. No one to stand for him. She was the younger sister, but she fought many of his battles. With her gone, he had no one on his side at home besides his quiet father.

The funeral was a painful ordeal for Simbai, who had vowed he would never cry at a funeral. But he found something in him, sobbing for his sister. If only he had given in to it. No, the tears inundated him as her adorable little coffin was carried through. It was so cute it reminded him of his sister in one of her beautiful floral dresses. He missed her dearly though she had been gone only a few days. And he sobbed uncontrollably and didn't even know why.

And then he had heard that his Uncle had been accused of killing his sister for black magic reasons. What can anyone do in the face of such an allegation? If you succeed, it confirms the charge. The only way to remain innocent is to fail. After the funeral, it made sense that the motel closed down entirely, and his Uncle had packed up and headed for the Zii river. And now Simbai was on his way there. He could not stand aside as the world's weight crushed his Uncle. Simbai felt empowered and heroic, thinking he would be his Uncle's champion. After all, it was not his Uncle's fault. And all the other nonsense was precisely that, nonsense.

His feet were crunching with such melody in the wet soil. It smelled so delicious. The wheels on his bag had trouble rolling, but that was okay. The wheeled traveling case was heavy because it had everything he needed to survive for months out there. Clothes, school supplies, and some books for entertainment. He had run from home using his saved-up pocket money. Simbai was pleased with himself.

This wasn't the first time Simbai had packed up to run away. He had put his sunrise reader in a bag in second grade, some maputi (popped corn), and some underwear to change. The underwear was so he wouldn't be stinky to the runaway girls. Don't ask; it's a second grader trying to find a better place to live. And those were the essentials he could think of at the time. So he hid the bag to get it when it was lights out at home. He had made it down the street when a dog passed by. The animal's eye gleamed, reflecting a distant light, which terrified him, but he kept going. Then, a few meters later, he met with more gleaming eyes, so many dogs roamed free in his hometown. He had never been out in the dark before and had never seen dog eyes gleaming. So he had run home in fright. But he hid the bag again for another attempt. Which was thwarted when he couldn't find the pack and knew he had been found out.

But now, he had packed up a traveling case. He had used his pocket money and even had some of it leftover. And he was willing to forgo boarding school and attend the rural school by the Zii river.

His Uncle was delighted to see him and much surprised. They had often come to the village together when Simbai was young, so it wasn't strange to have him there. But the older man's instincts made him invite Simbai to a fireside chat after dinner. A man-to-man conversation called a dare (d-ah-réh) was a huge honor in Zawe. The discussion by the fire had gotten heated, and they broke a Zii rule of no yelling.

"You are not a hero; you are just a child. And even if you were a hero, you don't even know what it means." His Uncle was saying, pacing back and forth by the fire. He must have wondered how Simbai's running away would be blamed on him. But Simbai tried to reassure him that he knew what he was doing.

"A hero, Uncle, is a noble person who saves people. He stands for the defenseless and is a voice for the voiceless." He replied confidently.

"No, to be a hero in people's eyes, one has to play the game of doing what the people want. To be a hero in people's eyes is to democratize your life and let the majority rule it for you. You are only a hero to the extent you do what they approve and no more. Do you feel like a hero if I sent you back home?"

"No," he mumbled

* * *

"What?" His Uncle asked, hand over his ear, cupping it like an inverted bull horn.

"No!" Simbai said louder, sadder, angrier.

"Then you are only a hero to the extent that I approve of you, right?"

Simbai nodded in resignation.

"Well, you get it now. First, be saved yourself; then, you can save others. You have to understand how painful and difficult your own salvation is. It would help to see how much collateral damage saving yourself will bring. Only then will you be able to walk with others through their pain as they walk their path towards salvation—a path that has many victims along the way. But you have to surrender those people you hurt to the healing of the heavens and keep walking your path. Only then, maybe, can you be a true hero."

He had paused to look at the boy. And Simbai had looked up to the man who had been an inspiration to him. The entrepreneur in the family had now been reduced to rural folk. His uncle started searching for something in the nicknacks around the fire. The two were silent for a long while. Then in an undecipherable tone, Simbai spoke into the silence,

"Do you?" he asked

"Do I what?" his Uncle replied, frantically looking around for something, for nothing.

"Do you understand how painful and difficult your own salvation is?" Simbai asked.

His Uncle stopped looking. He looked at Simbai and sighed. Then, he reached for him, pulled him to his feet, and hugged the shorter young man.

"Oh, you are just a boy, asking questions like that." he sighed again and chuckled, covering up his tears. "I wish the whole family were like you," he said. "Alright, I'll let you spend the night, but you are heading home tomorrow morning, okay?"

They laughed together easily as they embraced. Simbai held on to his Uncle tight. After all, the man was shouldering the guilt of the death of his sister, and Simbai wanted to let him know someone in the world did not blame him for it. Simbai looked at his Uncle, who simultaneously had tears and a smile on his face. The same Uncle who had just been furious moments ago. Simbai wondered if his Uncle was still sane. He puzzled over how someone could move swiftly from emotion to emotion. Of course, his Uncle wouldn't know if he was losing his mind. After all, people know they have lost their minds only after finding them. While insanity reigns, it's the world that looks strange and not the self.

It had rained that night, and the thunder and lighting made sleep sweet. All manner of distress was forgotten. And in the morning, he changed into new clothes and underwear. He chuckled to himself, remembering second grade. Before leaving he had visited Tambudzai's family compound. Then he and his Uncle marched back to the bus station through glorious after rain smells. He would google this phenomenon later and learn its name; Petrichor. The smell of crisp clean air and wet earth after rain. It was coined in 1964. Who knew words were being invented till that recently. The term was coined from Greek Petros, meaning "stone," and ichor, meaning "the fluid that flows in the veins of the gods."

WITH CHILD

Tambudzai woke up to an empty bed. The window was open, which was unusual. She walked over to shut it and turned away. She had a brief moment of feeling pins and needles all over her body. So she turned around, opened the window, and checked the pavement. She had to make sure her husband wasn't splattered all over it. Satisfied, she shut the window again and jog trotted over to the bathroom. She didn't throw up but felt nauseated. After her ablutions, she mosied over to the kitchen, expecting to find Simbai. He wasn't there. She looked down the hallways and noticed the door was locked from the inside, complete with the chain. When she tried his number, she was surprised to hear his phone ringing in the living room. They had a rule not to bring their devices into their bedroom. But they did try to keep them on their persons during the day.

Tambudzai decided to skip her walk that day. It had been several days of her feeling strange. She headed over to the kitchen to squeeze some oranges. Some fresh golden nectar, as her husband called it. Coffee was not an option that morning. Which was irregular for the coffee enthusiast she had become. She brushed the thought away, reminiscing about Simbai. He would make the gesture of offering the raised glass to her with both hands. "The golden drink of the gods!" She would chuckle and receive her bounty and then rub her then-pregnant tummy. She smiled, thinking of her husband, who was missing mysteriously. He was the one who had run around getting oranges and orange juice for her when she was pregnant with Leila. One of the things he was stressed about was when they ran out at home and the stores in Zawe ran out of orange juice as well. She was about to start worrying about him when she paused mid-squeeze and whispered to herself, "I'm pregnant."

She quickly opened the app on her phone, which helped her track her cycle. And yes, she was plenty late. She was furious that Simbai wasn't there to share the moment and carry the apprehension she felt. Finally, she left to pick up some pregnancy tests to confirm her suspicions.

As she looked at the results, she was biting her lip. At the same time, she was fixing to smack Simbai when he got back. When he appeared again from wherever people disappeared to behind locked doors. The digital test screamed "PREGNANT," The line test showed a positive. She did not know whether to be happy or sad. Would they survive this one? She went to drink more juice and water. As she downed the water, she chuckled at her choice of not drinking coffee that morning. A few hours later, she retook the test. And again, positives. The sun had run a good amount across the sky. It was towards late afternoon when she heard an unfamiliar noise. She made her way to the window.

The red Ferrari was making a racket. It stood out in the green Orange Valley area of hybrids and full electrics. Here, status was dictated by specific political and environmental values. Tambudzai was overly irritated by the noise and watched the car as it parked in a guest spot. Three people emerged from the red car. One of them looked like her husband, messy, bloody, and wearing dirty pajamas. The third man looked homeless, and the other man looked tall and very wealthy. It was a strange combination of humans, and they walked out of sight.

As they made their way to the door, Tambudzai heard her husband's voice and moved away from the window. "So this is where I live. The powers that be decided to give us one of their luxurious on-campus suites." Simbai was saying as she unlocked the door. "Apparently, we are special people from Uzu." He said as if this fact was something someone else had cooked up against them. He raised his hand to knock and alert his wife that he was back. Usually, he would have his key but not today.

She opened the door at that very moment. Without missing a beat, Simbai said, "And this is my wife. Wife, these are my two new friends. Learnmore, and Bishop Hooper."

"I'm not a Bishop anymore," Bishop Hooper protested.

Tambudzai leaped into her husband's arms, and her tears started flowing, surprising herself. Simbai winced in pain but held on to her tight. She cried in the silence, and he held her in the doorway without moving. And as she held onto her husband, she felt whole again. He was sad he had been scared of coming home rather than worried about how worried she would be. After a few minutes of standing by the door, they finally made their way into the apartment.

"Wow," Lenny remarked. "This is quite the apartment."

Tambudzai did not hear him but recognized the Zawe accent. She pulled her husband to their bedroom and shut the door.

"I can explain everything, love," he was protesting in whispers as he held her shoulders gently.

"Simbai, I am pregnant," she said.

The day could not get any more intriguing. He did not ask her to repeat the news; it was loud enough for him. He was petrified for a second, and then he looked at his wife's searching eyes. She was looking for the bold and courageous man squirreled away somewhere in his soul.

Simbai pulled her to their bed, where they sat down. He held her and kissed her on the forehead. "For to us a child is born, to us, a son is given?" he announced comically.

She slapped him playfully, "Who said it's a boy?"

"It has to be this time around. I need someone who can help and hold us together if I start faltering. Someone who can shoulder with you some things if I can't."

"Don't talk like that!" she said, disentangling herself from his arms.

He looked at her searching eyes again. She was looking for hope. The hope that this time they would do better. Then she shook her head:

"Okay, okay, that's out of the way; now tell me how you got out of a locked apartment. And why you're bloody and in your pajamas."

"Oh, that's a long story, love. Let's get into that later, but, but, but, can we just focus here. Congratulations, you are going to be a mother again!" he whispered, kissing her.

She sniffled, holding back more tears, and whispered back. "And you will be a father again." They embraced as they sat on the bed.

WHAT IF

"What if I can't shoulder it this time again?" Simbai asked as they held each other.

"We will find a way through love," she replied, smiling. "As long as we don't move to Uzu again, I think we will be fine."

* * *

"Oh my love, what happened there?" he asked her, referring to the move to Uzu.

"I don't know," she said, chuckling mirthlessly, "we had so many dreams. We had so many...a house, promotions at work, family..." she said, her voice trailing.

"So many dreams," he replied, whispering dreamily. Then he looked at his wife with a severe resigned expression and asked, "What happens to us when our dreams die?"

She raised her eyebrows and was silent for a minute. Simbai was quiet too. Then she sighed again. "I wish I could say we dream new dreams. But I think when our dreams die, we also..."

"Die," they both said in unison. They were quiet.

Then Simbai spoke in that silence, "I was afraid of that answer, but it makes sense. We died when we let my trauma push us out of Zawe. When we let Zawe's challenging socio-economic and political situation kick us out."

"We died when we gave up and ran away," Tambudzai added. They both looked at each other. Tambudzai was wondering if Simbai was getting stronger. And he wondered why he had never let her take the lead on the decision-making. She was brilliant, and he had such respect for her mind since high school.

"So what do we do?" he asked her, a weak smile posted on his face.

"First we come back to life, then we dream again," she replied thoughtfully.

"And how do we do that?" he asked. Tambudzai looked at him with gratitude in her eyes. He was asking for her thoughts, for her input. Perhaps he was growing stronger after all.

"We need to return to the scene of the crime. We have to loop back to the spot in time where we let fear and a desire for personal gain drive us out of Zawe. And then start thinking on a broader scale. My work with the UN has given me a broader vision of how we can think of the other people in Uzu and the other people in Zawe. A vision for more. We should never have left, but now we can return and breathe new life into ourselves by giving of ourselves."

He chuckled, acknowledging her beautiful reply, "Moving to Uzu was a dumb decision, wasn't it? Why did you let us do it?" he asked.

"Are you blaming me for that decision?" she replied, standing up and walking to the window. She started getting the pins and needles feeling again and asked in irritation. "What happened with this window last night?"

He stood up and turned her around to get her mind off the window. Then, looking her in the eyes, he said, " I am not blaming you for what happened, but I am blaming myself. And you, my dear, are so smart. You should take over the decision-making in this family."

"Stop, stop it, Simbai. This is not a time to feel all the self-pity and regret. We have had years to think about the past and process it. And I still trust in the vision you have for our family to be one. I believed Uzu would work for us. And look, it did for a time. We raised a super awesome baby girl in that village. Yes, she stayed, and we left, but that is not on you. She was brave enough to stand on her feet. Uzu worked for a long while. No matter what decision you make, it's bound to face resistance or a setback once in a while. Even if I make the decisions, the same thing will happen. It was 16 or so years before Uzu turned awful. And those two years to Leilani's 18th birthday were agony with the shells and everything. Nothing to do with you at all."

Simbai was soothed a little. The decision's fallout was not his fault. But his mental health was still in question. Not only that but his feelings of ineptitude at parenting. He did not know what a father would do, should do, especially with a son. He had figured it out with Leila, but now he didn't have Uzu's social structure. So how would he do well? And also now it would-be a son. Yes, Simbai had already decided the gender of the baby to worry about. It was a son he was always worried about raising wrong.

He cleared his throat. Tambudzai could see she had finally gotten through to him. But as usual, another objection was forming. She needed to add one last nail to this coffin, and they would bury the past. But he had to tell her what it was so she could speak to that concern.

"What if I am not cut out to be a father?" he asked.

"You wondered the same about being a husband, remember. My brother told me about how you confided in him when you considered proposing."

"What, he told you the stuff I told him not to share?"

"It was 20 or so years ago, love. And nothing you said then stopped me from saying yes. I believed you would be a great husband and father even with your past and your family's dysfunctions."

Now Simbai was close to tears. He had never needed to hide from this woman. She pulled him to the bed, and they sat down.

"Simbai, getting married has never been my ultimate dream like many of my girlfriends. I only dreamt of doing right by Adonai with whomever he sent me to help. You can be weak or strong; you can be crazy or sane. It won't spoil my dream at all. The dream of a healed and healing people of a great and infinite Kingdom. So stop worrying about letting me down or letting the baby down. Your worry makes me even more attracted to you because it means you care. I am not going anywhere, and you aren't ditching me either."

Simbai was grateful for such a woman and wife. He didn't understand what she had just said. It sounded like her faith came before him in order of importance. He liked that her priorities were in that order. She would not be alone if he faltered because she had the divine to lean on. He pulled her to him and squeezed her hard. "I can't breathe," she said moments later, and they both laughed.

"I will be back," he said as she expected. He needed time to water the seeds she had just planted in him. "I'll be making dinner," she called after him.

THE HOOD

Simbai walked right past the two gentlemen he had brought home with him. And right out of the apartment, still in the torn and bloody pajamas.

The other two men sat there for a few minutes before Tambudzai walked out of the bedroom, wiping away her tears. Bishop Hooper was on the floor in a corner, and Lenny was sitting in one of the white leather designer chairs.

"Please find a more comfortable place to sit," Tambudzai said. She walked over to Bishop Hooper, and she reached for his left palm and elbow to assist him up. He could not resist, and he rose as she led him to the couch. "It will get dirty," he protested. "And that is its telos," she replied, chuckling. "Why else would it be white? So, tea, anyone?" she asked.

"When will he be back?" they asked simultaneously. Tambudzai's hospitality made them very comfortable. Yet, it still was strange to be there with his wife, whom they had just met.

"I don't know, a few minutes, an hour, maybe more. He has a lot to think about because I am pregnant." as soon as she said that, the two-man looked at each other. Bishopp Hooper jumped up, and Lenny rose slowly, sighing for having to get up from the comfort.

"Tea sounds good," Lenny said as he followed Bishop Hooper out the door. They didn't have to go far to find Simba. He was sitting there on the hood of the Ferrari. People passing by were giving him dirty looks for being environmentally unconscious.

"What's going on, man?" Lenny asked when they found him

"She is going to be a mother," he said quietly.

"Yes, and just to be clear, you are the father." Bishop Hooper added, and Lenny gave him a reprimanding look. They didn't know that, and maybe that was the problem.

"But what is a father if he can't father? Am I just a sperm donor?"

"What do you mean?" Lenny asked, sidling up to him on the hood.

"You might remember Lenny, the baby in the Sta Soft commercial."

"Awwww, it was a cute baby, though," Learnmore replied, clapping his hands and smiling dreamily to the heavens.

"Sta-soft was a fabric softener in Zawe," Simbai said, looking at Bishop Hooper. "And in the commercial, the baby was wrapped in a soft blue wool blanket. The baby was held and raised to its mother's face. The music in the background was immersive. I wished I was that baby in those moments. Sometimes, I wished I had a baby of my own to love better than I was being loved. As the commercial came to a close, they would say the fabric softener was "as soft, as a mother's touch." This created a yearning in me for these mothers they were referring to since mine was not as soft. Oh, how I wanted to experience this soft touch. When I think of my mother, my memories say she is not the nurturing and gentle type. If you get hurt, she scolds you. If you fail, she criticizes you. So, there is only pruning and navy seal training. I used to ask myself, is she a real mother if she can't 'mother.' They say it is as soft as a mother's touch, but her touch is always rough. If she can't take her babies and comfort them, is she a real mother? If all she has to offer are cutting hurtful remarks day in and day out, is she merely a child-bearer but not a mother?"

"Hmmm, I see where your fathering question comes from. So you now wonder if by your standard of mothering and fathering..."

"Yes," Simbai cut off Bishop Hooper. "Fathering is protecting my family and being present for them in power. Providing is not so difficult; I can do that. The part that kills me is where I have led them astray and failed to protect them." he said, holding back tears.

The Bishop reached out; he was standing in front of the car.

"Simbai, you judge yourself the same way you judge your mother. The trap of judging is sadly circular like that. So we have to unwind it, straighten it, but we have to start at the beginning."

Lenny was surprised at Bishop Hooper's tone of voice and concern. He had sobered up quite a lot on their drive up. Now the wise drunk man was a wise sobber man.

"You see, there is no standard for a mother. Expectations of what mothers or fathers should be like are sad instances of a lack of acceptance of one another. There is no "should" when it comes to being or acting. Sadly, the western world has taken over ideas of truth. It's western to think there is one truth, and all should apply it in the same way. Yet, in wisdom traditions, we have opposing sayings all the time. Though the truth is true and singular, no human being can ever grasp it in its singular form. So no human can claim to have the truth though there may be one truth. So there is no "ideally a mother would" or "ideally a father should." But we have one true Father, and He is the ideal. But even Him, we all perceive differently. Furthermore, no one can tell Him what he should and shouldn't do because such concepts are beyond us. So we take what we get and do our best with it. Given this, then, we can remove expectations from our paradigm. And what do we have if not freedom to be and do?"

"Hurts, Bishop, I have pain," Simbai replied, pounding his chest.

"Yes, but hurts which no longer come with justifications. Hurts without justified anger or justified shame. Since there is no longer any ground to claim "she should have" or "he should have."

Lenny was silent, the Bishop paused, and Simbai was awed by the thawing he felt in his heart. This man may have failed his church, but he still had the touch. He still could minister to broken souls.

"Okay, I am listening," Simbai said, smiling weakly and optimistically. Maybe today, he could find a way out of the maze in his head. Tambudzai had already laid down the foundation.

"Alright, so now see your mother as you see yourself. A wounded person who was let down by her own parents. And then she passed on that wound to you."

* * *

"The mother-wound," Lenny murmured, remembering something he had read once.

"The sad part of the mother-wound is that it is often also the father-wound. But the mother gets the short end of the stick." The Bishop said, addressing Lenny and then turning his gaze back to Simbai. He was about to continue with another idea when Lenny interrupted and asked.

"What do you mean? You can't just drop that on me and expect to continue onto something else."

Bishop Hooper stopped and looked over. Then he sighed and began, "Well, usually it's a mother who had an absentee father. Such that her own mother had to make up for the absenteeism. Her mother - the grandmother - was probably both nurturer and disciplinarian in the family. So the mother now carries unresolved trauma, which creates low self-worth. She is no longer well attuned emotionally. She can no longer see her children's emotional needs. Neither is she capable of meeting them and helping them navigate life. So she ends up projecting her pain onto her children. She blames them for her unhappiness and unresolved outbursts. But then she usually gets married to an absentee man as well—one who validates her previous family dynamic. So the children grow up without a father but with a masculine mother who passes on her wounds. So it's the father who is absent. But this could be helped if the father were to stand firm and help raise the kids. It would go further if the father were also to call out his wife's behavior and help her heal."

"Aaaah, so the man has to stand next to his wounded partner and help her navigate her trauma. Help her not to pass it on to the children?" Lenny asked

"Yes, and in this case," The Bishop said, pointing to Simbai. He was signaling to Lenny to let them return to the man of the hour. "In this case, it's the son who is now in the position. But, first, he needs to forgive the mother and father. After all, she is merely wounded and bleeding all over. And the father was not taught how to help her heal. That's usually what ends the cycle, forgiveness. It brings about healing and cuts off the inheritance." he said, making the gesture of scissors cutting something.

Simbai liked gestures; they helped him remember ideas. Now he would think of scissors every time he thought of forgiveness. He was smiling weakly, thinking of Leilani and how she had become so strong and independent. Had he passed on to her the mother wound, or rather the father wound? Was she now trying always to be a masculine woman to make up for his absence in her life? Was she even a masculine woman? He was getting vexed as he thought about all this. He thought back to his upbringing, to who taught him to shave. His father had given him a quick tutorial way before he had a hint of a beard. He smiled briefly but quickly noticed that there weren't many other memories. But his mother had been the helicopter type, plenty of memories there. Maybe his dad had been absent somehow and shouldered a massive chunk of the dysfunction.

"Simbai, Simbai!" The Bishop was shaking his shoulder.

"Hmmm," he responded.

"You need to forgive your mother and forgive yourself. And start now to learn new ways of being a father. Learn more." The Bishop ended chuckling and looking at Lenny, and they all laughed, which dissolved the tension.

Tambudzai had been watching the three mean interacting. She was glad that her husband had some men to talk to. He had not had many male friends here in the USA, and he desperately needed a different perspective often. Not her view, though, but another man's outlook as well. Such relationships were hard to come by here unless it was a therapist.

GRUB

So Simbai brought the men upstairs again to the apartment. Simbai finally took a shower, and Bishop Hooper did the same in the guest bathroom. Tambudzai gave Bishop Hooper some of Simbai's clothes,

188

and they fitted on him loosely. He looked like an out-of-place rapper with baggy clothes. But he was clean and looked way better than in his previous garments. And that night, Simbai and Tambudzai's table and hearts were full.

They ordered in because it would be late when the food finished cooking. The group talked and exchanged failure stories. They laughed at how ridiculous living life can be.

In the morning, Simbai looked and sounded way better. Lenny and the Bishop had shared the guest bedroom. There was also a pull-out couch in the guest room, though not the most comfortable. They were laughing at breakfast at how Lenny had tried to tell the Bishop that in Zawe, up to five people could share a bed. The Bishop would have none of it and slept in the uncomfortable pull-out.

Seeing Simbai looking and sounding better, Bishop Hooper and Lenny felt like their work was done and so they planned to leave after breakfast. However, Tambudzai insisted they stay and eat the food meant for dinner the night before. So they stayed, and they hung out with Simbai, who skipped work for mental health reasons. They found out that Bishop Hooper had an apartment in LA during their conversation. The man had been punishing himself by living on the streets even though he didn't need to. He said he was ministering to the homeless, and it was better if he looked homeless anyway.

They also found out that Lenny had a mysterious Uzu source, and it was a woman. He refused to say much about her, but it was fun to tease him about the source. Finally, he said he had eyes for Letwin only. He was figuring out how to get her back.

HEADLINES

A couple of weeks later, Lenny texted Simbai a news headline. He and Bishop Hooper had been hanging out quite a bit. Some tabloid had published a piece on how Lenny was back on the prowl. Simbai did not hesitate but invited both men up to the bay to escape for a day or so. And they had a reunion of sorts which gave way to more hangouts as the months went by.

Soon, Tambudzai was showing. So Simbai sat her down to discuss the future of the baby.

"I think we should go back to Zawe to have this baby?" Simbai had said,

"Do you think or have you decided?" She asked

"What's the difference?" he replied

"Well, there is a difference when you decide and try to get me on board. And when you come to me to discuss this so we can come up with the best of both minds." She replied, reaching for his hand to reassure him.

"I hear you, but I am also confused. I thought you said it was alright for me to make the final decisions." Simbai said, visibly exasperated.

"Yes, but if you make the first and the final decision, isn't that redundant? Especially when both are identical." She replied, and Simbai relaxed. Her words made sense, but he did not yet know how to communicate well.

"Okay, then you make the decision," he said instead. "I will be okay with whatever you decide."

"Why would I deprive myself of your wisdom, my love. I want us to make the decision and not just you. It's not all on you, you know?" she replied, getting somewhat frustrated.

"I don't know how to take responsibility while not taking it all on myself. I mean, it's, it's my father-wound, right, right?" he paused, willing her to agree. But instead, she only waited for him to finish. "I believe it's my father and mother wounds that drove us to Uzu and which are now hurting Leila."

Tambudzai smiled, "Aww, baby, no. Our daughter is not suffering from a mother or father wound. I think she is suffering from common abandonment issues. Issues brought about by having different views from her parents. Challenging to recover from, but I think you can clear yourself of all guilt. It's on us. I was convinced then and still believe now that those shells were dangerous. I wasn't going to wear one even if you had chosen to."

"I'm not talking about that; I'm talking about her masculine energy!" he replied.

Tambudzai burst out laughing. She could not contain herself. "I'm sorry for laughing, my love. So you think your daughter's stubbornness and independence are because she has some parental wound?"

"Yes? Don't you?" he asked, puzzled by her laughter but relieved.

"No, no, not at all. That girl had two loving parents, and she and I may not have been close, but she had no such wounds. That girl was born knowing her mind, and though she took after you, I don't think you taught her to be stubborn. I think it's genetic?" She replied, smirking a little and teasing Simbai.

"Don't play Tambudzai. All I want is for you, Leila, and the baby to be alright. I want you to feel empowered and free to make decisions" he finished.

"Oh, Simbai, I am free and empowered already. The kind of freedom that no war or social justice can ever achieve for me. But let's get this straight, we are a unit, so there is no such thing as independently making decisions between us. You lead this home, and when I submit to you, all I need to know is you love me. I want to know you will guard and pursue a path that protects my interests even when they conflict with yours. That is why we need to discuss how we both see a situation. If you insist, even while knowing what's on the line for me, I will need to trust you. I know you love me; you wouldn't go against me unless you had good reasons. So all of this rests on love, really. And no war or social justice could ever achieve that for me. They can't give me standards to measure my freedom in love. So stop trying to be woke and start being my husband." she said, shaking her head and smiling.

* * *

"I hear you love," Simbai replied more cheerful, "But I don't want to look like I am the one pushing you around. Society is saying you need to make some decisions in this family."

"Simbai, that's a bad compass. Society is a bad compass. Within our framework, can we find our way? We don't need to break out of the paradigm; we need to do better within it. So please don't come to me with decisions, but come to me with your thoughts and ideas. And let me help you to think through them so we can come up with the best conclusion."

She looked at him as he was trying hard to love her well. He was trying to learn from all the new things he had heard in the last couple of months.

"So I submit my thoughts and ideas to you as you submit to our final decision?"

"haha," Tambudzai laughed. "Don't let society hear you use the word submit," she replied and chuckled. She eyed him as he smiled weakly,

"Do you remember the story you told me? Your dad left, and your mom left too, abandoning you to fend for yourself and your siblings.

Simbai's tears glistened in his eyes.

He looked lovingly at his wife, who was pep talking him into his rightful place, as she called it. "Remember you said the kids were hungry and you had to feed them. You had enough mealie meal for sadza (fufu) but no relish. You had exhausted every option for days before and did not know what to do now. As you walked in the garden, you remembered the story of your neighbors. They had been so poor they had eaten the leaves of sweet potato plants. But you decided you didn't trust that story as to the edibleness of the leaves. You decided, though, to dig up a few sweet potatoes. You picked a few green onions and tomatoes. Then you diced the sweet potatoes and added some green onions and tomatoes. And that was your relish. It had taken you so long to figure the relish out. The kids were crying from hunger when you started preparing the sadza. And instead of being angry with them and silencing them up, you told them that sadza cooks faster when you sing the Sadza song. So you taught them the Sadza song, which you borrowed from your high school fam. Sadzaaa, sadza, sadza rinonaka..." (sadza is delicious). And you would tell them to blow into the fire now and then to complete the magic of cooking faster. They stopped crying and started singing and laughing."

"Sadza nembambaira" he whispered. (sadza and sweet potatoes for relish)

Tears were streaming down her face, and he was sniffling trying and failing to hold back his tears. She smiled, though, like a ray of sunshine piercing through dark storm clouds and he started laughing a little. He opened his mouth to speak.

"But you forget how unjust I was, my love. That was one of the few days I had the mind not to beat everyone into submission. Wielding the belt as I had seen and experienced and beating up my own flesh and blood to get my way." Simbai replied

"Just like you to turn a word of encouragement into self-loathing talk, my love," she said, shaking her head.

"No, Tambu, it's the truth. I am not the hero of that story. They were the heroes; they were the ones who had to survive through it. And I was a villain in so many ways. I carry the shame of those days wherever I go. Why could I not know better? Why didn't I leave my siblings alone instead of being a disciplinarian as I sought to raise them? I didn't know how long it would be and whether it was fully up to me now to raise them. I had heard of child-led households and was at a loss to think this was us now. Why..."

Simbai was on his soapbox, and she echoed him.

"And just why would a teenager be the head of a family when both parents are alive?" Tambudzai asked, cutting him off.

"Yes, and why..."

* * *

Simbai caught himself, paused, and smiled. Tambudzai was doing the 'I'm on your side' echo. She brought it out to break him out of rabbit hole spirals. He looked at her as she smiled sorrowfully and murmured to him,

"You have carried a lot, my love; you are more than prepared to carry us. And you are no angel; I know that. I have lived with you for years now. And I am no saint either. You will always be a villain in someone's storybook. But you're not alone now like you were then. I am right here with you till the rivers all run dry."

He embraced her, thankful for her strength. He resolved to be strong too. So he extricated himself from her embrace and wiped the tears which hung on the corners of his eyes.

"I think it would be better to give birth to our son in Zawe. The health care is cheaper, and he will have a Zawe birth certificate. This means that the state here won't own him and take him away from us whenever they want."

"Wow, why would they ever take him away?"

"Baby, I worry I am still not all there mentally. And I don't want to risk losing our son if I do something stupid."

"Have you thought about opening him up to being an American president? If he is born here, he can be raised across the globe, but he will be able to run for president here."

Simbai chuckled. She had joined him on the "son" prediction. He jumped to embrace her, which took her by surprise.

"Careful, careful, I am carrying a tiny human"

"Oh yes, my bad. Okay, so what do we do?"

"Is that all you got, my dear?" she asked.

"No, but I want to leave room for your thoughts."

* * *

"Give me everything you have, and I'll keep adding my ingredients to the cake."

"Okay, if you give birth in Zawe, our savings from here are enough to keep you as a stay-at-home mom until you are ready to go back to work. And they stretch further in Zawe than here. We also will have nosy neighbors and relatives who may be able to help care for the baby. So it will be like Uzu, only no dragons, so better."

She chuckled; Uzu, but better was a terrible pitch, but he had made some good points.

CONFLUENCE

More weeks went by, and finally, Lenny had landed a small gig at a church in downtown LA. Bishop Hooper had pulled some favors. He had landed Lenny a stage director production job for the worship team. The same church had offered Bishop Hooper an assistant teen pastor position.. Things were moving along great. They invited Tambu and Simbai down for a celebration dinner.

At dinner, Simbai announced that he would be taking Tambudzai to Zawe to have their baby. The other two men were surprised and saddened. They had found belonging and a second chance in the community of Tambudzai and Simbai. The couple had a strange openness to others. It was undeniable that Uzu had a hand in it.

Bishop Hooper was a little envious that the two would be going to Zawe. He wished he could come with and see his family. As they ate and celebrated, Simbai's phone rang. He silenced it out of respect for the dinner, but a few moments later, it rang again. This time, Lenny's phone rang as well. Before long, Bishop Hooper's phone was ringing too. The three men exchanged glances, shrugged, and finally decided to pick up.

{ "Hello, is this Simbai?" Someone from the US embassy was asking. - "Yes, this is Simbai." Simbai replied.

* * *

* "Is this Lenny?" Riva asked

~ "Dad, dad," Timothy's voice came across his father's ears. Timothy's voice was filled with tears. Bishop Hooper had chills. His son had finally reached out. "Yes, I'm here, son; what's going on?"

~ "She is dying," Timothy said, "And it's all my fault."

~ "Who is dying?" Bishop Hooper asked

{ "Sir, I'm calling about your daughter Leilani. Unfortunately, she was involved in an accident. And she had you as her emergency number when she received her asylum in the United States." Simbai froze and lowered his phone involuntary. He looked at Tambudzai as he stammered Leilani's name. His mouth went dry.

"Leilani?" Tambudzai asked, furrowing her eyebrows.

* Riva looked down the hallway as her son sobbed into the phone. She paused,

* "Umm, Lenny, Leilani was texting you the most in the last couple of months. And so it's the first number I thought to call after the accident."

* "Who is Leilani," He asked

* "Oh, right, you might know her by "Lani"?"

Lenny looked across the table to Simbai. But unfortunately, he was busy over the phone, so his gaze landed on Tambudzai, who was looking at him askance. It was not a common name.

~ "Who is dying?" Bishop Hooper repeated as his distraught son kept sobbing and not replying. "I'm here, Timmy. Who is dying? Is it your mother?"

~ "Noooooo," the boy drawled and sobbed, "You, you, you don't know her. It's Leilani."

* * *

~ "Leilani, is dying?" Bishop Hooper repeated askance. The table hushed.

CHAPTER SIX

The Car Crash

WHAT DID HE SAY

"What did he say?" Leilani asked, enraged and surprised at the audacity of this man. She could not see the man because the angry crowd of protestors surrounded him. She didn't even know anything else about him but that he had said something offensive.

Her friend Biz whispered the dreaded words in her ear. "Blue lives..." Leilani was further inflamed and rushed to join the skirmish before Biz could finish the phrase. Leilani could not stoop to punch, so she threw her foot into the muck. The passionate activist was too livid to see how ridiculous her movements looked. She was kicking and thrashing about, straining to reach through the crowd. She pushed and shoved to make her opinion of the man's words known to him in a non-verbal way. The man needed to know that he was not at liberty to say those words, especially here. No, not without the consequences, which would make him think twice about it next time.

She thought she had landed a good one here and there. Some of her hits seemed to correspond to punctuated shrieks by the man on the ground. It was a cry from Zawe - Maiwee meaning "Oh mother." He sounded like he was saying, "My Way," which made the crowd even angrier. "The nerve of this guy, my way he keeps yelling," someone close to Leilani yelled. There was such a raucous, and it was impossible to hear everything clearly. Leilani was puzzled when she felt a strange tingle down her spine. The shrieks sounded muffled, distant, and yet familiar and not English. Yet, who would have thought the 'scoundrel' who had said the wrong color was an innocent person who wasn't speaking English. Of course, it was some defiant rabble-rousing right-winger. Blinded by her rage, Leilani dismissed her concerns and went along with the "my way" school of thought. The evil man was a murderer by proxy. "Say their names," she muttered breathlessly before yelling the words three times.

"Say their names!" The crowd echoed her call louder and louder.

With renewed frenzy, she continued reaching in with her leg, kicking about. Biz was watching as all this unfolded. Her spirited friend Leilani was deaf on all accounts at times like these. When Biz felt the moment of intractability had passed, she walked over to the crowd. She reached out to pull her friend away, dodging some blows as people drew back to strike. Leilani struggled against Biz's pull. When Biz finally let go, they were a few meters away. Leilani shook herself in frustration. She muttered, "I was about done anyway."

"I thought so," Biz said, shaking her head and smiling.

Leilani re-organized the clothes on her body, which had gone this and that way in the fight. If anyone could call, the crowd mobbing to hit the "blue lives" man a fight. Leilani picked up one of the posters on the ground. Several people had thrown their placards down to jump into the fray. They were still kicking and hollering at the man who had picked the wrong color. Suddenly, an uneasy feeling crept up in Leilani's gut. Maybe that man was having a mental health episode and decided to provoke the crowd. Or something else because now that she thought about it, something about the man had felt off. But had she even looked at the man excerpt through the blur of the crowd? Yet she thought she had. What had she seen? A weird feeling of apprehension was slowly settling in her stomach. She could not shake the feeling but decided to walk away fast.

She turned to go and took a few quick steps. Then she was lost in thought, remembering her mother and father. She was thinking back to the happy days of looking at a container with an identical label on either side. Her father indulged her and made sure the label was not moving. She fell back, dragging her feet as an eerie feeling unsettled her happy memory. Tears threatened to break free of their carefully built tide walls. The crowd was beginning to move on by degrees, but she was not moving much. Biz was waiting for her patiently and wondering what was going on.

After the last person spat on the man, the crowd left him the way clouds suddenly lift off the sun on a too-hot day, exposing the world to the blight. The group moved on as if nothing had happened except the renewal of their zeal. The man had added to their fuel - anger, from saying the dreaded color to screaming "my way" as they wailed on him. Many felt he deserved his beating. Chanting, marching, protesting police brutality, the crowd went on.

Leilani stayed back a little. She was not sure why. Then, finally, she tried to talk herself into marching on by addressing her words to Biz. "Biz, people like these make the world harder to live. That's why we are marching, to shame them and make it better. Let's go!" She whirled her body around to join the rest of the crowd. To face where they were facing and go where they were going. But after slowly walking a few paces along, Leilani felt something tug on her hair. She felt pins and needles. A feeling that was not physical, yet it crawled all over her skin. She turned, looking back to the man they had mobbed. Shock froze her when she realized the man wasn't white. Maybe she felt strange because they were punching a black man, she wondered. 'Was he a right-wing plant?' she thought further and looked at Biz, who was looking back at Leilani. Leilani's eyes screamed, "He is black, do you see this?" and Biz raised her eyebrows, clueless. Realizing Biz was not getting it, Leilani dismissed her friend with her hand and turned back to the man.

When Leilani turned around again, the blue lives man was almost to the door to the Varnish Bar. Though he had a limp, his gait reminded her of her father after a tiring day in the fields. She hadn't seen her father in over four years, but she could have sworn this man could be him. Was this the reason for all her pins and needles? Then he disappeared behind the door to the bar. Leila stared at the entrance to the Varnish. She felt her innards twist and turn themselves into the famous Gordian knot. She had to unravel this knot quickly before it rose to her chest and throat and forced tears to break their bounds.

She looked briefly at Biz as she reached to pull her phone out of her pocket. Her hands trembled as she tried to swipe the screen to unlock it. She found one of her hands rising to wipe away tears that had slipped through. She would not let those floodgates open, and distraction was always her best friend. She couldn't keep assigning her father's qualities to random people—especially this man who was a sellout.

She texted Lenny,

"I'll be going home with Biz. Also, watch out. A crazy right-winger is coming your way."

She shivered, put her phone away, and tried to shake the strange feeling off. Orange Valley was so far away from LA, where she now lived. So far away from the march. When she had received her asylum, she had made sure to choose a place far from them but also close enough. She would be close if they ever forgave her for staying back in Uzu and wanted to see her.

DRAGON PALOOZA

DRAGON PALOOZA

DRAGON PALOOZA

Leilani was eyeing the leaving airplane, which carried her defiant banished parents. She sighed, shrugging resignedly, suppressing an urge to smile. Her own will at last!

She was jolted by the commotion of the dragons bursting out of the houses. They shrieked and terrified everyone within earshot. Leilani was petrified as the sky was suddenly taken by a flying creature and then another one. She could tell the dragons had come out of the "scalers" houses. The houses from where the shrieks and screams had been heard often. It was clear to her, in all the panic, that the dragons were the "scalers" transformed.

Leilani only stood there horrified. Then, slowly, firmly, she felt the anger rise in her. She was angry that the plane had just left, only for her to now find that her father had been right. He'd been right to suspect evil of the dragon shells. And to think that many people were wearing the shell at that moment was nauseating! Each of them was slowly changing, metamorphosizing...the horror! Were the three flames trying to turn everyone into dragons?

Leilani dropped her mother's jewelry box, which she was holding. She bent over, retching but nothing came up. So, Leilani wiped her dry lips and reached into her blouse. She pulled on the shell and broke the fasten around her neck. She was about to chuck the shell when she paused. Maybe, the "scalers" would not destroy their own. She carefully placed the shell in the jewelry box and started her flight to Tawanda's house.

There was terror everywhere. The dragons flew around, shrieking, huffing and puffing, and burning down houses. A house would be fired, and the residents would flee. But each one of them was picked up from the ground and disappeared inside one of the dragons' mouths. People were screaming and running for shelter. But this was not a nuclear attack, and there were no bomb shelters. No one had drilled anyone on what to do if or when the dragons returned.

Leilani ran for safety through the chaos. The dragons seemed to hover over every part of the village state. They had so much reach in size; reach which was extended by the flames. They also skipped many homes in their attacks. When she arrived at Tawanda's house, she ran in to find terrified children but a calm father. He had faith the dragons would spare all the true believers. His calm demeanor had convinced Leilani. She needed to believe that only the believers were being spared and now had a compelling reason. The calmness of her father's former friend was that reason. She pulled back a curtain to look outside and confirm her newfound belief. The other family members shrieked and shrank back. Leilani ignored them.

The dragons did quick work ridding Uzu of its natives who did not wear the shell. Leilani was grateful then that her parents had been banished. Now she felt a tad bit abandoned. They would have become dragon fodder if they had stayed and didn't wear the shell. But she felt like blaming them for leaving her behind to deal with this new situation. They were the grown-ups; they knew better. Why had they not forced her to abandon the shell and come with them when they were banished. They should have grounded her or something. Instead, they let her run amok and do what she wanted. She was a teenager, for crying out loud. How could she know the implications of such worldly affairs? Leilani stared at her shell in the jewelry box. Her shell was beautiful and majestic, a little like the dragons themselves. She wanted to smack herself for still finding beauty in the creatures, especially as they had destroyed people's lives. People she once knew and cared for.

Many who were left felt the dragons had done well. The death of the unshelled was not only their fault but a boon to those left. The world had fewer unbelievers who did not care about the community. The world was that much better.

But to Leilani, the three flames were to blame. The chief of crops, the dragon head, and his son had done this to these innocent lives. First the scalers, then the people burned by the scalers turned dragons. The only crime these people had committed was independent thought. Leilani blamed all of it on the three flames. And the dragons were in on it too. They were the source of the authoritarian powers of these men. Leilani realized then that her defiance and independence as a woman would be her asset. She had stood against her parents and could stand against any other person. Then she realized her parents had been defiant, and she shook her head, smiling. 'Of apples and trees, right?' She thought. Then she vowed never to let herself be governed by men again. The Three Flames had done them all dirty. First: exposing them to the possibility of transforming into dragons. And now to the constant danger of being gobbled up. Who knew when a dragon would sense something worthy of firing someone up? The village state was directly under the government of the whims of brutal and remorseless beasts—animals that killed with impunity. Since the dragons ran the judicial system, there was nowhere else to appeal.

Life after the dragons was marked by destruction and loss of lives. Five more dragons had emerged on the days following the departure of the banished. The dragons had cut through the outside forest. They had burned again the territory marked by the first dragon. A massive expanse of charred remains of vegetation made up the Uzu border. Many trees also remained, and they made up the inner layer of the border. Food and much property had been destroyed in the dragon attacks. A few "believers" had been caught in the crossfire. You would think they would be immune to the fire. Others were killed by the falling walls of houses and the flying debris.

Weeks later, the three flames were rebuilding Uzu. They were helping to bury the dead and reassuring people that all was well. As long as people believed in the dragons and did not oppose the rule of the three flames, which included the dragons, everyone would be safe. The dragons had taken their rightful place in the trinity. The Dragon Head's son was demoted to the position of a regular citizen. The laws said only three in government, and all the seven dragons were considered one. There was a census and accounting of those still alive. The few children in Uzu who had not survived the dragon palooza were crushed by falling rubble or another similar accident. The dragons had spared even the children of the unshelled, which was a relief to the Dragon Head. He would have had a more challenging time with publicity if that wasn't the case.

Because Leilani had stayed and was shelled, she was saved from any firing. She became the poster child of faith in the shell for all children and young adults. She was even sent over the charred borderlands to speak on behalf of the children in Uzu. The village state needed to reassure the world that children were safe, especially if the world heard some things from the banished. People who may have witnessed things as their plane took off. Leilani also helped to settle the financial accounts of those banished. She allocated more money to her parents than other families. The three flames trusted Leilani so much she had free reign of some of these things.

On her 6th trip out a couple of years later, someone approached her. The agent had been sent to ensure she was safe and not working under duress. Leilani took this opportunity to apply for asylum in the USA, and it was granted swiftly. But they had to wait for her next trip out of "the charred borderlands," a new nickname for Uzu. Others in Zawe now called the village state "Scorched Earth" or Rustva in Shona. It wasn't long before she was sent out on another mission to spruce up the image of Uzu. Unfortunately for Uzu, she did not come back from this trip.

NOBLE AND BIZ

Leilani was told her parents had moved to Orange Valley in San Francisco, so she chose to be moved to LA. Not too far and not too close. She would be close if they ever forgave her for staying and wanted to speak to her. Unfortunately, her parents had not been informed of this development.

On landing, Leilani immediately began plugging into college life. She joined the student government and local social justice efforts. She was immediately enamored with the feminist philosophy. Moreover, she had Uzu history to back her views up. More female voices were needed in government the world over.

On one of the African Students' nights, she met up with two girls from South Africa; Nqobizitha (Conquer our enemies) and Nobuhle (mother of beauty). The girls were roommates.

"You are that girl from Uzu, right?" Nobuhle asked when she saw Leilani.

"Yes, that's me," Leilani replied without hesitating.

"You would get along with my roommate. She is a social justice buff like you." Nobuhle replied excitedly. She grabbed Leilani's hand gingerly and dragged her along.

Leilani laughed. She was not only the girl from Uzu, but she was a social justice buff. Not a terrible reputation, she surmised.

And so the two girls had walked together to find the said roommate.

"How are you liking your time so far in the States?" Nobuhle called back to her luggage.

* * *

"I love it. So many freedoms for women here. Uzu was a little..."

"Nqobizitha, you wanted to meet the girl from Uzu. Here she is?"

"Hi, yes! What's your name again?" Nqobizitha asked animatedly.

"It's Leilani?"

Nqobizitha told her that her name sounded like "lelilani," which means to cry. And Leilani looked somber, telling the girls she had cried plenty of tears in her short life. Nobuhle had jumped in and said it sounded more like "lalelani," which means listen. It was undecided which "sound like" would win. So, the two roommates agreed to call her Lani from that day forward. It was different from "Leila," which was how her parents shortened her name. It worked; it didn't remind her of Uzu, of them. It marked a new beginning for her, and she loved her new name. Unfortunately, Leilani could not get the two girls' names right. So, Nqobizitha became Biz, and Nobuhle became Nobu or sometimes Noble.

It was then that she started hanging out with Biz and Noble. She found it was better to discuss all the issues she was passionate about with Biz. But when it came to getting ready for a party, Noble knew how to get them all dressed in fabulous outfits with killer make-up.

Nobu taught her about make-up, and Biz was her sister warrior in arms.

Noble had the proverbial mic at one of the parties. She was regaling the girls with stories from South Africa. She described how the men at a taxi rank in her hometown whistled after her often because she was "hot stuff." Of course, Biz was against the whole idea of cat-calling. When it was explained to her, Leilani was too against it. No man had any right to make a whistle, shout, comment in a sexual way, or rudely flag her down like a taxi. "So, what do you do? It must be infuriating," she asked Noble. "Oh no, I am flattered by the attention. Of course, I make sure to be safe, but if the guys think I am attractive, I say gaze on gentlemen." Some of the other girls listening were laughing hysterically.

* * *

Biz had a different take on the situation: "I fight back and scold the men," she spoke up.

"Now that would be exhausting," Noble remarked. "Me, on days that I am too busy or just not into it, I tune it out. It's easy to switch off once you know how to hear them."

That made sense for Leilani. It would be futile and exhausting to fight the catcallers. But she could tune them out. The problem was that she had never been cat-called at all. Uzu had been tame on that front. The boys and men there were gentlemanly even as they were tyrannical. Since she had been in the USA, no one had gazed after her. Yes, she had been asked out on dates, but no one had cat-called her. It made her wonder if she was attractive. So, she hung out with Noble often and learned her tricks. She learned that one had to dress for the occasion, and then one had to walk for the audience. It became a massive endeavor for Leilani. She practiced her provocative walk, and she learned much about fashion and make-up. First, she had to get the men to cat-call her, and then she would see how it felt and go from there. She tried plenty of times without success. Soon her catwalk became her regular gait.

Leilani was late for a mid-morning class one time. The college was always under construction in one area or another. Leilani decided to take a shortcut through the construction zone. She walked past the scaffolding and through the makeshift walkways made for pedestrians. And as she made progress through the area, she felt pins and needles. It was an eerie feeling of being watched. And then a couple of guys whistled. Someone yelled something, but Leilani was distracted by the strange feeling. Another echoed something, and there was laughter. She unconsciously increased her pace. Then she realized she had experienced cat-calling. Her heart was racing; it was weirdly exhilarating. She felt accomplished and attractive. She wanted to turn back and walk through the construction zone again, but she had class. She could not wait for class to be over to go and tell Nobu. She even made sure to walk back through the construction zone, and this time she listened for the words. Finally, she arrived at her destination and burst into the two girls' room at lunchtime. She excitedly told Nobu all about the incident. Biz listened from her bed, disapproving of the excitement. Lani could not ignore the look on Biz's face. No one could dampen her excitement at the time, but the look gave her something to think about. So, Lani resolved that the next step was to be militant against the attention but use Nobu's strategy. Learn to tune out the words. She always had the freedom to let them in and enjoy the attention if needed. It wasn't long before she had learned what to listen for. And soon, she had learned to tune it out entirely.

LENNY

Lani and the girls were at a party in a sketchy part of town. The locals called the building Big Betty's, but its official name was Ivory Towers. Leilani had stepped out of the party and into the hallway to take a call. She was wrapping up when Big Betty and a tall, well-dressed man rounded the corner. She heard the man's Zawe accent and waited for an opening in the two's conversation. Then she said "zviri sei" - (how are things?)

Lenny's attention was immediately transferred to the girl in the hallway. He remarked on how fashion-forward she was for someone from Zawe. She laughed and commented on how he looked and sounded like the disgraced "gay man" she had heard about. He had laughed in turn and confirmed that it was he. They spoke with ease and eventually exchanged numbers. He, the underdog still looking for redemption, and her, "Lani," the warrior on a mission.

Lenny's reprieve from the ostracism was hanging out with Leilani. Besides Big Betty, no one else had been a regular contact in his life since the scandal. He spoke with Letty sporadically, but he had hope as long as she was single. Leilani had told him about the galling ignorance of the people of Uzu. She shared about thought control and all the gender roles. She had mentioned her parents once or twice but never went into detail about them. He laughed with her about her cat-calling project, which had turned out successful. He had given her many pointers on fashion, and they had so much fun hanging out. She had learned about the love of his life, Letty, and she hoped he could get her back.

* * *

208

A few weeks later, she had invited him to the march against police brutality. He chickened out last minute because he did not want his face as part of another publicity situation. But he had driven her downtown and dropped her off for the protest.

"Okay, so you will try and meet up with Biz. And if you can't find her, I'll be driving you back, right?"

"Yes," Leilani replied, her face determined. She stepped out of the car, pulled out her protest poster, and waved goodbye to Lenny.

"Lani, Lani!" he had called out. She turned around, "I'll be at a bar on the protest route if you need me. It's the Varnish."

She gave him a thumbs up.

She had managed to locate Biz in the chaos of the march. The two girls had decided to head to the protest after-party together. But they never made it. At least she had texted Lenny so he would not wonder what had happened to her. The protest had grown violent at many spots along the route. There were reporters along the route documenting all the chaos. Finally, the march arrived in a particular district of downtown LA. That's when someone decided to grab a TV from one of the stores. And the looting began.

When the police came, they rounded up many of the protestors. Leilani was part of those rounded up, unfortunately. She had not taken anything, but it didn't look good that she was caught in this chaos. This was not good for the asylum program, which had brought her and other Uzu people over. They weren't going to deport her, but she could lie low somewhere outside the country if she left of her own will. Of course, she was always welcome back but a year off from college was advised.

So Leilani flew back to Zawe and moved into Mbare.

LANDING

When Leilani landed in Zawe, she was quickly overtaken by culture shock. She was an Uzu-born and raised young lady. She was also halfway to becoming an American-educated woman. Being in Zawe felt like being brought back to her roots through a trial by fire. And, of course, she had chosen the iconic Mbare to live in so she could have an authentic gap year experience. She was not going to be a tourist in her father's house.

"Eh, sister," one of the touts said, whistling.

"Muri seiko yellow-bone," another yelled at her. (how are you, fair-skinned young lady)

One of the guys said, "aah boys, uyu ndewechirungu (she is fancy and knows English), you say - "bootylicious!"

Leilani was used to cat-calling, but this level felt slightly off the charts. Moreover, it landed differently because it was in her native language. She had practiced ignoring the familiar English words. And now she had to learn how to tune out this new breed of cat-calls with mixed languages. However, she had grown up in Uzu, where they spoke some Shona, so she was confident she would tune the words out soon.

She found a place to "lodge" with a cool landlord who wanted the reputation of her staying at his house. He was a married man who felt he deserved to live in the fancy parts of town but lived in Mbare nevertheless. Moreover, he relished the prospect of conversation with her. At first, she thought his enthusiasm was a way of flirting with her but soon realized he was simply eager to converse in English. It was also her opportunity for cultural exchange.

"Ah, sister," he would say in a heavy Zawe accent, "Donti leti iti geti to you. This hwindis actually mean no disrespecti. It's a complimenti, especially for someoney likey you ka. Enjoy it while it lasts, somedayi you will be old, and no one will call after you." And his wife would laugh with him at this last part. His wife was usually sweeping the yard as they spoke. Sometimes she would listen through the kitchen window as she cooked. The landlord joked like most people in Zawe.

Very little was sacred and immune to ridicule and laughter in this country.

"That's one thing about Zawe." She said in an email to Nobu and Biz. These people laugh about everything. They laugh at themselves, at hardship, and the pain. They even laugh right at a tragedy as it is happening or right after. It makes for a stress-reduced life, and I have found myself with little need for yoga or meditation. And they dance like no one is watching. But the cat-calling needs to stop."

She quickly settled into a routine. She was interning with an environmental organization. Her role was to help organize the Mbare recycling and waste recovery initiative. She found it bizarre that so many people had fresh fruit and vegetable stalls. Most of them were women too. It was remarkable not to get fresh produce from a big store. And to support people living right around her. One time she bought some bananas simply because the lady looked a lot more impoverished than every other stall owner. She then walked a distance and gave the bananas to the children playing hopscotch in the street. They were overjoyed. And she began to do that often, buying things simply to support the stall owners and then giving away her purchases. The children in the community loved her, and so did many of her neighbors.

Unfortunately, Leilani suffered more incidents of being cat-called. It put a damper on some of her positive feelings about her time in Zawe. But she had a way of coping. She turned the initiative into a personal women's empowerment recycling setup. With a few exceptions, Leilani sourced her labor and resources primarily from women. Leilani spoke as though her role was to be a freedom fighter leading a revolution. She enjoyed the feeling of power.

And then Leilani stumbled onto a Zawe dance party. A renowned local dancehall musician was shooting a music video in Mbare. And some people had joined the hired dancers as expected. Some people had whistled at Leilani to come and dance, but she ignored them and continued walking. Then she felt a hand on her wrist. She turned around, ready to blow some fire, only to find a young girl smiling at her and pulling her towards the dance circle. Leilani's heart melted, a little embarrassed. And she felt she could not resist much, and she joined in the merrymaking and discovered a new love; dancing. Or not so much dancing itself as dancing with these people. She found a new appreciation for her body, for movement. As everyone danced their hearts out and shook what evolution had given them, she felt she was one of them. At least for that moment. Her thoughts and observations amused her. And it looked like people were delighted that the "difficult" young lady was loosening up.

This lone day didn't stop the cat-calling. Leilani's mini dresses had earned her several extra whistles at the bus terminus. First, she had worn one because it was too hot. And then it turned into a statement, and she wore more in subsequent days. So, finally, she reached out to Nobu for mini-skirt reinforcement.

"Now, you must know, gender in Zawe is different."

She had written to Nobu, who laughed when she received the email. Nobu laughed at her sister educating her about gender in Africa.

"Here, men are men, and women are women, and there are no sex-less or gender-less rational creatures. Women here sway their hips the way you were teaching me, Nobu. And show what their mothers gave them proudly. They don't try to hide and tie sweaters over their pronounced behinds. And the way they dance! My dear Nobu, I have learned freedom and abandon as I move and dance. And watch for a video from Zawe with me in it. I'll wait for it to drop and send you the link. Oh, and the men are masculine - I wish I could explain further. But they somehow manage to make me feel seen sexually without objectifying me. It's thrilling, but all the same, the cat-calling needs to stop. So send more mini-skirts, please. We need to stick it to the patriarchy out here.

My neighbor slash landlord says it's a compliment. And that the touts mean no disrespect at all. And even though I have days I thoroughly enjoy it, a couple of days when I wore the mini skirt and dress, they went too far. So please do send over my summer beach box. How is Marcus?"

Marcus was the new guy who had asked Nobu on a date.

ODYSSEUS AND PENELOPE

Leilani had heard of another woman who was helping the underprivileged in Mbare. They said she was American, so she sought her out even more. Leilani thought this woman was a college student also taking a year off. She relished having one more like-minded friend when she went back to school. Also, if the friend were from another state, Leilani would have somewhere to go for winter or summer breaks. When she arrived at the Mbare church, she saw signs for the soup kitchen. When she walked to the soup counter, she was surprised to see a caucasian male. He looked very comfortable and greeted her, saying, "Sei sei sister?" She replied in English and asked for the woman she had heard about.

Riva was summoned, and she was very gracious and delighted to see Leilani. The same way she was with everyone who frequented the soup kitchen. It was called a soup kitchen, but they served other food instead of soup. They also did way more than food, and she had taken Leilani to the back and given her a tour of the operation. They became fast friends as Leilani shared what she was working on and her empowerment bent.

She learned that Timothy and Riva had been in Zawe for about three years. Timothy knew a lot of the customs and language. He hung out with the touts at the bus terminus now and then, even though Riva disapproved. She was grateful for how he had assimilated the culture. It was easier to help from the inside than from the outside. Riva credited Timothy for the various offerings they had developed. Offerings that met real needs but sounded weird on paper. During her tour, Riva had shared oodles and asked plenty of questions. Leilani felt like a student in the presence of her sensei. More visits ensued, which were filled with conversation and laughter.

Timothy had been biding his time, waiting for an opportunity to talk with Leilani. He had heard quite a lot about her from the touts. His mother seemed to like her, and that was a positive. So the next time she came by in the evening, he offered to walk her home.

Leilani accepted Timothy's offer to walk her home from the church. She was curious to hear more about his own assimilation experiences. He wanted to discuss life with someone who had some American influence and wasn't his mother.

Timothy began by teasing and telling some stories about her that he had heard about.

"What, you were there when that happened?" she asked, surprised at her not spotting him. She must have fixed her eyes to truly not see color. A caucasian young man should stand out in Mbare. That was not too bad an achievement. After all, her ears were trained to tune out cat-calls. "I have never spotted you at the bus terminus," she remarked as they closed the gate to the church.

Timothy only laughed and related more stories about her and her mini-skirts. And then the dancing which surprised everyone and delighted many. She was laughing too. Then he confessed that he had never been a part of the crew that called after her. Sometimes he would arrive right after she had passed through. The guys would regale him with tales of what they had said to her that day. He found it amusing and hoped that whoever was on the receiving end did not feel threatened. And now he had put a face and a name to the "whoever." And Leilani was quite incredible - he was saying.

"So you are okay with the cat-calling?" she asked pointedly.

"I was hoping you'd ask me if I was okay with the mini-skirts," he replied.

Leilani was surprised by the response, shrugged his mischievous smile off, and obliged, "So are you okay with the mini-skirts?"

He instead laughed, "I would have to see you in one to have an opinion."

* * *

"oooooh, I should have known?" she said, laughing.

"Yes, you walked right into that one," he replied, and they laughed easily together. Leilani found herself calculating in her mind how old he was. He interrupted her thoughts.

"But, but, but, I should say, it is my policy to refrain from having an opinion about other people's lives or actions. I am a fisheep, as my mom likes to say. Not telling others what to do, but like a good fish, swimming and waiting to be caught by the fishers of men who then keep the good and throw away the bad. And like a good sheep, being led by the good shepherd. I don't shepherd others as though I know better how they should live their lives. People have their own schedule for growth. In addition, there is only one teacher, really, and too many cooks spoil the pot. So fisheep."

"Hmmm, well answered. I don't even know what a fisheep would look like. But you sound like you have learned how to mind your own business." she replied

"Haha, not at all, if Zawe has taught me anything. Here my business is everybody's business. And everybody's business is mine. I only do my best not to believe I know better." He said, looking at her, and she was impressed and smiling.

"Interesting! So what's your business? How did you end up here in Zawe?" she asked, hoping to make it even more personal.

"Well, my mom went along with my dad's program for far too long. And then, finally, he pushed her away. So they are separated now, and she brought me here because I had been bugging her that we need to serve others across the globe. And so we are here now, and I am doing my best to assimilate integrate with the culture and help out. She worries about me learning bad habits. So I try to remain American when I am around her. But it feels a little like hiding and a lot like inauthenticity."

"Take it from me; it can be painful to find your independence from your parents. But, be yourself and do what you are called to do. Stop trying to please your mom. It's better to know you are where you are because of what you believe. Rather than finding yourself stranded somewhere for someone else's beliefs." she said, holding his hand and squeezing it.

He smiled at her and stopped. "I think I'll leave you here. I'll walk you all the way home next time you come by," he said

"Oh, there is a "next time" already, huh?" she asked, pleased.

"I already planned our future, Leila," he said, and she froze. No one had called her that in a long while. "Oh, was it too forward to shorten your name like that?" he asked, mortified.

"No," she said, shaking her head and swallowing. "No, not at all. Most of my friends call me Lani, is all."

"Would you prefer that then?" he asked.

"You are too kind to ask. I prefer what you prefer and will leave you to decide. Catch you later, Timothy!" she said, walking away.

Timothy was left scratching his head and watching Leilani walk away. He wondered if he had just messed up what seemed to be a positive interaction.

~.~.~.~.~.~.~.~.~.~.~.~.~.~.~.~

It was a couple of days before she visited the Soup Kitchen again.

Timothy walked her home again, and they were laughing and chatting. But, of course, some serious thoughts would waft through their light conversations.

"Has anyone ever told you they loved you? And you watch them, and you learn their idea of love. Or you ask them, and they tell you what their idea of love is. Then you think to yourself, how about you don't love me anymore?"

* * *

216

"How about "no" - Leilani chimed in, and the two laughed.

"Yes, how about no! I'm glad you get it." Timothy added

"Oh no, I get the part where there is something undesirable. But what do you mean rejecting another person's idea of love?" she asked.

Timothy paused, racking his brain for a way to phrase it so she could understand. "I am saying, sometimes people think they are doing you a favor or giving you a great gift when they say, "I love you." But when you learn what that phrase means to them, you would rather they don't love you."

"Hmmm, I'd have to think about that. Because, unfortunately, I haven't had a chance to wrestle with that one."

"Hmmm, don't wrestle with it; dance with it. Think of it this way." Timothy said, jumping around, trying to think.

Leilani found herself amused by his cute jump dance. She beamed at Timothy.

"Should I dance like that?" she asked, looking at him.

He caught himself and grinned.

"I could teach you if you like?" he replied

It was her turn to try the jump dance, and they were laughing and jumping around.

"Look, yes, here is an example. Some people's ideas of empowerment include isolating and wall building. In contrast, other people's ideas of empowerment include bridge-building and healthy interdependence. So when you hear someone championing empowerment, you need to pause and then listen to their definition of empowerment. In case you prefer this empowerment over that kind of empowerment."

"Oh, I see what you mean. When you put it in terms of empowerment, I can see how people may say the same word and mean different things. I can see how someone may say 'love' and mean the 'unconditional, perpetually forgiving open arms.' Another person could say love and mean the 'butt-kicking always correcting you so you can be better' kind of love. So sad, isn't it; when someone thinks they know better how to live your life, and they are always correcting you out of love. When their own life is in shambles."

"Correct yourself out of love, right?" Timothy asked, looking at her sideways.

"Yes! Your log first, then the spec!" she exclaimed and noticed his look. "What? What did I say?" she asked.

"I am only surprised at your choice of characterization. Are you sure you haven't spent too much time with my mom?"

"haha, I like your mom. I think she has some good insights into life, and she misses your dad quite a lot." Leilani replied, relaxing.

"Man, I don't miss that tyrant at all. All I wanted was to do good work in the world, and he was against every one of my ideas."

"My parents were not with my program. But they turned out to be right. I wish I had listened, and now I don't know if they want me back."

"Have you reached out to them?" Timothy asked.

"Have you reached out to your dad?" she shot back.

He smiled gently, "I mean well, you know?"

"Yes, I know. I'm a little touchy on that subject. Enough talk of parents. This is where I live." she replied

"Cool house. You rent a room here, huh?"

"Yes," was his one-word reply.

He noticed, and she saw that he had noticed the one-word reply.

"Well, I have done my part and made sure no lions attacked you on the way home. I hope to see you again, Leila...ni," he said, adding the last syllable in time. Leilani only shook her head, amused at the stumble,

"Stumbling over our words, are we?"

"I don't stumble; I dance," Timothy replied and bowed.

"Well, thank you, brave sir, you may return to your mommy dearest now," she replied, and they laughed and parted ways.

Timothy was over the moon. Finally, he felt he was making some headway in getting to know this woman. Maybe he could get married in Zawe and never have to leave. He would never have to go and confront his father.

Leilani was not sure how to think of Timothy. He was younger than her, but he seemed interesting and fun. And she felt they were like-minded in many ways. They could be Odysseus and Penelope or like her crazy parents, whom she loved and missed.

AT THE BUS TERMINUS

Finally, Leilani walked by the bus terminus, and Timothy was there. She could hear some remarks from the touts and quickly tuned them out. They liked how she ignored them, so more of them joined in. With precision, Leilani's ears caught the respectful greetings of market women and men. She responded cheerily to them and kept ongoing.

She walked in this mode when she felt a tap on her shoulder. She whirled around, hands ready for war. Timothy had jumped back to protect himself. The scene was dramatic and hilarious. All the touts who had been watching Timothy approach her burst out laughing. Leilani was relieved and she laughed, while Timothy grinned. "I'm sorry I startled you. It's tough to get your attention, apparently."

* * *

"Not to worry. I try to tune out all the trashy stuff and only respond to the good things."

"Gotcha! You do it so well." He replied.

"Thank you," She said, curtsying. "I have a lot of practice."

Timothy was amused. He asked her, "So can I accompany you wherever you are going?"

"If you want. I am heading to the small piece of land we are using for the women's project."

He raised his eyebrows. Leilani shook her head slowly and ignored his expression. "I call it that to remind myself that there are dangerous men out there, and I need to be wary and fight for my kind."

"And I am not your kind?"

"What kind is that?" she asked.

"Humankind, I would surmise?"

"Yes, you are, but the male kind has been oppressing the female kind for a long time now," Leilani replied resuming her journey while Timothy followed walking beside her.

"I have lived a short life but long enough to know that anyone who generalizes things has an agenda. Someone once said, to think globally, one has to level all the mountains and valleys to create a uniform world. To generalize is to do violence to so much in the name of making a point."

"You say that because the system is designed to benefit you," she replied.

"I don't feel better off than you. The system needs to be better designed to benefit me if it is truly designed that way currently. Men might need to organize and really structure this system to benefit them." he replied, smiling ridiculously.

* * *

"While you are doing that, I will fight the current system. First, I am going to get myself situated financially. Get some real estate, and start some businesses so I don't have to rely on a man for my upkeep. And then I will find a partner who will have his own stuff, and we will walk together."

Timothy had said, "these days, finding a woman who wants to do that is like the old days when women had dreams of family. Back then, it looked like most women could not dream without society cueing them. In the old days, they were cued to want family, and nowadays, they have been cued to want their own property. While men simply ride along free to choose."

"So you admit, men have been free to choose all along?"

"Haha, no. Man has no choice but to fill armies and do drudge work. All you hear is we need more female scientists and CEOs in the fight for equality. Have you heard them say we need more female ditch diggers and more female construction workers or more female miners? It's all about equality for illustrious jobs while the men take on all the other not-so-glamorous ones."

She shot back, "Which one is it? Either men can "choose freely without society cueing them," or society cues them just like it cues women. Privilege generally speaks the way you are doing right now, Timothy. Most women had to fight to be in the army or work in mines."

"You really are one of those people?" he replied.

"Whoa, what people?" she asked, stopping to look at him.

"There are people you shouldn't bother talking to..."

"What, why, why is that? This will be good," Leilani said, facing Timothy with her whole body. With her eyes, she dared him to continue with his line of thought.

Timothy paused and smiled ominously.

* * *

"Because you can ask them a question and open a woke magazine and get their answer. Their answers are prepackaged by thought leaders and social propaganda machinery."

"Wow, that is rich coming from you."

Timothy laughed nervously, ignoring her comment. "Critical thinking is all you need to realize that it's hard to find people who can produce original thoughts. People are yearning for things they have been conditioned by society to desire. They live out of an identity defined for them already by someone else. Everyone is thinking outside the box. The inside box thinkers might as well be the unique ones now."

"Who says I am going for unique?" she retorted, getting lost in Timothy's weird incoherent oration.

"I didn't realize you were going for ordinary." Timothy shot back gently. He had mastered his father's domineering, put-down nature without his father's emotionality. Before Leilani could reply, he continued pressing his point calmly, like the momentary silence before an explosion. "But in truth, we are all ordinary. But not the same kind of ordinary. And that's my beef with this idea that the human mind can comprehend the one truth at all. And that it does so in the same way if one is following logic. And if you don't agree with this one way, you become a bigot or illogical. And in one tradition, you are going to hell. But, at the same time, by another philosophy, you are evil because there is no hell but morality stands. Or your school of thought: either you agree with me, or you are an evil privileged man."

"So what, you believe there are no evil people?" Leilani retorted.

"I don't believe that at all. I believe that there are people in the world who are deceived. Some people choose evil because they mistake it for good. Some choose it because they are addicted, but we know now that's an illness. In truth, if you look at all the superheroes in the world, they tend to fight mentally challenged people. Superheroes save the world and destroy so-called "villains." And these villains tend to be mentally unhealthy people who need help. It's as though comic writers have been yelling for decades, "There is no boogie man, only mentally ill people; there are no evil people, only deceived."

* * *

"Tell that to the people who were lynched. And ask them to think it through like that." Leilani replied, crossing her arms.

"Oh yes, I would. If people treated each other better, more and more of us would be mentally healthy. And we would not need to victimize others. So it may come down to mental health, not necessarily empowerment or a lack of it. I am wounded by my past, so I appear to you as privileged. What I need is healing, not a lesson on privilege."

"You really are privileged," she muttered. "As a woman, I don't have the luxury to feel pity for the mentally ill or wounded if they attack me. At that point, I only have fear and self-defense for them. I can't wear my mini skirt in peace. I can't live my life without being concerned about the world and threats all around me."

"Sounds like you have left little room for compassion!" Timothy replied. He was gifted with compassion. He longed to help as much as he yearned to be understood.

"You church people have a weird view of compassion and grace. The world is burning down, and all you do is take the side with oppressors by being silent."

"We are not silent," Timothy retorted.

"So, what are you doing?"

"We are simply saying forgive them, Father, for they know not what they are doing. Forgive everyone on either side of every war, either the war of race, gender, or the wealth gap. If each side knew what it was doing while feeling justified, they would stop. This is not about sides. We are all on one side called humanity. To dehumanize those who dehumanize you is the same crime of dehumanization."

"That doesn't make the world a better place. It doesn't help anyone to say that. The church needs to take sides, or it's complicit. Even your Jesus said "to do" what he says. Action is key. The church needs to take more action, do more 'soup kitchen' stuff, and support the right side of the wars raging in the world."

* * *

"The church lost its way when it decided that responding to people like you was the way to get people in the door. It lost its way when instead of saying, "Forgive them, father," it started screaming along with all the woke people, "Justice!""

"You are so privileged. You have nothing to fear in this world because of your gender and race." Leilani replied with so much force it shook her body.

"I think I am brave to say all these things. They are true for me, and I know I have the potential to suffer for saying them because of the color of my skin. I should be afraid of you and what you could do to me, especially if there were many of you here." Timothy replied. He had fought with his father; he could fight with anyone. She had stood against her parents; she could stand against this young man.

Leilani remembered the blue lives man. She did not like how Timothy's words felt at that moment. How could it be wrong to think the world needed fixing. She wasn't wrong; the world was broken. She replied before she could even think. "You just don't get being a woman and being a woman of color, for that matter. The world sees me from afar and objectifies me or denies me opportunities before I even arrive on location. And when I walk home, I am always weary."

"Sounds like you never have fun. Or if you do, it's only on Saturday night with your girls, but the other six days, you are walking in terror. Which is weird for someone who claims to be empowered."

"I can be empowered and afraid," she retorted.

"But you certainly can't be empowered and a victim simultaneously." He replied

She was fuming, "I am woman, I am fearless, I am feminine, I am masculine, I am anything that I want. I am a hero..."

Timothy interrupted; it was a full-on fight now. "But the problem with today's heroes is they can easily be canceled. Even renowned authors can get sidelined and barred for not toeing the propaganda line. So to remain a hero in others' eyes, you need to keep playing the game. You need to say the right thing in the right way at the right time. Crack them right kind of jokes. Etc! You can't even say something positive about your enemy. Remember that orange-haired president of ours in the US?" Timothy asked and waited for Leilani's begrudging Zawe response of "hmmmm."

"When anyone said anything positive about him - anything positive - that person was instantly lumped in with "the basket of deplorables." A real hero stands for something regardless of society. And I dare you to have a view that doesn't mesh with your woke thought leaders."

Leilani could not think of an idea that she held contrary to the woke people she had met. She had even learned to dislike cat-calling to fit in with Biz and the other activists.

She was stumped. She stormed off! She dodged a car that was coming her way and kept going. Here, everyone saw everyone. The pedestrians and the drivers danced on the roads in these parts of Mbare. They dodged each other and honked a little here and there. Leilani did not look back.

LOVE TO SEE YOU WALK AWAY

Timothy was left standing in the dust. The once paved roads of Mbare had eroded such that large chunks of them were back to gravel. And as she walked away in a huff, she kicked up a bit of dust.

He remained standing there, blinking rapidly and staring blankly ahead. He was like a clueless man who had been smacked by life. And was now waiting unbeknownst to him for a kick in the butt. But instead, one of the touts came to shake him out of this stupor. He dragged Timothy back to the boys.

Timothy wondered a little how to recover from this situation. He was getting to like this girl. Their heated and indecipherable ideological fight was difficult to process.

* * *

"Why-i are you chasing-i that-i one-y chief?" one of the touts asked,

"She's tough, eh?" another one said. And the others were chuckling.

"She doesn'ty eveny turny aroundy when we press the the the the the the hooter at her in borrowed nice cars." someone called from the other side.

"Haaa, maBoss," (Bosses) Timothy replied, "I need a girlfriend inini (me). And she might be the one."

The guys laughed, and one of them spoke up,

"No one needs-y a girlfriendy Timmy. You only want one."

"Ehe," (Yes) one of the guys echoed, "The guy preaching at the square was telling us yesterday. If-u you thinki you need a girlfriend - it-i meansy you have issuesy ende you need eh, eh to deal with them."

"hehe, hanzi, if-u a girl say-zi, "I needy you" you shouldu run. It means she has issues, and she thinks you are the solution," and the boys laughed,

"Manje, ndiri seni, Timmy, (As for me, Timmy) If I had a sister, I wouldu be tellingy her to run from you righty nowu. Becaus-ie you said, "I need a girlfriend inini," he finished mimicking Timothy's accent.

And everyone laughed. Timothy joined in the laughter. It had taken him a little while to get used to truth-told in-jokes. He had gotten used to the truth spoken in front of you rather than behind your back. And that's how he had spoken to Leilani. No one had told him the Zawe saying, "Rume risinganyepi hariroori." (A man who doesn't lie won't get married.)

RETRACTION

The next time Timothy saw Leilani, she was cold towards him. He tried to tell her how he and his mom had left Arizona protesting his father's discrimination. He wanted to show her that he was for empowerment.

And she softened. So they began hanging out again.

They realized that they had opposing views on specific topics. So they tried to stay away from those topics.

"So you and your mom rebelled against the church?" Leilani asked on this particular walk

"Oh no, just me," he replied, "She is still a faithful follower of the imaginary. I am all about doing good, but I don't need God to do that."

"You sounded quite churchy when we argued at the bus terminus," she said, smiling and teasing. Timothy did not smile at her. So she pivoted, "So have you read any of the "new agey" stuff?" she asked.

"Why?" he asked.

"Well, it's usually the route for many people who leave the church. The spiritual aspect of life is not lost to many you know especially ex-church people."

He gave her a look. He felt found out and predictable.

"Yeah, I like Alan Watts the best," he replied after a long pause.

Leilani sighed, relieved, "Oh, I know Alan Watts. He is so profound, and his voice takes you to the next level." she replied, smiling.

"Oh, for me, it's not his voice. I like Watts because of his battle with alcohol. It makes me feel like it's okay to be flawed even as I continue to seek enlightenment."

She paused and looked at him, "And why can't you say the same about the church?

"I think the church needs to be better, and people need to stop being self-righteous." He replied.

"Naah, you are about to understand privilege. You can't say the same about the church because you were at the receiving end of the imperfections. You suffered through what your father struggled with, so now you can't say it inspires you. Now you see why I can't say, 'there are no evil people, only mentally unhealthy people or deceived people.' When you suffer through something, you can never see it purely intellectually."

"Really, you are going to bring that up?"

"I felt misunderstood last time. And I thought that now I could get you to relate."

"Well, I feel misunderstood right now. Your crusade and desire to be right stopped you from hearing my point," he replied

"Oh, I heard your point, alright. You are inspired by a flawed human seeking enlightenment and preaching things he struggles to practice. But that person is a new ager, and that works better because he is not from the church that hurt you. The irony!" she said, laughing at him. He didn't laugh with her.

"Well, now you feel how I felt. So now you understand why I stormed off then, huh."

Timothy laughed sheepishly. And Leilani closed the door to her heart. They had succeeded at being contentious, and he disagreed with the deep things she held to. Timothy felt the change, too, as they said goodbye. He had tried not to be emotional, but her comment about his dad was spot on. It didn't stop it from hurting, so Timothy walked home licking his wounds. He schemed on how he could get back at her. She was skimming on how to kick him out of her life. She liked Riva, though, so it would have to be delicate.

THE CAR CRASH

Timothy decided to exact his revenge when he saw Leilani at the bus terminus the next day. Her least favorite thing was to be cat-called. He was relishing the moment she would realize it was him cat-calling her. It would be the ultimate revenge. She had trained herself not to listen, but he didn't know how well she could ignore him.

"Eh, sister," he started, and the touts around him began to giggle.

"Mother vakatakura" (mother carrying a load), someone chimed in.

"Bootylicious" someone else yelled, and Timothy looked at the guy. Everyone laughed.

"Sorry, boss," the tout said, and Timothy smiled, "No problem, chief," and they went back to cat-calling Leilani.

Then they saw the car bearing down on the road as Leilani was about to cross.

Timothy whistled, as did some other guys, to try and catch her attention. But Leilani had tuned them out.

"Apo, yellow bone," Timothy called out. His voice was less confident and more frantic. She looked like she didn't see the car.

"Sister,"

"Hey, hey"

"Hona mota Iyo chidanger!" (look, there is a car coming, young lady)

Several people called out to her, but she could not hear them. She didn't have any earphones in her ears. She had responded to some greetings right before the touts had begun cat-calling her. To everyone watching, it was supposed to end well. But they had to make sure, so they called her and warned her of the car coming her way. The vehicle was blaring its horn, and Leilani thought it was another way of cat-calling as had happened once. Cars honked at her when she walked on certain streets.

Timothy finally gave in to his panic and decided he didn't want to annoy her anymore. So he yelled, "Leila!"

She heard it, and she finally decided to open her ears. She turned her head to look back at the only man who knew to call her that. That's when she heard the car, but it was too late. The car full of people and baggage crashed into her at full speed. The driver hit the breaks, but it was way too late.

If it was not anyone's fault, Timothy believed it was his for starting the cat-calling. He had tried to annoy her even as he tried to save her. No one else knew she would tune them all out but him.

AMBULANCE

Timothy rushed to the scene as people crowded around the fallen woman. The driver had his fingers crossed, hands behind his head, in the typical Zawe pose of lament. Tears were streaming down his face. He did not mean to crash into her.

He expected her to avoid him last minute. Everyone saw everyone here. It was the kids they watched for with great care. Grown-up pedestrians and drivers danced on the roads in these parts of Mbare. Close calls were a common occurrence, too, in these parts. Some pedestrians were defiant and moved last minute. And she was well known for her defiance, so the driver didn't expect it to end this way. He had expected her to dodge last minute, and the touts had expected her to hear them.

One of the touts, Timothy's friend, told him they needed a private car. It would most likely be too late by the time the ambulance got there. And that the government hospitals may not be equipped to handle the kind of trauma she had. They commandeered a kombi. One of the ladies gave her a reed mat to be used to help carry the girl like a gurney. People helped load Leilani into the 18-seater. The driver rushed to the nearest private hospital at Timothy's request. He called his mother on the way, and she rushed down to the West End Hospital. They expedited her case to the ICU on arrival, and she was gone from sight.

Leilani had her asylum ID on her and some other documents.

When his mother showed up soon after, Timothy was crying. He was trying to tell her it was his fault, but she could not understand how he had caused the accident. Riva comforted her son as much as she could. Several hours later, he was composed enough to join her in thinking of ways forward. They needed to reach out to several people but did not know their contact details.

Timothy had asked one of the doctors to unlock Leilani's phone with her fingerprint. It was cracked but still functional. He had obliged him even though it wasn't policy. He told him they needed to contact next of kin, but they didn't have anyone. They had already reached out to the US embassy since Leilani was an asylee.

When the doctor came out, the phone was unlocked, but the look on his face was not encouraging. It was already past midnight, and they had waited for news for hours.

"How is she doing?" Timothy asked instead of accepting the phone, which was extended towards him.

Riva took the phone and held her son as the doctor stood there, unsure how to answer. "How is she?" the young man asked with an impatient insistence on the question.

"Sir, who is she to you?" the doctor asked in a perfect English accent.

"Dog-gon-it, doctor; how is she doing?" Riva asked forcefully, surprising her son and the doctor.

He only shook his head.

"Is she, is she..." Timothy couldn't finish the question as his tears got the better of him.

* * *

"No, no, she is still fighting, but the prognosis is poor," he replied

Timothy walked away. He was overcome with emotion, and he needed his dad. Riva looked at Leila's phone over the cracks and tried to make sense of it. It looked like Lenny was the best contact to call from all her correspondence with him.

She talked with Timothy and asked him if he knew about Lenny. But the young man did not know. Riva had been taking numbers down from the phone. Nobu and Biz were part of the list. It was early morning outside.

Timothy walked down the hallway, pulled out his phone, and dialed his father.

The US embassy representative was there at the counter when Riva and Timothy were making phone calls. She, too, decided to call Simbai, whom Leilani had listed as her next of kin.

THE CALLS

{"Hello, is this Simbai?" Someone from the US embassy was asking. - "Yes, this is Simbai." The man replied

* "Is this Lenny?" Riva asked

~ "Dad, dad," Timothy's voice came across his father's ears. Timothy's voice was filled with tears. Bishop Hooper had chills. His son had finally reached out. "Yes, I'm here, son; what's going on?"

~ "She is dying," Timothy said, "And it's all my fault."

~ "Who is dying?" Bishop Hooper asked

{"Sir, I'm calling about your daughter Leilani. Unfortunately, she was involved in an accident. And she had you as her emergency number when she received her asylum in the United States." Simbai froze and lowered his phone involuntary. He looked at Tambudzai as he stammered Leilani's name. His mouth went dry.

"Leilani?" Tambudzai asked, furrowing her eyebrows.

Riva looked down the hallway as her son sobbed into the phone. She paused,

* "Umm, Lenny, Leilani was texting you the most in the last couple of months. And so it's the first number I thought to call after the accident."

* "Who is Leilani," He asked

* "Oh, right, you might know her by "Lani"?"

Lenny looked across the table to Simbai. But unfortunately, he was busy over the phone, so his gaze landed on Tambudzai, who was looking at him askance. Leilani was not a common name. Why was Lenny talking about a Leilani on the phone?

~ "Who is dying?" Bishop Hooper repeated as his distraught son kept sobbing and not replying. "I'm here, Timmy. Who is dying? Is it your mother?"

~ "Noooooo," the boy drawled and sobbed, "You, you, you don't know her. It's Leilani."

~ "Leilani, is dying?" Bishop Hooper repeated askance.

The table hushed.

Simbai told his caller to hold on, and Lenny also asked Riva to hold on.

They waited as Bishop Hooper wrapped up his call. He told his son he would call back soon, and they would talk some more. He got the name of the Hospital in Zawe and some more details.

Then Simbai went back to his cell and received the same details.

* * *

Last, Lenny went back to his call with Riva.

"Who is this?" he asked.

"My name is Riva. My son and I have been friends with Leilani for a few months now."

"You wouldn't happen to be Riva Hooper, would you?" Lenny asked, looking at Bishop Hooper.

"Oh yes, that's me. Leilani has spoken of me then," she asked animatedly.

"Yeah, yeah, yeah," Lenny replied. Lani had not, but Lenny didn't want to spook the woman.

Bishop Hooper signaled he did not want to take the phone call. So Lenny rounded up his call, and he hung up.

They all sat there for a few minutes. Tambudzai had overheard enough. "We need to fly to Zawe?" she said

"I have a jet that can be ready in two hours," Lenny announced, looking at his watch. Everyone around the table nodded at him. He passed Simbai and Tambudzai his credit card. "Go grab some clothes at the Taylors on my account. You won't be heading home to grab any."

Tambudzai snatched the credit card from him. She picked up her purse and rose, impatient to leave. She was patting Simbai on the shoulder, and he was looking at Lenny, waiting for more details.

"Oh," Lenny said, responding to Simbai's gaze. "Bishop Hooper and I are going to get ready as well. Meet you here at this restaurant in...," he paused, looked at his Rolex, and continued, "in one hour?"

66 HOURS

They drove straight to the West End Hospital from the airport, sixty-six hours later.

Timothy and Riva were shocked at seeing Bishop Hooper but glad at the same time. They all embraced and went over to the side.

Simbai and Tambudzai provided their identification to prove they were Leilani's parents. So they were the only two allowed into the ICU. As they walked into the hospital room, Simbai was shocked by how 1980s it all was. So clean and well kept, but it was like traveling back in time. They found Leilani wrapped up like a mummy. The doctors had managed to stabilize her, but she was not out of the woods. She probably needed some more complex surgery.

As Simbai watched his daughter on life support, he struggled to decide how to feel. Tambudzai wept while Simbai was fighting between anger and sorrow. She had not seen her daughter in years. They could not hold their little Leila, so they held onto each other. Tambudzai held her belly and thought about their coming boy. Enough of Leilani's face was unbandaged for them to recognize their grown daughter. She was a woman now. Simbai remembered the curse from the principalities. - "We are going to hide her from you until the end" Was this the end? He wondered desperately. He could not share his anguish with Tambudzai.

As they were sitting there, Leilani moaned. She turned to her parents, and tears started pouring down her face. Then her vitals began dropping. The doctors and nurses came rushing through. "Please give her room," someone was saying.

"We need an OR? Prep the OR!" the doctor was saying. There was one OR in this hospital, so there were no room numbers.

Leilani was trying to raise her hand to her parents, but it slumped.

"Get me the De-Fib, stat!" someone said. The next few moments were a blur. One with the soundtrack of a whirring defibrillator and a lyricist yelling "Clear" once in a while. People were shuffling in and out of the hospital room. Tambudzai and Simbai were clutching onto each other in the corner. Machines were beeping, and alarms were sounding.

The medical team tried mouth to mouth, and some more "clears" were heard. Simbai and Tambudzai were hanging on to each other all through it. She was in tears, and he was in terror. "Was this the end? They had hidden her till the end. They had kept..."

Tambudzai screamed and coughed and retched. The entire medical staff looked at her, including the doctor. A nurse stopped what she was doing and came over to the couple to usher them out of the hospital room. "You are disturbing the doctor. Your daughter is critical but let the doctor do his job."

Simbai struggled to decide on how to feel. He shuffled out of the room, numb, perplexed. Sorrow mixed with anger, and a desire for vengeance boiled around in his volcanic mind. His emotions were floating around like a butterfly at peace, roiling in the turbulence of a windy day. Then the feelings fluttered and landed on Uzu, and then they turned into a murder hornet. He had his target, and he had his orders. He would destroy that place and rescue the innocent people who lived there before they too were fighting for their lives in a hospital in Zawe.

CHAPTER SEVEN
Chimurenga

OSTRICH THINGS

When they walked out of the ICU, Tambudzai was inconsolable. Riva, Lenny, Bishop Hooper, and Timothy greeted Simbai and Tambu with anticipation. Simbai shook his head slowly, and Tambudzai would not look up. The receiving party assumed the worst. Riva embraced Tambudzai out of Simbai's arms and took her to the side. The two women sobbed and cried together. The guys came over to meet Simbai, who appeared to be seething more than he was mourning.

Meanwhile, Timothy was trying to take responsibility, but neither his dad nor Simbai would listen. Simbai looked at Lenny, who picked up that something was afoot. Lenny shushed Timothy to make space for Simbai to speak. Simbai spoke with hushed anger that scared Timothy and surprised Bishop Hooper. Simbai said he would end the reign of the dragons. That he would wipe out all their human avatars if it killed him. As the other men prepared to interject, the embassy representative walked up to them, and she asked after Leilani.

"Is she still with us?"

"Hanging by the hair of my chinny chin chin," replied Simbai to the visible relief of Timothy. Bishop Hooper and Lenny, too, were glad for the hope.

"Your daughter is a fighter," the embassy representative replied. And then she proceeded to tell them how Leilani had been spirited away from Uzu's clutches. Leilani had been brave, resourceful, and determined throughout the difficult and dangerous process. As the embassy representative told the story, she noticed the change in Simbai's expression and slowly trailed off her narration. Simbai pounced on the end of her story like a hawk snatches a little chick off the ground.

"You spirited her out. Can you squirrel us into Uzu then?" he asked without hesitation.

"What do you mean us?" Lenny asked.

The embassy representative looked at the four men, then back at Simbai. "What would be your intentions if someone were to sneak you into Uzu?"

Simbai replied in a cold surgical voice that rose from a whisper into an oration, "To do something about that bloody government. To do what would have saved my family, my mind, her life...". He looked in the direction of the doors to the ICU, grief flashing across his face for a moment before being replaced by the roiling face of wrath. If she hadn't made it, they would be out telling them by now. Maybe Leila had a chance.

Riva and Tambudzai stopped crying, their attentions stollen by the poignant moment and the conversation.

The embassy representative nodded, bit her lower lip, and said, "Hold on one second." She turned around and began dialing a number as she walked a little distance away.

The four men whispered loudly and gestured. Timothy looked sad and determined. He wanted to avenge Leila; he needed to blame someone else. While Simbai's eyes sparkled with rage, his face looked placid. Lenny and Bishop Hooper looked concerned.

* * *

"I will come with you," Timothy said, hoping to assuage his guilt and prove himself worthy of Leila. He was hoping by pinning the tail on Uzu and then destroying it, he could kill his feelings of guilt. Simbai felt obliged to refuse the tribute. But before he could speak, Bishop Hooper had grabbed Timothy by the shoulder. He was about to say something, and then he sighed. He brought Timothy in for a hug and murmured, "I'm sorry I can't let you do this, son."

Timothy wrested himself away from his father's embrace and replied, spittle flying everywhere. He was livid,

"Dad, you gave up on us a long time ago. Mom told me you wanted a divorce, not the separation. And you gave up on me long before that, never supporting me, always against my ideas and suggestions."

"Timothy, I'd take a bullet for you, you know th...."

"No, dad, no. Some people can take a bullet for you but don't have the courage to talk to you and make things right. They will, they will..." Timothy was overcome with emotion, and his tears started falling fast. Sniffling and gasping, he continued his rant, "They will take a bullet for you but don't dare to support you when it counts. Dying is easy, dad, but living is hard. So you can die for me, but it will never count for all the times you did not live for me."

Bishop Hooper was overwhelmed by his emotions. He believed he deserved his son's words, and he said as much. "I deserve those words, son. And yet I am still your father and will not let you go. And you know your mother will agree with me."

Timothy wailed louder and stormed off. Bishop Hooper was going to follow him when the embassy representative came back. She looked at Timothy, who was stomping his way to the door, shrugged her shoulders, and then addressed the three men.

"Regime change when dragons are involved is an unpredictable mission. The boss says they won't even touch this idea with a thousand-foot pole. They are not interested in..."

* * *

239

Simbai slammed the counter, cursing. The embassy representative jumped a little as she was not expecting the vehemence. Simbai whirled around and started pacing. Lenny and Bishop Hooper sighed in relief. "Well, there goes air support, back up, and logistics," Bishop Hooper chimed in a little more chipper. He was assuming the mission was over.

Simbai gave him an icy look. "My daughter is fighting for her life; I am in no mood to joke around. Those Uzu three flames need to pay for all they have taken from me," The Bishop froze. The Simbai he had known for months was not present in the body he was looking at.

Lenny, too, felt the cold and looked at Tambudzai, whose tears had dried. She signaled him to come over, and he slipped away as Simbai resumed his pacing.

"He is angry and stubborn, but let's try and talk him down from this ledge," She said, sniffling. Lenny nodded and walked back.

"Simbai, I know you want revenge, but your daughter might pull through. We could wait here and pray, and we will be here to support you."

Simbai just gave him a stern look. Lenny looked at Tambudzai again, who urged him on. Bishop Hooper caught the signal and joined in the efforts to talk Simbai out of going to Uzu.

"How about we inform your family first. And then we can have more people here supporting you. We can think about this Uzu issue after Leilani recovers?" Bishop Hooper said, reaching out to Simbai to try and grab his arm. Simbai stopped pacing. He eyed the Bishop's hand, which the Bishop lowered under his gaze.

"You don't get it! I failed; this is the end, and having my family here will only make this worse!!" Simbai yell-whispered.

"What do you mean the end? What will your family do to make this worse?" Lenny asked, puzzled and curious.

"I am the boogie-man in my family. Everyone is terrified of me."

Simbai replied

"Well, from how you are acting right now, I would venture to say it's for good reasons," Bishop Hooper chimed in. Simbai turned sharply towards the Bishop and started walking towards him. Lenny jumped in his way,

"Hey, hey, hey, hey, we are not the enemy here," Lenny said, providing the united front Tambudzai needed.

"Look, guys, I don't want to be the cross you or my old family must bear. But I never made myself the burden. They attacked me when I was innocent. I almost lost my mind. And then they labeled me a monster because of my reaction to their attack. It's not like I lost my mind willingly. When people blame you for something ridiculous, and all of them claim it's true, but you know it is not true, it messes with your reality, and you begin to doubt so much. Then things get interesting when you start finding things funny which are not," Simbai replied, retreating into his heart. He remembered the days when he was laughing for hours at nothing in particular. People thought he was drunk or high, while Simbai slowly marched towards insanity. These were some of the monster's limbs, the monster he had neatly tucked away in the cave. The beast whose other extremities made him afraid of being a father. The fiend whose face he now looked at and desired to destroy.

Lenny and Bishop Hooper moved in closer around him.

"Brother, that was probably a one-time situation. You can't be holding on to that for this long." Bishop Hooper replied.

"Yeah, you sound like the family historian. Every family has one of those. People who keep a record of every wrong that happened in the family and are ready to pull it out at a moment's notice." Lenny replied, chuckling. He was an only child, so he could afford to laugh at the stereotypes.

Simbai only looked at him with a sadness lodged deep in his eye like the log the carpenter of Galilee spoke about, "It was not once; they are still doing it. I am still the boogie man today, yet that label is the injustice I was initially fighting against. I earned the label when I fought back. I was not and am not the cause of their pain and suffering." He replied in a fit of quiet anger, which denied much consolation.

Tambudzai walked to them at that moment. She felt him calming down and wondered if this was the time to place the finishing blow. She had to hold back her tears and talk sense into this man.

"Simbai," she said, gently reaching for his shoulder. He turned around to face her. "Shaa, we went to Uzu, and I was with you, our daughter in tow in my belly. Then, we went to the rural areas, and I was with you. Then, we left for the USA, and I was there. I am still here, by your side. And now our son in tow, in my belly. What else do you want in the world?" she asked gently.

He pulled her close and finally broke down in tears. He cried like a sprinkle of rain at the fringes of a big storm. "It is not what I want; it's what I need," he replied

"And what's that?" she asked, sobbing with him.

"To trust, I am the man I believe I am, a good man willing to die for others. I have been a monster my whole life. I have been a failure to you and Leilani. I need to do this for myself. I want to be a good man for once in my life. To destroy the monster in me and the monsters in Uzu. And to give Uzu my life for the salvation of many if that's what it means. Remember, I need to return to the scene of the crime. We are back in Zawe, but there is also a crime in Uzu - we died there too. I need to come back to life and carry a vision for more for the people of Zawe."

Tambudzai recognized her words from another time. She sighed now, realizing she might need to argue against them. She had to tread carefully or undo whatever those words achieved in her husband.

"But, Simbai, so much more is on the line if you go to Uzu again. We have a son on his way, and we said this time would be better. But, it won't be better if a dragon has you for supper. I went with you to Uzu that one time because ultimately, I'd never leave you, Simbai. I'd ride with you through the worst of storms, even the ones you make with your own hands, because I know it's what you would do for me too. Don't let me and the baby lose you now because I couldn't handle it."

Simbai was sobbing too, and he was struggling to compose himself.

"But Tambu, I am scared you have already lost me. And you will lose more and more of me if I stay. I will be haunted by what became of my daughter because of me, haunted by my ideas. Will I ever be sure even of where to take you for dinner? It may sound small, but please let me do this. Let me make a man out of myself, my way." He said, looking at her, trying to wipe her tears off her face, which was futile as they flowed.

"But you are already a man to me," she replied, looking at him, her gaze going from eye to eye.

"And I am not ready to believe that. Either I escape into our nuclear family. Or I escape into wealth and pleasure. Or I face this monster within and without. This is bigger than any of us, and I want to be able to tell our son: When the dragons came and took Leilani away from us, I went back. And not only destroyed them but saved all the people they were oppressing. I want our son to know his father was not a coward. When my family came for me, I had no recourse, and when the dragons came for us, we were helpless. When the beings of light dropped me in enemy territory, I had no plan either. And so now must we wait for the next tragedy? No, I want my son to know I was not waiting for the next tragedy to befall me. This time I am taking the war to the monsters." He ended with tears drying up.

Tambu heard "the beings of light" and thought her man was off the hinges. She looked at him like he was crazy. And he smiled weakly as his tears began flowing again.

"Oh shoot, I did it, didn't I?" he asked.

"What?" Tambudzai replied, sad and puzzled.

"I said something crazy," he replied
* * *

And Tambudzai could not pretend. She nodded and embraced her husband murmuring. "I'm afraid you might have to go to a mental facility if you stay."

Simbai replied softly, "I am sorry I'm scaring you. But I need your support to go to Uzu. I need to face this, and I need to free those people and myself. I promise you; I am not planning on dying. I promise to come back, and when I do, I will go wherever you want me to go."

"But you can't promise me that!" she replied sharply.

"Yet you have to believe, my love. You have to believe. What is our love without believing in each other, especially in dark times? Unless you really think… But Tambu, can you carry me through the rest of our life together?"

"But this isn't just a dark time. It's a dark time you're making darker by choosing to go back to Uzu. If you stay, this could be a time of praying for Leila's recovery, and that's how dark it could go. But you dying and raising this baby without you?" she vociferated.

"And being in an insane asylum will be just like raising the baby without me," he replied quietly.

She closed her eyes tightly, sighing, as she slowly adjusted to their fate. He was going, and all she could do was help him think of ways to make this journey less dangerous for everyone involved, even though it felt like moving against common sense. He sounded like an ostrich refusing to face the facts.

She opened her eyes, licking her salty tears. It was weird, and they both smiled like the odd pair they were. Since Simbai was going, she hoped now, by a miracle, he would succeed at liberating Uzu or succeed at making himself the man he wanted. Both together wouldn't be too bad either.

"If you do this," Tambudzai said, her anger coming out. She, too, wanted vengeance. "If you do this, you might as well make sure those three flames pay for our daughter's life. And make sure you come back the man you are claiming or else. And the Bishop and Lenny must come with you," she finished hoping she was securing a considerable fraction of the possibility of success for their mission.

Now that they were on the same side, Simbai and Tambudzai relaxed. She was worried he was losing his mind and hoped he could overcome the monster invading his sanity. And he was praying he would survive and come back.

"Simbai, I would be remiss if I didn't register one more objection. Make that two, please." Bishop Hooper said, breaking Tambu and Simbai out of their embrace and reverie.

"Yes, go ahead," Simbai replied, turning towards Riva and the three men.

"If we go, can we at least agree that we are chasing the wind? I am comfortable jumping off a cliff if we don't pretend it's jumping off the bed or kitchen table. This is a suicide mission, and I can't believe I am willing to go along with it. But this is bigger than us. Can we still call it chasing the wind, pursuing emptiness, running after it, pursuing it; endeavoring to capture emptiness, striving to…"

"We get the picture," Lenny interrupted mirthfully.

Simbai looked at Lenny and shook his head, then he replied to the Bishop,
     "Maybe we are chasing the wind. But after I chase it, this might be the first wind to get caught. I may conquer and have a bucket full of freedom. I may die, but die fulfilled."

"The second objection is that I am a natural man. Violence is not my way of walking through the world."

"Except when you slam fists on tables," Riva interjected. The Bishop sighed and turned to Riva. They began talking amongst themselves, and the Bishop was preoccupied.

Lenny didn't need much encouragement. He had run from so many things, the collapsing politics and economy of Zawe and his own identity, to try and get rich. But it had all caught up with him. Nevertheless, he was not running from this near-impossible battle.

UZU

Lenny and Simbai decided they would pause as a Zawe gay couple fleeing the USA and unable to settle in Zawe for obvious reasons. They needed a place of refuge. Simbai was familiar with the immigration process. They claimed to be minimalists who had very few possessions but enough wealth. So they sailed through the immigration process with ease. Uzu had dragons now, so they weren't afraid of spies anymore. The Dragons were enough deterrents for most countries. The two were admitted into the village-state only a week after applying.

Bishop Hooper had matters to settle in Zawe with his family. So he said he would follow them later and use the religious exemption to be allowed into Uzu. Simbai and Tambudzai went to stay with Ruramai and his family as they waited on news of Leila. Lenny visited with his parents secretly.

When the plane landed in Uzu, Simbai and Lenny disembarked with their few belongings. Lenny was surprised at how simple and elegant life presented itself in Uzu. If there was a people who had taken to heart the words, "live and let live," it was the people of Uzu. It looked that way, at least. If these people were oppressed, they looked like they were enjoying it.

The roads were clean, and people were milling around, cleaning them even further. The vehicles were immaculate, with random stops to remove dust and wipe the cars down. There were even refreshment stalls along the streets, and people could pop in and grab something to drink or eat, all on the government's dime. People wore some bizarre fashion, but they all looked well dressed.

The one thing that was different since Simbai left was the new memorial. The driver said it was erected to remember the Uzu residents lost in the "war" against the unshelled. Simbai was gaping at it when Lenny finally asked the driver to stop. They gave the memorial a closer look.

An inscription was written at the base,
"Death is a fitting end for those who defy Uzu law. But the innocent, too, suffer when the chaff must go. A tragedy we now have to bear and not without shedding a tear. And remember the blameless we do while also keeping in mind what is true: death is a fitting end to those who defy the three flames; we shall gloat and never remember their names.

These words unsettled Simbai. They reminded him of when he was falsely accused of causing pain and unhappiness by his family. The family needed a scapegoat, so they had found a good one in him. Everyone needs a villain in their lives, and every family needs an ugly duckling. Every country needs an enemy within and an enemy outside its borders. The three flames required a scapegoat, and the unshelled fit the bill. Simbai was fuming, and he felt impatient for change in Uzu.

Simbai and Lenny looked around and saw people coming from working in the fields. Others were coming from the direction of the Gospel forum and supermarket. Some women were carrying crafts and looked like they were coming from the Women's Association of Crafts and Kids. While children - many of them orphans – who were too young for school played some games in the streets. Simbai sighed; these people were oppressed, but they did not look or sound distressed. They were waiting for more tragedy to befall them. It looked like little would change until more families and lives were destroyed. Their fear of dying for a better life would kill them like it ended his daughter's life.

They drove on to their new house. Lenny spotted the older men and women in their rocking chairs and some in their hammocks, relaxing and basking in the sun.

Simbai muttered something under his breath about ducks. Lenny didn't catch it. He was thinking back to Lani's comments about Uzu and compared them with what he saw. Lenny was enthralled by the sights before him. "I guess what you don't know truly doesn't kill you. Because if these people are oppressed, they seem ignorant about it. They embody perfectly the phrase 'ignorance is bliss,'" he remarked.

"Ignorance is not bliss." Simbai hissed. He turned around to face Lenny in the back seat. Simbai's penetrating gaze seized Lenny's attention. "Ignorance is the tragic pain and poverty of the soul. What you don't know won't hurt you because it will kill you. You can't be hurt when you are dead?" Simbai said, thinking of his daughter whose fate he didn't know.

The driver fidgeted uncomfortably. Lenny realized the folly of his comment, and Simbai remembered they were not alone. They smiled at the driver, and Simbai tried an excuse, "We like to argue for fun." The driver happily took that explanation because it was more comfortable and closed the door to thinking further about their comments.

Finally, they arrived at their new luxurious home. Lenny had presented a quarter of the left-over assets from the settlements. Even that little wealth had bought them some reasonable accommodations in Uzu, close to the higher-ups. Simbai hoped no one in Uzu would look for a spy there because the people of Uzu were positively afraid of the rich and powerful types.

The next day Simbai went to visit Shadreck. His long-time friend Shadreck recognized him quickly, but everyone else was duped. Simbai had to continue with his overly pronounced gay act in front of the family. When Shadreck finally got him alone, they relaxed. Shadreck expressed how he had found the exaggerated gay-act amusing.

Simbai was apprised about all the people they had lost to the dragon fires. Some of them were mere collateral damage. The others were unshelled and supposedly deserved their fate.

"How did you survive? I thought you were unshelled," Simbai asked.

"Oh, no, not with a grandmother like mine. She is skeptical but pragmatic. So, we all got shells in case it did protect us. You could say we went along with it. We were willing to."

"And we weren't," Simbai replied, sighing. Could he have saved Leilani had they stayed and gone along with the way things were?

"What is wrong?" Shadreck asked, and that's when Simbai told his old friend about Leilani.

The news tore Shadreck to the core. He loved Leilani like his own daughter. So the two mourned together in silence. "But she's not dead yet," Shadreck reminded Simbai. They remained quiet for a while, then Simbai shared with Shadreck his plan for revenge. The fiery rebellion and revolution to save Uzu.

Shadreck explained to Simbai how the possibility of a resistance army was tiny. Most of the unshelled who had the strength to resist had been banished. So the resistance was mostly in the diaspora. The few unshelled who remained had all been wiped out. Such that any remnant of resistance was terrified to make a move. Short of bringing those in the diaspora home, there was no one on the ground to give Simbai a hand in changing Uzu."

Simbai had to think of another plan. Maybe he could inspire those present and convince them to change sides. He went back to regroup with Lenny.

RAFI EL SHUMBA

It was two days before the full moon and five days since they had arrived in Uzu. The Dragons became weirdly restless. Simbai was afraid they were onto them. There were search parties sent around the village state. But, they did not know who or what they were looking for exactly. The Dragonhead had said that they would simply know when they found the person who was causing the dragons to be distressed.

This only served to add to Simbai's reasons to be sad and furious at the people's ignorance. They went along with ridiculous schemes like this one. A whole day had passed with no one being discovered, so the Dragonhead summoned everyone to a Gospel Announcement the next day. One day before the full moon, the dragons were extremely distressed. He announced that there was someone in the village who had entered undetected. But that the person was causing all the distress and the people had to be alert. But there was no description of the person, so there wasn't much to go with.

Simbai and Lenny returned from the Gospel announcement discussing this very search. Upon entering their home, they heard some noises in the kitchen. They wondered if Bishop Hooper had arrived, but they didn't see any luggage. So they cautiously made their way to their kitchen and were greeted calmly by a young man. He was preparing a peanut butter-and-honey sandwich. His head bowed intently with his dreadlocks pulled up into a distinct style.

"Zviri sei Simbai? I don't know you." the young man said, biting into the sandwich and pointing at Lenny. He pushed past the two men, sandwich in one hand and plate in another.

"I have been searching for your house for a couple of days now. I also needed a decent meal, and this snack will hold me over," he said, sitting down.

"Do I know you?" Simbai asked

"Aaah, not really. You are the guy who threw up on the side of the road when the police were holding me down." the young man said. He took a sip of the glass of juice he had poured before the two men arrived.

"But if you wait for me to finish eating, I can talk to you more efficiently." So they sat down and waited. Once he finished the sandwich, he went back into the kitchen for a fruit. Then after the fruit, he went back into the kitchen for another sandwich. Then the peach juice ran out, and he had to refill that. Then finally, he found a chocolate bar, ate that one, and chased it down with half a glass of water.

Then he looked at them and said, "I knew you guys would play ball and let me eat. I am here to destroy the dragons."

Lenny and Simbai looked at each other in shock. Another crazy person had joined the team.

"Who are you?" Lenny asked. Simbai didn't care as long as they would destroy the dragons.

"My name doesn't matter?" the young man replied

Simbai's interest was piqued at this response, "Well, you will have to tell us your name, now."

Rafi looked at them and smiled, "If you insist. Some people call me El Shumba. So, you can call me that as well."

"The Lion, asi unoyera shumba?" Lenny asked (Is lion your totem?)

"No, the dragon is my totem," Rafael replied and chuckled. Simbai smiled at his sense of humor.

"But that won't cut it, though. Unonyatsa kunzi ani chaizvo?" (What's your full and real name?) Simbai pressed on.

"Rafi, Rafi Shumba. Can we move on to killing the dragons now?" the young man asked, changing the subject.

"Why do you want to kill the dragons?" Simbai asked.

"Why do you want to free the people of Uzu?" Rafi asked, smiling. "All I know is I was sent here because you, Simbai, could help me stop the dragons. That's my job. The rest is on you; I am not here to liberate anyone."

"And who sent you here?" Simbai asked

"Call them the Elders or the ancestors if it helps. I have traveled very far to get here. And I will not be delayed. We have a short window to destroy the dragons and end their rule for a long while," he said, getting up and pacing.

* * *

"So, how do we do it?" Simbai asked

"Do what?" Rafi replied

"Destroy the dragons?"

"Oh, I thought you had come to Uzu with a plan" Rafi looked up and raised hands in despair. "Just like you to send me in without a plan, again?" he said, looking up at no one.

Simbai was encouraged by this young man's "can do" attitude.

"Okay, okay, let's think." Simbai said, "I know the dragons were once people. I also know that they were turned into dragons by some sorcery using contact with the dragon shell. So maybe we can magic them back into people somehow. What do you know about the dragons?" he said, looking at Rafi.

Rafi smiled. "I don't know anything. But, but...wait," he said, raising his finger, "Wait, but I have heard that there is an entity who can control them. In fact, this entity is in charge of them in some way. But you have to know its name to summon the being and then have a conversation. Names are powerful things. Each dragon has a name, and once you call its name, you can tell it what to do. So it is without a rider and with no master besides Uzu until someone calls its name."

"Okay, okay, that's what you've heard. Lenny, have you heard or know anything?" Simbai asked

"No, I had never seen the dragons until yesterday when one flew about in its restlessness. I also don't know about this entity, what it looks like or..."

"Yes, what does the entity look like?" Simbai asked, getting excited and looking at Rafi.

"Why, have you seen entities in the heavenly realms?" Rafi said mockingly. He had seen a lot in his temporal and spatial travels and felt he was the only one. When Simbai shrugged his shoulders, Rafi

252

answered offhandedly.

"Well, he is one of the lower heavens entities in charge of various invisible matters. And of all the ones I've seen, he is closest to human stature. He loves logic and enjoys talking a lot about human affairs. But I think he wishes he was human. The faces of light once told me that he loves the truth but..."

"Has been dispossessed of him!" Simbai finished the sentence shocking Rafi out of his chair.

"No ways, no ways!" the young man said, leaping.

"Yes, I think I remember Drogo. Its Drogo"

"Drogo," shrieked Rafi in excitement and twirling around. Then he stopped and said, "Into the shadows, Drogo," and boom, the entity materialized right there in front of him.

"Who told you my name?" the entity asked Rafi in disbelief. Then he looked around the room and saw Simbai, "Of course, I should have known you two would meet someday. So what do you all want?"

"We want to control all the seven dragons in this village state. I hear they are your pets." Rafi said, smirking and walking around Drogo.

"Hahaha, and what makes you think I will tell you that?" The being asked

Rafi laughed and bent over. Then he started making some marks on the floor...

"Haha, you think sealing the last seven doors of knowledge from my reach will make me talk. I have threats to make, too," Drogo said, chuckling.

Rafi smiled, then he got up. "I had to try. Anyway, Simbai?"

"What?" Simbai asked, surprised. How could he help in this situation?

* * *

"What happened to Leilani?" Rafi asked.

Drogo whirled around to face Simbai. And Simbai looked somber and close to tears. "She is hanging onto life by a thread. She was hidden from me until now."

"If you don't speak, you're risking the vengeance of this..." Rafi said.

"Sssshhh," Drogo said, "You know it doesn't always have to be all about arm-twisting. I can feel things too."

"Whatever works," Rafi muttered inaudibly. Then raising his volume, he said, "So, the seven dragons. How do we control them?"

And the being spilled the tea on how they could win against his pets.

"You will need three people. You always need three; that's why they have two people in government always here in Uzu. So it can't be three. Oh, and one of the three people can't be you, Rafi. You are touched and tainted, and you will have to find someone who has not yet eaten of the fruit. The three people can be from any generation and lineage. But to command and ride these particular dragons, you need someone of African descent. And for that one, I made the rules so you can ride them too, Rafi, if you want." Drogo said, then sarcastically added, smiling, "But sadly, you can't be part of the circle to call them."

Drogo then taught them the enchantment to make and say. Next, he showed them the positions the three needed to take around the circle to summon the name of each dragon. And then, once the proper noun was presented to them and called, the dragon would be harnessed.

Lenny was taking notes, and Rafi was simply nodding. Then Rafi said, "Alright, time for you to go. I release..."

"No, stop, Drogo, wait," Simbai said frantically. Then he sighed and took a moment, as though by delivering the question calmly, he could get a favorable answer. Then he asked, "Is this the end?"

Drogo looked at Simbai and realized he was not asking about the dragons. "I'm afraid it's the end," he replied and, without ceremony, turned to Rafi and asked. "Am I released,"

Rafi paused and looked at Simbai for confirmation. Simbai slumped into the chair behind him. The father was spent and looked sorrowful. Then Rafi looked at Lenny, who nodded, and so Rafi replied, "Yes, you are released."

There was an awkward silence in the room after the being left. Lenny looked from Rafi to Simbai, trying to ensure it wasn't a dream they had just experienced. He looked at his notes; they had remained there after Drogo disappeared. Rafi walked into the kitchen, remarking. "I am starving." This time he warmed up some other food with relish from the refrigerator.

"Why did you say into the shadows?" Lenny asked, puzzled as the young man prepared a second dinner.

"Because we live in the shadow," Rafi replied.

"The shadow of what?"

"You know, questions always carry the seed of their answer. They are like keys, and the right keys open the right doors. The right question is, whose shadow?" Rafi replied.

Lenny was very intrigued, "Whose shadow do we live in?"

Simbai perked up and murmured, "The shadow of the one casting the light?" Rafi walked out of the kitchen to look at Simbai. He eyed the man who had known the answer to the peculiar question.

Lenny turned to Rafi, "Is that the answer?"

Rafi nodded. "And no one can perceive the shadow because it has no end."

Simbai was no longer listening, lost in thought. Rafi respected such reveries since he was known to disappear into them from time to time. So he went back into the kitchen and hummed as he prepared the food. On the other hand, Simbai sat on the couch, pensively preparing to give Uzu, heaven through hell.

POOR BISHOP HOOPER

Bishop Hooper arrived the next day, and the dragons were extremely restless. Drogo's visit had churned them into a sort of frenzy. The creatures would fly around the village state shrieking and bellowing out fires. Of course, they weren't directing their flames towards anyone or anything. But they looked and sounded distressed. The Dragonhead and the Chief of Crops were at a loss as to how to soothe them. They had done their best to come to terms with the appearance of the dragons years before. But things were getting stranger even for them and their desire for power.

Bishop Hooper was driven to Lenny and Simbai's house from his clergy quarters. As the Bishop entered, he saw Rafi and exclaimed, "This is the traveler who told me about Uzu years ago."

"Rafi, my good sir, at your service again," Rafi replied, bowing comically.

The Bishop was appraised of the situation, and they told him about Drogo.

"So you have been interfacing with the principalities in the heavenly places?" He asked all three men. He was hoping it was a rhetorical question. Since the answer was yes, Bishop Hooper hoped to opt out of the deal because they had dealt with a devil.

"Just like when you pray and wrestle, pastor. You wrestle not against the flesh, remember. No human is our enemy but only the rulers and principalities. And if they can help us, a house divided...you know the rest." Rafi replied

Bishop Hooper did not like this answer, mainly because he could no longer use it to destroy the whole undertaking. So he took Simbai and Lenny aside, away from Rafi.

* * *

"Guys, think about what you are about to get yourselves into. We could die. Simbai, you have a pregnant wife, and I have a family to rejoin. Lenny, you have Letty to come back and fight for. This is a big deal." he ended.

"Some things are bigger than us," Simbai replied, "These people need to be liberated before suffering the same fate as my little girl. I am not saying I am their savior, but this system needs to be dismantled by someone. I am volunteering. I am willing to die for these people?"

"Are the people worth the fight?" Lenny asked.

Bishop Hooper and Simbai both looked at Lenny as though he was crazy.

Simbai smiled slightly as he realized Lenny had helped get Bishop Hooper to his side. "See, you believe they are worth the fight Bishop Hooper. If it was Timothy, would he be worth the fight?"

"But freedom cannot be forced on people, even Timothy. Freedom for people who don't want to be free is simply another kind of tyranny. Jesus did not force his freedom on people either. It's an invitation always. People are invited and allowed to say no." Bishop Hooper replied, borrowing from Riva's wisdom.

"I agree with Bishop Hooper. Never rescue anyone who doesn't want to be rescued, especially if it's a surprise." Lenny replied, thinking about Letwin.

"Don't you wish someone thought you were worth the fight? And that person was angry enough to do something about it?" Simbai asked.

"I don't wish any of that. You can fight without being angry. Anything you can do angry, you can do better without being angry. Especially fighting. It would be best if you had your wits about you to be able to shift the strategy in real-time," Bishop Hooper replied

"For the record, I am here for the dragons and not the Dragonhead, the chief of crops, or anyone else. I make no war against humans. No human is an enemy of another human. Only the thing whispering in the humans' ears, creating hostility, is the enemy of all humans. And no human can be a hero to another human. That is like saving yourself from drowning by pulling yourself up using your own hair. Only the Baron can do that." Rafi replied, chuckling.

The three men did not understand everything Rafi was saying. But his words gave Bishop Hooper an idea.

"Maybe we could destroy the dragons, and poof goes the power of the Dragon Head and Chief of Crops. Then, we won't need to find them and cause them harm."

Simbai, who had live-in Uzu for years, laughed out loud. "Even without the dragons, those people found a way to rule everyone here. The system must fall entirely. The three flames need to be extinguished! A reboot or reset, maybe even tearing down the walls that have kept these people of Uzu from the rest of Zawe. So they can all become one, suffer together, thrive together."

"The three flames are not our enemies, Simbai; no human is our enemy!" Rafi implored.

"If no one is my enemy, how am I supposed to love my enemy?" Simbai yelled out to Rafi. Bishop Hooper waited eagerly for the answer to this one as well.

"The carpenter from Galilee had trouble talking to us," Rafi replied, walking up to the window. He pulled the curtain back. Rafi eyed the full moon and continued. "If he had said, 'Love you loved ones', of course, we would all think he meant to love only those who love us. But he had to say, Love your enemies and do good to those who persecute you, so it was clear. Anyone you love is your loved one, right? When you love your enemies, don't they also become your loved ones? See, you have no more enemies when your enemies become your loved ones. But that would be unclear to many people. So the commandment reads, love your enemies. What he means is that other humans are not real enemies. Other humans are your loved ones. Your only enemies are the principalities. Love all humans; none of them are your enemies. Even when they seem to be, you change them into loved ones by loving them. So the real commandment should have been 'love your loved ones or love all people.' But again, it would be confusing for people who are angry, or hateful or feel hated."

The three men were silent.

"Bishop, have you heard that before?" Lenny whispered

"No, but it sounds true. It makes the not wrestling against flesh and blood more consistent." The Bishop replied.

"Guys, Leilani is battling for her life because of this place. Not only that, but families are falling apart, morals eroding, hearts breaking, all because of the corruption here. I will fight so no other father has to meet his daughter on her deathbed after years of separation." He finished.

"You can't free people who don't want to be free," Rafi called out. He stood up finally and walked into the kitchen to join the meeting. "If they were already fighting to be free and we came to help, that would be one thing. But these people are unwilling to emancipate themselves from mental, economic, and political slavery? There needs to arise a grassroots movement that says I am willing to die to bring freedom and good life to those around me." Until the masses awaken, all you are trying to do is become a martyr and a subject of legends and ridicule. I can even give you historical examples of people who became memes in Uzu. When Tongerai and others attempted what you are attempting - to change the seat of power - the dragon fired them up. You know the people you are trying to free will laugh at you when it all backfires."

Simbai was surprised that Rafi knew the history of Uzu but expected more mystery from this man anyways.

"We will educate the masses." He replied, "It's the way it's always been done when challenging the status quo. This is Chimurenga we are talking about, the war of liberation!"

"We don't have enough time for educating the povo. (The masses)" Rafi quipped.

* * *

259

That's true; we don't have enough time to rally the people and inform them so they can support us. So let's abandon ship. These people are complicit. Look, look, Simbai," Bishop Hooper said. "They say fool me once, shame on you. Fool me twice; shame on me. How about 'fool me for decades?' At that point, you can no longer accuse the con artist of committing a crime. At that point, the people being conned are to blame."

Lenny laughed and added to the Bishop's words, "At the point of people being conned for decades, we need to leave them to their plight."

"That's a bit harsh for someone who needed the world to be kind to him once," Simbai replied.

"Empathizing doesn't stop me from being critical and honest," Lenny shot back, shaking his head.

"I am sure that is not how empathy works," Simbai replied, shaking his fist.

"And just how does empathy work," Lenny replied angrily.

Simbai switched strategies and became a little more placatory. He needed Lenny on his side, but he was not backing down either. "Empathy is the first step towards forgiveness. It says if I was you and in your shoes, I would do exactly what you did and for good reasons. So now I need to understand those reasons, and in so doing, I will know you, forgive you, and love you.

"Don't let's get lost from the main point here. We are standing in the land of ignoramuses complicit in their own abuse." Bishop Hooper echoed.

"Shuwa, vakangoti tuzu as their lives and futures are squandered, and their families are separated," Lenny echoed. Bishop Hooper looked at Lenny, having not understood the Shona expression. The remark cut Simbai as it hit close to home.

Lenny looked at Simbai and Rafi, "How would you translate that, guys? How would you translate "Tuzu."

Rafi felt like Simbai was losing, and the other two were chickening out. But, the moon was approaching the position he needed for the dragon's name summoning ceremony. Instead of indulging Lenny with the definition, he said, walking into the living room,

"I am here for the dragons, and I was only given juice that expires in a couple of days. So, I need you three to stop with the pow wow and get into position. The dragons have been getting more restless by the hour and may sniff me out soon. So, if we don't do this now, we will have to wait until around the same time next year. But might not make it through. So let's get into position, people!" he said, using the customary imperative reserved for elders in Zawe.

Simbai did not wait for another word but went and stood in position in the living room. Lenny and Bishop Hooper stood there, shaking their heads. They wondered what could get through Simbai's thick skull.

"We might as well join in to mitigate the collateral damage," Lenny said, shrugging and walking into the living room.

Poor Bishop Hooper followed into the living room, trusting that he was there for a reason. He trusted that he had met Rafi for a reason. He had walked into the Varnish bar for a reason. Riva and Timothy had known Leilani for a season. Maybe, this was the reason. And so, poor Bishop Hooper joined the circle.

A TRIANGLE BY ANOTHER NAME

Many circles have been known to history. Round tables and fellowships of rings. From twelve to seven and so on. But a circle of three was a triangle by another name, yet they had to draw a circle.

"Alright, let's get you ready to chant, Bishop," Rafi said, smiling mischievously.

"How difficult can it be? I learned some Greek and Hebrew in seminary school." the Bishop said,

"Great, alright, the first word is "Zita.""

The Bishop smiled at all of them and repeated the word gleefully.

"Zi'tah"

He bowed like a man who had delivered an operatic performance.

"Mumumvuri," Rafi said

"Mumun...mumun...vhurrreee" The Bishop said panicking a little.

Twenty minutes later, they were almost there with this word.

"How many more words are in the chant?" the Bishop asked, hoping for fewer and easier words.

"One more," Rafi said to the Bishop's relief. Lenny was chuckling at the exchanges, and Simbai worked hard to be patient. Finally, the Bishop had enough of the pronunciations down, and they took their positions around the circle.

Bishop Hooper and Lenny were the two at the base of the arrowhead, and they were to join hands, so they did. Then with their free hands, they pointed to the center of the circle as Rafi directed. Simbai was the one at the head of the arrow in the circle, and he looked up. Then, all three chanted "Zita mu-mumvuri wechokwadi," condensed old Shona, meaning "Into the shadows, name, that is in the shadow of truth."

As they were chanting this, some furniture in the room started moving and shaking. The curtains rose somewhat like a gentle breeze was passing through them. And all four could feel tingling sensations on their skins. Soon, a word appeared at the center of the circle. Bishop Hooper could read it, and so could everyone else, but it wasn't in any specific language. It was more like a glow of meaning that appeared to each in their own way, but they pronounced it the same.

"Nungo," the name said; loosely translated, "Laziness."

"Nungo, huya pano," (Laziness come hither) Simbai, who was at the head of the circle, called out. They were silent and waited a short while. Then they heard the flapping wings of one of the dragons. It's important to note that not all of the Uzu dragons had wings, yet all could fly. This dragon landed not too far from the house. The four men walked out of the house to look at their handiwork. The bright full moon greeted them as though this was a most peaceful of nights. The night light illuminated the majestic creature which had terrorized Uzu since the beginning. They were the source of the power of the three flames, whether in lore or their actual existence.

"How do we know it's 'a friendly?'" Lenny asked as all four of them stood far from the creature. Other people in the neighborhood were peeping through their windows. No one dared step outside so close to the dragon. Simbai started towards the colossal beast.

"No, stop," Bishop Hooper called to the deaf resolute man.

He approached the dragon and reached his hand, willing it to bend down for him to pet its nose. To his surprise, the dragon did bend its neck. They did not know this, but this was the second-largest dragon in the land. Why it was called "nungo" or "laziness" was beyond them. Simbai was petting the animal and contemplating. To think this creature was once a human being and a staunch believer in the shell. He was reminded of their mission to save the people of Uzu. A mission to save them from themselves and the tyranny of the three flames. Simbai sighed and turned to the other men. "We have work to do," he said, walking past them back into the house and to the circle.

And they did the chants one more time, and this time it took twice as long but finally, "kukara" (gluttony) showed up at the center of the circle.

"Kukara, huya pano," Simbai repeated the calling card. (Gluttony come hither) Before long, they heard a distant shriek, which was answered by the bellow of the landed dragon. More calling and answering, and the second dragon descended with a thud. Rafi peeped through the window to confirm. The three continued chanting to get all seven dragons under their command.

Soon, "Hasha" showed up in the circle. A glowing furious ball of light. And so Simbai called again. "Hasha huya pano." (Anger come hither)

The three continued chanting, but a few minutes later, there was a commotion outside. Instead of one dragon coming on the third call, all the other dragons were on their way. There was loud shrieking and roaring, calling and answering—the dragons on the ground communicated with the ones in the air. The free dragons were breathing fire and looking for whoever was enslaving them to command.

That's when the biggest of the dragons bellowed so loud it shook the foundations of the houses.

There was a general panic in the area. People were screaming and fleeing. They were fleeing at the commotion of all the dragons converging in that area of Uzu.

The other dragons started burning and searching for the culprits. The fourth name was coming, and it made the house glow. The four men did not know that the light from the name could be seen from the outside. One of the dragons blew the roof over to investigate. Rafi yelled that they should break the circle and try and work with the three dragons they had. The four men ran right before another dragon smoked the place.

BURN BABY BURN

Rafi ran to the largest of the three dragons on their side. It was the second biggest dragon in the land. It rejected Rafi and rejected Lenny but took Simbai. He had bonded with it before.

"I feel for you, my friend. The darkness in your must be greater than the darkness in me." Rafi said.

* * *

"How do I control this dragon?" Simbai asked, ignoring the scary words.

"Use intention and the dragon's native language," Rafi replied and walked away. Simbai held on to the mane of the dragon. And it leaped into the air and started flying as he willed it.

"Then he saw the other dragon and instinctively screamed, "moto." The dragon bellowed fire in the direction of the oncoming dragon. And the battle began.

Lenny was soon airborne, and he joined in the fight, riding Hasha, who had no wings.

The third dragon, "Kukara," rejected Rafi, which was a shocker. It was true that Rafi could not participate in the calling ceremony, but eating the fruit did not prevent one from riding a dragon. It was a huge surprise, mainly because the dragon accepted Bishop Hooper. "You must be African in some way," Rafi remarked. "Only someone of African descent can ride these dragons." He did not waste time but told him some of the Shona words to command the dragon. He had to maintain a laser-focused, clear mind and communicate through intention for the rest of the commands.

Rafi watched as Simbai and the crew battled the other dragons. It was all happening right when the moon had risen. Though it was dark out, it was also bright. And the light from the dragon fire lit up the sky further. So the battle raged on for all the brave to see. Many in Uzu were behind locked doors, while some made a dash for the few public bunkers built after the first dragon situation. Some bunkers were made for the elite, but they were located far from the riffraff. The bunkers were created so that there would be shelter available if ever the important people crossed the dragons. This way, they could be safe in the bunkers until ways of appeasing the dragons had been established.

The challenge with the fight was that kukara was heavy and sluggish. It was third in the sky, but the two of the other dragons abandoned the fight with Simbai and Lenny to take it down. Bishop Hooper struggled with the command words. He landed some blows and some fire, but one of the dragons found his dragon's neck. The second one bit and burned the wings of Kukara.

Simbai ran down to the rescue and dealt some effective blows to the dragon, which had Kukara by the neck. Kukara and this other dragon both fell out of the sky. They landed side by side and did not rise. Rafi ran to the crash zone, headed straight for the dragons, and administered a potion. The dragons gulped, and they glowed from the inside. The heat and light soon subsided, and they turned into piles of ash. Then Rafi spotted Bishop Hooper. Half his body under the pile of ash from the dissipated dragons. Poor Bishop Hooper had been crushed underneath the weight of the dragons, and he did not look good. The potion had alleviated his pain by turning the dragons to dust, but he was in bad shape.

Back in the sky, Nungo was an energetic and a good fighter. Hasha was nimble, without wings, and returned fire for fire. The riders were novices to controlling these creatures. But the dragons they were fighting were battling out of instinct. The free dragons were fighting for survival and their homeland, Uzu. These dragons were once people who believed in Uzu so much they wore the shell and endured the transformation into full dragons. They had not been amputated and had been fortunate not to begin the transformation at chest level. A development that had a 100% mortality rate.

As soon as Kukara went down, the enormous lead dragon retreated. Nungo was about the same size as one of the dragons in the air. And hasha though nimble, was small compared to the other dragon in the air. It looked like the big boss would let the minions handle this one. They were chasing each other across the sky, blowing fire and fighting. Sometimes they would grip and wrestle and fall to the ground, crushing buildings. They would roll, tug, and bite each other's necks and wings while on the ground. Simbai and Lenny had to hold on and suffer bumps and bruises. Time raced by, and twilight was arriving.

Lenny dodged his attacking dragon's move. Then, he maneuvered to bite the tail of the dragon attacking Simbai. The creature coiled and swung but also knocked itself out of balance. It was spinning around with an extra wait biting its tail. Lenny managed to stabilize and let go, which sent the other dragon crashing onto the ground. Simbai and

Lenny swooped down with fire and more harassment, effectively ending that dragon. Now they had one dragon left in the air.

This dragon shrieked for help and even tried to flee to the mountains. But Lenny caught up with it and delayed it long enough for Nungo, who wasn't far behind, to catch up. They made quick work of this one, but something happened before they could deliver the final blows. The Dragonhead saw what was happening in the sky. The rumor that people were riding the dragons was confirmed as daylight lit the sky. Under the moonlight, they looked like shadows and a lot more like night witches. But with sunlight, they looked like regular men now. Whoever was riding dragons would be a new power in Uzu. The dragonhead ordered his handful of bodyguards to start firing on Lenny and Simbai. They began organizing the dragon catapult, hoping that the loyal Uzu dragons would not destroy them by wounding or killing the other disloyal dragons.

That's when Simbai turned his dragon on them. It was a massacre. He not only lit up the small army, including the dragon head. But went on to burn the man's palace and some other government buildings. Simbai's dragon, Nungo, sniffed out the elite bunkers and dug them up. Unfortunately, the beast's claws could not penetrate whatever material was used to build the bunker. So he ordered his dragon to burn the structure where it had been revealed. So, the dragon turned up the heat enough to get those inside to come out. The chief of crops, the dragon head's son, and their families perished that day.

Meanwhile, Lenny was fighting alone, and he successfully ended the dragon they had tag-teamed on. Rafi was by that dragon in no time when it crashed, and he vaporized it with his potion.

But the gigantic dragon was on his way. Even though Hasha, Lenny's dragon, was nimble, it was also tiny, fatigued, and wounded. And if he faced the coming dragon alone, he would lose and they could lose the entire battle. Simbai's dragon facing the huge alpha dragon without Lenny's support would also be a guaranteed loss. But facing it together they had a slim chance of victory. And right then Simbai was busy so Lenny had to be creative.

Lenny was but dodging and hiding. It was undoubtedly guerilla warfare at this point. Uzu buildings made for good cover and launching surprise attacks. The giant dragon flew low and crashed into some buildings along the way, searching for hasha. It didn't care much about Simbai and seemed to be confidently flying after hasha.

When Simbai was done, he turned to see Lenny's Dragon being hurled to the ground. The giant last dragon could use its front legs a lot like hands. Unlike the other dragons, this one looked a lot more humanoid. It was in hot pursuit,= to deliver the final blow after hurling hasha down. When Lenny said, "Pisa mama Pisa" (Burn baby burn), his dragon shot out blue fire. The big dragon was caught off guard by the blue flames so was everybody watching. Finally, the colossal dragon relented a little, swooping and looping rather than delivering its blow. This gave Lenny a chance to attack. Simbai managed to get his dragon to grab one of the spears prepared in the dragon catapult. And he and Nungo flew from behind the distracted giant dragon and drove it through one of its wings and part of its body.

The giant dragon shrieked in pain and fell with a crash. But it wasn't dead or out of the fight. The massive creature pulled the arrow out of its body and took to flight again. He was wounded but rearing for war.

The people of Uzu were shocked that there were people riding dragons. They did not even know that one of the sides was fighting for them. But some of them were entertained by the battle.

Simbai and Lenny regrouped.

"How did you make your dragon shoot blue flames?" Simbai asked, yelling in the air. They looked awfully comfortable for people who had never ridden dragons. The clarity was intoxicating, just like when Simbai had run from the dogs with his Uncle.

"Pisa mama Pisa," Lenny screamed. Lenny's dragon blew out blue flames at that moment.

Simbai laughed and suggested a strategy. They would swoop in as though they were going to attack from different sides. And they would swing in the same direction and send blue flames toward the dragon. Lenny raised a finger to signal Simbai to take a moment. Lenny swooped down and had his dragon pick up the bloody arrow from before. It was a quick movement for him, and Simbai shrugged. Then they put their plan into motion.

The giant dragon was poised to swing with its tail and front legs to defend against both attacks as they approached. But as it turned in anticipation of attacks from different angles, the two dragons swung to the same side. The two men were screaming "Pisa mama Pisa" loudly and repeatedly. Blue flames combined burned the colossal dragon, which looked away to prevent damage to its eyes. The giant dragon got Lenny's dragon knocking it out of the sky. It hit the spear out of the dragon's grip with the same blow. Simbai then realized Lenny's plan. He commanded Nungo to catch the murder shaft, and in the same flight swoop, right after the blue flames, he landed the spear on the neck of the enormous dragon. The creature bellowed in pain. The arrow's wooden part burned and disintegrated. The vast dragon tried to blow fire, but the substance was leaking through the hole in the neck. The big thing had to land, try and stem the bleeding and close the gap in its neck. It wasn't gone or dead. Nungo picked up some more spears and pinned the massive creature to the ground. The beast was panting and bellowing, but it was not going anywhere. It was finally over.

Lenny's dragon had been struck out of the sky and crash-landed, pinning Lenny to the ground. Rafi ran to Lenny. He gave Lenny's dragon a portion to drink, and the creature closed its eyes peacefully. Then, the beast started burning from the inside, turning to charcoal and almost instantly into ash. Rafi gave Lenny a once over. The poor, tall man was severely injured and unconscious. But Rafi could not stay long because he had another mission. So he ran over to the enormous dragon, and it, too, drank and turned to dust. By the time he returned to Lenny, he had found him cold to the touch. The tall Zawe man was no more.

TERRA FIRMA

Simbai was flying the last dragon around the village state in a victory lap. Soon, he landed his dragon and disembarked from it feeling invincible. He looked around, choking a little from the smoke and dust. He walked through the debris, and between bodies scattered like a medieval battlefield. There was a great commotion as some people were crying, especially children. Some people were limping around and trying to rescue others from the rubble.

He saw someone trying to get up, and he ran over to them. Holding their hand and elbow, he helped up the person covered in dust and blood. He started moving this person along when he saw another person in immediate danger. He apologized and let go of the person he was helping walk. He sat them down and ran to help the person at risk of being crushed by a beam hanging precariously above them. He helped several people and let them lean on him to walk away from the ruins. One of the helpers saw him running around and finally said, "You are one of them, aren't you?" The question was directed to Simbai as he helped an older man make his way to the safe spot where they were moving everyone.

The older man stopped, and so did Simbai. Simbai looked at the older man who was gazing back at him, and then Simbai sighed and looked up to reply, "One of who?"

"One of the dragon riders?" The other helper continued.

The older man looked to Simbai, waiting for him to respond. But unfortunately, Simbai did not know how to reply to the loaded question.

Finally, after waiting for too long a time, the older man repeated the question. "Are you one of the riders?"

"Yes, yes, I was riding to liberate…."

The older man made the usual Zawe angry sound with his tongue and cheek. The noise of the fed-up VaShona people. (Kuridza tsamwa) He pushed Simbai away and was about to fall over. Simbai tried to help stabilize the man, but he preferred to fall, so he pushed Simbai away again.

"Ndisiye," (Leave me alone). The man said from the ground as Simbai was bent over trying to reach him. "Usandibate, (Don't touch me) you caused all this!" The older man said, pointing to the destruction around them.

Simbai froze. He rose and looked around. The people he had just helped to the safe zone gave him looks of disdain. He tried to walk to another person to help, and that person raised their flat-faced palm to him in the universal "stop" gesture. The person said with a groggy voice, "Don't come any closer."

Simbai felt attacked without anyone saying much to him. People were whispering and pointing at him, as Simbai looked around. There was destruction everywhere. The smell of death was in the air, burning flesh filled his nostrils, and the sound of weeping was like a soundtrack to his panoramic gaze. A moment ago, he saw himself continuing the mission of helping and liberating Uzu. But now, in the face of their reaction, Simbai was at a loss. He did not know if this was the face of liberation or if he had mistaken his vision for a free Uzu. Was this the cost of doing business in the face of resistance?

He wanted to jump on the dragon and flee. He thought he could find a place to hide and defend himself from anyone. Maybe he could make more dragons and protect himself and his family. Was this the weight of the crown all liberators had to bear? He thought about the three flames making everyone wear shells and some of them turning into dragons. Had he just become one of the flames with this thought?

He turned around and saw Rafi walking towards his dragon. Without thinking, he yelled, "Get away from him!" Rafi heard the faint rebuke and looked in Simbai's direction. He saw the man running towards the dragon, so he made haste with his task. Simbai was about to yell, "moto" (fire) when Rafi put back the bottle he had extended to the dragon. Moments later, the creature closed its eyes in death. It burned from the inside, glowing, quickly turning into char and ash. Then a faint white substance was seen rising to the sky. It came from the spot where the dragon had been lying. Moments later, clouds were gathering around the area.

Simbai stopped running towards the dragon. It was gone; it was dead. It was now him and his thoughts surrounded by the destruction he had caused in the name of freedom. They would rebuild. They would, right? He thought about the people they had lost and how they could not rebuild that part. His thoughts went back to Leila and how he would feel if someone hurt her in the name of freedom. Would someone come after him as he went after the leaders of Uzu? It's all justified until your brother, sister, son or daughter is the one killed and then you want revenge. It's all collateral damage until your son or daughter is lost, and then it's personal. He shuddered at the thought and realized he was the monster he had neatly packed in the cave within himself. It was himself he had been afraid of all this time. Simbai had been afraid of living fully in his pain and anger and how they would play out in the world. He was scared of hurting others and being culpable as he held his family culpable. So he had rejected that part of himself, a part that he knew would cause harm. He called it a monster, and neatly folded and imprisoned it in the cave not knowing he was simply imprisoning himself. Now he was guilty of the violence at hand. The monster had finally broken free of the unjustified imprisonment. It had burst forth in the name of justice. And Simbai had fired up these people and had "gobbled them up" like a good Uzu dragon in the name of justice.

The clouds that had gathered grew dark and black. Seven dark clouds in total, and they rained down on Uzu. They were like a healing balm quenching the fires and washing the blood off of people. As the smell wafted up, the beautiful aroma of wet earth and rain, Simbai collapsed to his knees, sobbing. Petrichor, the smell of wisdom from his Uncle, filled his nostrils. "It would help to see how much collateral damage saving yourself will bring. Only then will you be able to walk with others through their pain as they walk their path towards salvation—a path that has many victims along the way. But you have to surrender those people you hurt to the healing of the heavens and keep walking your path. Only then, maybe, can you be a true hero."

Simbai now was himself a small Uzu, with blood on his hands in the name of justice. He wished the earth could swallow him up and wipe him from history. So much collateral damage and all not for the salvation of Uzu, but for his own. He recalled how a trail of bodies, tears, and pain, preceded the journey to Damascus. It sounded like the journey to being made whole was littered with other people's pain. Now he understood why his Uncle wanted him to first embrace his own journey of salvation. Simbai had caused harm the same way Uzu had caused harm and both in the name of justice. But to be Uzu's hero, he had to be willing to save it from his impatience, to save it from his brutal collateral damage type of justice. He had to save it from his selfish anger disguised as doing good. To be Uzu's hero meant walking alongside the village state even as it caused harm and trusting that change, was not only possible but was around the corner through a power greater than his. Hate and pain are instant but the change brought by love takes time. He had to give Uzu the benefit of the doubt, even as he desired the same now.

That's when he saw two blue flames approaching him in the rain. He was momentarily startled but on looking around, everyone had erupted into their spiritual flaming blue selves. Flames that rain could not extinguish. The two flames approaching him were Rafi who was dragging Bishop Hooper along. 'They were all blue fires,' Simbai thought remembering the bunker he had wiped out. Every one, a living soul burning the same color and doing their best to live life well with limited knowledge. Simbai was even more convicted in his heart. Rafi shook Simbai out of his kneeling reverie and the fires subsided all around him. They needed to find a place to hide, regroup, and do the ritual so they could leave Uzu.

Simbai looked up, his tears becoming one with the rain. Bishop Hooper was in terrible shape and seemed to be on the path to meeting the ancestors. Lenny was nowhere to be seen. Simbai's eyes were asking about Lenny. Rafi shrugged and shook his head, "He didn't make it," he said over the sound of the rain. Simbai looked down, burying his face in his hands.

"Amen," Bishop Hooper said with levity. And Simbai looked at the injured man looking down at him. Bishop Hooper's face was disfigured with pain and mirth. Simbai smiled weakly, tears continuing their journey with the rain, and the petrichor enveloping them aromatically.

Rafi pulled Simbai up, and the two of them helped prop Bishop Hooper, who groaned and half screamed, "Ouch, ouch, ouch, put me down, put me down, please." And so they had to sit him down in the muddy path. The rain continued to pour. Simbai decided to sit back to back with the man so he had somewhere to lean on. Rafi was looking around like a sentry. He was expecting some company and not the friendly kind.

"Not what you dreamed of, huh?" the Bishop asked, panting and wincing. Simbai smiled weakly, but the Bishop could not see the smile.

"I wish I believed that the ends justify the means because this is where that could apply, right?" Simbai asked, sighing and wishing he could believe it.

"I, I," the Bishop began saying. Then he groaned and began panting a little, "I don't know much, but maybe freedom for Uzu was the equivalent of the American dream. It looks good, sounds good, and sounds like something God would want. But...but..." The man broke his narration wincing in pain. "I think I broke my ribs," He said, and Rafi turned and knelt, feeling the Bishop's chest as lightly as possible. The Bishop was wincing with the kneading, and then he hollered out loud in pain. In the meantime, people noticed the caucasian dragon rider, and they were keeping an eye on the three as the rain began letting up.

"Where was I?" the Bishop asked.

"I don't think you should be talking," Rafi advised. The Bishop looked up and smiled weakly. They exchanged knowing glances, Rafi pressed Bishop Hooper's hand gently and moved away to give them some privacy. Rafi was still alert like a lookout at a bank robbery and pacing back and forth. Simbai didn't understand why Rafi was on the watch, but he didn't know much about Rafi, and Bishop Hooper wanted to talk.

"You were equating the American dream to the dream of freeing Uzu," Simbai replied. He needed to talk this out; Tambudzai wanted him back sane. He wanted to be in his right mind and be present in their baby's life and Leila's if she made it. Could he even go back to that after all this? If Bishop Hooper did not make it, what would he tell Riva?

"Uuuh, yeees," The Bishop said, wincing and coughing. He coughed up blood and shook his head. Time was running out; he looked up and said a silent prayer to finish ministering to Simbai.

"Maybe, those who equate freedom politically and socially with the divine dream have made political, social, and economic freedom their god. I believe are always to return good for evil and when we return evil for evil we become the people we are fighting." Bishop Hooper said, smiling. Simbai recognized some of his words from the Varnish.

"I see what you did there," Simbai said, chuckling but sitting with the wisdom. He could hide it, but he had been driven here by the anger at the possibility of losing Leila. He had blamed Uzu for being Uzu when it was the decision to move to Uzu that was the issue. And he had tucked on the freedom bit to make his cause righteous, just as he tucked on being "innocent" to make his crusade against his family justifiable. The same way many people tucked on justice or democracy to their trauma, paranoia, and desire for self-gain in order to justify their various wars.

"The Divine dream, huh" Simbai echoed, smiling weakly.

Bishop Hooper croaked and tried to clear his throat. He panted, "Just remember, not my dream but thine, and you'll be fine" The Bishop sighed and rested. Rafi muttered some things, looked at Simbai and Bishop Hooper, and bounded away suddenly leaving the two. Simbai did not understand.

That's when the men came. They seized Simbai and hoisted him up to his feet. He was about to protest that he was supporting his friend Bishop Hooper. He looked back only to see the Bishop's body plop to the ground. One of the men was taking Bishop Hooper's pulse and was shaking his head to someone. They dragged Simbai away and put him in the holding cell at the ruins of the Dragonhead's compound. Someone was in charge now, new power, same prison, same old system by the looks of things. Being in the jail cell reminded him of how hopeless, he felt when he carried his sister out of the swimming pool, knowing there was little chance of survival even as they snatched her body away. How weak and confounded he had felt when he was blamed for the pain and breakdown of his family. How powerless he was when he was losing his mind as they waited for Leila to join them in the world. He remembered how impotent he felt when he watched Leila fight for her life, and he could do nothing to help short of traveling back in time. He was in the jail cell now, waiting for the unknown and back to being helpless.

JAIL BIRD

JAIL BIRD

JAIL BIRD

Simbai's throat was parched. He had been locked up for three days and three nights, and no one had come to feed or water him and the other prisoners. His cellmate refused to talk or respond to any of his inquiries. He wondered if they were going to starve to death. He thought about how Tambudzai and the pregnancy were doing, especially after he abandoned them for his vendetta in the name of liberation. He shed a few tears for Leila, whom he hoped was holding on to life. Unlike him, he was beginning to let go of his life, counting himself among the dead. He felt he deserved to die, the monster to his family, the failure to his wife and Leila, and now a murderer in the name of liberation.

Finally, he heard footsteps approach the cell. He hoped whoever it was had some water at least. Or that they could end his life quickly. No thought was spared for the other prisoners who had been there longer. He saw Rafi's silhouette pass the door to the cell. The young man's dreadlock style could not be mistaken.

"Rafi, Rafi," Simbai croaked loudly. He cleared his throat as the young man took a step backward.

"Oh, I didn't think they would put you in the first cell. Cool, alright, that's easy then. So, who else is in here?"

"It's just this silent prisoner and myself," Simbai replied.

* * *

276

"I'm conserving energy," The prisoner whispered hoarsely. "They don't feed us or give us water often." He replied, then went back to his silence and minimal motion.

"Alright, I will put this explosive here on this lock. But we have to wait. I have another one on a timer somewhere, and I need the first one to go off and draw people away, and then we can set this one-off.

He was busy placing the homemade contraption on the cell door when Simbai started talking, "Do they know we liberated them?"

"I don't think they see it that way," Rafi whispered, fiddling with the explosive.

"Reminds me of when I saved the world from the Light Room guys," Simbai replied.

Rafi froze and looked at Simbai. "No wonder they wanted me to come to help you out. You know things."

Simbai shrugged, "and I save people."

Rafi chuckled, cautious not to get too loud, and said, "You did not save the people of Uzu. You are not their liberator but their enemy now. Ignorant cowards like these people are willing to go along for the ride. If you destroy their ride, you are crossing their will, and cross people nail others to the cross,"

"Is that why you didn't want to liberate the people?" Simbai asked, "You didn't want to cross them and "be nailed to the cross.

"No," Rafi replied, "I didn't want to liberate the people out of respect for their autonomy. I would do harm to them by disregarding their choice and giving them freedom. Remember the Galilean? First, he asked that man, "Do you want to be made whole?" Imagine spending your whole life crippled and begging for survival. You wake up mid-morning, head to a corner, and sit there all day begging. If you get healed, now you have to work for survival. You have to wake up early in the morning and be in bed late and tired from work. You have to be willing to be healed and make the necessary sacrifices that come with that. People need to consent to be healed as much as they need to consent to be freed. I know that these people were not willing to be freed. Thinking well and accurately is not an easy task. They weren't ready to do the work of reasoning or building a new world. And now, like the Israelites, they shall come after you, their self-appointed Moses. They will grumble and plot to kill you for setting them free from making bricks with their saliva."

"Humans are insane," Simbai said, shaking his head in disbelief.

"Haha, some may call it insanity, but these people here in Uzu chose to be here for a reason. And I respect that whether I agree with their choice or not." Rafi replied. Simbai sadly understood that reply. He had brought his family willingly to this village state. He had good reasons to do it too. He sat with those words for a while as Rafi continued working away.

Then Rafi finished placing the explosive and looked at his watch. Simbai felt like saying, "I'm conserving my energy," so Rafi would not think he was quiet because of Rafi's poignant words.

"Alright, step back," Rafi said to Simbai. "It's best to move into that corner and barricade yourselves with the single beds and mattresses." So Simbai and the prisoner did as he had suggested. The prisoner moved sluggishly like a happy sloth as they did this work. Rafi was egging them on quietly, hoping the first explosion would not come too soon. Simbai and the other prisoner were settled and waiting for a few minutes when the first boom was heard. It shook the prison, and they heard commotion above. Rafi whispered loudly, "Get ready!" He blew the cell open a few minutes later. Bits of metal flew everywhere as the door flung open.

"Alright, let's go, let's go," Rafi called out in a frantic whisper.

Simbai began to run out. He stopped at the open cell door and looked back, puzzled. The other prisoner did not move. Finally, the prisoner smiled weakly and said, "I'm not going to get far. I'm too weak to run."

Simbai looked at the man and played out the scenario in his head. The man would slow them down, the man could get killed in the flight, and the escape would do him harm if he came along. He decided against the noble feeling he felt to save the man. He was not a hero, and he needed to respect the man's choice to stay. Rafi looked at the man and nodded the way brown people do. The man smiled, a look of dignity in his eye, a twinkle of life in a body wasting away.

Simbai and Rafi made haste and escaped the Dragonhead's compound. They made for a nearby wooded area, and Rafi finally stopped them. He drew a circle and moved some leaves around, and then said, "That tree, let's walk backward towards that tree. And don't look back no matter what you hear."

They had started a few paces when Simbai's stomach growled. They paused and looked at each other, and Simbai made a gesture to brush it aside. He asked instead, "Will I ever see you again?"

"I don't know; it's not up to me. Also, please stop talking; you will disturb my chant." Rafi replied.

Simbai did not want to stop talking. He wasn't sure he had destroyed the dragon inside. He felt he needed to make sure it was gone before going back. But he shut his mouth as they made a few more steps. Rafi was muttering something under his breath, and it was repetitive and melodic. Simbai closed his eyes tighter and tighter to hold back his words. But he could not do it.

"What's going to happen when we get to the tree?" He asked

Rafi ignored him and continued chanting,

"I'll look back if you don't answer me," Simbai threatened.

Rafi looked at the problematic man and sighed, stopping the chants. "You turn back, the spell stops working, I stop the chant and the same. So answering you and looking back, both break the spell." Simbai smiled sheepishly. He realized he had given Rafi no options.

"If we get caught, it's on you," Rafi said. "When we get to the tree, one of the Rorodondo will come out and transport you out of Uzu to

279

another transport tree close to where you want to be. And I will be taken to the Elders for the debrief."

"Who or what is a Rorodondo?"

"Another being of the shadows," Rafi replied, drawing the circle again and arranging the leaves. He sighed, "We have to find another tree now; let's go." And he started walking, Simbai followed. Rafi was eyeing certain trees and drawing the circle, only to find it was not the right tree.

Simbai was agonizing over all that had happened in Uzu.

"Don't let it bug you," Rafi said without looking at Simbai.

"What?"

"Don't let the Uzu situation bug you," Rafi replied.

"It's not only that, it's my whole life too," Simbai replied.

"Your life, don't let that bug you either," Rafi said as he paused and scoped out another tree. Then he exclaimed, "Let me do the finder spell and not the confirmation spell."

"I am concerned; Lenny is dead, Bishop Hooper too. What will I tell Riva and Timothy? How can I live with the knowledge of all the people here in Uzu who are in pain because of my desire to free them? I am sad about all the people I have hurt already and am afraid to injure others in the future," Simbai replied.

"Hmmmmm, a noble fear," Rafi said distractedly. "You realize you did not only hurt people but also 'un-alived' several people, right?

"Thanks for making it worse?" Simbai replied.

"No, I didn't make it worse, I made it a little more accurate. You killed people; you didn't simply hurt some. How are you supposed to face things if you don't characterize them accurately?" Rafi finished with a question.

* * *

Simbai resigned himself to the truth and said, "Well, I guess to put it accurately, I am concerned my actions will result in more death and pain."

"Are you not a believer?" Rafi asked as he looked around.

"Oh yes, I believe," Simbai replied. He felt lost because of Rafi's unexpected question.

"Perfect then," Rafi said. "There is an oriental legend of the monkey king that may be helpful. Nancy el Gran was telling me about it last week." He said, chuckling. "Can I tell you the legend?"

Yes, yes, go ahead," Simbai replied impatiently.

Rafi stopped moving. He eyed a tree for a second, then sighed and continued walking, "So, the monkey king thought he was the best and could conquer Buddha the mighty and rule all the seven realms. The monkey king traveled across the different realms in the sky world and subjugated many other gods. And finally, he journeyed to the East to face Buddha the great. When he saw the two colossal pillars of the edge of heaven, he was overjoyed. The legends said that Buddha was on the other side once one got to the pillars. The monkey king arrived at the pillars and autographed his name so that any great passers-by would know he had been the first. It took him years to finish the autograph so that it was big enough and no one could miss it. The pillars were ginormous. Then he hopped on his flying cloud, and as he prepared to fly out, the pillars began to rise. The two pillars became three, and then five. Soon they curled around him, and that's when the monkey king realized the pillars were the five fingers of Buddha's hand. They menacingly loomed above him, and he felt a tinge of terror. It dawned on him that he had been flying around in the hand of Buddha the great all along. He had traveled for centuries to subjugate different gods in different realms. And all of it had happened in the hand of Buddha the great. The Monkey King was a puny creature in the hand of Buddha the great." Rafi finished chuckling.

"Uuuuh..." Simbai started to respond.

* * *

281

Rafi raised his hand to stop Simbai from speaking; They heard some people calling to each other from a distance. It was the search party looking for them. Rafi smiled and murmured, "Just when I found the tree." He bent over, drew a circle and other markings, and said, "Let's walk backward towards that tree."

"Wait, wait, I don't get the story, and I don't want to disturb our walk this time. Can you explain quickly, please?" begged Simbai.

"Oh yes, yes, the story. So you need to remember we are all simply creatures dancing in the hand of the Divine. He casts the shadow and provides the light. He is the one taking care of each of us. He can heal anything and anyone. So hurting others is not the worst thing you can do. I mean, it's guaranteed you will hurt someone in this lifetime. But the Divine is knitting together all our actions and mistakes, our hurts and failures, and even our successes to make a beautiful symphony we can't even begin to imagine. So stop dwelling on your past mistakes and your failures. All of us are stupid anyway, and none of us are the wiser. Yet, many of us are afraid of the stupid side of ourselves. But, it is also that same side that screams to the Divine. It's the foolish side that asks to be made well and asks for His presence. And it's that same stupid side that is the substance of many of our wonderful dreams. It also is the side that provides the groundwork for the mishaps in our lives. So you can see, I am not saying to stop dreaming of causing less pain, but you can see how inevitable it is for us to do harm. So maybe it's better to dream God's dream, not the dream of causing no harm."

"So it's okay to harm people?"

"Yes, yes, yes, you got it, it's okay…."

"What!" Simbai exclaimed.

"Yes, it's okay to do harm, the same way it's okay to not be okay," Rafi replied emphatically.

"But you refused to liberate Uzu because you did not want to cause harm," Simbai replied, frustrated.

"Yes, it doesn't change that doing harm is inevitable, and it's alright.

When someone says it's okay to not be okay, do you go looking for ways to not be okay? We need way more time to explain this, and we are running out of it." Rafi replied

"I can always ask you more when we get to the other side,"

Rafi stopped and sighed. "You forget we are not going to the same place."

"Yes, I remember now, you to the elders and me somewhere. So you better tell me more right now then." Simbai replied.

"Again, if we get caught, it's on you." Rafi paused, and Simbai nodded with impatience.

Rafi continued, "Okay, so, take everything you know about the idea that "It's ok not to be okay" and apply it to its okay to cause harm." Rafi smiled; he felt he had finished.

Simbai only looked at him blankly.

"Do I have to think about every detail for you? Okay, so..." Rafi said, pausing as they heard voices coming closer. He lowered his voice and said, "Imagine if a baby was learning to walk but felt like it was not okay to fall. That baby would never learn to walk because to walk means falling several times. So it is with healing. The journey to healing is a journey of causing harm. Many churches don't like that, but they are places of harm as much as they are places of being made whole. Unless one is instantly made wise, the journey to being less stupid is littered with stupid decisions and collateral damage. If you find yourself in a place where people are healing, you are also in a place where those same people will cause great harm unless they are instantly healed. And we know only a handful are ever instantly healed; the rest resist and grow over time. It's guaranteed you will do harm tomorrow, Simbai, the same way it's guaranteed a baby will fall as it learns to walk. It's okay to fall; it's okay to not be okay; it's okay to do harm."

Simbai was nodding, it was making some sense, and time was running out. He heard footsteps getting closer as the noises of people got louder. "And, my stupidity is the oxygen to my relationship with the Divine?" Simbai asked, puzzled but expecting another great explanation.

"Oh yes, as soon as we become wise, we are no longer in need of Him. But that's a paradox because He is wisdom, and no one can be wise without Him." Rafi replied thoughtfully. Simbai was worried as the search party sounded closer. He wanted to talk to Rafi but also wanted to escape. That's when Rafi looked at his watch and asked. "Are you done playing twenty-one questions? We need to start walking backward soon?"

"How can my stupidity be the oxy...." Simbai began to ask.

"Humility, humility or call it submission." Rafi jumped in impatiently. "First, we realize we are stupid. Then we notice that, in our stupidity, we act thinking we have agency. But we only cause more pain and suffering and try to escape it. But if we relax and accept that we are stupid, we stop being sitting ducks because we can humbly reach out to wisdom so we can have her. She helps us dodge life's pains caused by a lack of common sense while embracing the inevitable ones designed to grow us. And before you know it, we are wise only because we are no longer alone." Rafi replied, moving Simbai physically into position.

Simbai was mauling it over, and Rafi was looking at his watch. "Just remember," Rafi said, "Rejection of any part of the self is death. And when you kill yourself by rejecting your stupid parts, or the parts of you that cause harm to others, you need to return to the crime scene. Go back to the event, embrace yourself, and boom, you resurrect into wisdom. Simbai, accept you are stupid and that it's okay, now let's go!" Rafi said, hoping Simbai would hold onto any one of his hurried explanations.

They heard the guards' call even closer than before. People were looking for them, and they were getting nearer by the second. Simbai and Rafi began their walk backward. Simbai was deep in thought while Rafi chanted. Simbai realized that he could not escape feeling pain or causing harm no matter where he went. He needed to stop rejecting and fleeing from the parts of him that were stupid and hurt other people. They were the oxygen to his relationship with the divine and empathizing with others. Simbai felt a draft of cold air emanating from his back as they got closer to the tree. A cold skeletal hand covered his eyes, and another pulled him back-first into the tree. He gasped as he felt those hands, which disturbed his thoughts. His thoughts of oxygen and his Uncle's words were interrupted as he remembered.

"Fleeing from oxygen is not a sign of agency, but a sign of ignorance, stupidity even. And suffocation will show you that in acting this way, *you* are being stupid. So as you escape to the diaspora or into pleasure and money, you will get whacked by the consequences of your own choices and actions like a sitting duck. In the end, you can't escape pain and discomfort in life; that's why you have one option really; face it. Otherwise, you are a stupid sitting..."

Leave a Review

Thanks for reading *Tuzu - Stupid Sitting Duck*
Your support makes it possible for me as an independent author to continue creating. There is so much to rethink about our lives and to do it in a way that is entertaining.

If you liked what you read, please **leave an honest review,** especially on Amazon.
Amazon allows reviews even if you bought the book from me in person or from my website. You do not need a "verified purchase" tag to leave a review.

Your feedback is invaluable.

Newsletter

From July 2022, I will be living in Zimbabwe. Every month I will be sharing something from my experiences and releasing a short story or chapter for your perusal. I will also be sharing my plans both in the literary and art world and in the goat farming and waste recycling adventures I plan on having. There is an opera ahead, complete with African instruments and much more.

Please join the newsletter through my Patreon so you can be notified and support my work as an author and artist.

Link to the sign-up page

About the Author

Allen is a student of the human condition and an avid reader. He believes writing is not only a fun hobby but a calling for him. He has so many more works of art to write and compose and needs your support as an independent and growing creator. Please learn more about Allen on his website and find out about ways you can support his work.

Website: allenmatsika.com
Patreon: https://www.patreon.com/allenmatsika
Instagram: https://www.instagram.com/matsikaallen/

Printed in Great Britain
by Amazon

82179907R00173